D1643456

LIMERICK CITY LIBRARY

Phone: 407510
Website:
www.limerickcity.ie/library
Email: citylib@limerickcity.ie

The Granary,
Michael Street,
Limerick.

The Pleasure Garden

The Pleasure Garden

Caroline Davison

PIATKUS

Copyright © 2005 by Caroline Davison

First published in Great Britain in 2006 by
Piatkus Books Ltd of
5 Windmill Street, London W1T 2JA
email: info@piatkus.co.uk

The moral right of the author has been asserted

A catalogue record for this book is available from the British Library

ISBN 0 7499 0754 1

Set in Times by
Action Publishing Technology Ltd, Gloucester

Printed and bound in Great Britain by
Bath Press Ltd, Bath

Many thanks to all the people who read early drafts of the manuscript and offered advice and encouragement: Elspeth Barker, Amanda Brandish, Johnny Broom, Hayley Buckland, Sian Croose, Caroline Davidson, Simon Davison, Sally Davison, Helen Donovan, Andrew Gayton, Mary Kallagher, Jayne Ludford, Frank Meers, Eamonn OMahony, Johnny Phibbs, Andrea Rippon, Margaret Steward, Sophie Steward, Laura Tippler, Johnny Tippler, Frances Wilson, and especially to Pete Tolhurst for attention to detail and much more. Thanks also to my agent, Judith Murray, and my editor Emma Callagher for insight and support. And much gratitude to Pip and George for being Pip and George.

For my parents
... *there's only one Tom and Ina* ...

The scene is of a green and abundant garden. Lush leaves spill on to the verdant path. Trees rustle invitingly, casting rippled shade across the ground, and the breeze sets pendulous flowers nodding and swaying in rhythm. There is a perfume: sweet, curling, like smoke from burning incense.

A figure leans against the trunk of a tree, camouflaged at the point where the glaring sunshine dazzles the eye, and deepens the shade lurking under the branches. He stands stock still, listening to the garden murmuring. Then there is a sudden movement, a flash of decision. He steps into the garden and is lost at once, in amongst the green.

May

This is the season when the housekeeper begins to prepare for distilling. Plants are in their fullest perfection when they have grown up in their height and are budding for flower. Some of them will be just in that condition at this season. . .

> The British Housewife; or the Cook,
> Housekeeper's and Gardiner's Companion 1756
> Mrs Martha Bradley

Gretta and I are going for a midnight swim. The moon is full and the road is striped with shadows of trees. We have rolled back the roof of her old Citroen Dyane and turned off the headlamps. I am standing up on the front seat, the wind blowing my hair straight back. I am the figurehead of a ship as we plunge down the hill towards the sea.

The sea is glimmering mercury with a bright splash of moonlight, and it is crystal cold. We throw ourselves in, with no time for regrets. After the initial shock, to feel the soft water lapping against our skin is soothing; little whirlpools sliding down our bodies as we push our hands through the silk. I float for a while, listening to the push and pull of the waves on the beach. Afterwards, we wrap ourselves in our towels, enjoying the tingling of our skin in the night air, and we look up into a deep blue night sky, searching for shooting stars. My body feels as if it has a new skin, shiny and smooth, every little nerve vibrating. I feel brimful of longing, all this love inside me, and no one to lavish it on.

As we walk back up the steep slope of the beach we are both startled by the appearance of a figure at the top. A man standing very still, looking out to sea. Though the crunch of the stones is noisy as we walk, he does not seem to notice us. I wonder what he is doing there, standing alone in the dark? He could be a poet searching for his soul in the wilderness of the North Sea, or he could be a local fisherman looking at the weather and the tide. Perhaps he is a ghost. Or he could have been spying on us swimming. I hope not.

We say hello and he glances in our direction, murmurs an unintelligible greeting, and looks back at the sea. I can see just his profile, a dark shadow where his eyes are, the curve of his chin against the moon. But even these small signs tell me he is a handsome man. I feel a moment of disappointment. I will never see him again, but in a fairer life I might have met him and loved him. Perhaps I should run back to him and say: Let's go for a walk along the beach, through the marshes and out onto the sand spit. Let us talk and talk and then lie down together in the shelter of the dunes and marram grass.

I am too sensible. I dream these things, but on the outside I carry on as normal. Gretta is more likely to be impetuous, but she is too in love with my brother Jem at the moment to be thinking much about this stranger. She says: He looked mysterious, didn't he? I wonder where he came from? He'd be just the thing for you, Ruby. Let's go back and ask him to come and have a drink with us.

Luckily, she is joking. I don't mind being single. I am happy pottering along in my life, with my work, and my friends. It is better to be alone and retrieve my enthusiasm for living than to be stuck in the treacle that was life with my last boyfriend. The drawback is this surfeit of love I have inside me, great waves of emotion sloshing around in my stomach. I feel sick with it at times like this.

*

4

'I hope you don't mind the flowers, Mr Major,' said Professor Lal, as Charlie entered the room. 'It is like this. I am not at home in the city. The lack of plants distresses me. These flowers help me a little to maintain my equilibrium.'

Charlie said he didn't mind, but thought to himself: The man's a weirdo. The professor handed him a cup of tea, which he sipped while taking mental notes of his surroundings. Professor Lal's hotel suite was full of flowers. The hotel staff seemed to have experienced problems finding enough receptacles for the vast numbers, so fat bunches of madonna lilies stood in plastic buckets, and perfumed stocks were rammed into coffee pots. The scent in the warm room was thick and sweet. It struck Charlie that the professor's appearance was incongruous in this exotic setting: not another long-haired, pot-bellied, incense-burning guru as he had expected, spouting on about love and peace. More like an Indian businessman: slight, middle-aged, very soberly dressed in dark trousers and white shirt, his black hair cropped short, his face scrupulously shaven.

He wondered again why Professor Lal had invited him to do this interview. He had been aware of the professor's recently published book, and knew it had caused an enormous stir in the media, but he hadn't bothered to read it, as it wasn't his field. He had heard that the professor was shy of publicity and refused to give interviews. Then, out of the blue, Professor Lal's agent had contacted Charlie and offered him an exclusive. Charlie had no idea why. He was known for his writing on the visual arts, and he had no personal connections with the professor or his agent. Still, he did not hesitate to take up the offer, as he knew the interview would sell for a good sum. His preparation for the meeting consisted of reading some previous reviews of Professor Lal's work, and scanning through *Reaching Paradise – Gardens of Ecstasy* as he travelled down from Norfolk on the afternoon train. He was surprised how quickly the journey passed as he read all about fertility rites and sexual practices connected with agriculture throughout history.

Professor Lal was smiling at him. 'Please, sit down. Make yourself comfortable. Let us get this interview part over and done with, and then I have something I would like to ask you.'

Charlie felt a slight throb of foreboding, as though he had just seen the flashing light of a police car in his rear mirror. 'Oh yeah?'

The professor made reassuring noises. 'Don't worry, Mr Major. It is nothing to worry about. Now, please, sit.'

Charlie sat down on a chair enveloped in the scent of freesias. He took out his tape recorder, ready to start the interview, but the professor put up his hands.

'I would rather, if you didn't mind, that you did not record me. It will stop my flow. I am uneasy about my voice becoming the property of someone else. Silly, I know, but it is a foible of mine. A notebook would be preferable.' He smiled affably at Charlie.

Charlie scrabbled around in his briefcase for an old note-book and pen, thinking: bloody awkward bugger. He drank two more mouthfuls of tea, and tried to get himself into interviewing mode. 'OK?'

The professor sat down in an armchair opposite Charlie, and nodded.

'Right. *Reaching Paradise* is very different to your previous work. Where did the inspiration for the book came from?'

Professor Lal looked at the ceiling, as if the answer might be written there somewhere, then launched himself into a long speech, with the air of someone who has said the same thing over and over again:

'Oh, I am like everyone else, you know. Looking for a way to achieve happiness in the world. It struck me that the anger people experience every day has so much to do with the loss of a relationship with Nature. We do not have to look far to find historical texts, which help to explain this.

6

Genesis, Greek myths, or stories in my own culture. Paradise gardens are used as metaphors of a blissful, innocent state of being from which we inevitably fall. You know, the words for paradise in Arabic and Persian, *janna*, and *firdaus*, are both derived from the word for garden. As you will have read in my book, I believe that these ancient texts could offer us ways of returning to that blissful state. If we can provide the right context, perhaps we can come closer to the innocent ecstasy that was experienced by the first man and woman.'

The professor suddenly leaned forward in his seat. His face had lost its bored look, and was animated with enthusiasm. Charlie scrawled notes as the professor began to speak more quickly.

'It is like this. Through gardening in a spiritual way, we can cleanse our souls of the anger we feel. We can become close to the earth, we can become part of the cycle of the living year, we can escape the terrible tyranny of the worship of self and individuality, and become absorbed into the whole. The central idea in the book is that taking our natural place in this cycle will help us to retrieve our primitive souls. If we accept the inevitability of birth and death, and the fact of our rebirth through the soil, we may find contentment and peace.'

There were a few moments' silence as Charlie finished writing. Professor Lal stood up and walked slowly around the room, occasionally sniffing the abundant flowers. Charlie found himself struggling to concentrate. The warmth and the heady perfume made him feel sleepy, and he was not used to writing. With some effort, he forced himself to frame the next question.

'You can't be surprised that your ideas have caused so much fuss. What do you say to the charge that you are trying to create a quasi-religious sect, and are using sex as a way of ensnaring people?'

Professor Lal halted in his perambulation of the room, and shrugged.

7

'This is just silly. I am an academic, not a religious leader. Much of the material in my book, which you journalists seem to find so exciting, on reaching ecstatic sexual states, and so forth, is old news. My sources are historical texts. I merely brought them together in my book in order to illustrate the possibility that they represent an ancient memory, of a time before we lost our way.'

He began to walk around the room again, pacing backwards and forwards, as if he were lecturing on a stage.

'Of course, it is quite clear, to anyone who thinks for a moment, that the powerful influence of sex on every aspect of our lives cannot be overestimated. I think, in fact, that it is dangerous not to fully acknowledge the significance it has at the core of every human interaction throughout time. It is important, then, to find ways of making these experiences positive, life-enhancing moments. But this does not make me some tinpot cult leader. Whatever next!'

The professor caught Charlie's eye and laughed, but Charlie persisted.

'You must admit, though, that the content of your book is a long way from your previous work about farming.'

The smile faded and the professor looked weary. He stood behind his chair, his arms grasping the back, as if for support.

'My ideas have arisen quite naturally out of my previous work. The study of agricultural practices must bring us inevitably to the study of reproduction in all forms of life, and to the consequent human ritualised response. Gardening, or cultivation, though it may seem like a gentle pastime for the middle classes in your country, is essentially a combination of two primal needs: reproduction and sustenance. Through cycles of reproduction, we provide ourselves with food. Did you know, Mr Major, that the interplay between the moon and the sun, which has such an influence on the fertility of our world, is named in Greek *synodus*, which also means *copulation*?'

Charlie shook his head, but didn't look up from his scrib-

8

bling. He was struggling to remember the professor's words. What had he said about copulation? What was it in Greek? The professor began pacing again.

'The world has moved so far away from all this ancient wisdom. But if we can become intimate with these cycles, and follow them ourselves, we provide food for our souls. As I said, it is not a new thing. In all cultures, fertility of land and of women is interwoven in ritual and belief. We have all seen the ancient figures of Mother Earth, the Venus figurines, the so-called Sheela-na-gigs with the giant vulvas exposed. You find them even on your churches here, you know. They were not the result of some obscure sect but were part of the established belief. I am merely restating some ancient held truths.'

There was another long pause as Charlie made laborious notes, his mind clouded with billowing clouds of scent. Eventually he looked up. The professor was gazing out of the hotel window. Charlie saw him surreptitiously check his watch, and realised that his time might be running out. He tried to recall the main reason for the book's notoriety. He'd seen some bloody boring lesbian banging on about it on a late-night chat show, saying how it was all about women being barefoot and pregnant, so he said:

'You have been lambasted for focusing on the importance of female fertility in your book. What do you say to that?'

Professor Lal nodded briefly. 'That is one of the reasons I have been so reluctant to give interviews. The reaction has been ridiculous.'

'But the book does more or less say that women are here to provide sexual gratification and produce children.'

The professor shut his eyes for a moment, and shook his head. He sighed. 'I am, of course, saying nothing so simple. Though we are still ruled by those two driving forces of sustenance and reproduction, we have developed, as a species, many other, more complex, layers. We have spirituality; we have art, poetry. And we have developed

9

the pleasures of sexual intercourse unlike any other animal, well beyond the needs of reproduction. What I am saying in my book is that a ritualised harnessing of Nature could offer us a way back to fulfilment.'

He hesitated for a moment, and then came back to his chair and sat down. He looked intently at Charlie, and spoke quietly to him, as if sharing an important secret. 'I must say, however, that having sexual relations with the purpose of creation is an enormously exciting, powerful experience. The moment of conception is the closest anyone may come to oneness with the earth. Have you ever had children, Mr Major?'

Charlie shook his head, but then answered truthfully, 'Not that I know of, anyway.'

'Ah, then you will not know the feeling I am describing.'

Charlie began to ask another question, but Professor Lal held up his hand. 'I think I have given you enough for your article, Mr Major. Now I would like to ask you something. I understand you live at Oakstead Hall in Norfolk?'

'Yes, I do,' Charlie answered, surprised. He never gave out his home address in case people responded badly to his reviews, and turned up at his door. 'How did you know that?'

Professor Lal smiled secretively. 'Oh, these things are found out quite easily, Mr Major. I am interested in the garden at Oakstead – it has an intriguing history. I am working on a new book, and Oakstead may be relevant to it. In return for my favour to you, do you think it could be arranged for me to visit the garden while I am in England?'

Later that evening Charlie called up a woman he had met recently at a party. They went out to a club and then she stayed the night with him. It was all very nice and all very easy. But when he closed his eyes to go to sleep, a strange thing happened. A clear image of Professor Lal, with his intense, earnest eyes, popped up in his head. Charlie could even smell the pervasive aroma of the flowers from that airless hotel room. As he fell asleep the professor's words were swirling around in his head like a mantra: *Ah then, you will not know the feeling I am describing, you will not know the feeling* . . .

It is a beautiful clear blue day. I am looking out of the window over the familiar view of fields and trees. I think today, I will go out into the world. Often if I am working on a painting I stay at home for days on end, absorbed and anxious about whether I am any good at what I do. But, as Gretta frequently says to me, it is important to keep having experiences in the outside world, in order to develop and grow as a creative person. This is a very convenient excuse on a beautiful summer's day. I shall go out and seek inspiration.

I like the undulations of Norfolk. The salty air by the marshes seems to affect the light. The sky is a particular shade of blue I have only ever seen here, like a 1950s postcard. I am freewheeling on my bike, down the coast road, the heath rising on my left, the marshes and the sea spreading out to my right. It is still very early, only six o'clock. I am so pleased with myself on these days when I wake up feeling refreshed and full of verve.

There is no traffic on the road yet. Later it will be choked with slow cars trundling around the coast from tea shop to tea shop. I leave my bike at the bottom of the stony bank. It is already quite warm. I strip off and dash into the sea, and then run up and down the pebbles to get warm, making them clatter and crunch. The dripping water makes the round stones shiny and dark. I get dressed and sit on top of the slope, watching the evidence of my dance gradually evaporate.

All this makes me hungry. I head inland towards Holt, up the steep slope of the heath. Looking back from the top there is a stunning view of the tawny salt marsh, curbed by a flash of creamy shingle bank, and beyond that the sea and sky, indigo and cobalt blue. As I turn away from this view

11

to continue on down the other side of the ridge, I glimpse in the valley below a spark of reflected sunlight on something shiny. It looks like a copper roof on some kind of small tower. I've never noticed this before although I've been up here many times. The building is set in amongst a belt of trees, which forms the boundary to an estate. There is a gate here at the end of a grass track, which runs down to the copse. I've always thought it looked pretty. There are bluebells lighting up the gloaming, and in summer, if the breeze is in the right direction, you can smell the wild honeysuckle in the evening. It is still early. I have seen no one. I leave my bike by the bank and I climb over the gate and scuttle down the track to the cover of the trees.

It's the kind of wood that has mossy grass under the trees, a soft green blanket. Through these trees I can see the strange little tower with the copper roof. It stands on a solid plinth with stone plaques set into it. There is writing on them but I am too far away to be able to read it. At the top there is a wooden structure, which holds a small bell, sheltered by the roof of brash copper, not yet transformed by the rain into the more mysterious verdigris. Standing at the edge of the trees I can see why this monument has been built here. In front of it the ground drops away down a grassy ride. The grass has been left uncut on either side, and is spangled with red campion and stitchwort. Next to these wild-flower borders, lime trees have been planted to create an avenue. At the end of the ride, where the avenue leads your eye, there sits a rambling red brick house with big sash windows, nestled amid an orchard, and glossy green beech hedges.

Something inside me clicks. Not just, Oh, I wish I lived in a place like that. This is like recognition, this is home. A film rolls in my head: the big square rooms inside, filled with happy children, family and friends, the comfort of being protected by those aged red walls, the comfort of belonging somewhere with someone. I suddenly feel outside everything, all alone. Tears drizzle down my cheeks and I sit down, slumped against a tree trunk. The ground is dry and woolly. I give myself up to this sudden melancholy and curl up at the bottom of the tree, my head pillowed on my hands.

Ben Fitzmaurice was also feeling melancholy that day. He started the morning badly, coming down to breakfast to find the only bottle of milk had been left out all night and had turned into yogurt. The sink was full of dirty saucepans and crockery, the bread was stale and flyblown upon the table and the butter was crusted with crumbs and jam. Under his breath he cursed his friend and lodger, Charlie, for being so slovenly. He wondered again whether the benefits of having someone to share the house with him, to keep him company, actually outweighed the disadvantages of constant tidying up, washing up, and the general upheaval that Charlie and his social life left behind him. Is it obsessively tidy, he wondered, to want to be able to look at a room as a still-life painting, with all the beautiful objects in their right place? A slight tremor of irritation ran through him now as he came across a green chair which had been moved from the green drawing room into the blue kitchen, though of course he knew it was perfectly reasonable, if extra chairs were necessary. He picked up the green chair, sighed, and put it down again. I am becoming eccentric, he thought to himself.

After making some toast and brewing a pale herbal tea, he sat down to breakfast in the conservatory where the untidiness had not overflowed. It was warm, and his spirits rose a little. The scent of buddleia gently soothed him. Outside, the knot and topiary garden assuaged his need for some order in the day. A beautiful garden, a beautiful conservatory, a beautiful day, and beautiful toast. Ben considered all this and was annoyed with himself for feeling so bad tempered and forlorn, when really he knew he was a lucky man. But lonely. He went back into the kitchen, cleared the table, washed up and put the green chair back

13

in the drawing room. Then, feeling better, he went out into the workshop to start his day's work.

Loneliness would not leave him. He mused on how it had come to pass that he was on his own. His friends advised him that he was too nice, too obliging. Girlfriends seemed initially to be attracted to his kind manner, but then became frustrated or bored. Thinking over his past relationships, Ben realised that the women he had been involved with were usually escaping disastrous relationships, with men who took them for granted, and were cruel and callous. He took great pleasure in providing respite for these casualties, looking after them, cooking for them, entertaining them, and making sure they enjoyed their time in bed with him. But then they would start telling him it was all too easy. No arguments, no drama, no passion. Ben felt a moment of resentment as he thought about it. What was wrong with a calm life? He couldn't understand why this niceness of his was seen as a failing.

Laying out his tools carefully, he relived the sinking feeling that overcame him every time he realised the end was coming. Girlfriends would try to pick arguments with him, and he wouldn't be able to respond in the way they wanted. They would shout, and slam doors, and he would find himself planning a nice meal for them, to cheer them up. It was only three weeks since the end of the last doomed relationship and he was still feeling gloomy. Catching sight of his reflection in the workshop window, in his sloppy brown corduroys and frayed checked shirt, he wondered whether he was going to be left on the shelf forever. Always, between relationships, he felt how impossible it was that he would ever meet another eligible single woman. What chance was there that there would be mutual attraction? How would they possibly communicate it to each other?

He was working on a piece of garden furniture which required carved images of flowers entwined around the legs and arms. Yesterday's campion, which he was using as a pattern, was wilting, so he went round to the back of the house, through the shrubbery, and up the sloping ride towards the memorial to his parents. The novelty of this new building had not yet worn off. When he had picked a bunch of the wild flowers, he continued on, up to the top, so that he could sit on the stone plinth and contemplate his estate. I just need someone to share it with, he thought to himself: then he saw Ruby.

She had fallen asleep on the edge of the wood, lying on her side with her head resting on her hands. Fiery hair tumbled around her bare shoulders, startling red on the bright green moss. Her eyelashes looked long and black against her cheek and her mouth was slightly open. The sight of her hit Ben with the impact of a vision. He was paralysed for a moment as he tried to understand what she was doing there. Was she ill, dead? Was she a ghost, an hallucination? Was she something his fevered imagination had conjured up? He crouched down and touched her wrist to see if there was a pulse. Ruby was instantly awake and let out a scream of shock as she pulled away from him and scrambled to her feet.

'Oh, please,' he said in a hurry, 'don't be scared. I thought you might be ill.'

'No, no,' said Ruby, now fully conscious. 'I should apologise, I must've worried you, and I shouldn't really be here. I'm so sorry.'

They stood looking at each other for a moment and then they laughed. At the same time, they both experienced flickers of recognition.

Ben spoke first: 'Haven't we met before?'

Ruby scanned her memory. 'Are you Ben?'

Ben nodded. 'Yes. Ben Fitzmaurice.'

'I'm Ruby. I think you went out with a friend of mine for a short while. Helen. We were at college together.' Ruby recalled that the relationship between Helen and Ben had not ended well, and she felt uncomfortable, but Ben did not seem to be embarrassed.

15

'Helen! Of course. How is she these days?'

'She's fine. I don't see her that often now. She moved to London after college.'

'Married?'

'No.'

There was a short silence between them. Ruby was remembering that Helen had thought Ben was nice, but she had messed things up somehow. She couldn't quite recollect the circumstances. Ben's mind was more in the present, wondering if Ruby was single.

'How do you come to be in this neck of the woods?' he asked.

Ruby blushed. 'Well, actually, I live just down the coast. I was cycling and I noticed your new building here and I'm afraid I was being very nosy.' She smiled winningly at him. 'I hope you don't mind.'

Ben had inherited from his father an irritation with trespassers. But he could not find it in himself to be cross with Ruby. She looked too nice, and anyway, they had mutual friends.

'No, I don't mind. It's a memorial to my parents, actually. They were killed in a car crash a couple of years ago.'

'Oh no. How awful! I am sorry.'

Ben shrugged awkwardly. After a moment he said, 'So. We're neighbours, are we?'

Ruby gave him a relieved smile. 'Yes. I was on my way to Holt for breakfast. I'll leave you in peace. It was nice to meet you again.'

She began to turn away, but Ben was thinking fast.

'Haven't you breakfasted? Neither have I! Why don't you join me? You can tell me some more about Helen.'

She looked at him for a few seconds, and then said. 'OK. Thank you. That would be nice.'

They walked down to the house, Ben wondering desperately what he was going to give her to eat.

*

16

May 1st

The first day of May. Beltane. The book says this was the day when the triumph of light over dark was celebrated by the ancient people. They lit bonfires on hilltops all over the land to bring the sunshine down to earth, to warm the young shoots lifting their tender heads. They drank from the May bowl: wine infused with the fragrant blossoms of spring, to intoxicate the senses. All through the night the people made love in the woods. Shifting shadows, whisperings, fumbling in the dark, a bed of leaves and sweet-scented flowers: woodruff, the lady's bedstraw, offering up its heady perfume as the ardent lovers rolled amongst it. In this way they enacted the sacred marriage of earth and sun, reaffirming the fertility of the earth, showing the Earth Mother the way. Is it significant that on this day I saw the girl in the woods? She lay asleep on the bright green moss: a quiet promise, the beginning of the cycle.

What a day I had yesterday. I fell asleep feeling mournful, but when I woke up I was in a new world full of hope. I walked with Ben down the ride, through the orchard, and then into a surprise garden, hidden from above by the hedges, cool and green. Out onto a terrace at the side of the house where you could see the sweep of the river at the bottom of the lawn. Through French windows into a huge kitchen where he made me toast and herbal tea. We sat in his conservatory and ate. All this time we were talking, talking. It felt like we needed to know everything about each other instantly, as though it were urgent.

He wanted to know where I came from, where I had been, what my life story was. There were no doubts about what we were each thinking. Somehow, the offering and accepting of breakfast was enough for us to know. We spent the morning wandering around his gardens, then we had lunch in Holt and did some shopping, buying food together for the evening. It felt like a game, finding out what he chose, what I chose, which special things he likes.

Olives. Not taramasalata. Strong blue cheese. Special water biscuits. And baklava. In the afternoon we went for a swim, and then back to his house where we sat on the terrace drinking vermouth with nasturtium petals delicately floating amongst the ice. I began to feel very happy, and very warm towards him. We kissed, warm welcoming kisses, the smell of fresh air and salty sea on our skin, my fingers caught in the tendrils of fair hair in the nape of his neck. And then we went to his bed.

This morning I am sitting again at the kitchen table while Ben makes our second breakfast together. A man comes through the door, looks quizzically at me and then at Ben. Ben says to him: This is Ruby. Ruby, this is Charlie Major, my lodger.

Charlie? The name is familiar to me. He is a tall, dark, thin man, like a slightly wasted pop star. Scruffy hair and a Gitane smouldering in his fingers, before he has had breakfast. He smiles at me, a knowing, cheeky smile and says: Nice to meet you. I wondered who the redhead in the garden was.

He shuffles about making two cups of coffee, and then leaves with a 'see you later'. Ben says: Charlie often has friends to stay. He has what you might call a rather active social life.

Of course. I remember now. Helen got involved with Charlie while she was still going out with Ben. I never liked the sound of him but Ben says he and Charlie have been friends ever since they both worked on the school newspaper at their boarding school. Perhaps he has hidden depths.

After breakfast I feel that I must get my feet back on the ground, so I decide that, this morning, I should go home and do some work. I see a flicker of disappointment in Ben's face, but he masters it. He says: Oh, I see. Um, perhaps you would like to come back for supper?

When I say no his face drops. Then I say: You come to my house.

He smiles again. Amazing how we can affect each

other's lives so quickly. He agrees to come; we walk back up to the memorial, and through the wood up to the lane. My bike still lies nestled in the hedgerow. I cycle home. My heart is singing.

At lunchtime Ben was sitting in the garden drinking a cup of coffee with pictures of Ruby in his head, when Charlie plonked down next to him, and offered him a bottle of beer.

'Your shag gone, has she?' he asked.

Ben rolled his eyes. 'If you mean Ruby, yes. And your friend?'

Charlie nodded. 'Yeah. I just loaded her back on the train to Norwich.' He took a swig of beer. 'Was yours worth inviting back?'

Ben sighed. 'Really, Charlie. I don't know how you manage it. If I was a girl I'd give you a very wide berth.'

'Yeah, yeah. So anyway, where did the redhead come from?'

'I found her asleep in the wood. It was like walking into a Pre-Raphaelite painting. And I invited her for breakfast.'

Charlie nodded approvingly. 'Pretty fast going for you, wasn't it?'

'Can you blame me? Don't you think she's lovely?'

Charlie turned his mouth down. 'Not bad, I suppose. Nothing special. Red hair's never really appealed.'

Ben laughed. 'Well, that's good. I'll stand more chance with her if you're not interested.'

He sat musing for a moment, passing his bottle of beer from one hand to the other, appreciating the feel of icy glass on his hot palms. There was a huge bubble of excitement in his chest and he felt the need to talk about it. 'You know, I think this might be it. I really do. It feels like it was meant to be. Finding her lying there, it was such chance. I could have picked flowers from another part of the garden, I might not have needed to pick the flowers in the first place. If I hadn't had the idea of the memorial all those months ago she wouldn't have come, and I wouldn't have gone up to look at it.'

'Yeah, and if your father hadn't fancied your mother one night thirty-six years ago, you wouldn't exist and would never have met her.'

'Oh, you may mock,' Ben said with a smile, 'but when I saw her, it was like a thunderbolt. How else do you explain me having the courage to ask her to breakfast? I've never been so brave before.'

'True. It does sound more like one of my lines. Perhaps you've learned a few things off me over the years, after all.'

'God, I hope not.'

They sat in comradely silence, looking over the lawn to the river. Then Ben said, 'Do you never feel the need to find one woman to be with? You know, to be friends with, to live your life with, rather than all this one-night-stand rigmarole?'

'Nope. I like meaningless sex. It suits me. Got a problem with that?'

'No. I just wondered.'

There was a tense moment, both men embarrassed by the subject they had strayed into. Then Charlie swigged the last of his beer and said, 'Have you heard of this Professor Lal guy? You know, who's written this Zen-and-the-art-of-having-sex-in-your-garden thing.'

'I've read reviews of it. It sounds rather odd. Why?'

'I did an interview with him the other day, and he's coming for lunch in a couple of weeks' time. He's interested in the park here. Would you mind meeting him?'

Ben was surprised. 'Where has he heard about us?'

'I don't know. He's an academic as well as a nutter, so maybe he's read about it somewhere. Anyway, would you mind meeting him? He seems quite normal when you talk to him.'

'Well, I suppose so. Perhaps I'd better read his book before he comes.'

'That can be arranged. I'll go and get my copy, and some more beer. Don't go away.'

June

This is a good time for the planting out of those sweet herbs, which have been sown for the use of the kitchen.

Mrs Martha Bradley

Ben was waiting nervously for the arrival of Professor Lal. Charlie had suddenly found himself previously engaged, and left Ben to cope with the professor on his own. He was not sure what to expect. He thought some of *Reaching Paradise* was embarrassing, but he found the professor's obvious grasp of garden history rather persuasive. Though Charlie and all the other journalists had concentrated on the sexual aspects of the book, there was actually a sizeable section on the history of garden design and its links with religion and ritual throughout history, which was very interesting. He was quite keen to hear Professor Lal's opinions about Oakstead and its historical development. But he hoped that the professor was not going to bring an entourage of young women, as Charlie had implied he might. Ben feared he might find a mass orgy on his hands if the professor felt the garden was near enough like paradise.

In fact the professor arrived unaccompanied, except for his chauffeur. He looked quite ordinary, in a grey pullover, black trousers and black leather shoes. No open-toed sandals or rainbow shirts. He shook Ben's hand warmly and thanked him effusively for allowing the visit at such short notice. Ben offered him a cup of coffee.

'No, thank you, Mr Fitzmaurice, but no. I have been stuck in the city so long with all this nonsense publicity that I am feeling starved of greenness. Would you mind very much if we went straight to the view over the park? I would be so grateful.'

Ben said, 'Of course,' Professor Lal gave a brief nod, and then walked smartly off along the south façade of the house. Around the south-east corner, the view suddenly opened up to reveal the sweep of the terrace down to the river meadow, with the glittering artificial lake and its temple. Professor Lal stopped suddenly, took in a deep breath and spread his arms out wide.

'What a place, Mr Fitzmaurice. You are so fortunate to live here. It is a glorious sight, is it not.'

'Forgive me, but you seem to know your way around awfully well. Have you been here before?'

Professor Lal smiled his secretive smile. 'These things can all be found in books, if you look in the right places. It is no mystery. I understand you have Repton's Red Book for the design here?'

'Yes, I do. It was one of his earlier commissions, as you probably know. It's special here because so much of his design has survived. The lake, and the walks, and the views he created remain pretty much as he envisaged them.'

'Wonderful. Wonderful. May I be so bold as to ask to see the Red Book?'

'Of course. I've got it out ready for you. I'm sure you'll find it interesting.'

They stepped through the open French windows into the kitchen. The Red Book was lying on the table.

The first page carried an engraving of Repton's elaborate business card, showing an idyllic lake. Then there was a title page with 'Oakstead Park' written in careful copper-plate. This was followed by a short dedication:

22

Dear Sir

These few pages will contain little more than what passed betwixt us in our many conversations, yet my sentiments on the subject will, I hope, be more clearly demonstrated by reference to the map and drawings. I must beg your acceptance of this small volume as a tribute to the influence your own imagination and ingenuity has brought to bear on the plans contained herein.

An annotated map of the park showed where the best views were, particularly in relation to the main windows of the house, and where the landscape required improvement. Another page under the title 'Character and Situation' showed in more detail how the views from windows inside the house would be more restricted than those from the same position outside. After this came a painting of the Hall as it appeared in 1792, before Repton's design. Repton's trademark trick was to paint the existing look of the place onto flaps attached to the page. These could then be turned down, revealing a picture below which showed how his commission would transform the landscape. The picture on the flap showed the original east face of the Hall, which overlooked the river. Its plain brick face looked rather sombre, and several of the sash windows appeared to be either blocked or shuttered. The meadow in front of this side of the Hall was flat and grassy and the river ran its course through tussock-filled fields.

The flap turned down to reveal this hitherto dull façade rendered white, with a two-storey Grecian-style portico attached to the centre, and long sash windows. Another flap revealed the river course changed with the banks tidied up, and a large lake set in a landscaped park of carefully placed trees, where once there had been an unkempt water meadow. This was followed by a short outline of his plans for the park:

The View Explained

The sharp rise of the hill to the back of the house, and the encroachment of the river close by to the east are both aspects which require improvement, if we are to create a tranquil scene. In addition, it will be beneficial to introduce a bridge into the view looking south, not only for the convenience of crossing the river, but also to draw the eye towards this cheerful aspect.

Lake and Water Meadows

The improvement of the river and meadows to form a wide expanse of water will provide a view to the east worthy of the house, which overlooks it. To obtain this view it will be necessary to construct a long ha-ha to prevent cattle from trespassing on to the park to the east of the house and to preserve the walk to the lake.

Walks and Plantations

Another object of improvement is doubtless to cloath the hill behind the house so that it appears to cover and embosom the house. A screen of plantation may be brought around the west side of the building; this will afford a sheltered walk to the hill top and will serve to hide the back of the house in the view from the top of the hill. To obtain this view it will be necessary to give the upper walk the direction shown, so that it may break out in the front of the plantation and afford the prospect, which we always expect as the reward for our trouble in climbing to the summit. A further thin plantation screen will afford a sheltered walk to the kitchen gardens.

Kitchen Gardens

The substantial kitchen gardens required by your lord-
ship are to be situated close by the house to afford
convenient entry but sufficiently to the west that they
do not obstruct the views down into the valley and to
the village. The glasshouses will be as we discussed,
facing directly to the south in order to make full use
of the sun for ripening of tropical fruits and other
exotics.

Looking out of the kitchen windows now, the landscape
appeared to be almost identical to Repton's vision in the
book. Professor Lal seemed very pleased. Ben pointed out
that the proposed works to the house had never been carried
out. The professor nodded.

'Yes, I had noticed that. Also, I notice, the book does
not show the temple on the island. That is interesting. The
temple is by Repton, I believe?'

'Yes. My parents found the accounts, with the Red
Book. They record all the work carried out by Repton. I've
got them somewhere, and the temple is included.'

'It was Henry Faulkes who commissioned the park, was
it not?'

'Yes. My parents used to know all about this. Lord
Faulkes. He was very interested in agriculture, and applied
the new techniques coming in at that time. We always
thought that's why the kitchen gardens were built so close
to the house, and are so large.'

'Quite so. I know a little about Faulkes, and he was, as
you say, very dedicated to experimenting.'

They both stood looking out at the landscape which
Repton had created. Then the professor said, 'It is very
interesting, do you not think, Mr Fitzmaurice, that there
was suddenly in the eighteenth century this widespread urge
to create these magnificent parks. Idealised patches of
nature, seemingly unsullied by human hands. Grass and

trees, and the wild deer running freely. Quite a different – and sudden – change of direction after the fussy herb gardens and knot gardens, parterres and all that other baroque formality. Suddenly nature is welcomed back, wide open spaces, water, the sky. And amongst it all, the architecture of ancient worship, these temples. It is very inexplicable, don't you think?'

'Well, I don't know much about it, only what I studied at school. Wasn't it to do with the Grand Tours? People travelling to Greece and Italy, and bringing back all those antiques. The Four Graces, and such like?'

'Oh yes. I agree that the creation of landscaped parks was largely inspired by the desire to recreate the uncorrupted world of an idealised Nature, to try to go back to the pastoral simplicity of antiquity when order and tranquillity reigned. But it is my belief that there is a deeper symbolism to these parks. I am not satisfied that this sudden revolution in the way people treated their landscapes can be explained by a general liking for the landscape paintings of Poussin or Claude, or because the sons of the aristocracy had all visited Rome and become neoclassicists.'

Professor Lal stood musing for a few seconds, his hands up to his mouth as if he was praying. Ben had contributed all he could about the history of eighteenth-century art and stood trying to think of something intelligent to say. The professor suddenly clapped his hands.

'Let us continue the tour of the estate, if that is all right with you. And then, if I may, I wonder if it would be possible for me to see the accounts you mentioned, of the Repton work?'

The two men walked down to the river and around the edge of the lake, where the temple stood on a small island. Now they were closer, it was possible to see that the building was suffering from neglect. Stucco was dropping off the large triangular portico and walls, and there were cracks running up all the massive circular columns of the porch, revealing the brickwork underneath. The gaunt appearance

26

of this square, precisely symmetrical building was accentuated by the blank windows set high up in the thick walls, their glass broken. Ben felt embarrassed about the state of the building. He intended to repair it as part of his plans for the estate, but knew it was going to be expensive, and would involve English Heritage. This put him off. It was easier to erect brand-new buildings like the memorial to his parents. He was worried about the state of the building inside, because he was quite certain that the roof leaked. But as the old rowing boat had a hole in it and lay half submerged by the bank, the only way to get across was by swimming in the soupy water, amongst all the ducks and geese and the long weeds. So the temple stood forlorn. Professor Lal was very disappointed that there was no way across to the island.

'It is a beautiful piece, is it not, Mr Fitzmaurice. Have you ever been inside it?'

'A long time ago, when I was a boy. Even in those days I was told not to go there because the building was dangerous. So, of course, at the first opportunity, I swam over.'

'And what is it like inside?'

'Well, as far as I remember, there wasn't much to see. Just one large empty room.'

'No ornament at all?'

'I don't think so. It was all painted white. What do you suppose it was for?'

The professor rubbed his chin. 'These buildings were built principally as eye-catchers. Something to look at from afar. Hence the grandeur of the portico in contrast with the relatively small room behind. But no doubt there were little outings here on summer days, tea ceremonies, poetry reading, entertainments of different sorts.' He let his hand drop. 'I would have liked to see inside for myself. Another time perhaps?'

'Certainly, if you're really interested. I should get the rowing boat repaired anyway.'

'That is kind. Perhaps it can be arranged if I am long

27

enough in the country. Now, would you mind if we went to look at the walled gardens?'

The walled gardens at Oakstead were a striking feature of the estate: a series of gardens all surrounded by high red-brick walls, most of which were lined with glasshouses. Ben showed the professor how each one had been designed for a particular purpose. One glasshouse was completely filled by an ancient, bony vine, another with a venerable fig tree. Knobbly espalier fruit trees lined other walls. One garden contained several pineapple pits where this exotic fruit had once been raised on layers of fermenting oak bark and manure. Another had a beautiful glasshouse for peach trees, which still thrived. One garden had been used entirely for cutting flowers, and another, the largest, solely for vegetables. Ben explained how he had reinstated this tradition, selling cut flowers to a local florist, and the fruit and vegetables to a very good local restaurant and green-grocer in Holt. Professor Lal was thrilled to see the gardens flourishing in this way.

'It is just how Henry Faulkes would have liked to see it. All this food from the soil, the fruit of the earth, everything as it should be, the seasons respected and followed, the seed sown, the harvest brought in. It is an invigorating sight, Mr Fitzmaurice, a tonic to my senses after being parched of life in all these cities. But you surely do not manage this kind of perfection on your own?'

'Good heavens, no. I'd be lost without my gardener. I only lend a hand now and then when he asks me. Otherwise I let him get on with it. He's very good, as you can see.'

'Very good, very good indeed.' Professor Lal surveyed the beautifully kept vegetable garden that surrounded them. 'An artist, a genius. That is what he must be. I would like to meet him. Is he here?'

'No, actually, he isn't. He's delivering in Holt. Perhaps if you do come again, we could arrange for you to meet him.'

Exploring the walled gardens, and much of the landscaped park, took up the rest of the afternoon. The professor talked to Ben with great enthusiasm about the work of Repton, pointing out the effortlessly contrived views, the philosophy behind the planning, the merging of nature and artifice. His oratory was interrupted by the ringing of his cell phone. It was his chauffeur, anxious to be leaving in order to get back to London for a book-signing event. The professor snapped his phone shut with greater force than was necessary.

'This is most annoying. I am forever rushing from one event to another these days. There is no time for the important things.' He brushed his hand across his forehead, and smiled apologetically at Ben. 'Excuse me for my temper. You have been most kind, spending your valuable time with me. It is like this. I had hoped to look at the accounts of Repton's work before leaving today. But, as usual, I have allowed myself to be carried away, and not achieved all I intended.'

'You're very welcome to come back another time, perhaps when you are less busy. I'll organise a boat, and you can meet the gardener.'

'You are really very kind. I will certainly be in touch.'

They returned to the hall, where the chauffeur ushered Professor Lal into the black limousine and whisked him back to the capital.

A strange thing is happening to me. I have just seen a man, and I know we have had a life together. He is tall, and strong, and I have felt his arms round me; I know how his kisses feel. I have spent a life with him, a dark cottage somewhere, the fire in the grate, an iron bed-frame. I can smell the sweet herbs and woodsmoke. Together we have watched our children grow up and he has been tender with me in my old age. I have experienced his loss. It hurts, a sudden stab of bereavement, as he slips away. When he turns and looks at me I have tears in my eyes and I am paralysed with grief. He sees that I am not well and leads

29

me to the cool of a bench under an apple tree. He has dark blue eyes, I remember them. He asks me what is wrong. What shall I tell him? Perhaps I have sunstroke. I have been sketching all afternoon and it has been hot. Why is he here? Who is he in this life? He holds his cool brown hand to my forehead to feel my temperature. He says it feels normal but I do not feel normal. I am shattering into little pieces. He leaves for a moment and comes back with a glass of water. He says his name is George and that he works on the estate. He knows I am Ruby. Is that because of our previous life together, or is it in this world he has heard about me? I ask him whether I have met him before, as he seems familiar. He looks at me, his full beauty shining on my face, and says: You've probably seen me round the garden, when I've been working.

He doesn't recognise me in the same way that I have recognised him. And yet he sits with me under the apple tree and talks to me as if we do know each other. He tells me what he was doing when I stumbled upon him in the old glasshouse. He was making lamps for Midsummer's Eve, to light up his garden for a party. The lamps are brown paper bags with sand in them, to weigh them open, and one little night light each. He says they are transformed at night-time into fairy lamps. The party is this evening, he hopes everyone he invited comes. Some of his friends are going to perform an abridged version of *A Midsummer Night's Dream* at dusk. He says I would be very welcome if I felt better. He says he mentioned it to Ben and Charlie a few days ago, but he knows Ben is not really keen on big parties. Charlie will, of course, be going. I say I am not ill any more, it was just a funny turn, sunstroke. A Midsummer's Eve party sounds nice.

He insists on walking back to the house with me in case I feel ill again, not realising that he is the cause of my confusion. When we arrive, I see Ben lying on the front lawn, the papers all around him, and a drink by his side. He leaps up as we approach. He says: Hello, George.

Everything all right? Ruby? You look white as a sheet. Has something happened?

He looks at me with concern. His sweet face, with the cool green eyes that love me. I tell him I felt ill, but I'm all right now, and I mention the party.

Ben wasn't planning to go, but is happy to go with me, if I want. George leaves. I lie down in the cool shade while Ben goes to make me a cup of tea. He is so kind and good to me. Not just those things either. He is funny and talented. I have been madly in love with him for the past few weeks. Why has this other man been sent to throw me off balance? If George and I were together in a previous life, as I felt so strongly in the garden, does that mean we are supposed to be together in this life, too? Or is it just an inconvenient leftover memory, like a smudge between the past and the present? I want to just be happy with Ben. It has been so lovely to feel that I have found where I'm meant to be.

When Ben comes back with the tea, I say: Let's not go to the party tonight, I know you're not keen.

But he says he thinks we should, now we have said to George we would. Also, he hadn't realised there was going to be a play. He thinks it will be romantic to see *A Midsummer Night's Dream* on Midsummer night. So we get ready to go.

Charlie got to the party just before midnight, having spent the evening in the village pub. The night was warm and light, a half-moon shimmering in the clear sky. He was only slightly drunk. He had finished most of a bottle of wine with his supper and had followed this with several beers, but he noticed that these days drink didn't seem to affect him much. This vaguely worried him. His answer was to head for the party and find something stronger. The pulse of dance music travelled through the still night air, and there was an orange glow from a bonfire.

Usually as he approached a party he felt a buzz of

adrenalin, the excitement of the unknown, a surge of lust, at the thought of what might happen by the end of the night. The thrill of seeking, hunting, capturing and devouring. He didn't feel like that this evening. Something was missing. He wondered if he would be able to lay his hands on some coke at the party, to get rid of this nagging feeling he had, a kind of headache, constantly fuzzing his mind. For the past few weeks he had been struggling to silence the ringing mantra which had lodged itself in his head ever since his meeting with Lal: *You will not know the feeling*. Like tinnitus, making him irritable. He searched around in his pockets for his cigarettes, lit up, and sucked in a welcome boost of nicotine. Momentarily, his head felt better.

When he arrived at the party he saw Ben and Ruby talking to George in the garden. The two men were sitting on chairs and Ruby was sitting at Ben's feet, looking up at George with a beatific smile on her face. She was not Charlie's type. Not quite thin enough, a little bit too ruddy and healthy for his taste, and too scruffy. But for a moment Charlie caught a glimmer of what it was that Ben saw in her. He grabbed a bottle of wine from a nearby table, and swigged down a glassful. Then he walked over to the threesome and sat on the grass next to Ruby. He looked at her archly.

'You're looking particularly lovely tonight, if I may say so.'

'Do I? Thanks. Um, and how are you, Charlie? You look a bit glum.'

He laughed. 'Thanks for returning the compliment'

Ruby laughed too, and quickly laid her hand on his arm. 'Oh, you do look particularly lovely, but a bit glum.'

'I'm all right. What's been happening?'

'You've missed the play.'

'Oh, I think I'll survive that.' He suddenly put up his chin, held up his arms in a theatrical manner and started to declaim:

'"Over hill, over dale,
Thorough bush, thorough brier,
Over park, over pale,
Thorough flood, thorough fire,
I do wander everywhere,
Swifter than the moon's sphere;
And I serve the fairy queen,
To dew her orbs upon the green.
The cowslips tall her pensioners be:
In their gold coats spots you see;
Those be rubies, fairy favours,
In those freckles live their savours.
I must go seek some dewdrops here
And hang a pearl in every cowslip's ear."'

Ruby looked suitably impressed. 'You should've been in the play. You did it better than the girl did this evening.'

'I was the fairy in the school play one year. Believe it or not, I looked angelic in those days.'

'I'm sure you did.' Her gaze wandered off, looking at the people milling around the bonfire. Then she said dreamily, 'It must be nice being able to remember stuff like that. I wish I could.'

'It just stays in my head.'

She turned to him. 'Do you read a lot of poetry, then?'

'You sound surprised.'

Ruby flushed slightly. 'I suppose I hadn't imagined you were interested in that kind of thing.'

'Why do you think I became a critic then? It does involve knowing something about the arts.' Charlie smiled patronisingly at her.

She made a face back at him. 'I think it must be something to do with the way you act like a yob most of the time.'

He put a hand over his heart. 'Touché.'

Ruby laughed. 'Anyway, it was a beautiful play, in

amongst the trees and the moon coming up. Very romantic.'

She looked up at George and tugged at his trouser leg to get his attention.

'It was such a good idea to put the play on, and your little lamps look lovely.'

He smiled down at her and then returned to his conversation with Ben. They were talking about the garden. Ruby turned back to Charlie with slightly glistening, wide eyes. She laid her hand on his arm again and said, 'Can you recite me some more poetry?'

Charlie began to suspect that Ruby was drunk. She was being very friendly, and he had never noticed her being so physically affectionate before. He realised that the place where her hand brushed against him was tingling from the consciousness of being touched. He was suddenly assailed by the vision of Ruby naked beneath him, panting with excitement. He thought to himself: God, I must be drunk after all.

But a tiny spark had taken fire.

June 22nd

Midsummer's Eve. The long light evening for lovers, soft blue midnight dusk. I could see her moon shadow as she stood alone looking up at the sky. I wanted to lean her against one of the shimmering pale trees and kiss her. But the book says that midsummer is a time for ripening to begin, not a time for sowing. This is the season of the sun, when flowers fall away and wither and the seeds and berries begin to swell and sweeten. The cycle is slow but relentless. There was a look in her eye this evening, a far-off recognition. She is not yet mine to take but the time will come, the wheel will turn.

July

Many seeds will now be ripening, and they must be watched and gathered in due time.

Mrs Martha Bradley

Gretta and I are sitting talking in my garden, a small patch of shade under the apple tree protecting us from the searing noonday sun. We are stuffing ourselves with strawberries, and talking, as ever, about relationships: her and Jem, me and Ben. I tell her he is too good to be true, he is a dream, and I am still sleeping in the wood. Since we met my life feels like one long holiday. I do a little painting in the morning and then he drops by for lunch, bringing bread and cheese and exotic salad leaves from his garden and glasshouses: peppery mustard leaves, purslane, feathery fennel, coriander, lime-green oregano. An endless parade of explosive flavours. After this we may retire to the cool of my bedroom for a while. Then I do a little more work, we meet for an evening swim, and go back to the Hall for supper. George leaves us a selection of each day's crop from the garden, and we concoct delicious meals.

After supper we sometimes accompany Charlie on one of his many half-work, half-pleasure outings to private views, gigs and after-show parties. But often we stay at home, perhaps going for a night-time stroll through the gardens. We may take a bottle of wine to the perfume garden, which

35

is a bower of scent at night. Or we may walk across the meadow to the river. Sometimes we walk through the wood and disturb the roosting pheasants. They lumber out of the trees, fat black bomber aeroplanes, squawking and flapping. When it rains we sit in the conservatory and listen to the roar on the glass roof. A summer to remember all my life. But too soon, it will come to an end and I need to earn some money to take me through the winter. My cottage is easy to live in when the days are warm, but in winter the walls are damp and I have to scrabble around in the cellar, bringing up coal for the fire. My studio is freezing and I work wearing two woolly jumpers and mittens. Hard to believe now, when the weather is so soft and warm.

Gretta says that Oakstead has an amazing atmosphere, that when she first arrived here, she felt she was entering another world. The air is different, and everything seems lush and larger than life. She thinks I should abandon my independence and get married to Ben as soon as possible, so that I can become the princess in this magical land. I am not able to tell her about my complication, the distraction which is George. Is it fair to marry someone when you are still having these flights of fancy?

I do love Ben, there is no mistake. We are like two pieces of a jigsaw which fit comfortably. Once put together, it's obvious. My feelings for him are strong and level, as if he has always been part of my family, my circle. But the thoughts I have about George are like determined weeds, pushing up through everything I throw at them. I want to tell Gretta about it, but I'm too scared. If I say these things out loud the weeds will be fed by the attention and will seem more important. I would rather they wilted from neglect. I shove them into the shady corners.

Ruby was sitting on the terrace overlooking the lawn, which ran down to the meadow. She had on some sort of skimpy T-shirt with very thin straps, and her face was turned to the sun. An open book lay next to her on the step.

Charlie could see her from the kitchen, her back to him. The dishevelled look of her hair, tumbling down behind her, and the way her head was flung back, was very suggestive to him. He wondered, again, what she was like in bed. It was something which had begun to preoccupy him ever since Midsummer's Eve when he had suddenly seen her with new eyes. Since then he had been watching her more closely, and his desire for her had grown.

Once, when he had got back late from a party, he had been walking quietly along the corridor to his bedroom when he heard a muffled moan. He stopped and listened more intently until he was quite sure, and then stealthily made his way to the door of Ben and Ruby's bedroom. He listened as they made love, transfixed by the noises, little sighs, soft murmurings, the rhythmic creaking of the bed, the rising of Ruby's voice and the sudden cry from Ben. Ben sounded very happy. After this there was silence for some time, and Charlie was trapped. He knew that, when he moved, the floorboards would probably creak and give him away. So he stood like a statue outside the bedroom door for over half an hour until he heard gentle snoring from inside the room. Then he had crept away, his head full of the sounds of Ruby.

With this memory in mind, he stood just inside the open French doors looking at Ruby for a few minutes, trying to imagine her with no clothes on. Eventually she shifted her position and sat up straight, wrapping her arms round her knees. Not wishing to be caught staring, he called out to her: 'Ruby! Cup of tea?'

She turned round and smiled at him. 'Yes, please.' She stood up, stretched luxuriantly and stepped into the kitchen to join him. 'What are you doing this evening, Charlie? Are you out somewhere?'

'I'm going to a party, in Chelsea. Why?'

'Oh, I was just wondering whether you'd be here for supper.'

Charlie thought: I bet they love it when I go off for the

night. The whole house to themselves, no inhibitions. I wonder if they've ever done it here in the kitchen?

The kettle boiled, and he made a pot of tea. They went back on to the terrace to drink it.

'Where's Ben?' Charlie asked.

'He's delivering to the restaurant. I've been trying to do some work, but it's too hot, I can't concentrate. How about you? Are you working on something?'

'Oh, various bits and pieces.'

He glanced down at the book she had been reading. It was *Reaching Paradise*. Ruby saw him glance.

'After his visit, I thought it'd be interesting to read his book. It's a bit strange, isn't it? Such a funny mixture of academic analysis, and then these weird bits about having sex in your garden. Very peculiar.'

Charlie made a non-committal sound. Since his interview with Professor Lal there had seldom been a day when he had not dipped into his own copy of the book. There was something about it which had got under his skin. Certain paragraphs he read over and over again. The words elicited in him a thin little line of longing which he could not quite get hold of. Each time he read them he thought he would capture it. He had begun to be haunted by the claim that the moment of creation was the most intense sexual experience available, if the couple prepared in the correct way. For the first time, he had begun to wish he could fall in love. *You will not know the feeling.* In order to get the elusive experience promised by the professor, he had to feel love for Ruby. He had begun to feel things about her that were unfamiliar, but he didn't know if they amounted to love. It didn't make him happy. He felt agitated, almost persecuted, by these unwelcome feelings. He didn't even think she was beautiful, and she never flirted with him, even when he turned on the charm. In fact, she was quite rude to him a lot of the time, and she never seemed self-conscious about her appearance. He looked at her surreptitiously. She sat with her legs outstretched on the steps, her skirt gathered up around her knees, and the small T-shirt clinging to her shape. He wondered if she was really unaware of the effect it was having on him. In his experience, women usually knew. But she was pretty convincing. Why was he bothered with her? It was as if someone had spiked his drink and, under the influence of some mind-altering drug, he had begun to see new colours and new meaning in the things around him. He felt sick, unbalanced.

Ruby picked the book up and leafed through the pages.

'The bit that really makes me cross is this section where he goes on about the nature of men and women, and the supposed inherent differences. You know, all those stereotypes about women being fruitful and nurturing, and men being protectors and fighters. I thought we'd got beyond that kind of thing.'

'I think he's got a point.'

Ruby looked at him thoughtfully. 'But you're not a protector of women, are you? I suppose you're the predator type that the other men are trying to protect their women from. I've always thought it unfair that women have to be protected from men by other men. How are you supposed to know which ones are the protectors and which are the predators?'

Charlie felt a ripple of irritation. The trouble with Ruby was that sometimes she talked too much. She was always challenging him, trying to make him into some kind of reconstructed, emasculated new man. Of course, the fact that she was an old friend of Helen's didn't help. It was difficult to imagine this assertive, argumentative woman as the same one he had heard sighing and surrendering in bed with Ben. He wanted to know what the trick was to get past these barriers of hers and arrive at the soft centre.

Ruby saw the glazed look in his eye and said, 'Sorry. I know I bore you. I can't help it. You bring out the worst in me.'

Charlie blinked. 'What do you mean?'

'Well, I know the very word "feminism" gets your

39

hackles rising. I don't know why I bother.' She patted him patronisingly on the arm, stood up and stretched again. 'I think I'll go and start on supper. Are you sure you don't want anything?'

Charlie was not sure. She had this way of pushing him away and then drawing him back, so that dislike and desire got mixed up inside him. He wanted to shut her up by ravishing her, stopping her talk with his mouth. He sat on the step for a few moments, trying to master his rampaging feelings. He looked at his watch and saw it was time for him to go and catch the train to London. As he made his way to the station he thought to himself: Some girl's going to get lucky tonight.

I am sitting in the cutting flower garden, under the shade of a tree, sketching the flower shapes, and trying to catch their shimmering colours. I look up and there is no one to be seen. I look up again, and there is George, walking slowly up the side path away from me, slightly bowed, a basket on his arm, looking at the flowers. I watch him as he progresses deliberately. Now and again, his hand goes to a flower head. The shadow of his frayed straw hat hides his eyes, whenever his profile is turned towards me. I stop painting, expecting him to notice me, and say something. But he hasn't seen me. I must be camouflaged under the spreading leaves of my tree. So I watch him, his long brown legs and arms, his broad back, the delicate curve of his ear, his fluid movements, as he works amongst the flower beds. I start to imagine he is performing some kind of gentle dance, a ballet warming-up exercise, as he stretches out his arms, bends his knees, or stands on tiptoes to see something at the back of the border. Eventually I lose sight of him as he walks along the end of the flower border, screened by statuesque globe artichokes, silvery-grey leaves spraying out in petticoats.

I try to start painting again, but I can't concentrate, knowing that at any moment, he will start walking down my path, towards me. My self-consciousness freezes me, and I keep my eyes down, looking at my sketchpad, as if in deep reverie. I find I cannot make myself look up. Eventually, he is near enough for me to hear his footsteps on the sandy pea-shingle path. They stop. He says: Ruby? Are you OK?

I jolt myself, as if he has made me jump. Looking up, straight into his glittering blue eyes, there is a genuine lurch inside. He says he thought he'd better check I was well, after the last time when I had sunstroke. I say I have been careful to sit in the shade this time. He asks to look at my work, and comes to my side, kneeling in the brown earth under the tree. He smells of plants, and soil, a herby, musky scent. He likes my plant sketches, and asks me whether he can keep one, of an allium seed-head, with its mathematical sphere, a magic wand. He says he is collecting seeds. Today is a perfect day, hot and dry. In his basket there are more allium heads, and other crinkly brown seed-heads I can't identify. Some have bladder-like bodies, a star at their heads, set in a spray of tiny spikes. He tells me these are love-in-a-mist. Others look like grey, washed-out weeds. These are forget-me-nots. I feel a little pulse of excitement, realising the endless potential of the gardens to provide me with inspiration. I tell him this, and he invites me to visit his seed shed, to look at all the shapes there are. We walk out of the walled garden to where a long, low timber shed leans against the back wall.

Inside everything is soft shades of brown. Sunshine shafts through the undulating glass of the old windows, showering reflected ripples onto the earth floor. Illuminated dust creates dancing swirls of white light. All along one side of the narrow shed a wide slatted shelf is covered in collected seed-heads. He says there are poppies, honesty, foxgloves, columbines. They lie drying on the shelf, and then he will put them in brown paper bags and store them in a chest of drawers, which sits at the end of the long room, waiting for next spring. He holds a love-in-a-mist head over my hand and shakes it. Out of the little windows

41

pour a mist of tiny black seeds. He says: These were a really good blue, so I'll label them, and try to build up a bigger collection next year.

He takes my hand and gently tips it so that the seeds go into one of the paper bags. He smiles at me and says: You've got a halo.

I am puzzled, so he swings me round, and stands where I was. A shaft of sunlight lights up his head, irradiating his hair. He looks like some fantastical Greek god. Then he steers me round again and says: It works better with you.

I stand very still as he reaches up and takes a tendril of my hair. I think he is going to kiss me, and this seems the most natural thing to do in the world. I feel a moment of euphoria, of physical abandon. But then he brings the tendril in front of my face, so that it catches the light. He says: Look. Can you see? Like copper.

Then he lets it fall. We stand looking at each other for a split second before he turns, picks up his empty basket, and murmurs: I should get on. I need to make the most of a day like this.

He takes the sketch of the allium head and pins it to one of the timber window frames. And then we walk back to the cut-flower garden and I sit underneath the tree again. But I can't paint any more today.

Ben and Ruby were crunching along the shingle bank at Cley. It was hot, and a dry breeze brought them the scent of salty sea marsh. They were deep in conversation, talking about previous relationships. Ben's past was complicated. He had been involved with numerous women and was hard pushed to remember the names of them all. Ruby was outraged, and made him try to list them. They had got to the twenty-third.

'And how old were you at this point?'

Ben squeezed his eyes shut in deep concentration and then said, 'About twenty. I was still at university.'

'Twenty! I was only on my third boyfriend by then.'

42

Ben looked surprised. 'You were a late starter.'

'I wasn't inundated with offers.' Ruby squeezed his hand. 'Not everyone sees me the way you do.'

'How odd.' Ben smiled down at her. 'Well, anyway, you were probably much more sensible than me. I went to a single-sex public school, remember. Once I got out, I went rather mad. I look back on it now, and can't believe half the things I did. Still, at least I can remember the names of most of them. If you asked Charlie that question, he'd just laugh at you. It would be impossible for him to count or remember.'

'Why is he like that?'

Ben shrugged. 'I don't know. He's always had a self-destructive side, all the drinking, and drugs, eating rubbish, not sleeping. He thinks he's really living, and that people like you and me are unutterably boring and suburban.'

'And yet, he obviously has this other side to him. He quoted a whole lot of Shakespeare at me at George's party.'

'Did he?' Ben laughed. 'Well, he can be quite charming if he wants to be. He probably thought he would impress you. And he was right.'

Ruby stopped, and gave him a friendly push. 'All the same, he goes to these private views and plays all the time. There must be a more sensitive side to him somewhere, for him to be able to do that, and write about it coherently.'

Ben thought about this for a little while as they scrunched further along the gravel spit, hand in hand. 'I think Charlie is a bit of a Jekyll and Hyde. Intellectually, he's rather sensible and clever. We used to have some really good talks when we were younger at school. Before girls came onto the scene, I suppose. We talked about everything – love, life, the universe. We had an old string hammock we set up in a wood there, and we used to go over after lessons, with biscuits and stuff, and lie there just dreaming and rambling about anything.'

'I can't imagine it.'

Ben bent down, picked up a stone and threw it towards

the sea. 'He's got more bitter and twisted as he's got older. I'm talking about before he started abusing his body.' He looked intently at where the stone had dropped. 'So, he has this one side to him that's pretty sophisticated. But when it comes to relationships, or feelings, he doesn't know how to handle it, and he turns into a bit of a monster.'

'And what about you?' Ruby asked, smiling up at him provocatively. 'Are you good at handling relationships?'

Ben squeezed her hand. 'I hope I've got better. I've bungled things badly in the past.'

'Tell me your worst.'

Ben squirmed slightly. 'You might think less of me if I tell you.'

Ruby laughed, and stroked his arm with mock concern. 'You can tell me. It'll do you good to get it off your chest.'

Ben looked up at the sky, as he thought about which story to tell. Then he drew Ruby's arm through his, and continued walking. 'Probably the most caddish thing I've done was sleep with the fiancé of a good friend of mine, the night before the wedding. Poor old Duncan.'

'Oh dear.'

'Yes, and unfortunately, the new bride was unable to keep this terrible secret to herself, and told Duncan on their honeymoon.' Ben rolled his eyes at Ruby. 'The marriage didn't stand a chance after that. Duncan was always a jealous sort of chap. And he never spoke to me again, which is a shame, because I liked him. I just didn't think about the consequences of things in those days.' He looked down at Ruby with softness in his eyes. 'I'm better now. Honestly. I don't suppose you ever did anything so mean.'

Ruby laughed. 'I've had my moments. A couple I knew had a big argument once, and the man turned up at my house, looking for a place to sleep, and ended up staying for several weeks, mostly in my bed.' She gazed out over the pebbles for a moment, remembering. 'He was lovely, but I shouldn't have allowed it to happen. They were meant for each other.'

Ben narrowed his eyes at her. 'You're not still friends with him, I presume.'

'You needn't worry. I don't see either of them any more. That was another life. And you are much more gorgeous.'

They kissed, and carried on walking for a few minutes. Then Ben turned to her and said, 'I wouldn't want you to think I just slept around for the hell of it. After university I wanted things to be different. Every time I met someone new, I thought, "This is it." I was always searching for a real relationship that would last. I just wasn't very good at choosing. I think that was the problem.'

They looked at each other. Although Ben didn't quite dare say it, they both understood what he meant: this time he had chosen the right person. They hugged each other, both saturated with love. At that moment Ruby could summon up the image of George and feel nothing. She felt safe.

August

This is the time of providing for the winter and the following spring.

Mrs Martha Bradley

August 1st

Lugnasad. Or Lammas. The book says it means the feast of bread, when the Earth Mother gives birth to the first harvest of the year. Today is the day to go out and gather in berries, reap the first corn and give thanks to the goddess.

But the seed I thought was sown does not seem to grow quickly. This first harvest day is too soon, and I'm still unsure of her. Fruit only ripens when it is ready. We can beg the sun to shine, we can plead for rain, but there is no guarantee that we'll be heard.

Have I thanked enough? The book says that the pleasure of taking the berry must be balanced with a gesture of gratitude. But I don't feel grateful. My plate is still empty, and I feel the pangs of hunger. It's hard to resist the impulse to take her, but I know it's too soon. She is not ready and I would risk everything. It will be all the sweeter when the time comes for the harvesting.

Professor Lal's visit had made Ben ashamed of the way the temple was declining in his care. So he summoned up the energy to get the rowing boat repaired, then commissioned an architect to advise on the condition of the building and draw up a repairs specification. An inspector from English Heritage came to check the plans and to advise about grants. After visiting the island and examining the temple, she and Ben walked back towards the hall discussing the timing of the project.

'It could take at least six months for your application to be processed. So we're probably looking at early next year.'

'What?' Ben was aghast. What was there to think about for six months? His voice became clipped. 'That seems unnecessarily bureaucratic. Is there no way round it? My money is available immediately, and I don't want the temple to go through another winter in its present state. It would be quite ridiculous!'

The inspector looked thoughtful. 'It's true, it would be better to get the repairs started before the cold weather. It might be possible to argue that the works are urgent enough to warrant special permission to start, before the funding application has gone through. Particularly if you have your own money to fund it.'

Ben's frosty manner vanished, and he smiled glowingly at her. 'I'm sure I can rely on you.'

'Well, I'll sort it out back at the office. But I think you can plan on the assumption that works can start in the autumn. One of the grant conditions will require the temple to be open to the public once or twice a year. Will you be happy to allow that?'

'Well, yes, I think so. It might be fun.'

They had reached the side of the hall, and the inspector glanced up at the walls. 'Your ivy is getting out of hand. You should keep an eye on that. It looks like it might be damaging the brickwork.'

Ben followed her gaze. Ivy covered this wall, and some of the back of the house. He could see that it had begun to grow into the gutters at the top, and even started to creep up onto the tiles.

'If I were you, I'd get that cut and poisoned. Grow some Virginia creeper up there instead.'

After the inspector left, Ben walked over to the walled gardens to find George, and ask him to cut the ivy. As he went he imagined an idyllic open day, with teas on the lawn, and people wafting across the lake in boats. And, he thought to himself, they'll need information. Something about the temple, and Repton. A little booklet, perhaps. I could do it myself.

He decided to start his research that afternoon. He looked up the Hall in one of his parents' books, called *Country Houses of East Anglia*, published in 1962. There was a black and white photograph of the front of the Hall, with Ben's parents standing on the steps, young and earnest. Underneath there was a short text:

Oakstead Hall, Norfolk
Oakstead Hall was a minor seat of the Faulkes family. Built circa 1740. The original block was quite simple and not large. Two storeys of red brick with a low pitch roof. Five bays of sash windows to the façade, which faces south. Extensions to the original block were all completed during the nineteenth century, to provide a large kitchen to the west, a service area at the rear, as well as a single-storey service block running to the east, and an imposing cast-iron conservatory to the south-west.

The uncommonly well-preserved grounds were laid out by Humphry Repton in the early 1790s. The 'Red Book', with proposals for alterations to both the landscape and the buildings, is kept at the Hall. The park was designed for Henry Faulkes, the oldest son of the fourth viscount, whose seat was at Henford Hall in Derbyshire. Henry Faulkes moved into the house at Oakstead soon after he was married, and remained there until he inherited the main seat in Derbyshire in the early nineteenth century. In the 1840s the Faulkes' fortunes dwindled somewhat, and Oakstead Hall was sold to a businessman, Mr John Farrell. After this time the Hall changed hands frequently. It was the residence of the novelist G. J. Brunsworth from 1868–73; and the birthplace, in 1886, of Jane Kenneth, the internationally renowned soprano. In 1911 it became the country residence of Geraldine Fox, who was a friend of Roger Fry and, for a short time before the First World War, the house became a favourite weekend retreat for the bohemian artists of Bloomsbury. During the 1920s it was owned by another novelist, Margaret Ward. The present owners, Mr and Mrs Edward Fitzmaurice, acquired the Hall in 1956.

The large number of owners since the nineteenth century may explain the survival of the Repton park. Few remained long enough to make significant alterations. Those changes which were made to the park are being carefully restored by the Fitzmaurices. Their next major task is to be the restoration of the Repton temple, which stands on a man-made island in the lake.

Ben remembered his parents discussing the temple when he was little. It had seemed a magical building to him, a place where goblins might live. His parents always intended to repair it, but never found the courage. Though they were both knowledgeable gardeners, they were less well informed about buildings, and this acted as a disincentive to action. Ben recalled his mother telling him that an architect friend had warned of the likely expense of such a project. From a distance the temple did not look too bad, and so it was left to languish.

Ben found he wanted to know something more about Henry Faulkes, the man who had paid for the temple and had once walked the same walks in the park, slept, eaten, lived and loved in the same rooms that Ben now occupied.

He had never researched anything like this before, so he talked to Ruby about it, and showed her the piece in his parents' old book. She was fascinated to find that so many artists had been connected with Oakstead, and volunteered to find out more about them.

She looked up all the names on the internet. Nothing relevant came up about John Farrell, but she had more success with G. J. Brunsworth. He had been a popular writer in his time, although his fame had not lasted. Ruby worked out that while he was living at the Hall he had written a successful trilogy with the titles *Anne Hill*; *Summer Ends;* and *The Cold Plough*. According to the review she found, on the website of a second hand book-shop, the trilogy followed the 'trials and tribulations of a farming family in the mid-nineteenth century, starting with the matriarchal figure, Anne Hill, and continuing with her ramshackle children, and grandchildren.' Ruby wondered if the novels had been based on a real family, living nearby. The books had gone out of print long ago, and the original editions up for sale were well outside Ruby's price range. She moved on to the soprano, Jane Kenneth, and found a small website about her, put up as part of a music degree dissertation. Kenneth had been a child prodigy, born at the Hall, and singing from the age of two. Her first public performance at the Assembly Rooms in Norwich had taken place when she was five. At the height of her fame in her teens and early twenties she had been fêted all over Europe, singing at court, and in all the main opera houses. But then in 1910, at the age of twenty-four, she had collapsed and died while performing the role of Dido. There were no recordings of her voice.

The next owner, Geraldine Fox, appeared in several snippets to be found on the web. She was a background figure amongst the Bloomsbury set, providing occasional comfortable country weekends for the likes of Virginia and Leonard Woolf, Maynard Keynes and Roger Fry. Fox was the wife of a factory owner whose business went bust during the First World War. The Hall was sold on to Margaret Ward.

Ward was still in print and Ruby ordered a copy of *The Lost Summer* from the bookshop in Holt. The blurb on the back cover said that Ward 'blended the heat of human passion with a lyrical vision of the natural world'. The story was set just before the outbreak of war, and followed the developing relationship between a rich young woman, and a humble farm worker, who meet secretly in dark woods and on desolate heaths. At the outbreak of war the hero joins the army and is then lost, presumed dead. The novel had a tragic *Romeo and Juliet*-type ending, as the heroine kills herself a day before the man returns unscathed. Ruby enjoyed the book but couldn't help laughing sometimes at the imagery of throbbing and sappy nature, which laced the story with sexual innuendo. She finished it in bed one night, with Ben curled up around her, gently snoring. He woke up as she put the book down and turned off the light.

'Isn't it amazing,' she said, as he laid his head on her shoulder, 'that so many artistic people have lived in this house?'

'Mmm,' mumbled Ben.

'I wonder if any of them slept in here? Imagine if Virginia Woolf had stood looking out of our window at the lake. Or the singer, practising her scales. Do you think they're still here in some way?'

'Ghosts, do you mean?'

'No, not ghosts. But maybe memories, atmospheres, some kind of energy.'

Ben rolled over, half asleep, muttering, 'No ghosts here. I've never seen one, anyway. Night-night.'

Ben didn't like computers, so he looked Faulkes up in a historical bibliography for the county, which he had found amongst his parents' books. There were three references listed. One was a piece written by Faulkes entitled *A*

Treatise on the Nature and Properties of the Soil of Norfolk Chemically and Geologically considered in Relation to Agricultural Purposes. Another was called *An Essay on Agriculture, with a View to Managing Estates to the Greatest Advantage.* Copies of these were available in the local history library in Norwich. The third was a short memoir of Henry Faulkes, written by his nephew in the 1830s, when he had lived in Oakstead and had been rector of the parish. It was called *Memoirs of the Life and Character of Henry Faulkes by his nephew, Augustus Faulkes.* This handwritten document was held by the Faulkes Estate in Derbyshire. The only way to see it would be to make an appointment and go there. Ben wrote to the estate and was pleased to get a reply within two weeks.

Dear Mr Fitzmaurice,
Thank you for your recent letter of enquiry regarding Henry Faulkes, and your interest in his occupancy of Oakstead Hall in the late eighteenth century.

The Faulkes Estate archive is very large and has, unfortunately, never been formally catalogued. A few documents, such as the memoirs you mention in your letter, have indeed been abstracted from the collection over the years by interested researchers. These documents mostly appertain to the viscount's interest in agriculture, which was, of course, the principal reason for his fame. The rest of the archive consists of bundles of material which, as far as I can tell, were loosely sorted by subject matter in a hurried way prior to the occupation of Henford Hall by the army during the war.

As you know, Henry Faulkes only lived in Norfolk for a few years prior to his father's death, after which he inherited Henford and spent the rest of his life here. I am therefore not at all sure that there is any extant documentation which relates to his time at Oakstead Hall. However, you are very welcome to look through any of the documents we have, by appointment. In the meantime, I enclose a short booklet about the Faulkes family at Henford Hall, which may be of interest.

I look forward to hearing from you.

Yours sincerely,

Marjorie Sayer (Estate Secretary)

A few days later, Ben travelled up to Henford to see what he could find. Henford Hall was a vast house, much bigger than Oakstead. From the booklet sent by Mrs Sayer, Ben learned that the building had grown over several centuries. Somewhere, lurking at the back, was a wing from the original sixteenth-century hall. But his main impression, as he arrived, was of a massive Palladian mansion, built around a central courtyard. To one side he could see a further large extension, which the booklet said was built by Henry Faulkes during the early nineteenth century, when his agricultural prowess had brought even greater wealth to the family. It was only later in that century, when there was a general agricultural depression, that the family had been forced to be more restrained, and satellite properties such as Oakstead Hall had been sold to alleviate a cash-flow problem. This was the sole allusion in the booklet to the Norfolk connection.

Mrs Sayer was just how Ben expected an estate secretary to be. She was a lady in her sixties, with perfectly set hair and a tweedy twinset. She had lived in a spacious apartment in the eighteenth-century part of the house for over thirty years, and she had a proprietary air about her. She welcomed Ben in and made him a cup of coffee while explaining how she tried to organise the archive.

'I would love to catalogue it properly, but I simply don't have the time, and the present Viscount has other priorities. He lives abroad most of the year, now that the house is open to the public. So, as you can imagine, I find myself with my hands full dealing with all the day-to-day administrative business of the estate. All I can do is make a note of what people find when they come to visit, so that I gradually build up an index. So I'd be grateful if, before you go, you could write in my visitors' book which documents you've read.' She handed him his cup of coffee. 'I had a look in the book before you came, to see if anyone had come across documents connected to the viscount's time in Norfolk, but there was nothing obvious. Not many researchers have been here in the last few years. I think people are put off by the chaotic nature of the archive. Students these days seem to want an easier time of it.'

She led him down some back stairs into the old servants' quarters, dank and dreary. At the end of a windowless corridor she opened a large metal door, which looked like the entrance to a bank vault. Inside was a barrel-vaulted room, piled high with boxes. The light shafted in through small iron grilles positioned above head height, but which opened onto ground level outside. It was musty, brown and cold despite the sunny August day outside.

'I'm sorry it's such an inhospitable room, but we think it would be fireproof if the worst was to happen. If you go halfway down the corridor the way we came, there is a door, which leads up to a courtyard outside. Do feel free to take any boxes outside that you think might be interesting, in this lovely weather. By the way, the visitors' restaurant sends us some lunch over at one o'clock. Would you like to join us then?'

Ben said he would be very grateful, and Mrs Sayer left him alone with the boxes. Daunted by the vast number of them, he didn't really know where to start. He began to read the labels, which were stuck to the side of each one. *Kitchen accounts circa 1821–26 plus vegetable rotation plans 1823–1828*; *Wages books 1873–94 and tenancy agreements various*; *Stables accounts 1844–47 plus menu plans miscellaneous*; *Miscellaneous correspondence 18th century*. Ben looked inside this box as it seemed promising. The box bulged with crammed-in papers, notes, folded letters on thick vellum, barely traceable scrawls on crumbling tissue, torn-off scraps. He made a few attempts at reading some of them, but found it almost impossible. Always there was a word in each sentence which he could not discern and so the meaning was lost. He tried to read a letter, which had 'Roma, October 1793' written at the top. It was addressed to Henry Faulkes at Oakstead. But after the first few lines of greeting the writing descended into a scrawl and, when Ben looked closer, some of it appeared to be in Italian. He couldn't make sense of it. He felt deflated. He stood looking at the rows and rows of boxes and realised that the pre-war cataloguing had been very haphazard, and that he was going to be lucky to find anything of interest in the single day he had allowed himself.

By one o'clock, when Mrs Sayer came to fetch him for lunch, he was feeling thoroughly thwarted. He had spent two hours opening up dusty, smelly boxes full of meaningless accounts and barely legible lists. None of it brought him nearer to the personality of Henry Faulkes, and barely any of it related to Norfolk. He didn't even find any accounts for the Norfolk years. He guessed that they had just got left behind at Oakstead, and thrown away. When he told Mrs Sayer how unsuccessful he had been, she was very apologetic and said she always felt responsible when people came so far and went away empty-handed.

'However,' she said, 'you must not forget to look at the memoirs while you are here. They are rather diverting and won't take you long to read. I have put them out in my drawing room, if you would like to read them there. I think it would do you good, to be released from that dungeon for an hour or so.'

After his lunch and coffee, gently chatting with Mrs Sayer and her assistant at a table under an apple tree in the private garden, Ben felt slightly more optimistic. When the two ladies went back to work, he sat in Mrs Sayer's elegant drawing room and settled down to the memoirs. The book was bound in dark blue material with no writing on it. The edges of the pages were marbled. Inside, the paper was stiff and stained brown, and gave off the smell of damp sawdust, which wafted about the room. The memoirs were written in a large and uneven hand, which filled the pages with only three or four words on each line. They looked as though they had been written in a hurry, or in an agitated state. In places there were smudges, which Ben thought might be tear stains. He was not used to reading this kind of hand-writing and it took him some time to decipher it.

Memoirs of the Life and Character of Henry Faulkes, by his Nephew, Augustus Faulkes. 19th February 1834.

I sit down to write these memoirs of my esteemed uncle in a state of mourning, having heard of his passing yesterday. He was my patron and my guide in all things and I have been overwhelmed with the boun-tifulness of his generosity towards me and towards my family. My dear, gentle wife sits weeping in our dark-ened drawing room, unable to conceal her grief over the loss of our good and sweet protector. The wisdom of years which my uncle had gathered and which he utilised with such energy and erudition, will be sorely missed by all that were honoured to know him.

My earliest memories of him, when I was a boy, are of magnificent Christmas times, when the whole family enjoyed delightful holidays at Henford Hall. We were always invited to arrive on the 17th of December when celebrations would begin in prepara-tion for the special day. On the first evening of our stay there would be a remarkable ball, where the viscount and his family, and any visitors prepared to take part in the masquerade, would dress up as lowly servants, and would wait upon all the maids and footmen. We children would dress up as page boys and maids and would scurry about clearing tables and

bringing drinks. It was always a very happy and bois-
terous evening, and I am quite certain that this kind of
occasion was a principal reason for the popularity of
the viscount with his household. After the feast there
would be the ball, where people of all stations in life
danced together. When the first one or two dances
were over we children would be ushered to our beds,
but the ball would continue until dawn. Some people
may look with displeasure on such an entertainment,
but I believe that my uncle was following his Christian
duty by providing for his people so generously. My
uncle was always a kind and true benefactor of those
less fortunate than himself, and his charity was bound-
less.

On Christmas Eve all the members of the household
would go out into the woods with much merrymaking,
and collect baskets of greenery, singing carols along
the way. I remember the cold crisp air of the
Derbyshire moorlands and the plumes of steam from
the singers' lips as we walked through the woodland
paths of Henford Park. On our return from the woods,
the older people partook of a delicious-smelling drink
from the wassail bowl in the Great Hall. The sweet
smell of that drink haunted me and made my mouth
water. It was the aroma of warm spices and cream. I
cried heartily when my mother would not allow me to
take even a sip of the drink but, one time, when I was
ten years old, my dear uncle smuggled for me a small
draught of the concoction in a silver tankard, telling
my mother it was warm milk. Unfortunately, at so
young an age, I was not able to appreciate the mixture
of ale, apples, spices and cream which, despite the
addition of sugar, still tasted bitter to me.
Nevertheless, I drank every mouthful, not wishing to
displease or disappoint my kindly uncle.

After this hearty drink, the Great Hall entrance
would be garlanded with greenery from the woods so

that, as a young child, I believed a magical forest had suddenly grown up in our midst. I would hinder the maids and other helpers by trying to climb up the boughs of ivy, which would usually end in mishap and much howling from me, as I met with the sharp prickles of the holly. Then, with great ceremony, the Yuletide log would be a-lighted. The mighty old tree trunk was brought in one or two days before, by the men of the family and the servants. Once it was lighted on Christmas Eve, it was imperative that it stayed alight until Twelfth Night, if bad luck was not to be brought upon the house. We children would often times wake at night with the terrible fear that the Yule log had been extinguished, and we would creep down the long corridors from the nursery, and go to the top of the sweeping stairs which led down to the Great Hall. Though it seemed like the dead of night to us, when we reached the top of the stairs we would invariably hear laughter and music, the clinking of glasses and the rustle of dresses as everyone danced and celebrated the festive season. Sometimes we would venture far enough down the stairs to be able to glimpse the celebrations. It was a spellbinding sight, with hundreds of glittering candles lighting up the shiny leaves of the holly and ivy, and causing the chandeliers and the ladies' jewellery to sparkle. Of course, now I am in my mature years and am a servant of God in His church, I realise how foolish these superstitious customs were, but I believe my uncle was amused by the wonderment in the faces of the children and the women and servants, and he loved to be the provider of entertainment and joy. These little ceremonies, though frowned upon by some of my fellow brethren in the Church, were, I believe, harmless to us in our childish innocence. Indeed, my memories of these Christmas times are filled with awe and wonder, which are surely the best sentiments we can aspire to at that most holy time, the anniversary of the birth of our Saviour, the Lord Jesus Christ.

I cannot emphasise enough how kindly my uncle was to me and to my family. I am unable to enumerate the many miserable stories I have heard of arrogant heirs to wealth disowning their less fortunate brothers and sisters and failing to bring to bear the influence which they could so readily use to increase the happiness and comfort of their poorer relations. My uncle was instrumental in procuring positions in the army and the navy for my younger brothers, and he was most solicitous in promoting good matches for my three sisters, all of whom are now comfortably settled. To my great good fortune he bestowed upon me the living here at Oakstead which has been my home for four years. With the certainty of a home and an income I was able to marry Henrietta, who is the dearest and most amiable companion a man could wish for. Now that we have our sweet little daughter and, with God's blessing, a brother or sister expected soon, I could not be more happy, were it not for these melancholy tidings of my uncle's passing away. I am comforted by the knowledge that he is with God, and is in the perfect bliss that is the reward for all true Christians, in Paradise.

My uncle was always an active and interested man, who took his responsibilities seriously. He was very learned, and accumulated a vast library of books on every subject imaginable. He was, of course, always most assiduous in his studying of agriculture, which was his burning concern. But he also collected an impressive number of works on the subjects of natural history, religion and architecture. He found great amusement in engaging me in discussion on religious matters, particularly when I declared my intention to take holy orders. He loved to tease me with outrageous views, to test my knowledge and the resilience of my beliefs. I believe that these debates did indeed strengthen my commitment to the word of God, through rehearsing the truth of the Gospel under the onslaught of my uncle's provoking arguments. Any clergyman who came within his sphere was likely to receive similar treatment, and I know there will be bishops and archdeacons around the country who will remember being scorched by the fire of my uncle's oratory. No doubt this was the source of the malicious rumours, which once besmirched his good name.

My uncle's energies were by no means all directed towards his own self-interest. He was properly conscious, when he took up his place in Parliament, of the moral obligations he had towards the poor who depended on his benevolence. He understood the fears and anxieties of the people at a time when moral support from their betters was sorely needed, and was deeply saddened by the conduct of landowners who, unlike himself, plundered the land and starved the people for their own gains. My uncle was as a wise and judicious father to the people under his governance and never used them unfairly.

I would like to record the appearance of my uncle for posterity. As a boy I was deeply impressed by his fine figure. Though he must already have been in his forties, he was tall and strong still, with no trace of grey in his black hair. His eyes were a startling blue, and he had a strong and imperious chin. In my recollections of him he is always smiling and laughing, striding about the Hall, calling to his servants, to his dogs or to the children. He was beloved of everyone. It is very painful to me to imagine the world without him present in it.

Here the memoirs broke off. Ben imagined Augustus Faulkes sitting in a small dark room in the rectory at Oakstead, with the rain pouring down outside, and the

60

sound of weeping drifting up the stairs from the drawing room. He saw him sitting at a desk, his head in his hands, the pen discarded, and tears dropping onto the page creating little rivulets in the wet ink. Perhaps he had risen to go down to his wife and comfort her, meaning to return to the memoirs at a later date. Perhaps, once he rose, the impulse to write down his thoughts passed away. He may even have felt foolish for giving in to the impulse in the first place. Whatever the reason, there was no more. It was tantalising for Ben to think that the notes had been written in Oakstead, even though there was nothing in them about the viscount's time in Norfolk. Of course, Augustus had probably not even been born when the viscount spent those few years in Oakstead.

When Mrs Sayer returned to see how he was getting on, and to offer him a cup of tea, Ben asked her what she knew about Augustus.

'I know very little, unfortunately. He was rector at Oakstead during the eighteen thirties and then he went on to be an archdeacon somewhere. By the way, it occurred to me that you might like to see a portrait of Henry while you're here. We have one of him when he was just married.'

Ben followed her down various corridors and across courtyards and up several flights of stairs, until they came to a large gallery room devoted to portraits of the Faulkes family. Ben was impressed by the appearance of the newly married Henry Faulkes. The portrait showed him standing with one foot resting on a fallen tree trunk gazing straight out at the viewer. He had very dark hair, and a vibrant expression, his eyes burning from the canvas. Ben thought perhaps this was just a trick of the painter. Sitting sideways on the tree trunk was the viscount's wife, looking up admiringly at her husband. The setting seemed to be an imaginary landscape, with a distant perspective of a river winding through a flat meadow, and wooded hills rising in the background. Then Ben noticed that at the feet of the

61

viscount there was a roll of paper which, on close inspection, had a faint drawing on it, of sketchy buildings and three connected spiralling circles. The viscount's right hand, which Ben had at first thought was just hanging at his side, was in fact pointing at this drawing. He mentioned this to Mrs Sayer.

'Yes, that always gets people asking questions. No one knows for sure what it means, but it seems most likely that they are supposed to show plans, perhaps for the house at Oakstead. He has just married and he is indicating what he intends to do now, with the onset of new responsibilities. He was rather wild as a bachelor, and it's thought that the parents of his wife were very concerned that marriage would not reform him.'

'What kind of things did he get up to? It says something in the memoir about malicious rumours.'

'Well, the usual things, I think. Wine, women, gambling. His father had rather a reputation as well. So this picture may have been his way of showing that he was making plans for the future. Someone thought the circles were plans for a maze, but it wasn't possible to identify a real maze at any of the Faulkes' houses.'

'I've certainly never heard anyone talk about one at Oakstead.'

'And the landscape in the background hasn't been identified either. You'd think it might be Norfolk, as that is where they went to live, but the hills rather discount that, don't you think?'

Ben was not so sure. The landscape seemed oddly familiar. Oakstead did not possess a range of hills, but it did have one big one, which rose up to the coastal ridge at the back of the house. And there was a very similar meandering river at Oakstead. It seemed to him that the painting was an idealised representation of the best parts of the Oakstead estate, and that perhaps the plans at the viscount's feet showed how he intended to improve the landscape of his new home. He started to feel quite excited and he told

Mrs Sayer his theory. She was intrigued.

'Well, that is an interesting idea, Mr Fitzmaurice. Living there you would probably recognise things that other people might not notice. Yes, I can quite imagine that behind those hills there is the sea. Well, well. You'll have to send me some photographs of your estate so that I can see what you're describing. And perhaps we could then write a short article in our local archaeological journal. I'm sure people would be most interested in what you have to say.'

It was getting on for five o'clock by the time Ben and Mrs Sayer had finished discussing these new ideas over a cup of tea and biscuits. Ben began to feel anxious to leave, as it would take nearly four hours to get back, and he wanted to see Ruby. But as he was beginning to say his goodbyes, Mrs Sayer reminded him of the visitors' book. Though he had found nothing relevant, he had made notes of all the document references. He felt obliged to stay and write them in the book kept in Mrs Sayer's study, especially as she had been so hospitable.

Before he began to write Ben ran his eye down the few entries made by other researchers on the facing page. The first entry intrigued him. It was by a student who was researching her PhD, entitled 'Commercial Intercourse: the exchange of daughters for titles in 18th century Derbyshire'. The documents she had looked at all related to Henry's wife, Charlotte. Ben noted down her contact details, just in case they might be useful in the future. But then another name on the page caught his eye: Professor Lal, in an entry written some two years before. His list of documents was enormously long and covered what seemed to be miscellaneous subjects with no unifying feature.

'Do you remember Professor Lal's visit?' Ben asked Mrs Sayer, who was sitting on the opposite side of the table.

She looked up quickly from a letter she was reading. 'Yes, I do. Do you know him?'

'I've met him once. He visited Oakstead.'

'Really? Did you like him? I found him charming. So

much so I read his book, and was rather surprised by it. It's not what you would expect from so unassuming a man. Rather racy for my taste.'

'Yes, he is something of a surprise. Do you know what he was researching, when he came here?'

'Let me think.' Mrs Sayer leaned back in her chair. 'I believe it was to do with experiments in rotation of crops, and the way Henry Faulkes raised the fertility of the land, with his use of manure and suchlike. None of it got into the book though. He was here for days looking at numerous boxes. As you can see from his list, he just seemed to plough through box after box. Very useful for me'

'Do you know if he found anything particularly interesting?'

'Well, I think he must have eventually, because he stopped before he'd looked through all the boxes, as if he'd found what he was looking for.'

'But you don't know what it was?'

She made a rueful face. 'No, he didn't discuss that with me, I'm afraid. Do you think it might have been useful to you?'

'I don't know. It just seems rather a coincidence that he should have come to visit me, and he seemed to know so much about Oakstead. I was surprised at the time.'

'Well, the only thing I can suggest is that you look at the box which is the last entry in the list. I imagine he wrote the entries in the order he looked at them, and so the last box will have been the one where he found something.' She got up briskly from her chair. 'I'm prepared to stay for another half an hour if you think it would be useful to look in the basement again.'

Ben looked at his watch. Half past five. He was desperate to get home in time to see Ruby. A childlike frustration welled up inside him in response to this further delay; there was a hint of tears at the back of his eyes, an impulse to stamp his foot. He was so tired, the day had been a waste of time, and he could have spent it with Ruby. But this was the closest he had got to finding something concrete about Oakstead, and it had the potential to make the visit worthwhile. He took a deep breath, exhaled, and pulled himself together.

'That would be very kind of you.'

He noted down the number of the last box on Lal's list and the description of its contents: *Business letters and accounts for dairy 1834–37*. It did not look very promising. Mrs Sayer led him back down to the gloomy underground storeroom.

It was some time before they found the box. It had been wedged behind a stack of other boxes in the wrong place. Inside it there was a large wedge of brown, slightly greasy letters, bound with a ribbon. Ben untied the ribbon and carefully separated the letters from each other. Then he unfolded each one. Most of them were letters from other people to Henry. Several were requests for payment. Some were requests for financial help or investment. The majority were dated from the early part of the nineteenth century and were addressed to Henford. But Ben was excited to find that a few were earlier, and were addressed to Oakstead. The first two letters were from tailors in London requesting payment for items bought over two years previously. The third letter was more interesting. It appeared to be from the vicar of Oakstead, a Mr Joshua Rackham. It was dated 17th July 1794:

The Rectory
Oakstead

Sir,
I have been wrestling with my conscience since I saw you last, and I have been praying fervently for guidance. In the eyes of the Lord our God, I have no choice but to write to you. I am in deepest anxiety about the state of your soul, and I would beg you to take the contents of this letter as a token of my affectionate concern for your welfare rather than the

insufferable interference of a cleric, which I fear will be your first reaction. I have been pleased to think of myself as your friend, and I earnestly hope that you will forgive my boldness in addressing you thus.

My dear sir, that which you showed to me last week has shocked me beyond words. I cannot condone the nature of the work you have undertaken, and I entreat you, cease it now, and save your soul from perdition. I have prayed for you day and night since my visit, but I fear that only true repentance will save your soul from eternal damnation. I implore you, return now to the loving fold of our Saviour, the Lord Jesus Christ, and turn your face against this work of Satan.

I am keenly aware of the honour you showed me by taking me into your confidence, and I desire very much to continue the easy intercourse which has been our habit and which has been so precious to me. However, this intimacy cannot continue, if you insist on proceeding in such an unholy manner. All that I can do is to continue to pray for your soul, and for your return to the path of righteousness. I await your answer with a trembling heart, knowing full well how this letter will affect you, and you must believe me when I say that I am acting out of love and respect for your person. Nothing else in the world could persuade me to address you in this way.

Please believe me sir, to be your respectful servant,
Joshua Rackham

Mrs Sayer read the letter over Ben's shoulder.

'Goodness me,' she exclaimed. 'Whatever is that about, I wonder? What could Henry have been up to that made a clergyman write to him in that way? I'd be surprised if the vicar kept his job after a letter like that.'

'Would Henry have had any influence over the vicar?' Ben asked.

'Absolutely. The living at Oakstead was in the gift of the

viscount, who at that time would have been Henry's father, the fourth Viscount Faulkes. I'm fairly sure that if Henry Faulkes was displeased with the local vicar he could have got his father to do something about it.'

Ben tried to work out whether this was the document which Professor Lal had found so interesting and, if so, how it could possibly relate to the professor's research. The other papers in the box consisted of irrelevant bills, begging letters and accounts for cattle feed. He felt too tired to think through what he had found. Squinting at all these old documents had given him a headache. He looked at his watch. Half past six. An image of Ruby drifted into his head: Ruby, in her cottage, cooking something nice, pottering around in her kitchen, the radio on. A pang of longing shot through him. He wanted to be lying with his head in her lap, her hands stroking his forehead, her soft voice reassuring him that the visit to Henford had not been pointless. He hurriedly arranged with Mrs Sayer that he would send her a list of his notes and would phone to fix a time for another visit in the near future. Then he leaped into his car and drove recklessly fast back to Norfolk.

September

Few gardeners will have any great opinion of September sowings, yet there are some things to be done in that way very advantageous.

Mrs Martha Bradley

Today feels like the first day of autumn. The light is a translucent gold and the early morning air feels chilled. Last night I spent a rare night at home on my own and it has given me time to think, and to be melancholy. I am standing in my doorway, looking out over the view, the trees with their first hint of dying orange, and the pale blue ice-cool sky. I like being here in my little cottage on my own, having time to just contemplate. The summer has been hectic and confusing. I feel like I have been turned upside down and shaken. Meeting Ben, and then George, was like a series of explosions. I feel misused by fate. I don't understand which path I am supposed to take. I imagine dancing, Puck-like figures, mischievously ushering George into my life, just to cause a little mayhem.

I know that Ben is the right and sensible path, and yet, being on my own, I can't help imagining George here in the kitchen, standing with his arms round me looking at the view. I can control it when Ben is here, wrapping me up in his certainty. When he's away, these demons come back. I am still haunted by the knowledge that I have known

George before, and it tugs at me. It must mean something, for me to have these feelings? To ignore them may be such a mistake. But I am not very good at gambling; I let my imagination run riot, but in real life I am better at taking the safe and disciplined route. That is why Ben and I clicked together so easily. We have things we want to do. He with his wood-turning, me with my painting. Eating a lovely lunch of fresh salad from his garden is enough to make us both happy and then we go off again into our little worlds. I don't have to do anything but be myself to make him love me.

I have hardly spoken to George. A few chance meetings around the garden when we have only said hello and talked about the weather or the latest vegetable crop. It's laughable really. I am like a smitten teenager and I blush. The less I see him, though, the more powerful it is when we do bump into each other. It is something I have to control if I am going to stay with Ben and be happy, because George is not likely to leave. He loves the garden, and works every daylight hour and into the dusk. His nails are always dirty and he has turned walnut brown over the summer, like a romantic gypsy in an eighteenth-century landscape painting. He looks as though he has grown out of the soil here.

I don't believe I will ever get him out of my head unless I somehow find out the truth of him. I need to know what it is like to be kissed by him. I need to know that he feels something for me. I can't leave it alone. As I stand here looking out over this peaceful Elysian scene something inside me is moving relentlessly towards the precipice, where there will be no turning back. Even though I tell myself over and over again how foolish and damaging it will be to pursue George, there is some kind of deep-water monster swimming in my emotional depths, a stony-eyed beast after its prey. Is this the snake that Eve gave in to? Like her, I seem unable to resist.

Drawing helps me stop my mind; I turn to it for respite. This summer I have become fascinated by the produce from

Ben's garden. Or is it George's garden? Or Henry Faulkes'? I can't help feeling that the fertility he put into the soil here has remained, and seeped into the spirit of the place. The colours, shapes and textures have sparked a new energy in my painting. I am experimenting with flowers and vegetables. I don't need to make up the colours; they are dazzling in real life. This afternoon, I have been sketching courgette flowers. Beautiful bell-shaped and frilled, golden-yellow bloomers. It is getting late and the sun is beginning to go down. There is a light mist curling in over the garden. In the sky hangs a heavy full moon bathed in pink. The harvest moon, sliding up above the black tree branches. It means the summer is over, the crops have been brought in, the days are shortening. I feel cold, sitting here in shorts, the white sheets of my sketches becoming luminous in the deepening dusk. A bicycle ride will revive my circulation. I get on my bike and I cycle hard and fast. I cycle straight to George's cottage on the edge of the estate.

He is sitting in his garden in front of the mud oven he has been cooking in throughout the summer. A plume of woodsmoke perfumes the air. I stop in front of his gate and sit with my feet on the pedals, and I say hello. He is welcoming and asks me if I am on my way to see Ben, or whether I would like to stop and have some food with him. He has made a pizza in his oven. I am not on my way to see Ben. He has gone away to Derbyshire again for a couple of days. I bring my bike in off the road and I sit next to George on his straw bale. It is so lovely to be with him on my own, to have his attention, and to be unobserved by others. My heart expands with fluttering happiness. We are having a proper talk for the first time sitting out under the paper circle moon. We talk about the garden, and the cycle of work through the seasons. He says he doesn't mind autumn and winter, even though it brings an end to the frenetic summer fruiting and flowers. He says he loves digging. He likes digging in manure and feeling that the soil is absorbing it and expanding with nourishment. He says it's nice to make a clean start every year. A clean sheet, a slice of brown crumbly chocolate. I tell him about my painting and how it has been inspired by the fruitfulness of his garden. He is very pleased. He smiles at me, his teeth shining in the moonlight. A broad, inviting smile, with that lovely, plummy mouth and the small laughter lines either side. I want to run my finger along those little dimples. I say I will give him one of my paintings in thanks for his inspiration. Somehow, everything I say starts to have a double meaning.

We are drinking wine and I am beginning to feel reckless. I suggest we go for a walk into the evening trees, shimmering poplars at the bottom of his garden. The moonlight and the breeze make their leaves flutter silver. We walk together closer than we would in daytime. Then he grabs me, his arm hard around my shoulder, stopping me. I am confused for a moment, then realise he is looking up the row of trees to a fox standing frozen in our path. We stand completely still. The fox sniffs the air, but we are down wind of him and he can't pick up our scent. He stands stock-still for a few more seconds and then suddenly he is gone. George whispers: Sorry, I hope you didn't mind me grabbing you, but I thought you'd like to see the fox.

I say weakly: I am glad you grabbed me.

He laughs, but walks on, clearing a path to show me a twiggy wigwam he has found, a den made by village children. Then we jump down the bank into the lane and walk along the silver-grey road, listening to the night, the screech of an owl, the bark of a fox. I put my arm through his as we walk along. I probe a little, to find out about his life. He has been here only two years, working like a Trojan to bring the garden back to life. Before he came here he lived with a woman who was also a gardener on another estate in Kent. When the relationship failed, he had to leave the house and the job as well as her. He says he was angry at the time, but he is grateful now, because of the opportunity it has given him to work on such a special garden. He doesn't ask me personal questions. He knows,

71

after all, that I am with Ben. A cold little droplet of an idea enters my head: George will never do anything to jeopardise his way of life here, so he is not likely to enter into clandestine dealings with his boss's girlfriend. I am making a fool of myself flirting with him in the middle of the night, when I should be at home and thinking about Ben. I shiver. He notices and says: Maybe we should head back. It's cooling off.

I suddenly feel miserable about the way I have been behaving. Why did I come here and why did I drink? George must be thinking I am silly and vain. When we get back to his house, he invites me in for a warm drink, but I say: No thanks, I've taken up too much of your time already. I think I'll go straight home.

I am cycling fast, hoping the breeze will blow away this terrible feeling I have, of my treacheries, my vanity, my weakness. I burn with embarrassment. My head prickles with the disagreeable consciousness that I cannot erase my behaviour and make George forget it. It is done and cannot be undone. His impression of me must be something like a dog on heat. I feel so distressed about the way I have exposed Ben. I want so much to be happy and content as we were, but there seems to be some kind of poison in my blood. I need Ben to be here, to save me with his certainty.

Ben returned from his second visit to Derbyshire newly inspired by his research and his discussions with Marjorie Sayer. He had taken photographs of Oakstead park with him to Henford, to compare with the background landscape of the Faulkes portrait. Although he could not absolutely confirm it, he felt certain that the painting was an exaggerated version of the Norfolk park. He and Marjorie spent a morning together, comparing the photographs and the portrait, and chatting about Henry Faulkes.

'I think he was one of those brilliant people who don't quite know how to use it to the good, and it made him a little mad,' said Marjorie.

'What kind of things did he do that were mad?'

'Well, I think he fought numerous duels. He was very quick to take offence, which was unfortunate for people who crossed him. It's known that he was a very accomplished swordsman and a good shot, and he never lost a fight. One of the reasons he spent so much time abroad in his twenties was because he was forever running people through or blasting holes in them, and then having to flee the country.'

'Did he actually kill anyone?'

'It's not known for certain, but it seems quite likely, when you think of the state of medicine in those days. Presumably the power of his father protected him from prosecution. Perhaps we would have heard more about it if Henry had killed someone important. I don't know.'

Ben frowned. He felt that the pieces did not all fit together. 'In those memoirs of his nephew he sounds like this rather lovely, cuddly man who wanted everyone to have a nice time.'

Marjorie looked up at the portrait affectionately. 'He was obviously a man of many parts. I imagine he mellowed as he grew older, and perhaps the duties of being the fifth viscount calmed him down somewhat. Also he married and had the responsibilities of a family to think of. And perhaps his interest in agriculture cured his restlessness.'

'It doesn't sound as exciting as gambling and fighting, does it?'

She laughed, a short bark. 'True. It's something we'll probably never get to the bottom of.'

Before he left, Ben studied the portrait of Henry Faulkes for a long time. Faulkes looked out imperiously at him. He was dressed in a long blue jacket and waistcoat, with a ruffle of white neck-scarf around his throat. His knee breeches were a dull yellow, and his shins were sheathed in glossy white. The clothes were late eighteenth century, but his face had a strangely modern expression. He looked like a person you might see in a magazine, a singer or an actor, with an arrogant, challenging stare. He did not resemble the usual pale-eyed, stiff-limbed figures that Ben had seen hanging in many National Trust houses. How did it feel, Ben wondered, to be suddenly brought to heel by his father, after his itinerant life on the Continent? Is there a hint of desperation in his eyes as he glares out at us? Perhaps he is wondering how he will survive in this godforsaken backwater, with his clinging wife whom he cannot love. He will immerse himself in ambitious plans. He will transform this hamlet in the furthest flung corner of England into an exemplary estate, with the finest of everything. He will bring society to his doorstep, the finest artists and designers, the best minds and intellects. This will save him from death by tedium.

Faulkes' wife, Charlotte, drooping on the tree trunk by her husband's side, was less vividly drawn. She looked more like an eighteenth-century stereotype of beauty, with her small rosebud mouth, high forehead, and sloping shoulders. Life for her must have been very hard. Surely Henry did not give up his previous vices just because his father decided to marry him off to a merchant's daughter? Perhaps the portrait was an accurate depiction of an already exhausted and disappointed woman, trying dutifully to please this difficult man. Perhaps she loved him. He was the kind of man women adore. Difficult, but handsome.

Looking so closely at the portrait kindled in Ben a deeper interest in Faulkes' wife. A new sympathy for her grew in him as he studied her defeated demeanour and the rather puppy-like eyes. It can't have been easy, he thought to himself, to be married to a man with such a temper. He went to find Mrs Sayer in her office, and asked to see the entry made in the record book by the PhD student who had researched Charlotte. His heart sank as he looked through the list of documents she had recorded: menus, bills, accounts, invitations. What could they tell him? He pictured the strongroom where all the old boxes of documents were kept, so cold and dark, and he thought, I can't face riffling through all those old boxes in that dungeon, and coming up with nothing again. Clapping the book shut, he looked up at Mrs Sayer. 'Do you remember this student, Jayne Greene?'

Mrs Sayer mused for a moment. 'Yes, I think so. Perfectly nice girl, as I recall.'

'Do you think she was the kind of person who would mind me contacting her, to see what she found out?'

Mrs Sayer rustled her papers slightly impatiently. 'No harm in trying, I imagine.'

Ben drove home considering the differences between the Oakstead that Henry had known, and the present-day estate. In Henry's time, he presumed, the house and park would have been teeming with people, but most of them would have been unworthy of Henry's attention. Instead, he would have relied on bringing people from London, from his aristocratic circle, to entertain him. Ben thought about his own friends, the people he spent most time with. Apart from Charlie, they were from very different backgrounds: teachers, businessmen, café owners and shopkeepers. He wouldn't have given them a second glance in the eighteenth century. There must have been times when Henry was desperate for good company on the estate. No wonder he turned to his near neighbour, the vicar, for entertainment.

Charlie was working in his room when there was a knock on the door. He called out, 'Yeah?'

Ruby came in. 'Sorry to disturb you. I just wondered if you might know anything about this Geraldine Fox who lived here.'

Charlie pushed his chair back to look at Ruby. He noticed that she was wearing a tight-fitting T-shirt and a long skirt, with nothing on her feet. He wondered momentarily whether she had anything on under the skirt, or whether he could just lift it, perhaps lean her against the door, press himself up against her, nothing in the way ...

He gazed at Ruby for a second longer than was comfortable. She made an apologetic face. 'Sorry. Have I

75

interrupted a train of thought?'

Charlie shook his head, to clear away the image. 'Sorry? Who?'

'Geraldine Fox. She was apparently something to do with the Bloomsbury set.'

'Was she? Never heard of her. But then I've never really been into the whole Bloomsbury thing. Bunch of shirt-lifters and mad women. I've got one or two books you could borrow, though.' He stood up and ambled over to his bookshelves.

Ruby had never ventured into Charlie's room before, and she was amazed by the vast number of books he owned, stacked neatly on shelves lining an entire wall of his large room.

'You've got a whole library here!' she exclaimed.

'I like books.' He lifted two large hardback books off the shelf. 'There you go. Have a look at these, see what you can find.'

Ruby was looking at the rest of the shelves. 'This is amazing. They're all in alphabetic order.'

'Of course. And in chronological order, and in separate subject categories. Otherwise I'd never find anything.'

Ruby took the books from him. 'You never cease to amaze me, Charlie.'

'How d'you mean?'

'Well, look at you. You're like a monk in his cell, with all your books, and your computer, tapping away about some-thing esoteric. It doesn't go with your party animal image.'

Charlie snorted. 'I have to earn a living.'

He returned to his desk, where he stared at the computer screen. Ruby followed and leaned over him slightly. As she did so, her left breast brushed against his arm.

'Are you writing about something interesting?'

A cold little shiver travelled along Charlie's arm, down his spine, and into his groin. He placed his hands in his lap to disguise what was happening there and sat quietly, hoping to feel again the soft rub of Ruby's breast, as she shifted position, reading over his shoulder. After a couple of minutes she stood upright again.

'It sounds like a good show. I should go. I haven't been to see anything in London for months.'

'Come with me sometime. I always have extra tickets.'

Ruby had begun to walk towards the door. Over her shoulder she said, 'Yes, maybe. Thanks for the book.'

After she had gone, Charlie got up and locked the door. Then he sat on his bed, unzipped his trousers, and enjoyed a five-minute fantasy, Ruby's skirt flapping against his thighs, those soft breasts rubbing against his chest.

September 23rd

Equinox. Here is one of the days of perfect balance with the night: half light, half dark. Yin and yang. Male and female. It's also the second harvest, before the nights draw in. All living things prepare for the winter, filling the cupboards and storehouses, the cellars and barns. I store away my moments with her, the times when I have felt she is close to me, that I could reach out and make her mine. I store away the look in her eye, the curve of her shoulder, the sway of her hips.

The book says that this is the season of thanksgiving, for celebration of the generosity of the goddess. Offerings should be made, the best of everything given back to Mother Earth as a sacrifice. In ancient times, when the harvest was a time of intense anxiety, a matter of survival, the sacrifices were human. And so this time of thankfulness must have been shadowed with fear, of sudden death or slow starvation. Joy and fear, light and dark, a balance. This is how I feel: a tentative hope, a feeling that there is a possibility of survival, of living with this desire, of it being met. But weighed against it, the fear of disappointment and loss. I will weather the long dark nights with my store of memories, and dream of spring.

October

Gather in fruit that is to be kept for the winter.

Mrs Martha Bradley

Professor Lal rang Ben one day early in October, from New York. He wanted to arrange another visit to Oakstead on his return to England. Ben told him about the impending repair of the temple and could sense tension in Lal's voice as he replied:

'I would very much like to visit before the repairs begin, if that would be possible. I would like to be able to experience a sense of place, without the interruption of scaffold and builders climbing around the place. Would it be possible, Mr Fitzmaurice, for me to come as soon as I am back in England? I would be so grateful.'

Ben said he was welcome any time he liked. The professor arrived very early in the morning, only three days later. He had made special arrangements to fit in a day in Norfolk between lecture dates in Europe. Ben was puzzled by the professor's extreme enthusiasm for the garden. It obviously stemmed from an interest in Henry Faulkes, but Ben couldn't see how it connected with Lal's other work. He decided to try wheedling the truth out of the professor before the day was over.

It was a pale Indian-summer day, thin sunlight washing through crisping leaves, long shadows stretching across the

78

dew-wet lawn. Ben had organised the repair of the rowing boat in order to take them over to the temple, but insisted on having breakfast first. The professor attempted to hide his impatience but was not very successful. He nervously jingled some coins together in his pocket, and repeatedly put his hand up to his forehead and pushed back his hair as if trying to smooth away a headache.

'I know you've come a terribly long way to see the temple,' Ben said, 'but really, you must be hungry yourself, and I can't do anything properly until I've eaten in the morning.'

He decided they should take breakfast in the orchard under a wizened tree, like an old man dancing. As they carried out trays of toast and jam, tea and coffee, muesli, fruit and yoghurt, Ben explained to the professor how the orchard had been one of his parents' successes.

'The trees had been neglected for years. They'd grown into thickets of impenetrable twigs, and the fruits were full of disease. My parents pruned and cosseted them like children. They used to do things like putting greasy rings around the tree trunks to deter codling moths, and brushing the aphids individually with methylated spirits. They tried to enlist my sisters and me to help, but it was terribly tedious, we never lasted long. We'd be off around the park, leaving them to do all the hard work.' Ben paused, and surveyed the surrounding trees. 'Now, of course I feel sorry I didn't spend more time with them. You take these things for granted when you're young.' He placed the tray of cutlery and plates carefully on the table.

The professor looked sympathetic. 'Your parents died quite recently?'

Ben nodded. 'In a motorway smash-up a couple of years ago.'

'That must be a great sorrow to you.' The professor shook his head. 'The loss of a mother or father is very hard.' Then he smiled encouragingly at Ben. 'But of course they live on in the trees and flowers, and the meadows they created.'

Ben sighed. 'Well, they certainly did a good job here.'

Ruby arrived with the cups and saucers, and they all sat down. The professor stretched and let out a long breath. The he chuckled. 'You are quite right to make me stop,' he said. 'I have been rushing, rushing, these past few weeks and I have forgotten how to just be. What an inspired idea, my dear Mr Fitzmaurice, to make me sit in the embodiment of the first garden, with these fateful fruits hanging above our heads. There is nothing so beautiful and yet so simple as the orchard. Beauty and fruitfulness, form and function united. It makes me think of that remarkable clergyman, William Lawson. He understood so well the significance of the garden and the rewards to be reaped from it. He wrote as long ago as the seventeenth century, something like this: "Now pause with your self, and view the end of all your labours in an orchard: unspeakable pleasure and infinite commodity." A man of great insight, I think you'll agree. "Unspeakable pleasure". Absolutely, absolutely.'

Ruby poured him a cup of coffee and asked, 'Do you know much about apples, Professor Lal? There are so many different ones here, and there seem to be more than one kind of apple on each tree.'

'I know a little. Though, of course, the fruit hanging on the tree of knowledge was probably a pomegranate, the apple still holds a special place in the heart of western culture.' He stood up and walked around the tree under which they were sitting. 'Yes, there are some very ancient apples here. Perhaps some of them are even descendants of trees planted by Henry Faulkes. They do not look as though they are commonplace apples.'

'My parents would have known.'

'I think it would be worth your while to have someone come look at these to identify them. I think you might find that you have an invaluable collection here.'

He turned to Ruby. 'You are right about the different types of apple on the same tree. This was common practice, to graft varieties on to the same rootstock. It allowed a wider variety of fruit on a smaller number of trees. As there is no shortage of space here, I imagine that this orchard may have been set up like an experimental laboratory, to test different fruits for flavour, pest resistance, and so on. Very interesting.'

'Ruby has been looking closely at the apples because she's using them in her paintings.' Ben beamed proudly at her. 'You should have a look at some of her work before you go. She's been painting all the vegetables from the garden. I think they're lovely.'

Professor Lal looked politely interested and said, 'Oh, are you an artist, Ruby? So much to inspire you here, I am sure. The park certainly seems to stimulate the creative spirit of its occupants. A remarkable place.'

After breakfast, they walked down to the lake and clambered into the rowing boat. Ben rowed while Ruby and the professor sat squeezed together on the seat opposite him. It only took two minutes to glide across; the boat nudged into the grassy bank. Ben climbed out and then helped Ruby and the professor. The temple looked very shabby at this close proximity. The door was unlocked. They stepped inside.

The lead on the roof had failed many years previously and rain had been leaking through onto the ceiling, causing large areas of it to collapse. Piles of clammy plaster and rotting ceiling laths were strewn across the floor, together with large amounts of pigeon droppings. Rising damp had forced the surface paint to peel off at the base of the walls and there was a thin sheen of grey mould all over the rest. Thick cobwebs with dead spiders hung across the windows making the temple even gloomier.

'It's awful, isn't it,' said Ben apologetically. 'If I'd known quite how bad it was I would have done something sooner.'

Professor Lal looked about him with a preoccupied air. 'It is a mess, that's true. But nothing irredeemable, I am sure.'

'That's what the architect says, thank goodness.'

'Can you tell me, Mr Fitzmaurice, what exactly the builders intend to do inside here?'

'Well, they're going to restore the roof, obviously. And then they're going to remove the modern paint from the walls, which will allow the damp to escape.'

'Do they plan to strip the walls completely back down to the brick, or will they attempt to salvage the plaster?'

'I'm not sure. I've rather left the detail up to the experts. Why do you ask?'

The professor looked thoughtful, raising his hands in a characteristic prayer-like movement to his pursed lips. 'I am working on a theory.'

He went up to one of the walls and scraped it with a small knife produced from his jacket pocket. He made one or two more scrapes in different areas and then stood looking pensive. Eventually he said:

'Mr Fitzmaurice, you remember my request to see the accounts for the work, which I unfortunately had no time for on my last visit? Would it be possible to see them now? I think it would be very interesting for me.'

The three rowed back over the lake and returned to the house where Ben had laid out the accounts for the Repton park. Then he and Ruby left the professor to look for whatever it was he wanted to find.

Sitting in the kitchen, Ruby said, 'Are you going to ask him about his research at Henford? Considering how loquacious he is about every other subject, he's been very reticent about that, hasn't he? I think you ought to ask him straight what it's all about.'

'I keep nearly asking. He's obviously harbouring some secret theory that he doesn't want to share with us. It's probably something terribly esoteric, like Henry's innovative ideas on manure. Perhaps that's what the vicar objected to. A viscount experimenting with different forms of cow dung.'

Ruby smiled, but then her brow creased. 'I don't really take to him. It may be that I'm influenced by that book he wrote, but he gives me the creeps. I'm sure he was squeezed up against me more than he needed to be on the boat, and then when you were helping me out onto the bank he put his hand on my bottom.'

Ben let out a surprised laugh. 'He didn't!'

'He did. I mean he may have been trying to help me out, but I didn't like it.'

'Well, I never. The cheeky so-and-so. Right then. I have no qualms about making him uncomfortable now. Fancy doing that to you under my nose, after all the help I've been giving him. Sorry, Ruby.'

When Professor Lal emerged from the study a couple of hours later, Ben was quick to lead him into conversation. 'Did you find anything interesting in the accounts?'

'I did. I am really beginning to think I can come to some conclusions.'

'Are you able to tell me what it's all about? As you can imagine, I'm rather intrigued.'

The professor sighed through his nose. 'It is like this. I do not feel ready yet to disclose my ideas. It is a harsh world, the world of academia. I am working on a new project and it is important that it is successful. I do not want other people to be on my trail.'

'Are you suggesting I'm not trustworthy?' Ben was affronted by the professor's implication. Lal spread out his hands in front of him and made an action as if he were smoothing out sheets on a bed.

'Mr Fitzmaurice, please do not be offended. To be frank with you, it is particularly important to me that my next publication is well accepted in my own world, the academic world. The ridiculous furore over the last book has been very exhausting. The amount of publicity it brought was too much for me to carry on my other research effectively. My next work must be more firmly rooted in my subject. But people already want to know what I am up to, and I am not ready yet.'

The professor smiled at Ben and continued. 'I know you

83

are full of English integrity, but think of all the academics who will descend upon you once the restoration of the temple is underway. I do not want to burden you with a secret. Far better that I keep it to myself. I would like to take home what I have found out today, put it together with what I already know, and think about it further, before making my conclusions known. At any rate, it may not be long before I have to talk to someone about it. I wonder, could you tell me the name of your contact at English Heritage? I would like to discuss some things with her.'

Ben was not going to be put off. 'I will tell you her name but I rather feel I have the right to know a little bit more about what's going on. The temple is my property after all, and I am putting a lot of money towards its repair. And while we're on the subject, I'd be interested to know what you found out at Henford Hall when you were there a couple of years ago.'

The professor looked slightly startled by Ben's new assertive tone. 'I was at Henford some time ago, that is true. May I ask how you know this?'

'I went there recently trying to find out a little more about Henry and his temple so that I could write a leaflet for visitors.'

'I see.'

'Mrs Sayer said you found something you were rather excited about.'

'Did she? I wonder why she thought that? I was researching for *Reaching Paradise* which, as you will remember, deals in one chapter with developments in raising the fertility of the soil through history. As an innovator in this field, I obviously was interested to know more about Henry Faulkes. I don't like to rely on published material for my information. So much is missed by closed minds. They publish, and their interpretation of the source material comes to be regarded as fact. Usually it is only the tip of the iceberg. There are so many hidden voices lost to us through the myopia of pompous historians. People live

84

shallow lives, you see, and so they only know how to read the surface of these documents. Deeper meanings, numerous possibilities, escape them.'

Professor Lal stopped suddenly, and laughed. 'I must apologise. This is something I feel rather strongly about. You asked me if I found anything interesting. As I remember, I spent several days there, ploughing through innumerable documents, and found little that was of particular relevance. It seems his published texts on farming remain the main source of information on him.'

'What about the angry letter from the vicar? Didn't you think that was interesting?'

The professor looked puzzled. 'What letter was that?'

'You know, the letter from the vicar here, saying he couldn't continue to be acquainted with Henry if he carried on doing whatever it was he was doing.'

'Oh, yes, that letter. I think I recall it. I read so many documents, you must understand, I cannot always remember every one. Somewhat of a mystery, I would say. But it did not seem to be relevant to my research. What do you think it meant?'

'I have no idea. But it seemed pretty extraordinary to Mrs Sayer and me. She thought it was the letter that you were excited about.'

'Well, I am afraid that inestimable lady is wrong. Any excitement I manifested was probably only due to being released from that dungeon of a place where the documents are kept.' A sparkle came into the professor's eye. 'Did Mrs Sayer show you the magnificent portrait of Faulkes just after he was married?'

'Yes, she did. Why do you ask?'

'Oh, I am just interested to hear what you thought of it.'

Now Ben became cagey. He didn't see why he should share his ideas about the idealised landscape in the painting when Lal had been so evasive about the letter. So he said, 'What did you think?'

'Well, I was rather puzzled by the little drawings.

85

Weren't you? What could those spiralling circles be?'

'Mrs Sayer said they might be of a maze.'

The professor nodded contemplatively. 'Yes, yes, this is true. But I think it may be more interesting than that. Now *there* is something you might like to think about, Mr Fitzmaurice!'

Just then there was a knock on the door and George stepped into the large entrance hall where Ben and the professor were having their discussion. Ben introduced him.

Professor Lal shook George's hand enthusiastically. 'Ah, Mr Buchanan, I am so pleased to meet the genius who has raised this garden from its slumber.'

'Thanks. Of course, Ben's mum and dad had done a lot of the groundwork before I arrived. I can't take all the credit!'

'But the abundance in the walled gardens, this is your work, I know. I would be very interested to walk round with you, if that were possible, to talk about your methods. I am intrigued to know just how you achieve so much with so little help.'

Ben interrupted. 'It is actually lunchtime, if you'd like to join us, George. Ruby and her friend are concocting something for us in the kitchen.'

Ruby and Gretta were making thick root vegetable soup and two enormous apple pies. Charlie and Ruby's brother, Jem, who had been roped in to peel apples, had stayed in the kitchen drinking beer and pretending to help. The kitchen smelled of freshly baked bread and pastry. Everyone suddenly felt very hungry. They all sat outside around the table on the terrace overlooking the river meadow.

'We should really appreciate this,' Ruby said. 'It may be the last warm day we have this year.'

The professor turned to George. 'It must be so satisfying, Mr Buchanan, to be able to eat food that you have planted as seeds, nurtured and harvested all your self.'

'It is. I like to eat what's in season. I like the idea of self-sufficiency.' He paused, and then said, 'Mind you, I must admit, I do go to the supermarket now and then. Well, every week to be honest.'

They all laughed. It was a jovial lunch. Almost everyone was in love with someone else sitting at the table, so it could hardly fail.

Feeling frustrated with the professor for being so unhelpful, Ben tried to think of ways of furthering his own research. He decided to contact the PhD student, Jayne Greene, because he guessed that when she was studying Charlotte she must have learned things about Henry too. It turned out that Dr Greene was still attached to the University of Derby, but as a lecturer rather than a student. Ben spoke to her on the phone.

'Sorry to trouble you, but I am the owner of Oakstead Hall in Norfolk, and I'm trying to build up a picture of the life of Henry Faulkes when he was living here. I wondered whether, while you were researching his wife Charlotte, you found out much about their time here.'

'Oh yes. Poor old Charlotte Wainwright. I've often thought I must go back to her, and do her justice.' She sounded as though she smoked, her voice slightly husky, with the faint hint of a Yorkshire accent.

'Really? Was she an interesting character, then?'

There was a pause at the other end of the line. 'Well, I'm not sure she was an interesting person herself. My impression was that she was a bit silly, and out of her depth. But studying her did offer insights into the alliances between merchant and aristocratic families in this area during the eighteenth century.'

'What kind of things did you find out about her?'

There was another pause, and a sigh. 'Look, I don't want to be rude, but I haven't really got time to talk to you about this. It was a few years back now, and I would have to go and look up stuff for you. Probably the best thing is if you read my thesis. It's available in the library here.'

Surprised by this sudden rejection, Ben gabbled to cover his embarrassment. 'Oh, I see. It was just that I saw your name at Henford, and apart from all the work Professor Lal did there you were the only other person who seemed to have carried out relevant research. I'm not so much interested in the politics of her marriage, but in what it was like being married to Faulkes.'

'Professor Lal? What's he got to do with it?'

Her voice was sharper, more abrupt. Ben sensed that he had caught her interest. 'Do you know him?'

She snorted. 'No, I don't *know* him, but I know *about* him. That ridiculous book he brought out recently. Gives historical research a bad name.'

'Ah. Well, he is working on some theory about Oakstead at the moment, and so I have met him a couple of times.'

'Is he researching Charlotte? Are you working for him?'

Her voice was openly hostile and suspicious. Ben realised quickly that her plain dislike of Lal could be advantageous. 'No, quite the opposite. He is, in fact, being very obstructive, which is why I have decided to try and find out some things for myself.'

'I see.'

Ben could not tell what Jayne was thinking. He tried again to pique her interest. 'I'm concerned that you think he is not a good historian. I would obviously be very interested in ensuring that any research carried out on the estate is of the best standard.'

'Hmm.'

Ben could hear her tapping her fingers, during another pregnant pause in the conversation. Then she came to a decision.

'OK. Tell you what. I've got a conference in Petersham in about a month's time. You come and meet me down there at the record office, and I'll maybe point you in the right direction. In fact, in the meantime, you could start

88

trying to find out what you can about Joshua Rackham at
your end.'

'The vicar?'

'That's right. You know something about him, do you?'

'Only the letter I found at Henford.'

'A letter?'

'Yes, did you not come across it when you were there?'

'Hmm.' Ben could tell from her non-committal answer
that she had not. 'OK, Ben. Let's make a deal. You do a
little bit of research on the Reverend Rackham for me, and
I'll see what I can do to help you with Charlotte. Agreed?'

Ben agreed, and they set a date to meet.

Charlie began to take an interest in Ruby's work when,
after much encouragement from Ben, she had shown him
one of her new paintings, of voluptuous dark red raspber-
ries on a blue delft plate. Charlie had been pleasantly
surprised and had asked to see more, which was why he
now found himself over at Ruby's house on a dark, rainy
October afternoon. Her paintings were stacked in the tiny
spare bedroom upstairs. The canvases were large and each
one had to be struggled with, in the constricted space,
before it could be balanced against the wall above the
narrow single bed. The sky was black with rain clouds, and
hardly any light managed to find its way through the small
north-facing window. The light from the single bulb
seemed to be swallowed up in the shadows. They were not
the best conditions for assessing a new artistic talent but
Charlie could see enough to feel it would be worthwhile for
them to visit a friend of his who owned a gallery in
London. He felt a rare stab of happiness at the prospect of
spending time with Ruby, sorting out the paintings and
organising an exhibition. It made him nervous.

'Do you mind if I smoke?'

Ruby frowned. 'If you don't mind me opening a
window.'

She climbed over the bed and struggled with the ancient

timber casement. After a few moments he clambered alongside her, and they pushed the window open together, then collapsed back on the bed and laughed. Her arm brushed his, her hair momentarily tickled his ear. He lit his cigarette, trying to regain his usual cool.

Ruby was beginning to occupy most of his thoughts. He didn't know why. He remembered the night when something woke up inside him, when he saw her smiling at George, soon after he had interviewed Professor Lal. Somehow the two events had got muddled up in his head. He longed to feel the ecstasy that Professor Lal had described. But somehow he had to persuade Ruby, he had to find a way of talking to her, convincing her. He didn't know where to start.

Looking back on his previous liaisons was no help. He knew he was attractive, and he was very practised in the art of choosing women who were susceptible to good looks and surface charm. He had never cared about whether they were interesting, as long as they were compliant in bed. But his looks had not worked on Ruby. He realised that in order to get her into bed with him, he had to work harder. He had to make her like him, and relax with him. Then perhaps he too would hear her soft moaning in his ear, feel her surrender.

'So how are things between you and Ben? Everything going well?'

He thought he noticed a moment of hesitation before Ruby said, 'Yes, of course.' She chuckled. 'He's very absorbed with all this stuff to do with the temple, isn't he? He's obsessed with it.'

Charlie thought, Aha, she's bored with him and his strange obsession with an old monument. There are chinks in his armour. He replied, 'Yes, the boring old tosser.'

Ruby smiled, but said, 'He's not boring! He's interested in things. You've been his friend for years. You know what he's like.'

'Yeah. More interested in reading and being philosophical

than coming out and having a good time, as I remember it. No wonder all his girlfriends turned to me for solace.'

Ruby pursed her lips, then turned to lift one of the huge paintings onto the bed. After a few moments, Charlie tried another direction. 'So what made you start to paint all these fruit and vegetables?'

Ruby laughed. 'Do you think it's an odd subject?'

'No. I just wondered what made you change from the more abstract stuff you were doing before.'

Ruby put her hand up to her mouth and ran her index finger along her lower lip. She often did this when she was considering something, and Charlie found it very unsettling.

'I suppose it allows me to add a bit more structure to my work, but because of the shapes and colours I can still experiment with abstract forms.'

'But what made you move away from the abstract form in the first place?' Charlie persisted.

Ruby put her hands over her ears and pretended to be in severe pain. 'Questions! All these questions! Is this going to be reported in the tabloids tomorrow? OK, I admit it, I'm in love with a carrot!'

Charlie temporarily lost his sense of humour. Why wouldn't she let him get through to her? 'I was only making polite conversation. Why are you always so suspicious?' It came out before he could stop himself.

Ruby looked puzzled. 'I was joking. I just don't know why my painting has changed, that's all. I'm not suspicious of you. Why should I be?

'You always think I've got some ulterior motive for everything.'

Ruby took hold of both his arms and playfully shook him. 'Come on, Charlie. You must admit that's often true. But it's not your fault, it's the journalist in you. I don't hold it against you.'

Charlie struggled for a moment with several impulses. Her grip on his arms, and her close proximity after shaking

91

him, tempted him to throw her on the bed right there and show her what he knew about women. At the same time, her words made him want to storm petulantly out of the room, slamming the door behind him. The third impulse was for self-preservation. He muttered, 'I thought it was the journalist's job to be provoking.'

Ruby smiled, relieved that he had returned to normal. They spent the next couple of hours choosing the paintings which would be most appropriate for the London gallery, and then Charlie left, feeling the pleasure and pain that is caused by being scrubbed with a rough pumice stone.

Ben felt very pleased with the way his talk at the Henford local history society went. He mulled over his success as he drove home. Since his previous visits to the Hall he had been working further on the theory that the backdrop to the portrait of Faulkes represented an idealised version of the Oakstead estate. He had been reading the opinions of art historians for further insight, but they always dismissed the backdrop as an imaginary landscape. They were more interested in analysing the symbolism of the painting and, in particular, the strange little sketches depicted on the sheet of paper. One writer suggested that they were plans for a maze, which might have been constructed at Henford out of gravel or grass, and would therefore no longer be easily traceable. Another went further and suggested that the patterns did represent mazes, but that they were intended to be symbolic of Faulkes' personality, and were not intended as serious plans. One article theorised that these shapes might have had some darker Satanic meaning, in the light of the wicked reputations of both Henry and his father. Ben did not feel that any of this rang true.

He decided to stick to what he knew, and wrote a short article, identifying the backdrop as Oakstead, which was to be published in the Henford History Group newsletter. Mrs Sayer had arranged his talk as part of the group's annual general meeting. It was all potentially very dry and stuffy, with a number of retired old ladies and gentleman falling asleep in the back row while he showed them slides in the dark, but Ben loved it. He began to gain some insight into the professor's possessiveness about new theories. He could see how frustrating it would be, not to receive recognition for an original idea. He had discovered a whole new part of himself that was completely consumed by the thrill of research, and he was increasingly intrigued by the character of Henry Faulkes.

After his conversation with Jayne Greene he had looked through more of the documents in the collection at Henford, for anything else connected to the vicar, but had found nothing of further interest. He read the letter over and over again, trying to understand what kind of behaviour had so outraged the vicar. He realised that much would depend on what kind of a man Joshua Rackham was. If he had been very proper and starchy he might have been offended by the viscount's interest in the earthy side of farming, and its embarrassing preoccupation with rams and bulls. On the other hand, the implication in the letter was that the two men had been used to spending time together perfectly happily until the event which caused the letter to be written. Perhaps Henry had confided in the vicar about some kind of immoral act, such as sleeping with a maid-servant. This seemed to be common aristocratic behaviour. The letter mentioned Henry showing something to the vicar, though, and it seemed unlikely that he would go as far as parading a fallen maidservant in front of a man of the cloth. The same would apply to any pornographic material that Henry might have acquired. It was surprising, considering the dramatic effect of whatever Joshua Rackham had seen, that Henry had not anticipated a bad reaction. The more Ben thought about it, the more he felt it would be useful to find out something about the character of Joshua Rackham for himself, as well as for Jayne Greene.

Ben reached the Lincolnshire fens, stuck in the pouring rain behind two large lorries crawling through the bleak, flat landscape. He mentally made a note to avoid driving up to Henford again for at least a few months. Then he wondered how long it would have taken Henry and his entourage to travel up from Oakstead to Henford in the eighteenth century. He imagined Henry galloping ahead on a snorting, sweating horse while his wife trundled through the Fens in a carriage. Ben was fascinated by the way Henry Faulkes had seemed to relish life. There he was in the painting, embarking on his new married life, and already his head was full of ideas for changing the whole landscape and experimenting with new technologies. Unbidden, an image drifted into Ben's mind of himself and Ruby posing for a painting in front of the park at home, her sitting on the trunk of a fallen tree, him standing looking out at the painter. She was in a beautiful silvery silk wedding dress with wild flowers in her hair. A pulse of heat ran from the top of his head down to his little toes. The feeling was so strong, he almost thought he heard a voice whisper in his ear: You must marry her.

He got back to Oakstead just after nine, but instead of going to the Hall he went straight over to Ruby's cottage. He found her sitting in her small living room watching television, wearing two woollen jumpers and drinking hot cocoa even though a coal fire burned in the hearth. She had not expected to see him that evening but was pleased to be saved from the television.

'It's cold,' she said.

'Let me warm you up. Come and sit on the sofa with me.'

They cuddled up together for a few minutes, until his body heat from the long drive in a hot car gradually seeped through to her.

'How attached are you to this cottage, Ruby? I know it's lovely in summer, but it does seem rather silly, you shivering away here all on your own now that winter is coming.'

Ruby drew away from him a little and looked into his face. 'What are you suggesting?'

He suddenly felt very nervous. It was all very well having a flash of inspiration in the snug confines of your car, but it was another thing to be faced with the reality of an inscrutable girlfriend.

'Well, I was thinking on my way back, about you, and me and, you know, how good we are together and everything, and I thought, well, I just thought perhaps you might think about, um, marrying me.'

Ruby looked into his eyes, but he could not read her face. Then she said: 'I don't need to think about it. Let's get married.'

October 31st/November 1st

The Celtic day began at sunset. At the point where October merges with November the Celtic New Year started. The ancient people named this moment Samhain, the summer's end, the beginning of the season of darkness. It marks the third and final harvest of the cycle, symbolised by the apple, the late ripener. Apples are the fruit of the Otherworld. They were buried in the ground for those who had passed on, so that the departed might eat. They symbolise fertility, love, and knowledge. The taut, rosy-green skin and the sweet, moist flesh sitting heavy in your hand, round, perfectly shaped to fit into your palm.

I've waited impatiently as the first and second harvests passed, but now the season of the third harvest in the cycle has come, and she has given me apples. A symbolic offering, the acknowledgement of temptation, the promise of knowledge to come. A different kind of succulent flesh.

If eaten on Samhain, an apple will bring the dream of a future lover. I will eat the apple, and look for her in my sleep.

Gretta has come to visit. We are getting ready to go to a Halloween party that Ben has organised so that he can announce our engagement. I am embarrassed by the idea, but Gretta thinks it's lovely. We are walking through the orange leaves that lie on the floor of the little wood at the back of my cottage. I am feeling melancholy about leaving this place which has been my small haven for so long. I have got used to being cramped, and wearing coats and gloves indoors, and finding condensation on my bed covers when I wake in the morning. Though I know it is probably silly to believe such a thing, I can't help worrying that when I leave here for the comfort of the Hall I will lose that raw edge which artists need to be creative. I have read too many books about starving artists in garrets and I have come to believe that you need to suffer to find inspiration. Gretta is scornful and says I should pull myself together. She has never understood my attachment to this place. She likes to be warm and nurtured all the time. She points out that the ideas for my latest work have come from the kitchen gardens at the Hall, and that it will probably be the source of many new inspirations.

We start talking about the wedding. Gretta is thrilled by the whole idea. She wants a huge white dress, horse-drawn carriages, choirs, marquees, fairy lights and candles, fireworks, an orchestra, opera singers, forests of flowers, famous people, poetry, flamenco dancing. But I am not very good at making a public spectacle of myself. I wish Gretta could do it for me. She is frustrated by my attitude and there is a small pause as we continue walking. Then she says suddenly: I know what I've been meaning to say to you. That man, the gardener who had lunch with us the other week. I knew I'd seen him before and I was racking my brain trying to think where, and then it suddenly came to me – the man on the beach. Do you remember?

She turns to look at me. Can she see the inside of my head collapsing, I wonder? It is as though she has just burst a big balloon in my face. The man on the beach. How did I not realise? All these months I've been believing that I met George in some other life, and it turns out I just walked past him one evening. I imagined then what it might have been like to spend my life with him, and somehow those thoughts must have crystallised and remained in my memory. It was such a vivid reality, the truth is jamming my mind. I am not quite able to hide my confusion from Gretta. She says: Are you all right? You've gone very quiet. What have I said?

I tell her I'm just amazed that I hadn't realised that George was the man on the beach, and that sometimes I worry my mind is going. She laughs and tells me to lighten up. She says it doesn't matter about some guy on the beach and that what I should be thinking about is getting married. But then she looks slyly at me and says: He is rather lovely, isn't he?

I can't answer her. My voice will give me away. The fact that I have not known him before hasn't lessened my feelings for him. Instead, it makes the deep connection I feel all the more remarkable. I wish I could find a way of getting under the surface difficulties we have in communicating, and find a way through to him. I am thinking about this, even as Gretta goes back to talking about the wedding. I hate myself, sometimes.

People run about the house wearing grim masks and black cloaks. There are candles on all the tables and windowsills, gently melting and flickering as people whisk past in hysterical high spirits. I am stumbling about in the semi-darkness, bumping into friends and having disjointed conversations, while I collect drinks for one person, food for another, sticking plaster for another. Ben has disappeared somewhere outside. I am feeling the isolation of responsibility, and I am embarrassed by the constant jokes and innuendo about my impending marriage, which Ben announced earlier: 'Here's the blushing bride-to-be,' or, 'It'll be the pitter-patter of tiny feet next,' or, 'Make the most of your last weeks of freedom.' It's crushing me. I feel an arm round my shoulder, and turn expecting to see Ben, but it's Charlie. He says: You looked like you needed a drink.

97

He hands me a glass of champagne and smiles at me: Cheer up. You're supposed to be celebrating.

It is dark in here, only a few candles flicker. His eyes are glittering, and his arm feels heavy. Drunk, I suppose. I say: Aren't you supposed to be helping Ben with the fireworks?

His arm slips down to my waist, but I step away so that it falls to his side. He grins: Ben doesn't need me. But I think you do. Come and smooch with me. We can wear masks and no one will know.

I mutter something about maybe later, and pretend I am busy. Outside there is a huge bonfire sending orange fizz up into the sky. I find myself a quiet corner of the conservatory where I can see what's happening outside, but they can't see me. I look on at the celebrations but I am sealed away in my glass box, voices are muffled and my vision is muddled with the bright spots of torches and the spray of sparklers.

A hand touches my arm. It makes me jump. I turn to look at the person, but my eyes have been dazzled by looking at the bright fire. He says: What are you doing hiding away in this dark corner? I thought you'd be partying outside.

It is George's voice, close to my ear. His breath smells of beer and cigarette smoke, a welcoming scent like a familiar pub. My eyes are beginning to adjust back to the darkness and now I can see his face. He is not smiling. He slumps down on to the bench behind me and swigs a bottle of beer. I can't think of anything sensible to say to him. This party should be my final renouncement of him but here he is in all his melancholy glory. I say: Can I have a sip of your beer?

He holds the bottle out without looking at me. I take it and sit down next to him. I ask him if there is something the matter. He stares down at his feet for a long time and then he says: I suppose Halloween's a good time for an engagement party.

I don't think so. It feels rather macabre, as if we are celebrating the release of all these ghosts and ghouls. Like a Pandora's box.

He looks at me for the first time, and says: I was reading something in the paper yesterday. It said that Halloween is left over from some kind of ancient festival about renewal. A time for leaving behind the old year's troubles, and looking forward to the cleansing cold of winter.

There is something about the way he is looking at me, the way he is speaking. Electricity is passing between us, crackling and burning. Adrenalin is running through my body, and I feel pressure and lightness, my heart beating loudly. I put my hand up to my chest and can feel the vibration. There is meaning behind his words, a message to me. I say: What troubles are you leaving behind?

Another long pause. Then he says, without looking at me: I think my troubles have only just begun.

I am tongue-tied. I cannot be sure that he is telling me something about his feelings for me. Why should he be? There has been no precursor to this. Only my own clumsy attempts to get close to him, which have left me feeling stupid and humiliated. Blood is pounding in my ears, making me dizzy. If I don't say something, he will think I don't understand, and then maybe he will never be open to me again. I struggle to find words. Then, suddenly, his mood seems to change and he says brightly: So when *are* you getting married? Soon?

I wince inwardly, as if I have been slapped. The little bubble that held us is burst and the sound of the party returns. I can hear my name being called. Ben is looking for me because he is about to start the fireworks. They crash up into the sky, symbols of wild freedom, glittering showering fantasies turning into fluttering soft black ash.

November

Frosts become severe and crack the earth about the stems of plants; this lays the roots bare and a continuance of the same weather utterly destroys them.

Mrs Martha Bradley

The day after Halloween, Gretta and Ruby spent the afternoon pottering about in the antique shops of Holt, looking at beautiful things and talking about the party.

'I'll tell you who I was surprised by,' said Gretta.

'Who?'

'Charlie! He was really turning on the charm last night. If I didn't know better, I'd be quite smitten.'

Ruby laughed. 'I must admit, I've been slightly reconsidering my opinion of him lately. He's been very nice about my painting.' She picked up a teapot and scrutinised it for cracks and chips. 'The trouble with Charlie is he can be nice when he wants to, but I'm always wondering what his motive is. You remember what he was like with Helen.'

Gretta nodded, put down one teacup and picked up another. 'That's true. I think it's classic displacement of affection.'

'How do you mean?'

'You know, when men who are good mates share the same girlfriends. It's the closest they can get to having sex with each other without being gay.'

Ruby snorted. 'You've been reading too many women's magazines. Surely it's more to do with being competitive, always wanting the toy your friend's got.'

Gretta put down the second teacup. 'Either way, he was flirting openly with you last night.'

Ruby frowned. 'Did you think he was? I did feel a bit uncomfortable about the way he was being, but I guessed he was just very drunk.'

'He was. But that's when the truth comes out.'

'He was a bit odd with me when he came over to select some paintings the other day.'

Gretta opened her eyes wide. 'In what way?'

'Just a bit awkward, and he got cross and said I was always suspicious of him.'

'He sounds like someone who doesn't want to be rumbled.'

'How do you mean?'

'I mean, it sounds like you're right to be suspicious.' Gretta pursed her lips. 'I rather think you'd better keep an eye on him. You don't want to be another Helen.'

Ruby snorted. 'Don't be ridiculous. I wouldn't touch him with a bargepole.'

'But, as you say, he can be very nice.'

'I know! That's what's so odd about him. One minute he'll be having a literary discussion with you about some obscure poet or something, and the next he'll be looking at naked women in a magazine and talking about what great tits they have.'

Gretta looked around the shop swiftly, and said, 'Shh!' They both giggled. Then she whispered, 'His trouble is, he spent too long in a public school with no girls. In my experience, men come out of those schools either gay, or desperate to bed as many women as possible.'

Ruby laughed. 'Which is Ben?'

Gretta made a face. 'He's the exception that proves the rule. So don't let Charlie fool you.'

'He's the least of my worries.'

Gretta's expression sharpened. 'What else is there to worry about?'

Ruby shrugged her shoulders, and said nothing.

Ruby's reluctance to make a fuss about the engagement only endeared her more to Ben. He liked the slight awkwardness of her, the inability to just go with the flow, the slight scratchiness of their progress. She is more real, he thought fondly, than all the county-set girlfriends I've encountered, all gushing and over-the-top, and then gone. She weighs up every dilemma, struggles with it, chews it over and then when she makes a decision she really means it.

He was clearing out one of the outbuildings to make Ruby a studio. As he carried out numerous piles of old tools, newspapers, flat tyres, rusting bicycles and broken toys, he meditated on the mood of his girlfriend. He could sense there was something tugging at her that made her not quite sanguine about the wedding, but he couldn't put his finger on it. When he tried to talk about it with her she would say there was nothing wrong, or that she was a bit scared of the responsibility of being the lady of Oakstead Hall, or that the prospect of the actual wedding made her nervous. Ben thought there was probably some truth in these things, but he didn't believe it was the whole truth.

He found a pile of his sisters' teenage magazines mouldering under some old coats, and flicked through a couple, amused by the old-fashioned graphics, the dated language, the articles all about how to get a boyfriend, how to please him, understand him, and then how to get rid of him. But then the meaning seeped through, and made him feel insecure. Perhaps she's not sure it's the Real Thing? Perhaps I have moved too fast? Do I cramp her style? He completed one of the multi-choice quizzes, which purported to tell you whether you were a selfish, over-generous or normal lover. He was relieved to find he was normal. Then he sat with his head in his hands thinking: If she leaves me I won't recover from this one.

He threw himself into creating a beautiful space for Ruby. The pile of her canvases, which had taken up the whole of the spare bedroom at the cottage, disappeared into one corner of her new room. The walls were freshly painted and light came through two large skylights. There was a wood-burning stove, a sink and a kettle. Ruby loved it, and thanked him over and over again, and he felt better. At least he had done this right.

One evening, soon after Ruby had moved in, he tentatively brought up the subject of setting the date for the wedding. She was leaning against the door frame of the sitting room watching him as he walked round plumping up all the cushions and straightening the throws before going to bed. He tried to sound nonchalant, and preoccupied with tidying.

'You know, we ought to start thinking about fixing a day, if we want it to be next summer. We'll want people to keep the date free a long way in advance.'

Ruby came in and sat on the arm of the sofa. 'I suppose. Is it going to be a great big wedding then?'

He glanced up at her. 'Not if you don't want it to be. But even a small wedding needs lots of planning.'

Ruby suddenly grinned. 'You've been talking to Gretta!'

Ben picked up their two empty wineglasses and carried them through to the kitchen, Ruby following. Over his shoulder, he said primly, 'I did talk to Gretta last week, but she only confirmed what I'd already been thinking.'

Ruby laughed and put her arms round him from behind. 'Between the two of you, you'll have me dressed like a princess, with full orchestra, and pink roses.'

He put the glasses down, turned and hugged her. 'I want the wedding you want, what ever it is.'

'Well, there's no need to rush, is there?' She was speaking into his shoulder, so he couldn't see her face. 'A year and a day has a nice ring about it. Since we met.'

They looked on the calendar and circled the first Saturday after May 1st. Then she said, 'And let's not rush off afterwards. It's not as if the wedding night's going to be a big surprise for either of us.'

This rang in Ben's ears. Although they had only been sleeping together for a few months, it was true that the wedding night would not be very different from any other. He lay in bed, thinking. How could he surprise and delight Ruby on the night? A bed full of rose petals, perhaps, or hundreds of candles and perfumed oils. He surveyed the bedroom as it was, with the pale wallpaper and the sanded floor, the creamy muslin curtains and the Shaker-like furniture. But for his wedding night he wanted it to be sumptuous, with swathes of red velvets, Turkish carpets, and incense. And some kind of magnificent centrepiece. In a flush of excitement, he decided that he would make a bed: a fantastical, exotic, voluptuous bed, created with his own hands, with his love.

On the following day he hurriedly drew some preliminary sketches in his workshop, but then he wanted to share his feeling of inspiration with someone. He had heard Gretta arriving earlier, and thought she would be the perfect person to consult, so he went over to the house. There were voices in the room at the end of the landing, which Ruby had adopted as a study. He knocked lightly on the door and began to walk in but was met with screams of 'Don't come in! Don't come in!' and the door was pressed shut against him. Then the door opened again slightly and Ruby peeped round.

'Sorry. This is all Gretta's idea. She has a friend who designs clothes and she's asked her to show me some wedding dresses.' She made a face at Ben, which said: I think this is a stupid idea but I can't say no.

'That sounds fun. Can't I see?' Ben was much more enthusiastic about the wedding rituals.

Gretta's voice shouted out, 'No you can't. It's bad luck. Anyway, it'll be a lovely surprise for you on the great occasion. Go away!'

Ruby grinned at him. 'You know Gretta. You might as well give up. She'll fight you tooth and nail before letting you come in and bring bad luck on us all.'

Ben retreated and found himself thinking how exciting it was not to know what Ruby would look like on the day. She, on the other hand, would know exactly what he was to wear, how the day would proceed, where they were going on holiday. There was no mystery in it for her. Ben realised, with a jolt, that this really was what was spoiling it for Ruby. No mystery or magic. He would make her a bed from a fairy tale! A re-creation of the wood he had found her in, with soaring tree trunks, a canopy of branches, wreaths of flowers, and leaves. A place of passion to start their new life together.

Repair work had progressed quickly at the temple so the English Heritage inspector came to check the quality of workmanship. Ben went over to the island with her, to help with the boat. The pristine new lead cupola roof was a shade lighter than the leaden sky. Inside, all the rubbish had been cleared away revealing a good-sized room. The high ceiling was reinstated, and the interior given a preliminary wash down.

The inspector looked closely at the walls, and said, 'I don't know if you know about this, Mr Fitzmaurice, but I have been contacted by a Professor Lal.'

'Have you now? And what did he have to say to you?'

'Well, he was rather cagey, but he seems to be concerned about the way we might tackle the walls here. He seems to think there may be something on the original surface that could be of historic interest.'

'What kind of thing, exactly?'

'He wouldn't be specific, but I suppose it could range from a piece of graffiti up to a whole pictorial scheme.'

'You mean some kind of painting?'

'Well, yes, there could be, although it would be very unusual.'

'Would it? Might it be important, then?'

'That is rather difficult to say, as we have no evidence at all. I haven't seen any sign of colour on the walls. But of course, if there is good documentary evidence, we must take it seriously.'

Ben peered at the wall where Professor Lal had scratched it when he visited. There was nothing to be seen except dusty white paint. The inspector went outside to inspect the exterior, and he followed her out.

'Did Professor Lal tell you how he arrived at this idea of paintings?'

'He said he had carried out some research which suggested that the walls were not originally plain as had been previously assumed. He was rather anxious that we might start works to the interior of the temple and risk destroying whatever he thinks is hidden there. I said we would like to have more information but so far he has not been very forthcoming. He said he is in the middle of further research and was not able to be more specific at the moment.'

'Oh, honestly!' Ben exclaimed. 'He's always got some excuse.'

The inspector took a couple of photographs of the repairs and made some notes while Ben sat on a freshly felled tree and distractedly picked away at the bark, fuming about the behaviour of the professor. Then they walked back to the boat.

'So what does this all mean?' asked Ben, after they had negotiated the lake and clambered up the bank on the other side.

The inspector sighed. 'Well, obviously, if there is something of importance underneath the layers of paint it makes life a bit more complicated. We could get wall-painting conservators in to uncover some small sample areas, and then if we do find evidence of decoration there will be philosophical issues to resolve about whether to uncover it or not. It could rather slow things down, I'm afraid.'

'I see. I wonder what the old goat is up to.' As they turned and began to walk towards the Hall, an idea popped into Ben's head. 'Do you know anything about the three spiral circles on the Faulkes marriage portrait?'

The woman looked blank. 'No. What are they?'

'They're on a piece of paper in the painting. The professor made a cryptic allusion to them last time he was here. Do you think it might be something like that under there?'

The inspector looked mildly interested, but said, 'At this stage, there is not enough evidence to make an informed guess about what might be concealed. Do you mind me asking how well you know Professor Lal?'

'Not well. Enough to know he is rather an odd character, and I don't really trust him. Why do you ask?'

The inspector stopped walking and looked off into the distance, her face slightly flushed. 'I didn't want to speak out of turn but, to be honest, we are rather sceptical in the office about Professor Lal's credentials. We should, of course, seriously consider involving conservators, although it would increase costs, and that is something we would have to discuss. To justify that extra work, we really need more information.' She turned her gaze back to Ben. 'It's odd that he's not been more specific, particularly to you, as the owner.'

Ben nodded his head vigorously. 'Yes, and I must say I'm rather annoyed about it. If he thinks it's something important, why doesn't he just come out with it?'

'We can't help feeling he's trying to work up some kind of hype for his next book, rather than taking a conservation approach.'

'That may be true. I know his research to do with the estate and Repton's work is important to him, to re-establish his academic status. He more or less told me so.' There was a pause before they resumed walking, both thoughtful. Then Ben asked, 'What can we do to find out more?'

'As I said, I think it would be as well to carry out some sampling of the paint surface to see what's there.'

'Is that something you would do?'

'No. I'm afraid you would have to pay for it. Then if you find something of interest we may grant-aid a scheme of conservation. We would really need to monitor the environmental conditions of the temple for a time, to establish any fluctuations in conditions, such as dampness, temperature and so on. Those kinds of things could adversely affect the paintings if they were uncovered. At the moment, if there is anything surviving underneath, it is at least receiving some protection from the elements.'

'But the roof has been made weathertight, and the windows repaired. We could install warm air blowers in there to dry the place out.'

'Drying the interior out too quickly could damage the paintings. Believe me, Mr Fitzmaurice, I am as keen as you to find out if there's anything there, but we must do things properly and, unfortunately, that can take time. But we could help initially by writing a brief for you.'

'A brief?'

'Instructions on what needs doing, which you could then give to whichever conservator you choose. I'll send you some names of good firms.'

As they reached the house, she said, 'I'm glad to see you took my advice about the ivy.' Sections of the thick stem had been cut out at the bottom of the plant, and now all the leaves were wilting and turning brown. They walked round to the back of the house to see progress there. The inspector put her hand over her eyes, to shield them from the light. 'Can you see that blocked window?' She pointed at the corner of the house, just below the eaves. Next to an old timber casement in the top left-hand corner, Ben could just see a line running through the brick bond work, as if some kind of alteration had taken place.

'Gosh. I never would have noticed that.'

'I expect it relates to some internal alterations. You might find all sorts of other things when the ivy comes off.'

After the inspector had gone, Ben went upstairs to see if he could find evidence of the window inside. The little room, on the attic floor, had been part of the original servants' quarters, and had no particular use any more. A few old bits of broken furniture stood around the walls, and the window was clouded with cobwebs. But what Ben noticed was that there was no space next to the casement where the blocked window should have been. Instead, the opening was jammed up against the wall that formed the side of the room. With some difficulty, he managed to move the old latch on the window, and force it open in a shower of spiders and splinters. Then he stuck his head out and looked at the exterior wall. There was the faint line that marked the blocked window, just where he expected it to be. The hairs on the back of neck tingled as he realised what this might mean. He withdrew his head and tapped his fist against the wall under the casement window. It made a dull, heavy thud. Then he tapped the side wall. It made a lighter, more resonant sound. A hollow sound. It was clear that this wall was not the solid outside wall, as Ben had first expected. This one was timber and plaster, and on the other side of it was a hidden space. A secret room with no doors or windows.

He went to find Ruby, who was working in her studio. 'Come and look at this!'

He took her round to the back of the house, and showed her the faint line in the brickwork, and then he took her to the cold little servants' room under the eaves, and pointed out the position of the window. Ruby immediately understood. 'There must be a secret room in there. How spooky.' She shivered. 'I don't like it. Why would there be something like that here? Is it a priest hole?'

'No, I don't think so. They were earlier.' He rubbed his chin. 'I can't imagine what the reason would be. Shall we open it up?'

Ruby looked panic-stricken. 'No, don't! It gives me the creeps.'

'Wouldn't it be better to open it up and find it's nothing horrid? And then you'll feel better.'

Ruby hunched up her shoulders and folded her arms around herself in a defensive motion. 'I wish you wouldn't.'

Ben could see that she was genuinely shaken. 'All right. Let's leave it for now. We'll think about it again another time.'

Ruby nodded, and half ran out of the room. Ben followed, laughing at her reaction, but thinking: I'll open it up when she's not here.

Ben had picked Charlie up from the station and they were in the village pub having a drink. After two pints they had strayed into difficult territory.

'This wedding's a bit sudden, isn't it? You hardly know each other.'

Charlie sounded irritated, but Ben didn't notice. 'You can see how well we get on. I feel certain we're right for each other.'

'What about when the sex gets boring? Won't you want to move on?'

Ben tutted. 'When will you grow up? There's more to a relationship than just sex.'

'Is there?'

Ben rolled his eyes at Charlie. 'You know there is. Don't give me all that stuff. One day you'll meet your match.'

Charlie chose to ignore this idea. 'But sex with the same woman forever? Could you really do that?'

Ben looked down into his empty glass. 'Yes. Because it's not sex, it's love.'

Charlie laughed out loud. 'You don't believe all that crap!'

'Sex is only one part of it.' Ben was very serious. 'She makes me feel good about myself. I want that, all my life. I know that she's The One.'

Charlie said, with genuine interest, 'How do you know? What makes you feel that? You're bound to get in a rut.'

'No! We might baffle each other sometimes, but that's

110

all part of it. She is constantly interesting to me. We're best friends as well as lovers.'

Charlie thrust his fingers in his mouth and made vomiting noises. 'Spare me, please. You can't be best friends with a girl. They're always after something.'

Ben looked up. 'You've got to get over that one, Charlie. Women aren't a different species, you know.'

Charlie stood up. 'Yeah, whatever. Let's go.'

Ben's senses were too befuddled by the drink to be safe, so Charlie drove them home. He looked at his drunken, snoozing friend, and felt a claustrophobic shudder at the thought of being trapped with one woman for the rest of his life. But at the same time, floating over this, the image of Ruby persisted, muffling his normal instinct to run. He carried on in his usual way, sleeping with casual acquaintances he picked up at parties. Women who knew how to present themselves, who laughed at his jokes, flirted, and came up with the goods. But he felt a numbness creeping over him. The flirting and the sex were no longer supplying him with the buzz he needed. He began to wonder whether he was in love. Had feelings like this inspired all that poetry? Turned his perfectly sane best friend into a wet blanket? A strange invading virus that makes you turn an ordinary, slightly annoying gingerhead into an obsession. That stops you enjoying yourself.

He had read Professor Lal's book so often he knew large chunks of it by heart. He thought he might find an answer in the book, something that would explain what he was experiencing, and make it feel safer. He read of 'ecstatic union', and 'utter pleasure', sharp little darts, pricking his skin. How much more powerful could sex be, sex with Ruby? Would it be an explosion, a raging fire? He wanted to know. Not knowing was eating away at him.

The wedding plans increased the pressure. It set Charlie a deadline by which he had to make Ruby want him. He guessed that invoking gratitude would be a good way of getting through to her, so he worked hard at organising a high-profile exhibition of her work in London. He managed to fix up a show for her, just before Christmas, when people would be keen to buy. The gallery was a small but prestigious establishment, owned by an old school friend, John Bernard. Bernard thought Ruby's work was very sellable, he was always pleased by Charlie's reviews and he was also in sympathy with Charlie's pursuit of Ruby.

He said, 'Once we've sold a few paintings for her, we'll see just how grateful she is towards you, my son. I expect to hear the details.'

Normally, Charlie would have laughed along with his friend, but now that he had elevated Ruby above all other women he felt protective towards her. He didn't like hearing her talked about in that way. Even so, he was confident that a successful exhibition would bring her closer to him.

The day before the opening of Ruby's exhibition, Charlie drove her down to London to oversee the hanging of her paintings. He had looked forward to this day for some time. Three whole hours ensconced in his car with her, when she would be feeling particularly warm towards him. He felt sure he would make some progress. Ruby was very excited, but was also feeling nervous and insecure about her work.

'I'm really grateful, Charlie, for all the help you've given me. I just hope my work lives up to your faith in it.'

Charlie's happiness expanded like a big balloon in his chest. 'Of course it will! Your work's great. You'll be raking it in!'

They talked for a bit about the space at the gallery, and ideas about how the paintings should be arranged. Then Charlie felt that he needed to direct the conversation to more personal matters, to give him an opportunity to open her eyes.

'How are the plans going for the wedding?'

Ruby looked at him suspiciously and said, 'Fine. Why do you ask?'

112

Charlie felt the familiar stab of irritation he always experienced when Ruby put up her defences. 'I'm just making polite conversation, Ruby. Why else would I be asking?'

'I don't know. I suppose I'm assuming, perhaps unfairly, that you think getting married is sentimental and soppy, and people are fooling themselves if they think there is such a thing as love. Am I wide of the mark?'

'I'm not as cynical as you think.'

Ruby raised her eyebrows. 'Aren't you? Is there really a forlorn Romeo inside you, waiting to be released by the right person?'

Charlie's grasp on the steering wheel tightened, and he spoke through his teeth. 'Is it necessary for you to be so bloody rude?'

Ruby looked surprised, and exclaimed 'Charlie! What's got into you?'

He remained silent, glaring straight ahead.

'Look. I was only joking. I'm sure you must have a sensitive side. You just tend to hide it rather well.'

Charlie sensed that he had wrong-footed her. 'Yes, I do. And can you blame me? I did go to public school, you know. You show any sign of weakness there and you're done for. The first thing you learn is how to hide your feelings.'

'But Ben. . .?'

'Ben was all right because he was good at cricket. If you're good at sport, you can get away with a lot. He was really popular.' Charlie took a deep breath and stepped out into the void. 'He didn't ever get cornered in a room and buggered, I can tell you.'

Ruby was shocked. Without thinking, she rested a sympathetic hand on his arm for a second. 'Did that really happen to you?'

'Once or twice. I was a bit girly-looking in those days, and I was weak. It was only when I got into writing the newspaper that things looked up a bit. I had somewhere to go.'

113

'It must've been very difficult for you.'

Charlie shrugged. After an uncomfortable silence Ruby suddenly returned to the original question about the wedding:

'Well, anyway, the plans for the wedding are going as smoothly as can be expected considering I'm petrified by the whole thing.'

'Are you? Why? Do you think it's a mistake?' Charlie pounced on this possibility.

'No, of course not! I love Ben and that's what matters. It's all the pomp and circumstance that scares me.'

Charlie smiled, but he was suffering the terrible pain of unwanted truth. The words 'I love Ben' rattled noisily around his brain, and he felt as though he had walked into a solid brick wall.

They drove on silently for several miles. Charlie was feverishly trying to decide what to do. Should he grasp this opportunity and declare himself? It was becoming so difficult to withhold these great truths, that they should be together, and that marrying Ben was a mistake. Like the feeling before being sick, he felt it would be better to get the unpleasant moment over and done with, and deal with the consequences once he had got rid of this awful agitation. He edged towards the revelation.

'I sometimes think that ultimately I will be saved from myself by finding the right woman.'

Ruby was startled by this sudden, rather curious, declaration, but she was careful not to sound sarcastic. 'What kind of a woman would that be?'

Charlie looked at her, and tried to sound casual. 'Oh, probably someone a bit like you.'

Ruby was shocked into a burst of laughter, and said, 'You *are* joking.'

Charlie struggled to control his face as it crumbled for an instant and then resurfaced with a fixed smile. He turned, and looked straight ahead through the windscreen and said, as if he were talking to himself:

'Why is that so funny? Don't you think I deserve someone like you?'

Ruby blushed, and put her hand nervously up to her forehead.

'It's not that I don't think you deserve someone. Really. But not someone like me. You need someone more like you.'

Charlie realised he had gone too far. He flailed around in his mind, trying to find a way out of the situation. A moment of inspiration came. He glanced disdainfully at Ruby.

'Don't get your hopes up. I didn't mean you. I said someone *like* you. I was thinking more of Gretta, actually.'

'You're being ridiculous. Anyway, she's very happy with Jem. I think we should change the subject.' Ruby turned her head away from him, and stared out of the side window at the blurred banks of the motorway.

As they drove through the centre of London in silence, Charlie went over the conversation again in his mind. It had been pretty disastrous, he knew. She was angry, and he had humiliated himself. It felt bad. His only hope was that Ruby's interest would be piqued by his rejection of her. He had always had a lot of faith in the 'treat them mean, keep them keen' school. He shut out the painful feelings by planning his evening. A club, some coke, some sex. Familiar pleasures.

In preparation for his forthcoming meeting with Jayne Greene, Ben went to the central library and asked the assistant how to find out more about Joshua Rackham. She got out for him a large book called *Crockford's*, which was published each year and listed all the clergy from the mid-nineteenth century onwards. The earliest edition was published in 1840 and in it he found an entry for Joshua Rackham, listed as The Right Honourable and Right Reverend Joshua Rackham, Lord Bishop of Petersham. Ben was pleased to find that his subject had achieved such an important position, as he thought it would make it easier to research his life. A later edition of 1860 gave fuller entries on each member of the clergy, listing their educational backgrounds and previous posts. Ben did not expect to find an entry for Rackham in here, as he would have been so old. But he was in luck. Joshua Rackham, in his late eighties, was still holding on to his post twenty years later. The entry noted the name of his college at Oxford and then listed the posts he had held during his career. It showed his first as Oakstead where he held the living from 1792 to 1794. He then moved on to a place called Burntbridge in Derbyshire, where he stayed for ten years before becoming an archdeacon and then Bishop of Petersham in 1836. Ben realised that this was probably why Jayne Greene had arranged to meet him there.

Ben asked at the enquiries desk where he should look next and was directed to the records office on the second floor where he spent two fruitless hours searching for a reference to Rackham. He went back to the help desk where it was suggested that the record office at Petersham would be a better source of material on Rackham as he had been bishop there for so long, and had died there. Ben wondered whether he had found out enough to fulfil his part of the bargain with Dr Greene, but hoped that the photocopy of Rackham's letter to Faulkes would clinch the deal.

The record office at Petersham was small and stuffy despite the cold grey day outside. Sitting at the tables, which filled up most of the space, were an assortment of elderly people, all deeply absorbed in their work. All apart from one young woman, who sat on the corner of a table in a short stretchy skirt. She was gazing out of the window in an abstracted manner, swinging her legs, which were clad in stripy red and black tights. Ben asked the assistant whether he knew who Jayne Greene was.

'Oh yes.' The man nodded towards the young woman, a hint of superciliousness in the movement. 'The lady with the stripy tights.'

116

Ben found Jayne's appearance difficult to match with her voice. On the phone she had sounded like a smoker of twenty a day, and her abrupt manner had led him to imagine a short and stocky forty-something with a sensible haircut. In fact, she was young, perhaps in her mid-twenties, with green eyes and sleek black hair. She put Ben in mind of an elf. He went over to introduce himself.

'Hello. Jayne Greene? I'm Ben Fitzmaurice.'

Jayne turned to him and blinked. 'Oh, Mr Fitzmaurice! Nice to meet you.' She laughed, an incongruous smoker's cackle. 'I'd imagined someone much older.'

Ben also laughed. 'So had I.'

She slipped off the table, and put out her hand to shake his. 'So, have you managed to find out anything about our Reverend Rackham?'

Ben brought out his file from his bag, and showed her his notes. She scanned them quickly.

'Oh yes, I've already looked at *Crockford's*. Pretty straightforward stuff, although . . . a bishop from so lowly an academic background *is* unusual. He only has an ordinary honours degree and nothing else. Usually a priest would have had a doctorate in divinity before he'd be considered for such an elevated post. That's a bit strange. . .' Her voice trailed off, and her gaze met Ben's. 'Well, anyway. I think you mentioned a letter?'

Ben removed the photocopy from the file, but held it to his chest for a moment. 'Am I to understand that we are going to work collaboratively on this? You said you would point me in the right direction about Faulkes?'

Jayne smiled and snorted at the same time. 'Yes, yes, of course.' She pointed to a folder lying on the table. 'I've got this out for you to read. See what you think.'

Ben handed over the letter, and then sat down to read the document in the file she had ordered. The file was labelled *A notebook of sermons by Joshua Rackham 1792–1836 (Bishop of Petersham 1836–60)*. Ben handled the book reverentially. As his hand touched the cover, he felt a connection, almost physical, with the hand of the vicar who had held it over two hundred years ago. It was bound in some kind of stiff cloth of faded blue. Inside, there was a handwritten title page which read *Notebook of Sermons. Guide Thy servant, O Lord, to preach Thy gospel Faithfully. April 1792.* The book was full of notes written in scrawling faded brown ink. At the beginning of each sermon was written the number of the chapter and verse from the Bible upon which it was based. At the end of each, Rackham had noted the dates and locations of where he had preached it, in order, presumably, to avoid repeating himself to the same congregation.

Ben began to read through each text. The early ones were difficult to understand, with numerous crossings-out, and insertions in tiny writing, running in between lines and up the margins. Gradually, Rackham seemed to become more confident and his words flowed more freely. By 1794 most of his sermons were clear of corrections. His style changed too. It became more passionate and florid, and Ben could imagine the haranguing tone of the vicar, up in the pulpit at Oakstead, trying to instil some religious feeling into his unenthusiastic flock. Ben was amused to find that several of the sermons referred directly to people in his congregation. One, on the theme of abstinence, mentioned the ungodly behaviour of local men on the previous Saturday night. Another, which dealt with the sin of sloth, seemed to be directed towards the maids in his own household. Then, in August 1794, Ben came across a sermon, which was again covered in alterations and erasings, as if the vicar had struggled over its content. This made it difficult to read, but as Ben ploughed on he felt a little pulse of excitement. This sermon seemed to be addressed to Henry Faulkes himself, squire of the parish:

Thou shalt have no gods before me. *Exodus xx:3*

118

And God spake to Moses and he charged him to tell the people of his sacred commandments. And Moses went down unto the people and he spake unto them. And his first words were thou shalt have no gods before me. And his second words were thou shalt not make unto thee any graven image, or any likeness of any thing that is in heaven above, or that is in the earth beneath, or that is in the water under the earth. Thou shalt not bow down thyself to them, nor serve them; for I the Lord thy God am a jealous God, visiting the iniquity of the fathers upon the children.

Dost thou think it a matter of chance that these are the first two of the commandments our Lord God set down for his people, the children of Israel, delivered from the tyranny of Egypt? Dost thou think that Our Father knows not all things, the past, the present and the future? The words of the Lord are the Truth and the Way. He madest the world and all the things contained within it. He hath foretold the destiny of the world, of the coming of Christ our Saviour and of the apocalypse, when the righteous shall be saved forever, and the sinners shall be damned in hell for eternity. Dost thou think, then, that the commandments He entrusted to Moses were the matter of mere prittle-prattle? Did Moses not slay three thousand men in His name, when the people bid Aaron to make a molten calf? The Lord God said unto Moses, Go, get thee down; for thy people, which thou broughtest out of the land of Egypt, have corrupted themselves. But Moses first sought to save his people and turned away the Lord's wrath, saying, Wherefore should the Egyptians speak and say, 'For mischief did he bring them out, to slay them in the mountains and to consume them from the face of the earth?'

But Moses did command the slaying of three thousand of his people. Why, when he had besought the Lord to spare the people, did the wrath of Moses wax hot, and bring death to those same people? Because of Aaron, his brother, who had been appointed by the Lord to guide the people while Moses was on the mount, learning the word of God. While Moses was away, the people turned to Aaron. He was entrusted to care for them, as a father tends to his children, or as a squire may have regard for the comfort of his tenants. But he followed not the way of the Lord. The people said, Up, make us gods, which shall go before us; for as for this Moses, the man that brought us up out of the land of Egypt, we wot not what is become of him. And Aaron said not, Have you not heard the commandment of our Lord God, that thou shalt have no other gods before Him, and that thou shalt not make unto thee any graven images? He leadeth not his people on to the righteous path, as a shepherd leadeth his flock. No, he followed not the way of the Lord. Aaron allowed sin to lead his flock onto the rocks and perish. Rather than guiding his people to follow the commandments so lately laid down for all to follow, he fashioned the graven image himself, a frippery of molten gold, the image of a calf, and afterwards he led the people in the building of an altar, and the making of burnt offerings. He caused a temple of graven images to be built, and brought upon the heads of his people the terrible wrath of God. And the Lord plagued the people because they made the calf which Aaron made.

Thus, when a man entrusted with the care of his people treadeth not the righteous path, but rather indulges in the making of graven images and the worship of other gods, so will the Lord strike him down, as he did the followers of Aaron, and the sinners of Sodom and Gomorrah. A temple made to false gods is indeed a temple of wickedness, whose worshippers will suffer everlasting misery in the burning fires of hell. For the Lord our God set out these two commandments first, to signal their importance and to offer a warning of the great punishment that shall come, if they are transgressed.

There are those in this parish who dare to challenge the word of God, who dabble in Satan's work, following superstition and false gods, who rise up and play rather than following the one true God in solemn worship. Let this be a warning to all leaders of men, and to those that follow false leaders. Beware the wrath of God. He sees all and he is a jealous God. To escape the fires of damnation it is required of you to escape the corruption that is in the world through lust. This was an admonition which the apostles judged the more requisite, considering the vicious neglect of so many who claim to be called Christians, who yet lack faith or true belief and so remain barren and unfruitful in the knowledge of our Lord Jesus Christ. Nay, all manner of husbandry cannot bring down the grace of our Lord, where belief in an earthly paradise casts a shadow upon our Lord's glorious heaven. Christianity calls you to a life of righteousness, and has commanded you to cast off the pollutions of a corrupt nature and a wicked world, and for encouragement hereunto, all men's sins are remitted in baptism. Christ assures you of the assistance of His grace to sanctify you for the time to come, a grace which renders all sins, especially wilful and presumptuous ones, the most inexcusable. We have need to take care to correct evils of so terrible and destructive a consequence while God allows us time for it.

Beware the whispering serpent in the garden who beguiled Eve away from the righteous path even as that miserable sinner enjoyed the perfect paradise of Eden. Even amidst the heavenly garden there was evil afoot. Do not forget the pernicious ways of Satan who would turn the absolute law of God topsy-turvy

121

without us perceiving of it so that the forbidden fruit of knowledge becomes a sweetmeat which brings sin upon us all. Just as that first paradise on earth was polluted by sin, so too are the beauteous pastures of our present abode corrupted with wrongdoing and Satan's work, as a canker which eats at the heart of a shining red apple, all unseen and undiscovered. It is requisite to utterly extirpate these bad fruits that grow so fast, to suppress their viciousness in the bud. It is required of us to strive for that heavenly paradise which has been made for us in our Lord's infinite mercy, rather than investing our belief in the fleeting pleasures of this world, and the beguiling appearances of Nature and its fruits.

Lord, what is man that Thou hast such regard unto him as to visit him with Thy salvation, to call such weak and miserable creatures as we are, tied and bound with the chains of our sins, to raise us from a captivity to sin and Satan to the glorious Liberty of the Sons of God? To be called to glory and virtue from shame and pollution, to have the exceeding great and precious promises of the Gospel offered to us, to be called from a Nature so infected and vicious!

We must be upon our watch to escape the pollution which draws us to worship worldly idols and follow false gods. If they who despised the word of Moses were met with the greatest severity of temporal punishment, then they who despise Christ shall meet with punishment much more terrible from the God, who in his vengeance, is a consuming fire, for whom, therefore, we must labour to serve acceptably with reverence and fear. We must cast up our eyes to the heavens and place our faith in the righteousness of our heavenly Lord. Above all we must follow the commandments set out for us by our Lord if we are to reach salvation and escape the eternal fires of hell, through His infinite mercy, granted through our

Saviour, Jesus Christ, with the Father and the Holy Spirit, to whom we ascribe all honour and admiration, henceforth and forever. Amen.

Ben read through the text twice. He was sure that the allusions to a temple, the squire and the leaders of men must have been aimed at Henry Faulkes. It seemed to criticise Faulkes for worshipping false gods. Ben hurriedly skimmed through the following few tracts but none of them seemed so significant.

The sermon had been delivered about a month after the vicar's letter to Henry. Ben wondered how the squire would have reacted. It seemed likely that a man of such passion and energy would not sit quietly and accept such public humiliation. It was obvious why Joshua Rackham had only held the living at Oakstead for a few months more.

He examined the scrawled writing with its numerous corrections and blotches and he could almost feel Joshua Rackham entering his body, sitting in his seat, in his black frock coat, struggling with the words which he knew would outrage his patron and probably ruin his career.

He looked up at Jayne Greene, who had been sitting making notes on the opposite side of the desk. 'This is fascinating. What do you think it's about?'

'Why don't we go and grab ourselves a cup of tea, and talk about it.' She chuckled again. 'We'll get thrown out of here if we talk too much.'

They went round the corner to a small café. While they waited to be served Ben told her what he thought the sermon might mean.

'It seems clear, doesn't it, that the temple at Oakstead offended Rackham in some way.'

Jayne leaned forward. 'A temple? I didn't know there was one. What date is it?'

'Late eighteenth century. It was part of the Repton design. It's on the island in the lake.'

'Oh, so something for the ladies to visit and have tea in.'

'That sort of thing, I suppose.'

She looked at him sideways, her chin resting on her hand, and spoke as if she were thinking aloud. 'So . . . a real temple. When I read the sermon I was just struck by the way it's obviously directed at Faulkes. It sounded like the vicar was accusing him of worshipping false idols. I thought, maybe, that the vicar had found him up to dubious tricks at one of his parties. Drinking chicken's blood, or something like that. Satanic stuff. Those young aristocrats did get up to some dodgy things when they were drunk and on the loose.' She leaned back in her chair, and narrowed her eyes. 'But now I'm thinking, perhaps he was up to something fishy in the temple. It couldn't have been the building on its own that upset Rackham – classical temples in landscaped parks were commonplace.'

The waitress came and took their order, while Jayne picked up a teaspoon and began playing with the sugar in the sugar bowl. Ben noticed how perfect her nails were. She looked up at him suddenly, and he felt conscious that he had been staring, but she didn't seem to notice. She said, 'So what do you think he might have been doing in there?'

'Well . . . perhaps it had something to do with what was on the walls. Professor Lal thinks there may be something surviving under the paint, so I've booked in some wall-painting conservators to come and have a look in the next couple of months. He suggested to me, in his roundabout way, that it might be something like those spirals on the wedding portrait.'

At the mention of the professor, Jayne screwed up her face in a frown. She was not convinced. 'Lal is prone to making huge leaps of imagination based on very little fact. If it was to do with the real temple, I bet the vicar was more worried about what was going on inside it than what was on the walls. And, of course, it may not be referring to the real temple at all. It may be metaphorical. Let's not jump to conclusions.'

124

'True. What about the letter? Do you think it's connected?'

'Definitely. They are so close together. I wonder what Rackham was worrying about? It's not really what I was expecting.'

'No? What did you expect?'

They looked at each other, and for a moment their gaze locked. Ben felt a little lurch in his stomach as he identified the fact that he was very attracted to her. But her face was inscrutable. She broke the moment, blinking her eyes, and straightening her back. 'I'm not sure. I'll come back to you on that one.'

The tea arrived. Jayne ate a large piece of sticky chocolate cake with great relish, which prevented her talking for several minutes. After delicately sucking the chocolate from each of her fingers she leaned forward, and fixed him with her stare. 'So tell me a bit more about Professor Lal. How have you got mixed up with him?'

'I met him through my lodger, who's a journalist. He asked to see the garden, and I didn't see why he shouldn't. But since then he's been rather mysterious and murky, and I don't know what he's up to.'

'Hmm.'

Jayne screwed up her face into a frown again. Ben could see that this was habitual, as she had two incipient vertical creases at the bridge of her nose, where her eyebrows drew together. He found this rather touching. They seemed to be a sign that she was often puzzled. 'What is it you dislike about him so much?'

'He brings historical research into disrepute.'

'You didn't like his last book?'

She made a 'humph' sound in the back of her throat. 'No, I did not. It was unforgivable.'

'In what way?'

She looked at him in surprise. 'Well, it was just obviously rubbish. Haven't you read it? He takes post-modernism to ridiculous extremes. He mistrusts

125

language to such a degree, he denies the possibility of there being one meaning for anything. We no longer have history, but rather *his story*. Do you see what I mean?' She had become angry, and her voice had lost some of its huskiness as she spoke more loudly. 'His message is that there is no truth, only a load of myths handed down through partisan channels. He more or less denies the possibility of there being any known history. Which means, as a society, we're like a person with Alzheimer's, unable to understand our present because we have no past.'

'But he seems to be taking his research at Oakstead very seriously, just like you or me.'

'Yes, but wait until you get his interpretation of whatever he finds! Then you might see what I mean.'

He studied her slightly flushed cheeks. 'Why does it make you so angry? Hardly anyone who read his book would have picked up that he's a radical post-modernist. It was just a good read.'

She flared up again. 'That's the whole point! Historians like me are desperate to encourage people to take an interest in the past, and to make it more relevant to everyday lives. But Lal uses these pseudo-scientific methods which give academic weight to what are essentially fairy stories. And it makes fools of his readership. They think the fairy stories are true, when really what he is saying is that there is no truth. If he had his way the world would just become fogged with innumerable stories, with no indication of which is based on the actual, and which is pure make-believe.'

Ben sat back in his chair in reaction to her onslaught. 'But what would be his motivation?'

She shrugged. 'Fame. Notoriety. A sense of intellectual superiority. A best-seller.'

He smiled at her, trying to lighten her up. 'Well, I will endeavour to carry out my own research and give the professor a run for his money. We can tell our own story.'

She continued to frown. 'Hmm. Maybe.' Then her mood

seemed to change abruptly, and she turned a glorious bright smile on him, the creases in her forehead smoothed away. 'Anyway. I ought to be getting back to the conference – it's the posh dinner this evening. You could come if you like. Keep the old men at bay.'

For a moment or two he entertained the idea. He imagined entering a dining hall with this earnest elf-woman on his arm. But he knew it would not be right, because he liked her too much already. Something about the strength of her ideas, her battling against the world, drew him to her. So he declined the offer. She did not seem too disappointed. When he asked her what he ought to do next, she pursed her lips while she thought about it.

'I'll tell you what, Ben. I'm going to think about this. I'm very busy, and this isn't really relevant to my main line of research.' She tapped her fingers on the table and spoke quietly, as if to herself. 'I did always want to get back to Charlotte, though ... and I would be interested in having a go at Lal.' She pushed her chair back, and stood up to leave. 'I'll get in touch with you about it. Meanwhile, why don't you keep an eye on what Lal's up to and let me know if you find out anything else. Is that a deal?'

After she had gone, Ben remained sitting in his orange plastic chair in the café, and let out a sigh. He reflected on the arbitrariness of life's course, and the impossibility of knowing where each road might take you. There was a chance that Jayne might have been the perfect partner for him. He would never know. The picture of Henry Faulkes drifted into his mind. Ben wondered again what his predecessor at Oakstead would have got up to in the temple. Was it some kind of love nest? Ben guessed that Faulkes would not have hesitated with Jayne. He would have scooped her up on his horse, taken her away, and ravished her somewhere in a hayloft, or the temple. Ben couldn't help admiring the audacity of the man, even though he didn't approve. He could almost hear Faulkes' voice goading him for being so prissy.

On his way home he tried to steer his thoughts away from Jayne and back to Ruby, and the wedding. His mind became filled with designs for the bed he intended to make. Driving on through the night, Jayne's image faded and he became preoccupied instead with the qualities of seasoned oak, the smoothness of beech, and the hardness of cherry.

December

This is a dead season of the year for gardening.

Mrs Martha Bradley

I am sitting in the wood behind my old cottage, looking out at the familiar view, leaning back sociably against the spiralling bark of an old beech. All the trees are bare and the wind blows through them, making that beautiful comforting white noise which prevents me hearing anything else. I am cut off from the rest of the world, cocooned in a blanket of rustling swirling wind. Occasionally it brings me the smell of woodsmoke from weekend bonfires. I nestle in amongst the crackling orange beech leaves, which cushion me from the damp, cosy in my great overcoat. Looking across the wavy furrows of the winter field, I watch the puffed-up white clouds speeding across the sky, and the sun flashing on and off, like a lighthouse. The coldness of the skin on my face and hands contrasts with the warmth inside my coat, and there is an exhilarating cool shiver on my shoulders, the characteristic feeling of a bright, blustering winter's day. I cling to the hope that this bustling breeze will clear my head of the ache that resides there. My instinct is to hibernate. I would like to dig a snug hole here at the base of this beech, framed by its roots. I will curl up on a bed of leaves in the dark, musty warmth and dream under the protection of this old, old tree, which has witnessed things far worse than my muddled life. It must have seen shipwrecks and floods, fires and famine. Perhaps other people have leaned here against its trunk, people starving, hiding, loving, lonely. I am, after all, only a very small speck in the world and in time. But somehow that is no comfort. My feelings loom uncontrollably big and infinite, as if they have been there always and fill every corner of the galaxy.

I have been thinking about this for so long now that my head feels scraped and battered inside. I go over it again and again. I love Ben. I love George. But the resonances around that word 'love' are so different, like two shades of blue, sea and sky, both necessary.

At the end of the ploughed field I can see a figure. He is leaning against the gate at the corner. It is George. As if he realises I have seen him, he moves. He opens the gate, and passes through it, walking slowly up the side of the thick earth clods. I feel frozen to the floor, and I begin to shiver. He is looking down at the ground, finding his way through the mud, and then he reaches the edge of the wood where the ground lifts and the earth is carpeted with orange leaves. He raises his eyes to mine. There is no smile of greeting. He walks up the gentle slope, looking at me, I looking at him. I can feel the tree trunk pressing in against my spine as I brace myself against it, tense with anticipation. Then he is beside me on his knees, his arm curled round my back, and he is kissing me. He is hot from walking, and I inhale the scent of his body. His mouth is warm, a warm glass of red wine. With my eyes closed, I float in the black-red tunnel that is our mouths, joined in a warm flood. This kiss is two butterflies chasing, interweaving, fluttering, nectar-drenched. Two humming birds, hovering, seeking in the centre of the flower. Floods of sweetness, sugar falling on our tongues, warm streams of liquid honey. My back dissolves under the pressure of his warm hands. I sink back onto the ground, cushioned by the welcoming leaves, and he lies beside me on his side, with his hands in my hair, and these soft, soft kisses raining down on me. Then he stops, and he runs a fingertip down the side of my face. He says: Sorry.

I have no words. I am not sorry. I want more. His beautiful mouth so close to mine, I have to taste it again. But he stops me and says: I shouldn't have done it.

A bubble of panic rises up inside me. I ask: Why not? Why kiss me so beautifully and then spoil it with this? It was good that we kissed. Now we know. Not knowing was half the trouble. For me anyway. I never knew if it was just me.

He sits up and looks away from me, across the field and mumbles: It wasn't just you. But this wasn't right.

This cycle of pleasure and pain again, of joy and humiliation. Why does he do this? When I speak I can hear the tremor of desperation on the edge of my voice: You can't just leave it like this. This was beautiful. There is something between us. Don't you want to find out more?

His hands are in amongst the leaves, scrunching them up, gathering them. He mumbles something about it being wrong, and then gets up suddenly in a flurry of crackling orange: Let's walk somewhere together.

We spend the rest of the afternoon walking in the wood, onto the heath, down to the comfortless, cold shingle of the beach. The wind sears our faces and makes me cry. We do not touch, because someone might see us. As we walk back up the rise to the house it is already dark, a twinkling crescent moon in an unforgiving black sky. The wind feels icy in the dark, and we seek shelter for a moment in one of the cart sheds. Despite what was said earlier this afternoon, we kiss again, but this time it is a kiss brimful of loss. Then he slips away and I enter the glare of the house, and the friendly warmth of the kitchen, where Ben is making supper. I go and stand by him as he cooks, and he puts his arm round me, the other hand expertly manipulating the frying pan. He says: Have you had a good day? Did you do any painting?

131

Hot tears of confusion blur my vision and threaten to spill onto my cheeks. So I bury my face in his shoulder and say, incoherently: No. It was cold. I love you.

Crisp white snow, open fires, and the resinous aroma of the tree were the essence of Christmas for Ben. He loved wrapping up presents in fresh sheets of wrapping paper, and piling them up like big sweets, and he looked forward every morning to the arrival of piles of coloured envelopes rustling through the letter box, bringing friendly greetings. This year there was ample reason to feel buoyant. Ruby was there with him, buying presents with him, jointly signing his Christmas cards, and lying cuddled up in bed with him, looking out of the windows onto the frost-bitten lawn. At the opening of her exhibition in London he was so proud of her, he lost the ability to speak coherently.

In the week before Christmas, he and Ruby went for a walk around the park. It was a clear blue day, with a nip in the air. Their route took them past George's lodge house, where they could see a man working in the garden, digging over a flower bed. As they got closer they were shocked to see that it was Professor Lal. Ben felt his hackles rising. What did the man think he was doing, roaming about in someone's garden? What was he doing here, without telling anyone he was coming? He strode up to the gate and said in his most clipped voice, 'Professor Lal. May I help you?'

The professor visibly jumped, and stumbled slightly in his haste to stand up straight.

'Mr Fitzmaurice! How nice to see you. And Ruby. What a lovely day! I am so lucky to be able to come and stay in so pleasant a spot while away from home. It is so rejuvenating, to be back in touch with the soil!'

Ben felt his face flush. 'You're staying here with George?'

'Yes, yes. He has very kindly offered me his home as a bolt-hole for the few days over Christmas I am not busy. Such a relief to be away from London and all the streets chock-a-block full of people shopping. One gets a much better sense of the Christmas spirit in the countryside, don't you think?'

Ruby said, 'I didn't realise you and George knew each other so well.'

'Oh yes, we have been in regular correspondence since my last visit. I was so much impressed with the way he runs the gardens, I have been very interested to find out more about his working practices. It has been most illuminating. He is, of course, very interested in the history of gardening. So we have found plenty to talk about. He is inside making a cup of coffee. Would you join us? It would be a pleasure.'

Ruby tightened her grip on Ben's hand and looked at him with anxious eyes. But Ben was feeling ashamed of the way he had spoken to Professor Lal. He had sounded just like his father, that stern, proprietary voice, ensuring tres-passers knew their place. It made him feel a bit sick. So he ignored Ruby, and said, 'That would be lovely.'

They trooped inside. George didn't quite manage to disguise his startled look when he saw Ruby and Ben come through the door. 'Ben! Ruby! Welcome! I bet you were surprised to see the prof?'

'I was,' Ben said, opening his eyes wide, to express his doubts over George's sanity. George, standing behind the professor, shrugged and made a face as if to say he had been given no choice in the matter.

They sat down and drank coffee and talked about the forthcoming Christmas festivities. The professor was keen to experience an English Christmas, as he was very inter-ested in its pre-Christian origins.

'Did you know, for instance,' he said, 'that your kissing under the mistletoe custom is probably a sanitised allusion to its sexual significance in pagan worship. The white juice of the berry, I think you will agree, is very like semen in colour and consistency.'

Ben, Ruby and George all shifted uncomfortably in their seats.

'Even now,' he continued, unabashed, 'mistletoe is often banned from churches, where holly and ivy are welcomed, simply because it cannot shake off its strong associations with pagan sexual rites. Pliny, you know, wrote that if a woman wished to conceive, she should carry with her mistletoe berries taken from an oak tree.'

Ben could not help being interested in what the professor had to say. 'I remember, in your book, I found the part about the pagan origins of Christmas terrifically interesting. It was so audacious, to replace a fertility rite with a sanitised virgin birth.'

The professor laughed. 'Yes, the timing of Christmas Day was chosen so carefully by those early Christians. The original *Saturnalia* was an outrageous ancient Roman festival held in the week before Christmas. Saturn, you know, was the Roman god of agriculture. His name comes from the Latin *sator*, a sower. His sickle did not only signify the inevitability of death, as is generally understood, but rather the cycle of time, through seed to fruition, and harvest, when the time was ready, then a return to the soil. The winter festival celebrated the birthday of the unconquered sun. Everything was turned topsy-turvy. Servants and masters would change places, the greenery of outside would be brought inside, light would burn all the time to banish the dark.'

He paused and smiled. 'Look how I am giving you a lecture. It is my affliction to always want to teach. Anyway. It is like this. George and I were saying it would be super to have our own yule log over Christmas. We are going to walk into the wood in search of a suitable log, in the next day or two, and bring it in ceremoniously, tied in ribbons as they used to do, and after lighting it on Christmas Eve, keep it burning until Twelfth Night. This is supposed to bring great good luck, and the ash from the fire, mixed with the spring sowing, is supposed to bring great fertility. I would love to see if this is so.'

It was this side of Christmas that Ben had always liked

134

best, the strange little customs and rituals that had no link at all to the story in the Bible. Why mince pies? Why the Christmas tree and Father Christmas? He could still easily conjure up the special feeling he had experienced as a child at Christmas time: a mixture of cosiness, magic and excitement, which enveloped him like a scent, from the opening of the first window on the Advent calendar at the beginning of December until Twelfth Night when all the decorations came down.

'It sounds fun,' he said. 'Perhaps I could help you bring in the log?'

George raised his eyebrows at Ben. 'I've told the prof that he's asking a lot. My fireplace is too small to take a log that'll burn for twelve nights.'

'Oh no, of course. What a shame!' It only took a few seconds before Ben's natural sociability took over, and he said, 'Look, why don't we have the log burning in the entrance hall at home? It's perfect for the job and it would look lovely. We'll make a celebration of it, and decorate the place with holly, and have mince pies and mulled wine. Just like in Henry Faulkes' time. What do you think?'

Ruby and George studiously ignored each other as Professor Lal accepted the invitation with great enthusiasm and clapping of hands.

Later, when Ruby and Ben were a few steps down the front path, breathing in the chill air, Professor Lal called to them from the front door.

'Mr Fitzmaurice! Before you go, I have an apology to make. I expect you have heard from the lady at English Heritage about my thoughts on the temple?'

Ben blushed, embarrassed by Professor Lal's sudden forthrightness. 'Well, yes, actually, I have.'

The professor shook his head at his own bad behaviour. 'I should have told you myself, I know. It was very remiss. It is like this. I have been so busy, I have not had time to be courteous. I had to be sure that any paintings that survive would not be damaged, and I knew I had done what

135

was necessary to achieve that. I'm sorry.'

After feeling so angry with Professor Lal, Ben was suddenly disarmed, and made some spluttering noises about it not mattering. The professor smiled and nodded, and then closed the door. Ruby and Ben looked at each other.

'Well, I never,' said Ben.

Everyone was putting on boots in the hall, and passing round a hip flask of whisky to set them up for the expedition to the wood. Ben was trying to persuade Charlie to join in the yule log celebrations. 'Come along! It'll do you good to get some fresh air.'

Charlie had been drinking steadily since breakfast time. He muttered irritably,

'Look, I'll have a swig of your Scotch, but all this jolly Christmas spirit stuff is really not my thing. You go and leave me alone.'

Ben gave up. 'All right. Off we go then! We'll leave Mr Scrooge here to meditate on his glumness. Ruby can catch us up.'

Gretta, Jem, George and Professor Lal all trooped out of the door leaving Ruby speaking on the phone in the kitchen. Charlie wandered in and sat looking at her while she wrote down a message. She was dressed in a huge shapeless coat, which she had bought second-hand, and baggy green trousers tucked into muddy black wellingtons, ready to join in with bringing the log back to the Hall. Only a few months ago Charlie would not have given her a second glance. But now he no longer saw the clothes. He knew the shape of her, underneath this disguise, and he knew her face, and its characteristics and expressions. This is all he saw now.

He realised that the conversation with Ruby on the way down to London had been a terrible mistake. She had withdrawn from him again, and avoided his company. The strange pressure he felt inside, this 'in love' feeling, was becoming too much to bear. He tried drinking from the moment he woke up until last thing at night, but the alcohol seemed to have no effect. This made him panic. What if he could never get rid of the pain? Even harder drugs only gave temporary relief. Every minute was filled up with the knowledge that only Ruby could bring him the ultimate bliss described in Professor Lal's book, and he had bungled it.

Ruby put the phone down and smiled at him. She looked concerned. 'Why don't you come out with us? It'll be fun, and we need as many people as possible if we're really going to lug a great big tree back with us. You look as if you need some fresh air.'

Charlie's resolve wavered. Did she want him to come for her sake? Would she be made happier if he was one of the party? Wasn't that progress? Ruby left the room before he could articulate an answer. The sinking feeling in his stomach made him realise that now he very much wanted to go with her into the wood. He jumped up and shouted, 'Ruby! Wait!'

She was standing in the hall, holding his coat ready. 'Come on then. We need to catch up with the others.'

They walked in silence for a minute or two then Ruby said, 'By the way, that was the gallery on the phone. They've sold another of my pictures. One of the really big ones. I can hardly believe it.'

'I knew they would sell well. They're great paintings.'

'Well, I wasn't sure to start off with, whether you really meant it, but after all this, I have to say I really appreciate the faith you put in me.'

Charlie felt the pain of tears arriving at the back of his eyes. Ruby's words and her kind, genuine face suddenly made the pressure inside insupportable. He could say nothing, and he looked down at the ground, trying to pull himself together.

'I mean it,' Ruby said. Then she saw tears were running down Charlie's face. 'Oh no, what's the matter? What's happened?'

137

She placed a hand on his arm. Charlie felt a tidal wave of agonising self-pity rise up inside, and a huge sob convulsed him. He took a breath and, with his face behind his hands, tried to compose himself. Ruby's anxious face was near to his, he could see the dark fringes of her eyelashes and the shape of her mouth. In a thin little strangled voice, he said, 'Hold me.'

Ruby made an awkward attempt at comforting him by placing her arm behind his back, barely touching him. But Charlie turned and pulled her tightly to him, burying his head in her shoulder. Ruby stood stiffly, holding her head away from his whisky breath. After a minute or so she tried to loosen his grip, and said, 'Come on Charlie, what's this all about?'

But he still held her tightly. He was inhaling the scent of her hair, feeling the contours of her body against his, listening to her breathing. He was not ready to let go. This new feeling of love was streaming around in his blood, carrying some kind of amphetamine to all his nerve endings. His mouth was against her neck, and he kissed her. She pushed him away with full force, thumping him in the stomach to make him let go.

'What the hell do you think you're doing! What's the matter with you?'

Charlie doubled up, winded. 'Oh God, Ruby, oh God, what am I going to do?' He slumped on the floor.

Ruby became alarmed. 'Are you ill? What's the matter? For heaven's sake, Charlie. Speak to me!'

But he lay on the floor, curled up in a ball, his hands covering his face, sobbing. The barrage of emotions felt like physical assaults, a battery of slamming walls of water crashing about him.

Eventually, when he seemed to have stopped crying, Ruby ventured a question. 'Can you tell me what this is all about?'

Charlie slowly lowered his hands. His face looked crumpled and blotchy. He said, 'You must despise me.'

'Why, because you cried in front of me?'

'Maybe.'

'I don't despise you for crying. Why are you so upset?'

Charlie struggled with this new person inside him, infected with love and pathetic softness, smothering his old self, a great weight inside him, suffocating. He opened his mouth, to say, 'Oh, forget it, I'm drunk, someone died,' to get himself out of this crushing situation. But instead he found unknown words falling out of his mouth:

'I love you.'

There was a pocket of silence and stillness as they sat looking at each other, both sharing disbelief in what had been said. Then they heard someone shouting.

'Ruby!'

Ben emerged from the edge of the wood, calling her. Charlie scrambled up and muttered, 'Tell him I'm drunk or something,' then he ran off down the track back to the Hall. Seconds later, Ben arrived puffing at Ruby's side. 'What's the matter?'

She was still sitting on the edge of the track, stunned by the hysterical scene she had just witnessed. Ben offered her his hand, and pulled her up. She smiled a weak smile at him and said, 'Oh, nothing, really. Charlie thought he would come with us, and then felt ill. Don't worry. Let's catch up with the others.'

Ben shrugged. 'I'm not surprised, the amount he's been putting away over the last few days. He needs to slow down a bit, or he'll be unconscious for most of Christmas.'

'Perhaps you should have a word with him.'

Ben laughed. 'I wouldn't like to get between Charlie and his drink.'

They turned and walked along the track to the wood.

Gretta had been Ruby's friend for many years and she knew her very well. Her suspicions already aroused by their previous conversation about George, she watched the way Ruby behaved towards him while everyone crashed around

139

in the wood trying to find a suitable log to take home. She saw how Ruby stayed close to Ben and clung onto him when she could. She noticed that when everyone gathered around George as he chainsawed the chosen tree trunk, Ruby stood back, outside the group, distancing herself. She also saw the effect this had on George. He looked everyone in the eye, except Ruby, when they were all gathered together, but when everyone was dispersed looking for holly and ivy, he watched her.

That evening when the log had been brought in on an old cart and deposited in the huge fireplace, and the hall had been smothered in greenery, Gretta cornered Ruby in the bathroom.

'Is there something you want to tell me?'

Ruby, already rather thrown by being locked in with her, looked confused. 'How do you mean?'

'I'm worried about you. I've got a feeling you're in a muddle.'

'You don't think there's something going on between me and Charlie?'

Gretta looked concerned. 'No. That wasn't what I was thinking. There isn't, is there?'

'No. Not in the way you're thinking, anyway.'

'Meaning?'

Ruby told Gretta about the terrible scene with Charlie. She responded with words of disbelief. 'He didn't! Oh my God, no! You're joking!'

'Do you think I should tell Ben?'

Gretta thought for a moment. 'Well, yes, I do. How could you not?'

Ruby winced. 'It's so awkward. Ben would feel like he had to do something about it. Can you imagine how embarrassing it would be? Him and Charlie trying to have a heart to heart?'

'But you can't carry on as if nothing has happened. What if he does it again?'

'I don't think he will.' Ruby recalled Charlie's shocked

140

face after he'd said he loved her. As if someone else had said it, and he was listening. 'I think perhaps he was very drunk, or stoned, or something. Why else would he behave so strangely? He can't really love me. There must be something else going on in his head. I think I'll wait and see what happens. I don't want to cause unnecessary trouble.'

Gretta looked unconvinced but said, 'We'll see.'

Ruby started to open the bathroom door, but Gretta put her foot in the way.

'Not so fast. I haven't finished with you yet.' She narrowed her eyes. 'It was another muddle I was thinking of.'

Ruby looked puzzled, but Gretta was not put off.

'Come on, Ruby. It's me. You have to tell me about George.'

'Do I have to?' She winced. 'You won't like me any more.'

'Don't be silly.'

Ruby slumped on the floor and leaned against the bath. 'Oh, why do you have to know me so well?' She heaved a big sigh. 'Don't jump to conclusions, though. We've only kissed.'

'Hmm. Kisses can be enough to do the damage. What about Ben? Have your feelings changed about him?'

Ruby rested her head on her drawn-up knees. 'No. But it's like when I try to see him, there's this thing in the way all the time, like my fringe has grown too long, or I've got a hat falling over my eyes so I can't see properly. And it's George.'

Gretta came and sat down next to Ruby and they held hands companionably. 'When you say you've kissed George, what do you mean? Have you been seeing each other often?'

'No. That's one of the stupid things. We hardly see each other at all. He avoided me for ages, then he turned up one day and kissed me, and then he started avoiding me again. It's terrible.'

141

'Strange behaviour.'

'Not really. He doesn't want to hurt Ben. He's nicer than me.'

Gretta did not jump to her defence. 'Ben is a lovely man, Ruby. You'd be mad to mess things up. I agree this George character's rather gorgeous, and being a gardener is very romantic, but, you don't know him. You know Ben. You make each other happy. You'd regret it so much, if you lost him. I'd hate to see that happen. You don't seem to realise how lucky you are.'

Ruby rested her head on her friend's shoulder. 'I know you're right but somehow, knowing what's right doesn't make me do the right thing.'

'It's because it's clandestine.'

'How do you mean?'

'It's the secretiveness, and the unknown, and the stolen kisses, which make it so alluring. You don't need to tell me, I've been there. But if you split up with Ben and end up with George it won't be clandestine any more, and you won't have gained anything.'

'I'm not going to split up with Ben.'

Gretta squeezed Ruby's hand. 'Just be careful, Ruby. Try to draw the line at kissing.' She struggled up from the bathroom floor, adjusted her skirt, and smoothed her hair in the mirror.

'This place!' she exclaimed. 'It's like a zoo, all these men on heat, prowling around. What's the matter with them?' She leaned down and offered Ruby her hand, to pull her up.

Ruby's brow creased in thought. 'I don't know. In the past, it was always you that got the men going. I'm not used to it. I don't know what to do with it.'

'Not that you don't deserve their attention.'

Ruby gave a slight snort. 'Well, it's kind of you to say so, but I don't think I've suddenly become irresistible. Do you?'

They gazed for a moment at their images in the mirror:

Gretta with her sleek blond hair and lipstick, Ruby dishevelled, with a smudge of dirt on her cheek from collecting the ivy. As they turned away, Ruby muttered, 'It must be something in the water.'

They both giggled, but then Gretta said, 'Seriously, I do think there's something about the park, an atmosphere, maybe just how beautiful it is – it stirs things up. Jem and I always feel it when we're here.'

Ruby put her hand to her mouth, pretending to be shocked. 'Is that so?'

Gretta blushed faintly. 'Perhaps you don't need to know about that. We should go now.'

Ruby laughed. 'Perhaps we should.'

They returned to the hall, where everyone was sitting in front of the blazing fire, drinking each other's health, the picture of Christmas conviviality.

December 22nd

It's wrong to attempt the kindling of heat in the dead time, but sometimes my longing overcomes me, it overflows. The human spirit fights back with celebrations and light: Yuletide, Christmas, Saturnalia, New Year. Anything to roll back the night. From now on the days lengthen, the light grows and we can look forward to summer, and the return of plenty. In the dark season I lost my way. This day marks the return of the sun, but it's a long and slow process

I feel that Nature is on my side, that the cycle of life will overcome the obstacles. Things will become clearer when there is more light. She will come to me and we will praise the goddess together.

I am walking along the beach, watching toddling children careering around the wide expanse, intoxicated by the space. Ben runs after his young nieces and nephews, and they scatter, squealing, to their mothers, who laugh and gather them up protectively. How good it will be to have our own little family, warm and secure. Why does George get in the way of this, kissing me and making me feel so much? He has drawn out this great longing in me, but now resists it, leaving me feeling like a panting dog. I am not even able to enjoy the innocent pleasures of a walk with the family. He is there in the back of my mind, clouding my thoughts. Him and Charlie. How has this happened, this awful mess, every way I turn a complication? Sometimes I think maybe it is all part of some great set up that Ben and Charlie have planned, and they are just waiting for me to take it seriously before having a good laugh at my expense.

Ben runs about the beach, oblivious. He is like a dolphin, a smile forever on his face, swooping and diving through deep water, so smooth-skinned, no troubles seem to cling to him. I want to swim in his slipstream, in amongst calm waters with him. He is straightforward and true, and assumes everyone else is. We repay him with weakness, and treachery. A terrible aura envelops Charlie, like a bad smell. It does not feel like love coming towards me. He resents the way I have made him feel, just as I resent George for affecting me. This constant unevenness, these undesired feelings foisted on the wrong people, it goes round and round. I want to break free from this cycle, and walk hand in hand with Ben, along the open sand, our eyes to the horizon, the clear expanse of the beach before us, the comforting scrape of the waves erasing all other sounds.

After a dewy start, the last day of the year turned clear blue, with no wind. As darkness arrived, a thick crust of ice formed over every outside surface. A sliver of frosty moon floated in a clear black sky, spangled with clouds of stars. When the party revellers stepped outside the hall the air was still and thin, as if they were at the top of a mountain. The grass crunched underfoot, and the driveway was milky glass, smooth and slippery. Tree branches were coated in white; the leaves on the evergreens were encrusted with sugary granules. A group of people from the party made their way towards the river, slipping and sliding, laughing hysterically. The pearly ground reflected all the light of the moon and stars, making it easy to see the way.

Earlier in the evening, someone had mentioned a way she had heard about of wishing for things in the New Year. It involved writing down a list of your aspirations for the coming year on a piece of paper which you then made into a boat and set sail on a river, or in the sea, in a symbolic gesture to fate. This idea had been pounced upon by several people, and Ruby had been sent off to find large amounts of scrap paper for the purpose. Dreams and desires were easy to think of, but making the boats proved more difficult and took some time. Nevertheless at five to midnight a large number of partygoers stood ready to launch their boats into the oil-black river.

Ruby stood holding Ben's arm, drunk, gazing at the glittering meadow. Charlie was draped over a young woman she had never seen before. Professor Lal and George were milling about in the crowd. George was avoiding her as usual, under the pretext of looking after the professor. Ruby clutched her little boat in one hand, anxious that no one should see what she had written. Writing down what she wanted was dangerous.

At midnight, everyone toasted each other with champagne; then there was a flurry of white paper, dropping softly into the water, and everyone cheered. Most boats became tangled in the weeds at the bank edge; others sank, a few caught the current and gently swished down the river. Ruby couldn't see what had happened to hers. She hoped that, if it was one of the boats caught in the weeds, all the writing would be too smudged to be legible to anyone. Some people were lying on their stomachs leaning over the river, trying to free their boats, others went looking for sticks to try and prod them. There was much laughing and screaming and no one seemed to notice how cold it was.

Some hours later, the party began to slow down. All

over the house, people lay slumped in chairs and sprawled across sofas. Ruby was wide awake. She felt as though the piercing cold air outside had seared the drunken fuggi-ness from her nerves, and she was alert, like a cat on the prowl. She stepped silently around the house, observ-ing the wreckage, seeing the night's work. Ben had fallen asleep in a chair in the early hours until Ruby had shaken him and persuaded him to go to bed. Charlie and the girl had disappeared soon after the paper boat ceremony. Ruby didn't expect to see them again until very late the next day. She crept through the downstairs rooms, check-ing candles were blown out, and that guards stood round the embers of dying fires. Then she went into the dark-ened kitchen to make herself some soothing cocoa, to try and overcome her wakefulness. She stood mixing her cocoa into a paste, gazing out through the French windows over the glowing white lawn, musing on life and the bitter-sweetness of it. Suddenly a face appeared at the window, and Ruby screamed and jerked her arm, spilling cocoa paste and milk all over the floor. Even as she screamed, she realised it was the professor and not a ghost or a murderer. He stood outside the window, with his hands up to his face, mouthing 'sorry' as she unlocked the door to let him in.

'Oh, dear, Ruby, I am so sorry. I had no idea you were in the kitchen. You have no light on, you see, I could see nothing.'

'What were you doing outside?' Ruby allowed her suspi-cion of him to break through in the tone of her voice.

As usual, the professor either did not notice, or ignored, the implied criticism. 'It's so beautiful, so white, so pure. I have been walking around the park, dazzled by its splen-dour. Really, you must come and see. There are icicles hanging from the trees, and the lake has frozen over. Come. Look.'

He stood in the open door, gesturing to her to come outside. Ruby was already regretting her rudeness to him.

She disliked the effect he had on her. He made her skin prickle with irritation, but his perseverance in the face of hostility made her ashamed of herself. So she picked up her coat and stepped out into the freezing night with him. They set off towards the crystal wood to one side of the lake. As they moved, the trees twinkled at them, moonlight caught in the frozen droplets.

They walked in silence for some time and then as they entered the small wood the professor said, 'I went to see your exhibition while I was in London, Ruby. It was super, really very impressive.'

Ruby was surprised that he had known about her exhibition. 'I'm flattered you made the effort to go and see it.'

'Oh yes, I liked it very much. In fact, I bought one of the large paintings. The one showing those succulent red summer fruits on a big dark blue plate. You know which one I mean?'

'Yes, of course. It was one of a short series I did using that lovely plate last summer. I painted the fruit and vegetables as they came into season. It was such an eye-opener. The colours of the fruit, when you really look at them, are amazingly complex.' Ruby stopped abruptly, realising she was getting carried away.

'Tell me,' said the professor, 'what was it that inspired you to start using fruit and vegetables as your central subject? I understand that before this series of paintings your work was much more abstract. Why this sudden return to a more traditional form?'

'I've been asked that before and I don't really have an answer. I simply woke up one morning last May with this idea in my head. I suppose I'd just seen these fantastic gardens for the first time, and Ben had shown me the walled gardens and explained how they produce food all through the year. I caught this powerful sense of the seasons, eating whatever happened to be ripe, finding out about vegetables that I'd never heard of before. There are so many extraordinary shapes and colours! This autumn

147

George brought me a huge basketful of squashes. Do you know what I mean?'

'I do. Very delicious.'

'Well, yes, they are. But I'd never seen such things before. They're like fruit out of a fairy tale, so small and perfect, and with those unreal patterns, as if they've been painted. I suppose I just became intoxicated by the bountifulness around me.'

'Ah, yes. Intoxicated. That is certainly the sense I get from your paintings. As though you have absorbed the colour and the perfume of the garden into your veins and it is driving you to paint, to create.'

Ruby gave him a startled look. She was unnerved by the intensity of his response to her work. 'I wasn't aware that I had put so much passion into them.'

The professor stopped walking and turned to her, excited, his hands clasped in front of his chest in supplication. 'In all creative acts there must be passion, for the thing to succeed. There must be the meeting of souls, fire in the blood, a pounding heart, a sensuous intoxication, whether it is a work of art you create, or another human being. Do you see? That is what is required of us in this world. Joyous moments of fruitful creation.'

Ruby tried to think of something appropriate to say after such an outburst. She suddenly felt very isolated, standing in the middle of the wood, out of sight of the house, with this strange, excitable man. The cold began to seep through her coat. She shivered and then began to walk again, murmuring over her shoulder, 'Well, anyway, I'm glad you like my work.'

He quickly caught up with her, and laughed as he said, 'Yes, yes, as usual, my enthusiasm gets the better of me. It is interesting though, is it not, that a chance meeting should lead to such a change in your life's direction, including so radical a change in your work? Some people might argue, I suppose, that it was not by chance that you were drawn to this place, to this park, but that it was your destiny. It seems remarkable, do you not think, how many of the occupants here, over the years, have experienced a kindling of the creative spirit? Novelists, an opera singer, painters. What do you make of this idea?'

'I don't know. The sensible side of me thinks that life is probably just a series of haphazard chances. But then, another part of me senses that something is controlling what happens, playing with us. Some coincidences, some meetings, or events seem too surreal to be chance. I'd like to believe that.' Her own mistaken feelings, when she first met George, flitted through her mind. 'But in the end I suspect there is usually some more prosaic reason for things happening.'

'But you made your little boat this evening, you wrote down your hopes and desires, and you launched it with all the rest of us. Did you not believe on some level that it may influence the course of your life?'

'I suppose, deep down, there may be a childish wisp of hope that these things really do work sometimes.'

'Do not ignore that child, Ruby. The child represents all that is instinctive and natural in us. We should treasure any fragments of childish intuition inside us that have survived the onslaught of the world. Do you not agree?'

Ruby sighed wearily. 'I think it would be better if I was more grown-up.'

The professor chuckled. 'Compared to me, you are a spring chicken. There is plenty of time.'

They had reached the end of the lake where the wood petered out into water meadow, and they began to follow the track which ran along the lakeside. The professor seemed to want to change the subject and began talking amiably about the wonderful holiday he was having here, and how much he felt reinvigorated.

'I am itching to get back to writing my book, which has been languishing so long on the back burner. All this silly hoo-ha about *Reaching Paradise* has kept me away too long.'

149

'What's your new book about?'

'Aha.' The professor tapped his nose with his finger twice, meaning it was secret, but then he continued, 'Oh, why not tell you, I know you are someone who can keep a secret.' He looked at her in a direct way, which made Ruby blush. She wondered what George had been telling him. He continued: 'I have a theory, which I have been developing for some time now. I am exploring the more obscure influences on garden design across Europe in the eighteenth century, including, of course, developments in England.'

'Hence your interest in this estate.'

'Exactly so.'

'Why do you have to be so secretive? What is so monstrous about your theory, that you have to be evasive all the time?' Irritation had crept back into Ruby's voice.

The professor smiled at her. 'I am aware that you and Mr Fitzmaurice are rather, shall we say, frustrated by my carefulness on this point. But you see, Ruby, it is like this. I have a reputation. It is expected of me to come up with radical, colourful ideas. It is an unpleasant fact, but the academic world can be a cruel place. Everything depends on the work you publish, and there is tremendous pressure to be always producing new theories, new angles, new arguments. My last book annoyed people. It was too subjective for some of my fellow professors. They like everything to be catalogued into neat little boxes. They did not consider my work to be legitimate history, and I feel now that I am in danger of not being taken so seriously.'

He turned briefly to Ruby. 'Ridicule, you know, is a very efficient way to silence dissenting voices. I am much more interested in giving voice to peoples and cultures that have been passed over by centuries of narrow-minded historians than in making my fortune selling commercial books. That is my main mission. To look at the past in an alternative way, to reveal all the hidden layers. But to do this, I need to be taken seriously. My approach has always been

150

radical, but when I was writing dry texts about the evidence for agriculture in obscure corners of the world, I was tolerated more. Since *Reaching Paradise* was published I have been criticised for my approach to the notion of truth.'

'How do you mean?'

'It is like this. I do not believe that truth is an objective matter. You will know yourself, Ruby, that one event experienced by four people will be interpreted and retold in four different ways. No one is qualified to arbitrate in such a matter. Most historians do not like this idea. It does not allow for fact. It transforms history into fables and tales. I find this very liberating, but most of my colleagues do not. It leads me to places that are closed to other historians, and that is why I have been so successful.' He stretched his arms out wide, as if embracing all these possibilities. 'But, Ruby, people do not always like it when you are so successful. There are people who would be very happy to see me fail. I am aware of that and to remain successful I have to protect my ideas right up to publication. My rivals are always very keen to undermine me, to steal my thunder. I have become careful through bitter experience.'

He took in a deep breath of thin, crisp air and then puffed out little clouds of white steam, which curled off into the night. His face shone again with that ecstatic expression, as he exclaimed, 'But tonight, walking around this marvellous place, I feel so close to the mastermind who designed it, it makes me want to tell the world of my discovery. It is as though his spirit is here with us and wants me to speak the truth about his magical creation.'

'You mean Repton?' Ruby asked.

'No, no. It is not Repton who is the genius of this place, who is present in every tree, every blade of grass. No, no, it is Henry Faulkes, of course.'

'But I thought Repton drew up all those plans in the Red Book, those before-and-after paintings?'

'Yes, he did. But I have become quite convinced that Faulkes directed Repton very strongly throughout the

151

works. For example, the temple is clearly designed by Faulkes.'

'Henry Faulkes designed the temple?' Ruby said with surprise. 'Ben would be very interested to know that. He's been doing his own research on the building, as you know. How did you find that out?'

The professor was looking slightly anxious. 'Well, this is something I perhaps should not have told you. I should say no more.'

'Oh, for heaven's sake. What harm can there be in Ben knowing that?'

'No, I must apologise. I am carried away by the beautiful night, the park, too much champagne, and the pleasure of your company. Please, do not press me further.'

Ruby bit her lip and looked away from him to conceal her annoyance. They stood at the edge of the lake, looking over the water to the temple. It sat glimmering on the island, its newly rendered walls reflecting the cool moonlight. The frosted ground and the clear night sky combined to throw up a shimmer of milky white on the windows, high up in the walls of the temple. Then the light flickered. Ruby looked hard at the light. It flickered again. The sky was clear and there was no wind to blow clouds across the moonlight or shake the trees or their shadows. Ruby realised, with a slight tremor of anxiety, that the light was coming from inside the temple. Flickering candlelight. Without thinking, she grabbed the professor's arm.

'Look! The temple. There's someone inside it!'

The professor gazed over at the island, as the light flickered again, but he did not seem very concerned. He smiled a knowing smile.

'You have had a super party here tonight. New Year's Eve is a perfect time for starting things anew, do you not think? I am sure it will just be two people having a romantic experience on this most beautiful of nights. I do not think we should disturb. Let us go back to the house.'

Ruby thought he was probably right, although she

wondered how romantic a dusty old temple could really be on such a freezing cold night. They returned silently to the house, after which the professor disappeared off into the night, towards George's lodge. Ruby went to bed and was lulled to sleep by the warmth of Ben's sleeping, comforting body.

January

Grafts for early fruits are to be cut at this time and laid in the earth in a warm, dry place.

Mrs Martha Bradley

On the first morning of the New Year Ben woke up feeling only a little fuzzy from the effects of alcohol. He lay for some time, complacently watching Ruby asleep. Then he began to feel very hungry, so he slipped out of bed, gathered up his bundle of discarded clothes and crept out of the bedroom. He had an invigorating shower, made himself a huge breakfast of bacon and eggs and fried potato, and drank most of a whole pot of tea while listening to the radio. Now and then someone would poke their head round the door and say, 'Tea! How lovely!' and they would come in and make two mugfuls, and go away again to wherever they had made their nest on the previous night. Ben knew himself well enough to avoid looking at the state of the rest of the house. He would be overcome by a frenzy of tidiness, and would only annoy people and make them feel unwelcome. So he decided to complete his recovery programme by going out for a brisk walk in the sparkling frost-bitten morning.

Outside, the grass was crunchy, like crystallised sweets. The ice compacted under his feet and made a satisfying squeak. He walked some way, just relishing the sound of

154

the scrunching. The landscape was white on white. A hoar frost had powdered everything, bleaching out colour, blending in the familiar features of the landscape, merging sky and earth. Ben felt slightly vertiginous, as if he might at any moment slip off the ground and fall into the sky. He walked down to the river to see if it had frozen.

The river was shallow and flowed slowly through the park and so, whenever there was a cold snap, it froze over quite easily. A thin pearlescent layer skimmed the darkened waters. Ben bounced a couple of stones across the surface, and they clattered into the opposite bank. A few ducks made their way hesitantly across the ice towards him, slipping and sliding, looking very puzzled and chilly. Gazing down at them as they struggled to clamber up the shallow bank, he noticed a bedraggled white heap. Looking closer, he realised that the heap was all that was left of several marooned New Year's wish boats from the night before. He tested the edge of the ice with his boot. It was rock hard. So he stepped down to gather up the mess. Some of the boats were reduced to mush, others had survived intact and were frozen crisp. I won't look at what's written on them, he thought to himself, I'll just clear them up. He managed to collect most of them without prying, only half looking at them, picking out the odd word. But then something caught his eye. In large capitals he saw the letters UBY. He could not think of any word that contained these letters, other than Ruby. It made him curious. He knew it might be Ruby's boat, and if that was so he would not allow himself to read the contents. But if it was someone else's boat, what was their reason for writing about his girlfriend? He carefully unpicked the folded paper. There was very little written on it. Just these words: I WILL HAVE RUBY.

When Ben got back from his walk Ruby was up, sitting in the kitchen, having breakfast. They hugged, and then chatted about the previous night.

'Charlie was with some woman I've never seen before. She was utterly legless. God knows what he'd given her.'

155

Ruby winced. 'Don't. Quite a few people overdid it last night.' She laughed. 'Did you see your sisters dancing? They were more or less propping each other up.'

'They'll feel terrible this morning. They never could take their drink.'

'And guess who I went for a midnight walk with.' Ruby put on a mysterious face.

'I've no idea.' Ben thought of the least likely person. 'Charlie?'

Ruby snorted. 'You must be joking. He was in no state to walk. No. Professor Lal.'

'Really?' Ben felt a jolt of anxiety. 'How did that come about?'

'He turned up outside the kitchen and nearly scared me out of my skin, but then he invited me to walk with him because it was so pretty.'

Ben raised his eyebrows. 'And did he behave himself?'

'Yes, he was fine. But he let something slip that you'll be interested in. He said the temple was designed by Henry Faulkes, not Repton.'

'Did he?' Ben's eyes opened wide. 'But how does he know? Did he tell you?'

'No. He went all secretive, and said he'd gone too far.'

'That man drives me mad sometimes. I still haven't managed to pin him down about the wall paintings and nothing can happen at the temple until he lets English Heritage see his research.'

'Well, it occurred to me this morning that he was very pleased with himself that day, when he came and looked at the accounts. Do you remember? He'd obviously found something he was excited about.'

Ben screwed up his eyes, remembering. 'That's true. Perhaps I should have another look at them. I'm rather better at reading old writing than I was. I might pick something up this time.' He sipped his tea and glanced up at Ruby. 'So the professor didn't flirt with you, or try anything on at all. You know, he didn't make you feel

156

uncomfortable, like he did before?'

Ruby looked at him quizzically. 'He got rather over-excited about my paintings at one point, but no, he didn't try anything on. Why?'

Ben brought out a soggy piece of paper from his coat pocket and gave it to Ruby.

'I didn't know whether I should show this to you, because I thought you might be alarmed, but then I thought you ought to know.'

Ruby read it out loud. '"I will have Ruby." How weird.' She felt a fluttering in her chest. 'Who could have written that?' She was thinking, this must be Charlie.

'Do you think it might have been the professor?' Ben asked

'No. I don't think it would be his style. He's too direct. Anyway, I haven't felt he's taken a particular shine to me, have you?'

'Well, I hadn't, but then we hadn't realised before how much he liked your painting.'

'True. But I don't think it's him.'

'Who, then?'

'I don't know, but let's not worry about it. It was probably someone having a joke, or it could be about someone else called Ruby. It doesn't have to be about me.'

'I'm not convinced. I don't like it. There's something about those capital letters that gives me the creeps. Mad people write in capitals'

'Ben! Don't say things like that! I'm sure it's nothing.'

Ben decided not to push it any further, but later that day he walked over to George's to see Professor Lal. He wasn't sure how he was going to approach the subject, but he wanted to find out somehow whether the professor really was nurturing some kind of obsession with Ruby. He also wanted to make Lal reveal more of his research on the temple, and his reasons for believing that wall paintings were hidden there. But when he got to the lodge only George was there, looking rather worn out, having indulged

157

too much on the previous night. The professor had left earlier in the day to catch a flight to New York.

'Damn the man!' Ben exclaimed, but he felt relieved, not only that the professor was out of the country away from Ruby, but also that it had excused him from a potential confrontation.

'So what did you get up to last night?' he said to George, looking at his pale face and scrumpled hair.

George smiled weakly. 'Well, I must admit, I mixed it a bit. Charlie was handing out speed and I drank a lot as well. Not good. I puked.'

'Oh, dear. Not a promising start to the year then. You shouldn't let Charlie lead you astray. What did the upstanding professor think of your behaviour?'

'Oh, you know, he's pretty open-minded about what people get up to. He likes people to enjoy themselves.'

Ben voiced something which had been puzzling him for some time. 'Do you really like him then, George? It wasn't an imposition, him staying here all this time?'

George laughed. 'Yeah, I do like him. I know you don't, but I think he's all right. He knows everything there is to know about garden history, which has been really useful. And he's quite a laugh. And I like the way he deals with people being rude to him.' George looked Ben in the eye.

'Well, I would feel rather more sympathy for him if he didn't go out of his way to annoy people in the first place,' Ben said defensively.

George held his hands up in front of his face as if he was fending off a blow. 'OK! OK! I'm not up to arguing with anyone. Do you want a beer?'

Ben made a face. 'No thanks. I'm on a strict diet of tea today.' He followed George as he went into the kitchen and put the kettle on then fetched a cold bottle of beer for himself from the fridge. Ben found he couldn't stop himself asking more about the professor.

'Did he ever say anything to you about Ruby?'

George looked vacant. 'Who?'

'Professor Lal.'

'What kind of thing?'

'I don't know. Whether he thought she was attractive, or something like that.'

'He never said anything like that. I know he likes her paintings. Why do you ask?'

'I have a bad feeling about him.'

'I don't think you need worry about Ruby running off with the prof, do you?'

'No, of course not,' Ben said, slightly irritated by George's flippancy. 'But I don't want him worrying her.'

George flopped down on to a chair and pushed his hair back from his forehead in a gesture of exhaustion. 'Well, he's out of the country now.'

He put the beer bottle to his mouth and glugged down most of it in one go. Ben watched him with concern.

'Do you think that's a good idea after last night's experience?'

'Yes.'

'You've been spending too much time with Charlie. Why don't you come over later for a meal? You need some proper food inside you.'

George took in a long breath and then sighed a long sigh. Ben thought he was going to say no. But he said, 'OK. Why not? I'll bring some beers over.'

Ben walked home in the brittle afternoon darkness, wondering why the conversation had been so strained and irritable. The aftermath of too much substance abuse, he decided, and went back to the kitchen to indulge in some therapeutic cooking.

The kitchen is cosy, steamed up and fuggy, and there is a lovely savoury smell curling from the oven. Ben has been chopping and whisking and mixing and is in the last frenzy of bringing everything together. I am sitting with my feet resting on a chair, comfortably reading a week-old Sunday

159

paper and sipping at a cool crisp glass of wine. I am feeling content. Even the knowledge that George will soon be here does not seem to worry me. Today I feel that I understand him and why he has felt the need to distance himself. He is trying to do the right thing, and I should be grateful to him for saving me from myself. Perhaps over time I will really believe this.

Charlie comes in, looking like death. Ben asks him politely if his companion from the night before will be joining us for supper. Charlie says in a scowling voice: I sent her packing hours ago.

His misogyny is like a slap in the face. Where does it come from, this contempt he has for women? Ben looks exasperated. He is embarrassed by Charlie's behaviour in front of me.

Charlie has hardly spent five minutes in my company since the yule log expedition. I know he must feel painfully self-conscious in my company, but he pushes the possibility of sympathy away with his anger. He looks at me to see my reaction to his remark, and mumbles something crude under his breath about feminists. Then he puts on a squeaky, whining voice: 'Ooh, it's not nice to treat wimmin like that, they are not objects, they are intelligent, creative people.' Well, this one wasn't, OK? She was asking for it.

Ben looks shocked, and tells him to shut up. Charlie is still looking at me, ready to duel with me. I don't want to get drawn in. I am thinking about the phrase 'I will have Ruby' and what Charlie would have meant by it. I turn my back on him and stand at the sink washing up.

Charlie doesn't shut up. He says: She wasn't even a good lay. Too out of it.

I watch as Ben walks briskly over to the table where Charlie is sitting and leans over so his face is a couple of inches from Charlie's. He says in a low voice: I mean it, Charlie. If you don't stop being so disgusting, I will throw you out. You've gone too far. Do you understand?

Charlie stares back at him sullenly, but says nothing. I

160

have a chilling picture in my head of Charlie soullessly mauling a half-conscious woman, only a short distance from my own bedroom. My stomach turns. Is that what he means? To have me? For the first time I feel scared of him.

The doorbell rings. It will be George. I am not feeling so calm now, and the thought of Charlie and George glowering together in the kitchen makes me panic. I wish Gretta and Jem were here. This place feels like a madhouse. Ben asks me to answer the door, as he is in the middle of serving up. George stands on the doorstep, looking wan and dishevelled. I say: Why have you come?

He takes my hand, and smiles at me: I wanted to see you on the first day of the New Year. To try and make a new beginning somehow.

He constantly pushes and pulls me, breaks down my resolution, ties me in knots. His smile blazes at me, his hand, holding mine, sends warm jets up my arm. It makes me feel nervous. I say: Let's not talk about it now. Come in.

We walk back into the thick atmosphere of the kitchen. Charlie is tenaciously keeping his place at the table despite Ben's anger. Ben is clattering and banging saucepans. I look at all three of them, Ben, George, Charlie. All the emotions that they demand from me suddenly well up like fountains. Guilt, desire, anger fill my head in a sudden flood of pressure, pressing on my temples. After a moment of paralysis, I walk out into the hallway, where it is cooler. Then I open the door. Outside is a calm, black sky, with diamond stars. The moonlight shows me the track, winding off to the walled gardens. I breathe in the air like icy water and my head feels better. I picture myself, huddled up in my coat, leaning against the garden wall, looking out at the silent park. I quietly lift my coat from off its hook and put it on. Then I am walking.

Ben was worried about Ruby's behaviour. The following morning he tackled her about it, but she reassured him.

'It was just a mixture of Charlie, and tiredness, and too many parties. Forget it. Let's get back to normal, back into work. I need to do some painting. Practical things.' She smiled encouragingly at him. 'You were going to look at the old accounts for the temple. Why don't you do that?'

He was vaguely conscious that she was changing the subject, but he agreed that a return to routine would be welcome. The market garden, the wood carving, and his research. That afternoon, he got out Repton's accounts. He felt more practised at deciphering the writing, the familiar broad, swirling brown-ink copperplate of the eighteenth century. He ran his finger down the list of items: wages for labourers, shovels, lists of shrubs and trees, glass, sawn timber. At the bottom was a note confirming that the work had been completed, with a request for the account to be settled. The date was December 1793. The accounts for the temple were on a separate piece of paper. Ben had assumed before that this was because it was a building, completed once the main landscaping was finished. Now he tried to look at it afresh, to be open to suggestion.

He lay the two accounts next to each other, and suddenly it was blindingly obvious. Both documents were written in the educated hand of the eighteenth century: the loops of the *b,d, l* and *h*, the strange double balloon of the *f*, the harp shaped *s*, and the shepherd crook *p*, the horizontal flags on the capital letters, the slight tilt always to the right. These characteristics seemed to be shared by all the writing he had looked at so far. But set side by side, personality emerged from the different extracts. The handwriting on the Repton bill was small and even in shape, and leaned less to the right. The other was more jumbled, more sweeping, less desirous of making an impression. The loops and tails of the letters on each line tangled with those above and below, making it less legible. Previously Ben had just thought this was the same hand but in more of a hurry. Now he thought: This must be the hand of Henry Faulkes himself. Here is the evidence that he took sole responsibil-

162

ity for overseeing the building of the temple. A temple that so outraged the local vicar, he felt driven to preach against the lord of the manor, and the source of his living, from the pulpit.

Ben scanned the temple accounts but, as before, could only pick out a few words, the writing being so intermingled. Now, though, he felt it was vital to decipher what lay hidden there and settled himself down to analysing every letter on the page. He tried to think what words he might expect to read in a list of materials for a temple. Bricks, stone, lime, lead, plaster, tiles, glass and timber. Once he had identified one or two of these words they acted like code-breakers, and he was able to recognise individual letters in amongst the scrawled squiggles. Having transcribed most of it, there was one word that eluded him. It looked like *Piymneit*. He looked at it for some time, substituting different letters, trying to think of words with the same pattern of letter shapes, but it defeated him. He wondered whether perhaps the word was a name of someone who had been brought in to do the work.

He heard Ruby come home, and called down to her. She came up to his room, rosy-cheeked from walking around town in the brisk air, and sat on his lap. 'How did you get on?'

He showed her the two sets of handwriting, and how he had been deciphering the temple accounts. 'There is just this word I can't make out. I can't think what it would be.'

Ruby glanced at it and said: 'Pigment.'

'What?'

'Pigment. Look, that's a *g* not a *y*, he just hasn't finished the circle off properly. And that's a drawn out *m*, not an *m* and *n*. And that scrawled line before the *t* is supposed to be an *n*, only his pen hasn't worked properly on the down stroke. And the dot above it belongs to the *i* at the beginning. See?'

Ben did see. '*Pigment* hadn't occurred to me. I suppose it's a word you use all the time.'

163

Ruby put on a complacent, pursed-lip smile, like a child who has just won a conkers competition, but then said, '*Pigment*, of course, means that they were using colours. Do you think this is the evidence the professor found which made him think there were paintings?'

Ben experienced a sudden rush of blood to his head, a hot swish of inspiration. He hugged Ruby tightly and then held her shoulders, gabbling excitedly into her face,

'Of course! The presence of pigments proves there were paintings inside the temple!' He let go of Ruby, and said, 'I wonder what they were of? Something shocking, no doubt. That must be why the vicar was so upset. A classical temple wouldn't normally raise eyebrows, but some kind of risqué subject on the walls, safe from prying eyes – that certainly would.'

'Some kind of titillating scene, you mean? Like a Fragonard? Looking up the skirts of a girl on a swing?'

'Yes! Why not?'

Ben had heard nothing from Jayne Greene and he presumed she was too busy to become more involved. But he thought she might be interested in the pigment clue, so he rang her at the university. She recognised his voice immediately.

'Ben! It's really nice to hear from you! Did you have a good Christmas?'

That strange smoky voice again. Ben pictured her sitting on the edge of her desk, her legs swinging, her glossy black hair pushed behind her ears. Something like a cool shadow flitted across his skin and made his hairs stand on end. I like her too much, he thought to himself. He returned a standard answer. 'Yes thanks. And you?'

'No, not really. It's not my favourite time of year.'

'Oh, I'm sorry to hear that.'

There was an awkward pause. Ben didn't know whether he should enquire further.

She broke the silence. 'Don't worry about it. I'm just not

164

good around forced cheerfulness. Makes me feel very serious.'

An image of a Christmas party bubbled up in Ben's mind, with drunken lecturers and secretaries, popping crackers, and party hats, and Jayne in the corner with her creased forehead and tapping fingers. He wanted to put his arm round her.

'So, anyway,' she continued. 'What can I do for you? What's Lal been up to since we last spoke?'

'Funnily enough, he was here over Christmas.'

'Oh really?' Her voice was abrupt.

Ben tried to avert her suspicion. 'I had no choice. He was staying on the estate with the gardener. By the end of it, I was jolly glad to see the back of him.'

'Hmm.'

'Yes, really. I have good reason to think he had dishonourable intentions towards my fianceé.' There was another silence, as the word 'fianceé' clattered down the phone line like a stone. Ben wished he hadn't said it, then felt glad that he had. It was best to be honest. He hurried on. 'The important thing is, while he was here he let slip something about Faulkes being the designer of the temple, and that made me look again at the accounts we have here. I think I've found evidence to show that there were definitely paintings of some sort on the interior walls, and that's maybe what outraged Rackham so much.'

'I see.' She didn't seem very excited by his news.

'You don't think I'm right?'

'Oh, yes, I'm sure you're onto something there. In fact, I meant to ring you ages ago about those spirals you mentioned. I asked a colleague about them and she said it sounded a bit like the labyrinthine patterns found on prehistoric monuments. There's a famous one in Ireland. She said some people think it symbolises the cycle of life. You know, birth, death, rebirth.'

'Really?'

'Yep. They're found all over the world, apparently. I

165

thought, perhaps Faulkes used it as a code on the painting to symbolise turning over a new leaf when he married Charlotte. It's possible, I suppose, that he used the same symbolism in the temple?'

Ben sighed. 'I don't know. I think the professor would be perfectly capable of sending me on a wild goose chase. They were probably just interesting to him because they're about fertility. But we'll find out soon because the conservators are coming to do their sampling next month.'

'Hmm. It's puzzling. The thing is none of this really fits in with what I know.'

Ben's ears pricked up. 'What *do* you know?'

She laughed her smoker's cackle. 'Well, that would be telling.'

'You sound like Professor Lal.' Ben was irritated.

She laughed again. 'You know how to hit a girl where it hurts. Me sounding like that tosser! Hang on.' Ben heard some noise in the background, a scraping of chairs, and voices. 'Look, Ben. I must go, I've got a meeting. But I'll tell you what. Maybe you can do some thinking for me. Go back to Petersham and ask to see Rackham's private papers. There are some letters in there. See what you think of them, and we'll talk again. OK?'

Ben drove up to Petersham the next day. He soon found the reference for the letters in amongst the catalogue entries for Rackham and they were delivered to his table in a cardboard box. The familiar, musty smell of old paper rose up from the letters. The sheets were stiff, folded twice, with a ribbon round them. Ben sat down to read them with relish, as if he was about to eat a sumptuous meal. The first letter was undated but appeared to be from the vicar's sister.

Dearest Brother,

Only imagine what a sensation your last letter has wrought upon the household! Your brother is become very grave and has shut himself up in his study with orders not to disturb him. I think he is writing to you and I will slip this missive in with his. He was against me reading your letter in the first place but I plagued him, as I could see it was something important, and I must know everything that pertains to you, my dearest Josh! How insupportable it must be for you to find you have been so misled by Mr Faulkes and he turns out to be a man who is beyond all that is decent! However, I expect Edward will know what to do and will instruct you in his letter, and all will be well.

I wish you were here to share in our amusements, instead of being in such a pickle.

Write again soon, dearest Josh, and God be with you,

Your affectionate sister,
Mary

15th June 1794
Dear Joshua,

I am, as you may imagine, horrified by the contents of your letter, and I am deeply concerned about the difficult circumstances in which you now find yourself. What can have possessed the man, to show to you such abhorrent works, when it is quite clear that you would never condone such behaviour? You are right to believe that it would be wrong to take no action, but I am keenly aware that any displeasure you cause by remonstrance will likely jeopardise your position in the parish. I think you must talk to your bishop and seek his advice. Do not carry the burden alone. I write no more now so that this letter can be dispatched, but be assured we are all praying for God to send you His guidance.

Yours as ever,
Edward

25th July

Dear Joshua,

I am shocked to hear of the advice given to you by the bishop. Has he no conscience? It is all very well for him to argue the case for Faulkes' youth, but we only have to look to the viscount to see how the sins of the father are visited upon the son. I feel somewhat responsible for encouraging you to take up the Oakstead living, when I knew perfectly well how that family was already tainted. At the time, coming after the death of our beloved mother and the unfortunate termination of your academic studies, it seemed the best course, but I now have cause to regret the decision bitterly. I have always had your interests at heart, dear brother, believe me.

What to do now, is the question. If the bishop does not support you in taking action, you have only two choices. You must either confront Faulkes yourself, or you must give up the living. Giving up your parish may seem a drastic action to take but I am sure in time you would be able to find another position. In the meantime you must come and live with us. I am troubled by the thought of you facing this trial alone, and I wish you would give me a better account of its effect on your health.

I cannot foresee any fruitful conclusion from a confrontation with the man. He is obviously lost to debauchery, else he would have known better than to show you his devilish works. He patently has no moral sense left in him. I therefore entreat you to come home at all speed and sever the connections with this corrupted family as soon as is possible, for your own sake.

God be with you.

Edward

Joshua – I write in haste. I have read the copy of the letter you mean to send to Faulkes, and I entreat you not to send it. It cannot produce any good for him, and will only do you harm. Please do as I say and come home as soon as is possible.

Edward

My dearest Josh,

We have not heard from you for several days and would wish that you send us word soon of how things go on in your parish. How did Mr Faulkes receive your letter? Edward thinks that you should not have sent it. He is worried about the effect all this is having on your constitution, which you know, dearest brother, has never been very strong. I, on the other hand, think you did right to attempt to save the poor demented creature's soul. If you considered yourself his friend you had a duty to petition him, as well as your duty as a man of God.

But was he very angry, or did he come to you on bended knees and beg for forgiveness and absolution? I fear it will have been the first course, as I have been privileged enough to hear some quite chilling history of Mr Faulkes and his family. One of my new friends is a relation of some sort to Mr Faulkes, a second cousin or some such, and he has many an interesting tale to tell. Do not fear that I told him anything of your present circumstances. I merely mentioned that you were the vicar at Oakstead, and my admirer – whose name is William, and who is as poor as a church mouse – could not be stopped from burning my ears with his stories. You will not believe it, Josh, but Viscount Faulkes was a renowned rake in his youth and was a member of that terrible cauldron of vice, the Hellfire Club. Do not be shocked by my knowledge of such a club! The satanic practices of Lord Dashwood and his fellow sinners are quite common knowledge in London circles, and we ladies must find something to talk about when we withdraw. Only think! Your patron was a member of the most notorious band of sinners England has ever known! Is it to be wondered at, then, that his son is also a lost soul? But did not you find his father to be an amiable man when he interviewed you? It is difficult to comprehend. I fear you find yourself in a den of wolves, my dearest brother. Can not you leave the place and come to us? I am full of concern for your predicament, and would feel happier if you were safely in the bosom of your family.

Write to us soon, or better still, arrive at our door, as Edward has entreated you.

God bless you
Mary

24th August 1794
Dear Joshua,

Am I to believe you have actually spoken the words of the sermon you included in your last letter from the pulpit? Although I am in the greatest sympathy with you in your horror of that man's scandalous behaviour, I cannot but feel that preaching against him may have desperate consequences for you. I am become very concerned that your health is suffering under this terrible burden. Your letter does not convince me that all is well with you. You know that this kind of event matched to your nervous disposition can only bring you more trouble. Leave the man to God's wrath, I beg you and come home. If I do not receive either your assent in writing or in person within the week, I will come for you myself, with all the attendant embarrassment such a visit would cause you.

Your brother
Edward

Dearest Josh,

I would have given much to see the face of Lord Faulkes when you preached your sermon to him. Did

170

his face turn red? Did he splutter and fidget? How audacious you have become! But I hope he did not confront you afterwards and beat you, as I know that you would be no match for him. I have heard that when he was in London, before his marriage, he was forever challenging gentlemen to duels for all manner of petty faults. See how much I have learned about the pastimes of wicked men during my sojourn here! Edward does not like it but I think it is best to be instructed in the ways of the world, rather than being green and more than likely duped by some handsome scoundrel. I could not help telling Edward about the present viscount's wicked past and was quite put out to find that both you and he had known all about it for an age. In any case, it would appear that Lord Faulkes has inherited all the vices of his father, and was apparently a most renowned gambler and liber-tine before he married and took up his residence at Oakstead – I hear this all from William, who is become a very good friend. William says that the viscount practically rusticated Faulkes because he had accumulated enormous debts. There was also talk of some terrible fight between him and a fellow gambler, which ended with the near death of his adversary. It seems that Lord Faulkes then fled the country for some time. William says that on his return the viscount summoned the reprobate and gave him a terrifying dressing down, threatening him with disinheritance or exile, unless he married and retreated to the country. I pity his poor wife, who I believe is from a very genteel family. They were assured by the viscount that his son would mend his ways once wed, but it appears that the stain of sin cannot be so easily expunged.

Do come home, Josh. You have surely done all you could for a friend who has betrayed your trust so inju-riously. Edward is become so stern and cross, our

171

melancholy household would be greatly improved by the benefit of your company. Besides, I would be pleased to have the opportunity to introduce you to William, whom I think you will like very well, as I do.

God bless you,
your affectionate sister,
Mary

We have just heard of the attack. My dear little Josh, how cruelly you have been treated! Edward is leaving at this very moment to attend your bedside, and I will be with you tomorrow to nurse you. I will not sleep until I can be sure you are recovered. God be with you.

Henford Hall, 30th August 1794
Dear Mr Rackham,

The behaviour of my son has once again been brought before me for censure. I cannot be anything but impressed by the intrepid nature of your public attacks upon my son's character, knowing as you do of his renown as a prodigious swordsman combined with that dangerous character trait which I fear he inherits from his excellent mother, a hasty temper. I trust that my physician has eased your situation and rendered you more comfortable.

In connection with this matter, I have had the honour of interviewing your brother, and it has been decided that it would be propitious for my son and his wife to embark soon on an extended tour about the country, to widen his study of agricultural innovation, which, as you know as his sometime friend, is a genuine passion of his. He has expressed a wish to revisit those ancient sites in Italy, which seem to have engendered his perverse love for a particular kind of architecture, but in the circumstances I think this unwise. In any event, you will no doubt be relieved to

172

hear that his departure from your vicinity is imminent.

I am very conscious of the service you have attempted to render my son under the most trying of circumstances. Such constancy and diligence in the face of threats against life and limb deserves to be honoured and so you will be gratified to hear that I am offering you the living at Burntbridge here in Derbyshire. There is a fine parsonage there and a church in good repair. I have instructed my agent to make all the necessary arrangements so that once you are quite recovered you may avail yourself of the place at your leisure. I have also taken it upon myself to discuss your merits with a certain lord bishop of my acquaintance, and you may rest assured your name will not be forgotten where there is opportunity for furtherance.

I am sure that you will be as anxious as I to prevent this sorry adventure from becoming the subject of tittle-tattle. I could not guarantee your own immunity from censure, were news of these events to become more widely known.

Faulkes

As Ben read this last letter, he could hear the voice of Henry Faulkes' father in his head: light, but threatening. He imagined how frightening a dressing down would be coming from such a powerful man, even if you were married, and well versed in the ways of the world, as Henry already was in 1794. Ben read the letters three, four times, not quite able to believe their content. He went outside and rang Jayne.

'Why didn't you tell me about these before?'

'I didn't want to play all my cards at once.'

'What?' Ben barked at her.

She also raised her voice. 'Look! I didn't know you from Adam. I thought you might be working for Lal. I wanted to check you out!'

'What do you mean?'

She spoke more quietly. 'Any half-decent researcher would have already looked Rackham up at Petersham, but it was pretty obvious to me you hadn't seen the sermon before.'

'Of course I hadn't!'

'OK! Just calm down a little bit. So what do you think about the letters?'

Ben took in a deep breath, and exhaled slowly before speaking. 'Well, they seem to confirm that the vicar was outraged by something Faulkes showed him – probably some paintings in the temple – and then he preached against Faulkes, and was beaten up for his trouble.'

'Yes. And that's what your Professor Lal will be thinking as well.'

'What else could they mean?'

Ben could hear the fingers drumming on the table, as he waited for her reply.

'Are you still at Petersham?'

'Yes, I'm standing outside the record office.'

'OK. What about this. I've got something I want to show you. It'll take me about an hour to get there. Can you wait?

Ben looked at his watch. It was three o'clock. 'All right. Shall I meet you in the tearooms?

'Yep. I'll see you there.'

Ben wandered down the street looking for somewhere to buy a sandwich, then he sat in his car and thought about his conversation with Jayne. He was offended by her suspicion of him, but it made him wonder what she was hiding. Perhaps she knew something about Oakstead that Lal didn't? This was an exciting possibility. He sensed that Jayne would be very interested in undermining Lal's research, and that she might therefore let him in on the secret, if she trusted him enough.

After an hour of waiting he walked round to the tearooms and found a table by the window. Soon he saw her small figure walking up the road towards him, wearing a long green coat which flapped in the wind, and knee-high leather boots. He felt a flicker of desire, of possibility, followed by a moment of regret. Cups of tea together in obscure towns would necessarily be the limit of their relationship. He knew throughout his life he would meet other women with whom he might have had happy times, but he also knew that Ruby was the one for him. It was as though she walked through the crowd with a halo. After all these years of disappointment, he was not interested in jeopardising his chances with her. So when Jayne entered the café he smiled politely, and ordered her some cake.

She threw her coat and bag on the floor by the table, and stretched. 'What a drive! I always forget how horrible that road is.' She flashed a smile at him. 'Are you still cross with me?'

Ben started to deny he was ever cross but she interrupted him. 'So anyway. Tell me what you're going to do now that you have the evidence for paintings of some sort in your temple?'

'Well, the conservators will be arriving in the next few weeks and then we'll know more.'

'Hmm. I wonder what the paintings would be of? The temple is neoclassical, so presumably something with a classical theme.'

'But why would that upset the vicar?'

She leaned back in her chair and looked at him directly. 'We don't know for sure it was the paintings that upset him. But I suppose some of the stories were pretty risqué. You know, gods coming down and impregnating women in shafts of golden light, sex with bulls and swans and all sorts, incest, rape. Maybe Faulkes just pushed it a bit too far.' She paused and bit her lip, while their tea and cake was delivered. Then she said, 'Have you ever been to Pompeii?'

'No. I'd like to. Why?'

'Well, I went there when I was a teenager, and we were taken round by a guide, who kept going on about this special room, and how if we wanted to see it we'd have to pay extra. We thought it was going to be some kind of amazing mosaic, something like that. But it turned out to be a brothel, with all these pornographic paintings around the walls, of enormous erect willies, and people having sex in different positions. It was very embarrassing at the time. I was with my mum and dad. They didn't know where to look.'

'Oh dear.'

'Exactly. But the point is, maybe Faulkes was keen on the seamier side of classical art? Perhaps he'd seen things like that when he was in Italy?'

Ben looked at her with big eyes. 'To think that there may have been something like that lurking under the paint all this time.'

'It might not be there, of course. It might've been destroyed in some way. Don't get your hopes up too high.'

'No, you're right. We'll have to wait and see.' Ben poured them each a cup of tea, while continuing to talk. 'I can understand why something like that would upset the vicar, but it doesn't explain why Henry would show him the paintings in the first place.'

'No. That's true. Why would he?'

Something else occurred to Ben. 'Do you think Rackham would have become a bishop if he hadn't been taken up by Henry's father?'

'Good question. I don't think so. Most bishops-to-be would have been higher profile, and more academic. They would've published things to get noticed, or would've tried to get some kind of upmarket living, perhaps in a London parish, or at the Palace in some capacity. Rackham was very under-qualified to be a bishop. That suggests he received a lot of strong patronage from a very influential person.'

'I wonder how badly hurt he was. Henry Faulkes sounds like he could be a nasty piece of work.'

'Hmm. Well, I have something here which might help

you there.' She rustled around in her bag and brought out a thin cardboard box file.

'What's that?'

She placed the box on the table and rested her hands on it. 'It's something I came across when I was doing my PhD. I went on the local radio and talked about how I was researching old Derbyshire families, and then I asked people to let me know about any stuff they might have been hoarding in their attic – old family trees, portraits, that kind of thing. It's a good way to find new material.' She patted the box. 'And this came through the post.' She looked up at him. 'You *are* sure you don't work for Lal, aren't you?'

Ben fixed his eyes on hers. 'I promise you, I can't stand the man. I would be very pleased to obstruct him in any way possible. If you don't want him to know about whatever this is, I will take the secret to my grave. Could I be any clearer?'

She gazed at him for a few more seconds, and he noticed how the green of her earrings matched her eyes.

'OK. The thing is, there is potential for a really juicy little book in here. I've wanted to get round to it for the last couple of years, but haven't had the time. I would hate to have my thunder stolen by that waste of space.'

Ben was beginning to lose his patience. 'What is it, for heaven's sake?'

She opened the box, and inside was a pocket-sized book bound in soft, almost black, leather. 'It's Charlotte's diary.'

'What?' Ben's voice came out as a hoarse whisper.

'Yep. Faulkes' wife, when she was at Oakstead, and after as well. The lady who sent it to me said that it had been handed down through the generations from Charlotte's maid. The story goes that when Charlotte died the maid hid the diary because she knew what was in it, and wanted to protect her mistress's reputation.'

'Why? What does she say?' Ben put his hand out to pick the diary up, but she stopped him by laying her hand on

177

his. 'It doesn't do it any good being handled. I started typing it up when I did my thesis, and I've printed out some excerpts for you.' She withdrew her hand, rustled around in her bag again, and brought out some A4 sheets. 'Have a read.'

I shall write this diary to unburden my heavy heart, as to a friend, having no such amiable companion with whom to share my days. My governess – dear Miss Palmer! – would always say that the keeping of a diary was a ladylike pastime, and it will give me the opportunity to improve my hand. How I wish Miss Palmer was with me now! She would no doubt have a quicker understanding of my husband's temperament, and would guide me in the ways of wifely duty. I know that I try him sorely every day with my clumsiness and my dull speeches. Whenever he enters the room, I blush as red as a Robin's breast, and my voice is as squeaky as a mouse. I could be a good wife to him, if only I could master my agitation of nerves in his presence. I am sure that he is good and kind and that it is finding himself wedded to a simpleton that puts him into such black moods. It is my most earnest wish to be deserving of his radiant smile, which I have seen shine upon others, but not upon me.

I have not written for some days, as my duties as hostess have kept me occupied. Henry invited some of his friends from London to stay for the shooting. They were our first guests, and I was terrified at every moment of making some mortifying mistake. I am certain that they thought me to be a rattle-brain, as, try as I might, I was forever forgetting their names. I uttered barely a word at dinner, overcome as I was by the company of so many gentlemen, and no other lady with whom to converse. The party was made up of very high-ranking gentlemen from the oldest families in the land, but my mother and father would have blushed to hear the talk at table, and observe their manners. I am afraid my timid ways did not please Henry. He called me his 'grey mouse' at dinner one evening, and the whole company laughed at me. I was unable to eat a single mouthful after that, and could not raise my eyes to his again for more than two days. Then he came upon me as I was making my way to bed alone one evening, weary from yet more rowdiness at dinner, and he held my chin in his hand and said, 'Poor little grey mouse,' and stroked my hair in the most affectionate manner, so that tears came to my eyes. And was so kind to me that evening that I am now pleased to be named his 'mouse'.

I write from my bed as I am unwell – but from such joyful cause! I am to be the mother of Henry's heir, and I am proud beyond all measure. Henry has been uncommonly attentive to me and the house has been free of noise and disorder for some weeks. Everyday, despite the sickness, I have the comfort of recalling his smile of joy when I informed him of the expected event, his eyes glowing at me, his arm fast around my waist. I will never forget it. At that moment I saw how I can be a comfort to him, and bring him happiness. Now I must take every step to remain strong and well, to prepare myself for the coming trial. I could not bear to disappoint him again, and lose the privilege of his smile once more.

Today, I being too indispos'd to attend church, Mr Rackham came to visit me. He is a kind young gentleman, with a pleasing countenance. He put me in mind of my brother, John. It was a pleasure to speak with someone so amiable. Henry came in as we were drinking tea, and took Mr Rackham off to view the new lake excavations, and afterwards he stayed for dinner. They spoke of Henry's plans for the park with great interest all evening. It gave me real pleasure to see Henry so animated, but without the riotous mirth which often accompanies his mood in company. I nurse the hope that Mr Rackham will exert a moderating influence on the behaviour of my husband. To be sure, the plans for the park have already dispelled the ennui that seemed to have settled upon him since our return from the Continent.

My son is a blessing from heaven! Nothing can bring me more pleasure than to be in his innocent company. Sweet Freddie! I have had no time to write these pages, occupied as I am in tending to his needs. I could wish that Henry took more interest in the boy. Lately, however, he has been occupied with his building schemes and we have little of his company. He and Mr Rackham discourse endlessly upon designs for the park which, I must confess, vexes me somewhat. I miss the gentle conversations that Mr Rackham and I shared.

I am just now enduring the company of another party of Henry's friends from London. He has been away for some weeks, and, on coming home, has brought these friends with him. The conduct of these gentlemen has been even more riotous than before. I have used the preoccupations of motherhood as justification for excusing myself from most of the duties of hostess, and I do not apprehend that I am missed. Tonight I am kept awake by these inebriated guests, who seem to be stampeding around the servants' quarters above my head. Now and again I hear terrifying bumps and thumps, and I have been tormenting myself with the notion that they are murdering the maids. I dare not venture out of my room in case I am embroiled in their devilish games. I would not trust Henry to defend me.

Since his return his demeanour towards me has changed. He seems to take little pleasure in the company of sweet Freddie, and his behaviour is reckless and wild. He is drunk every night, and spends the days in idle pastimes, playing foolish tricks upon the servants. Yesterday evening, he and his party were in high glee having doused a manservant with a pail of water, which they had balanced on a door above his head. I long for the company of Mr Rackham, and his gentle sympathy. But he does not come to visit when Henry's London friends are here. Their behaviour is too ungodly. Even he could not attempt their deliverance!

These last few weeks have been the worst torment of my life. My beautiful boy, my own precious Freddie, has been perilously sick, so that I thought we would lose him. The agony of observing his suffering almost overturn'd my senses, and only the burning desire to see him well has kept me from my own sickbed. Henry has been inexplicably cold and distant, as though hardening his heart against expected misfortune. He is not disposed towards the softer emotions which have assailed me with full force in these agonising times. Indeed he is disgusted, I think, with my weeping. My single consolation during these black days has been the dear company of Mr Rackham, who has attended every day to offer us comfort. My esteem and affection for him has grown so great that I cannot imagine happiness without his solicitous company.

God help me in my present anguish! Joshua torn from me, his poor sweet face disfigured and broken! I am terrified of Henry and his violent temper, and have kept to my room with Freddie safe by my side. My husband prowls around the house at night, under the exciting influence of excessive wine, and I hear him moaning, and speaking angrily, as if he has a companion. But there is no one there. Last night, I heard a terrifying howl of despair, as if a wolf had entered his heart. He is lost to me, and Joshua is lost also! My heart can hardly bear its burden. Never did I imagine that my husband was capable of so much jealous feeling, or that my conduct could throw him into such paroxysms of anguish. I sorely feel the loss of Joshua's affectionate attendance, his quiet ways, his good sense. How terrible it was to see him struck down, falling senseless to the ground. And then to see him no more!

Ben put the paper back down on the table and looked up at Jayne. 'Well I never!'

She chuckled. 'Interesting, don't you think?'

Ben closed his eyes for a moment to focus his mind. 'This implies that Henry attacked Joshua because he was having an affair with his wife. Nothing to do with the temple or paintings at all.'

'That's right.'

'But . . . then Joshua was playing a very dangerous game, preaching against Henry.'

'And in the letter you showed me from Henford, he was obviously upset about something Henry had done. Presumably the paintings. That's been puzzling me, too.'

'Poor old Joshua. He was in a muddle.'

Their discussion was interrupted by the waitress, who came to clear their table and told them the café was closing. They stood up reluctantly, and Jayne began to put on her coat. She glanced at her watch. 'Listen. I don't really feel like driving straight back to Derby yet. Let's go for a drink.'

Ben was torn. Ruby would be expecting him back, but he and Jayne had lots more to discuss. He wasn't ready yet to relinquish her company. Oh God, he thought to himself, this is not sensible. What am I doing? But Jayne didn't seem to doubt that he would do as she asked, and so he followed her obediently to a dark and smoky bar close by, where it seemed like midnight, even though it was only five o'clock in the afternoon.

Charlie came across Ruby reading by the fire in the sitting room. It was the first time they had been on their own together since Christmas. He had avoided her, trying to ignore these insistent feelings which made him lie awake at night, imagining her hair tangled in his face, her legs locked around him, his hands on her skin. He had started to watch hardcore pornographic videos to try and expunge these sentimental images from his mind, kill them dead.

Ruby drew her legs up into the armchair, and held the book to her chest. 'Oh, hello Charlie.'

He attempted a smile. 'Where's Ben?'

She looked at her watch. 'I should think he's on his way back from Petersham.'

'Still banging on about all that history stuff, is he?'

Ruby smiled. 'Yes.'

He stood silently, looking at the fire, trying to think what to say next. After a few moments Ruby went back to reading her book. He felt again that nausea, a prickling of the skin, blood thumping in his ears. Something impelled him to move towards the fire. Ruby looked up at him, as he stood over her. Her pupils were very big, her eyes almost black, open, scared. His head filled up with a muddle of images: of holding her to him; pushing her legs wide apart and taking her rough and hard; kissing her gently on her eyelashes; kneeling astride her, his cock luxuriating in her soft mouth; resting his head in her lap.

Ruby withdrew further into her chair. 'Are you OK?'

He leaned over, his hands either side of her on the arms of the chair, his face close to hers. His voice was hoarse, scoured out of him. 'You're ... torturing me. Just let me, please, just once. I need to know. Just once.' He lifted one hand to her breast, and bent down to kiss her.

Ruby pressed herself back into the chair, and tried to slide out from underneath him, but he was in between her legs. He pressed down all his weight on her, his hands holding down her arms, and began to kiss her neck. Ruby shouted at him. He vaguely heard the sound above the rushing and whizzing of blood bursting through his veins. But then another sensation found its way through. An intense pain, hot needles through his flesh. He leaped off her, and put his hand to his ear. There was blood. 'Shit! You nearly bit my ear off!'

Ruby was behind the armchair now, armed with a poker. 'What do you expect!' she screamed at him. 'Get out of here!'

As he stepped towards her again, she brandished the poker in his direction. 'Get out!' Her voice was cracked with rage. He saw her face distorted with disgust, and knew that he was lost. A violent nausea overtook him and he stumbled out of the room. In the doorway of his bedroom he doubled up and was sick; afterwards he lay on the floor completely desolate. He would never have Ruby. He heard an involuntary moan leave his mouth.

Then a tide of bitter rage flooded through him. How could he have allowed himself to be reduced to such depths by a woman? What was the matter with him? Was she a witch? She had blighted him, reduced him to a gibbering wreck. How had it happened? He searched back in his memory trying to pinpoint when this disaster had begun. He remembered all the times in the summer when Ruby had flaunted herself in front of him, seemingly oblivious to his gaze. Now he started to wonder. Perhaps she had known all along how it was affecting him. She had done it on purpose so that she could reject him and make him appear foolish, and pathetic. Bitch!

An image came into his mind of a demon, possessing his body, screaming against exorcism, against banishment, tearing out his guts, clinging onto his organs, splitting him open. Disappearing in a foul, stinking puddle.

184

He stood up shakily, his stomach still lurching, and clambered onto his bed. He felt as if his sight had returned. Now he saw Ruby as she really was. Not beautiful, not an angel amongst women. Just an ordinary, manipulative, run-of-the-mill flirt. He needed to sleep, to get away from the humiliation. As he was about to lie down he noticed *Reaching Paradise* open on his pillow, where he had been reading it that morning. With an angry shout he picked it up and threw it across the room. Then he smoked a cigarette, and gulped down several swigs of whisky, before keeling over on his bed, in his sick-spattered clothes, sinking into exhausted unconsciousness.

In a drab corner of a cavernous pub, Jayne was telling Ben more about the contents of Charlotte's diary.

'The affair with Rackham, or whatever it was, was just the start of her career. She went on to have several more scenes with other men.'

'Really? So she wasn't very prim or proper then.'

'Nope. I think she started off as an innocent northern girl, and ended up a serial mistress. I want to write a book based on her experience, which draws out the differences between northern and southern society at the end of the eighteenth century. The effects of the industrial revolution, and changing attitudes to class and money. It could be really interesting.'

'But what did Faulkes think about it? Surely it was awfully dangerous for her to be so unfaithful?'

Jayne shrugged. 'She must have got more careful, or maybe he turned a blind eye. It's not as though he was a saint, by all accounts.'

'No.' Ben sipped at his beer. 'We might find out more about that, if we uncover some paintings.'

'I expect it will be a lot of naked ladies – a series of page-three girls dropped into some sort of classical scene to pretend it's Art. Critics always direct you to look at the beauty of the human form, the symbolism, whatever. But,

185

let's face it, why was the rape of the Sabine women painted quite so often? Or Venus taking a bath?' Jayne tapped the table in front of her. 'It's pornography, plain and simple. Are they trying to tell us that eighteenth-century men didn't get turned on by naked women, just the same as they do now?' She turned to him slightly, so that their knees bumped together, and she looked up at him through her eyelashes. 'Tell me truthfully. When you look at one of those paintings of a naked woman, aren't you drawn to her breasts, her curving stomach? Don't you try to look behind the gossamer barely concealing her fanny?'

Ben swallowed hard. He rarely drank alcohol during the day, and one pint of beer had gone straight to his head. The prim space which had separated them on the bench seat when they first arrived had disappeared. They had drawn closer, cocooned in a haze of smoke and low lights. In this pleasantly befuddled state, Ben now saw in his mind's eye a classical nude, and it was Jayne, the drapes of her Grecian dress revealing her nakedness beneath. She was still looking up into his eyes, and it seemed to Ben that the space between their mouths had become charged, pulling him towards her. He managed to stutter. 'Yes, I suppose so. Of course. One can't help noticing.'

She drew away slightly, and clapped her hands on her lap. 'Exactly. And they were just the same two hundred years ago. If not more so. They didn't have any hang-ups about objectifying women. That's what we were there for. People forget how frank they were then about sex. Look at *Tristram Shandy*, one of the first proper novels. It opens with a graphic description of his conception and how the sperm travelled up inside his mother.'

'Does it really?'

'Yep. Have you ever read any pornography from those days?'

'Er, no. No, I haven't.'

'Well, they loved all that perverted sex in Greek myths. Can you imagine what fun it was? Pretending you were being

186

learned and studying Greek and Latin, and all the time you're reading stuff about gods coming down and impregnating women as they lie sleeping, gods spying on women bathing, bulls, eagles and swans raping them. It's outrageous.'

'Yes, I'd never thought about it before.'

'That's one of things I hated about Lal's book. It was a barefaced commercial venture, appealing to people's prurient interest in sex, dressed up as an academic treatise. I wouldn't have minded if he'd been upfront about it, and just said it's a book about sex. I'd have nothing against that.' She leaned towards him again. 'I wouldn't want you to think I'm a prude. I'm not. I'm as interested in sex as the next person.'

Ben felt sure that she was flirting with him, and was troubled to find how much he was enjoying it. He felt no resistance at all, and wanted her to keep talking, to keep drawing him in. He said, 'I'm sure you are,' his voice a broken whisper.

She leaned back again, but their legs were still touching. 'I've read some beautiful historical texts about sex which aren't offensive at all, because they're not being disingenuous. The *Kama Sutra*, obviously. Taoist sexual teaching. Jade stalks and cinnabar grottoes. I like all that.'

Ben closed his eyes and murmured, 'Cinnabar grotto. Yes, that's nice.'

Then Ben's cell phone rang. It was Ruby. She sounded worried, her voice quavering. 'I was just ringing because I thought you'd be home by now. Are you going to be long?'

Ben blinked, and looked at his watch. It was nearly seven o'clock. The noise of the pub, the music and the slot machines all came back at him, full volume.

'Sorry, Ruby. I should have rung you. I'm just having a bite to eat. Then I'll be on my way.'

A cold bucket of water could not have been more effective. He turned to Jayne, who had shifted in her seat and was sitting very upright. She smiled ruefully at him and said, 'Oops.'

'I should have rung her. It was stupid of me. Look, I'd better be going. So sorry.'

She stood up. 'That's OK. I'll get myself some chips, and be off home.'

He shook hands with her rather awkwardly. 'Thanks so much for coming all this way, and for sharing the diary with me. I promise I won't tell Lal.'

She held his hand in her firm grip. 'No problem. Let's stay in touch. Let me know if anything happens about the paintings.'

Ben walked back to his car, and began the drive home to Ruby. He tried not to think about Jayne, but Faulkes' voice popped up again in his head, like a little demon. You could've had her. You wanted her, you spineless dog.

Ben attempted to blot out this intrusive voice by thinking hard about the paintings in the temple. He tried to imagine the circumstances which might have led up to the vicar's outrage. Perhaps he went to supper at the Hall one evening, happy as usual to be honoured with such an invitation, looking forward to seeing Charlotte. Henry Faulkes might have been particularly pleased with himself, having just completed his series of erotic paintings in his beautifully designed private temple. Perhaps, after dinner, the two men had strolled along the terrace drinking their port. This, combined with the wine during dinner may have made them pleasantly drunk, and perhaps engendered a feeling of fellowship. Perhaps the vicar complimented Henry on the design of his temple, which was such a pure distillation of the neoclassical style. He was probably being careful to keep on the good side of Henry, so that no suspicion fell upon him. Henry would have been brimful with his knowledge of the interior. With the beautiful evening, the drink, a feeling of comradeship with his fellow classicist, and his head full of sensual imagery, he might have ambled down to the lakeside with the unsuspecting vicar, lapped across the

188

lake in the waiting rowing boat, and triumphantly thrown open the door of his temple for viewing. How would the vicar have reacted?

Inside, the temple would be dark compared to the light evening. There would be the smell of paint and varnish. Perhaps there were boxes of paints and brushes, and sheaves of cartoons lying about the floor to be tripped over. Gradually, as his eyes grew accustomed to the light, what did Rackham see looming out at him from the dark recesses? Flesh, contorted muscles, phalluses, naked bosoms, grinning eyes and gaping mouths? Ben could not quite imagine what was lurking under that sanitising whitewash. But something shocking. Did the vicar stumble back outside, there and then, and make his feelings known to the drunken Faulkes? Or did he hold his counsel and make polite comments about Henry's clever execution of such ambitious work, before making his excuses and rushing home to spend the night wrestling with his conscience? Another thought flashed into Ben's head. Perhaps Faulkes already knew about Rackham and Charlotte? He might have shown the paintings to the vicar to shame him. Or even to welcome him into his amoral world as a fellow traveller.

Something nagged away at the back of Ben's mind, some little piece of knowledge lodged in its furthest corner that he had picked up along the way and filed as not relevant. But now there was a connection, a little light flashing in his head, saying: Look at this! When he first started his research at Henford Hall hadn't he found a letter written to Henry from Rome, dated exactly at the time he was building the temple? And hadn't Henry's father mentioned Italy in his letter as the possible source of his son's scandalous interests? Ben felt sure that this could well be worth revisiting. He mentioned this to Ruby when he got home, but she didn't seem very keen.

'You're away too much at the moment. I don't see you enough.'

He laughed, and ruffled her hair with his hand. 'Sweet of you, Ruby. But things will settle down and then you'll probably be sick of the sight of me.'

February

Most of the summer crops are to be sown this month, therefore let there be great care taken not to lose the opportunity.

Mrs Martha Bradley

February 1st
This is the day when life is brought back after the dead of winter. The Earth Mother wakes and from her fingers the first shoots begin to emerge. Her energy seeps through the soil, stirring the seeds and the roots, coaxing them. I can feel a difference in the air, a change in flow. The cycle of the year coming round again, the rejection of the dark, the movement into new life. It reawakens the pain of longing. The winter cold helped to numb it, but now it creeps through my veins, and it hurts to see them together. When she loves me, he will already have seen the tender expression which I hope to see. The same laughter, the same anger, the same look of passion. It will all be second-hand.

But today the old woman of winter is reborn as Bride, the Young Maiden of the spring, goddess of regeneration and abundance. The virgin. She will make everything shiny and new. We will forget every other kiss, every other sensation. The Bride's power is stronger than any pointless secular wedding ceremony. We will be united with the

191

blessing of the goddess. Adam and Eve, the first lovers, cradled in the bosom of Nature, filled with life's longing for itself, reborn.

I am looking for peaceful respite this morning. There is a softness in the air, a brightness in the sky. Perhaps spring is on its way. I would like to think that, just under the ground, green shoots are pushing up their glossy heads towards the sun. I have been wondering about Ben. Since Christmas he has seemed slightly distant, not quite completely here with me. Nearly every day he goes off and works at his friend's workshop in Glandford nearby. I don't know why he doesn't use his workshop here, and I feel abandoned. When I suggest cycling to meet him at lunchtime, or after work, he always thinks of a reason why I shouldn't. I could just turn up, of course, but if there is something he doesn't want me to find out, I don't want to stumble upon it. Why do wives search through their husband's pockets? I would rather remain ignorant. But without him here there is always the possibility of Charlie finding me alone again, more out of control than before. A constant shadow of anxiety. I should tell Ben, but the words won't come. Sometimes I think I imagined it, it was so quick, so ridiculous. If Ben knew, there would be rows, upset, anger. I can't face it, I am already brimful. My mind is incapable of stirring my body into action, doing the rational thing. The same thoughts go round and round my head, but I never manage to do anything about them. As if I am wrapped tightly in cling-film.

My painting has also ground to a halt. I have been trying to do something with oranges, but the colours keep going wrong. I have blood oranges – that startling, dripping red – but they make me feel queasy. I come out into the struggling sunlight to eat bread and cheese, leaning against the warm red wall of my studio, looking across the front lawns. The winter drabness of the flower borders is being gently ousted by clumps of snowdrops and aconites, although the avenue of limes still looks cold and chapped by the wind, bare-skinned, stiff-fingered.

I am pretending to myself that I have come out here to sit quietly in the rejuvenating sun, but despite myself I am always, always conscious of where George may be. I try not to think about it, I try not to walk in those parts of the garden I know he is working in, but somehow I still find myself doing it. Today he has started digging over the vegetable beds in the walled garden. I find myself thinking how nice it would be to go for a short stroll along the top of the water meadow, sheltered by the high walls of the gardens. Perhaps this would get my sluggish blood moving and would bring me some inspiration.

I am walking past the front of the house, rosy in the long-rayed February sunshine. As I pass the perfume garden I am stopped in my tracks by a powerful scent, sweet and intense. Just inside the entrance to this enclosed area there is a bush, bare of leaves but covered in tiny pink flowers. I step inside and put my head next to the branches and inhale, my eyes closed. When I open them, George is standing next to me. He says: It's pretty, isn't it? *Viburnum bodnantse.* Such a strong smell from such tiny flowers.

At this sudden sight of him, so close, my heart leaps, but I try to sound nonchalant. I say: I didn't expect the garden to smell so sweet at this time of year.

He says there are lots of plants which flower in winter, and they all have a lovely scent to attract insects. He says he was having his lunch. I turn and see that he, too, has been eating bread and cheese, nestled against the garden wall, between two bushes of shrubby honeysuckle spangled with scented white flowers. He has whisky in a flask, and chocolate, and he says I should share them with him. We sit huddled together on his jacket, which is laid on the bare earth, and we both take sips from his silver hip flask. Then we sit quietly for a little while, feeling the whisky melt the inside of our throats. He offers me chocolate. He breaks off a square from the bar and places it in my mouth. Our faces are very close, we are looking into each other's eyes, and his warm hand seeks out mine.

And then there is a sound. A cough. A clearing of the throat. In a ridiculously obvious sudden movement we jump backwards away from each other, confirming our guilt. I turn and see Charlie, his face twisted with malicious glee. He says: Very interesting, Ruby. Very interesting.

He is walking away. Searing cold fear ripples up my back. George says: What shall I do? Shall I go after him?

I shake my head, and close my eyes trying to think, but my brain has crashed. I am swamped with panic. George sits quite still, next to me. He says: Do you think he'll tell Ben?

I try to imagine what Charlie may be thinking in his strange, warped way. I am scared of him and what he may be capable of. The thought of Ben hearing the news of my infidelity from Charlie's cruel mouth makes me feel ill. What can I do? What can I do? Thoughts fly around like leaves in a whirlwind. I can't catch hold of any of them. George says: It's not so bad. He only saw us holding hands. Nothing much more has happened between us.

This is true, and makes me begin to feel calmer. I have gone such a long way with George, in my mind, I forget that we have only kissed a few times. I still feel we have lived a whole life together. I take my hands from my face and look at him by my side. He looks worried about me, and goes to take my hand again, but I can't. I feel watched now. He says: Don't take yourself away from me.

I look into his eyes, and I feel his hand caress my neck. He leans forward and kisses me, whisky and chocolate and canvas and woodsmoke. I feel myself sinking into it, and panic. I say: I've got to go. I'm too scared.

I run away, into the house, into the bedroom, and hide under the comforting darkness of the duvet.

Charlie had been on his way to the pub when he saw Ruby and George in the garden. The image was printed some-

194

where on his retina, like a photograph: Ruby looking up into George's eyes, their hands entwined, mouths so close. This new pain was like a long sword thrust into his chest. It was a relief to feel the full force of it erupt after the long weeks of nagging anger. A liberating feeling of unconditional hatred. Ruby was available to other men for sexual favours. She really was a slag after all, just like all the others, and Ben had been duped. What a laugh.

He sat in a dark and smoky corner of the pub, gulping down whiskies, and chain-smoking, thinking about how to use this information. How could he make Ruby suffer most? He could threaten to tell Ben, unless she slept with him. Or he could just go home and tell Ben now, and watch the promise of wedded bliss disappear down the drain. Or he could do both. When the pub closed after lunch, he ambled home with a comforting sense that he had plenty of time to play with this little bombshell. While he delayed acting, Ruby would be tortured.

Ruby heard him come in, and after a moment's indecision decided she must face up to him. She slid out from the protective warm bed and walked down the hallway to Charlie's bedroom. She knocked, and waited for an answer. Charlie did not respond, but she decided to open the door anyway. He was lying on his bed in an after-lunch torpor, his hand down his trousers. The curtains were drawn closed, and piles of clothes and newspapers, overflowing ashtrays and empty bottles littered the floor. There was a thick smell of old air and nicotine. She stood holding the door handle, ready to flee.

His eyes barely opened to look at her. Ruby was scared, but she felt compelled to speak. 'I wanted to talk to you.'

Charlie rolled luxuriantly onto his side, to face her, his hand still ostentatiously thrust down his trousers. 'I bet you did.'

Ruby steadfastly ignored all his body below his chin. 'I don't know what you think you saw, but you may have made a mistake.'

He met her look with his old cynical stare. 'Well, if that's true, there's nothing for you to worry about, is there? On the other hand, you might like to consider a quick shag with me. I bet I know a bit more about it than your gardener friend and, I can tell you now, I've got a bloody huge hard-on down here.'

Ruby turned away in disgust. As she started to close the door she muttered, 'Blackmail won't get you your New Year's wish.'

Charlie's leer faltered slightly. He slurred, 'What d'you mean?'

She paused. 'Oh, nothing. Just that Ben found your stupid boat in the river the next day.'

Charlie looked even more puzzled. 'What boat? I haven't got a boat. I can't sail. Too bloody dangerous.'

Ruby clicked her tongue in exasperation. 'The wish boats, we did them on New Year's Eve.'

Charlie frowned. 'I don't know what the bloody hell you're talking about. I didn't do one of those bloody silly boats. Hippy claptrap. I had other things on my mind.'

He looked genuinely confused. Ruby could see that. A ripple of apprehension ran through her body. If it wasn't Charlie, who was it? She closed the door, but as she walked down the hall he shouted after her, 'Ruby! Think about what I said. The offer still stands!'

Ben has gone out already, to his workshop at Glandford, before I have even finished breakfast. I am sitting munching away on cold toast, wondering what it is he's doing over there that takes up so much time. It is so unlike him, to keep things to himself.

Charlie comes into the kitchen, with just a dressing gown on. He looks pinched, ill. But he sits opposite me at the table, and laughs. He says: Well, if it isn't the house whore. Business a bit slack this morning?

He says I am a hypocrite, preaching at him about his amorality, while all the time I have been sleeping with the gardener. I try to tell him he is wrong, that nothing has happened between George and me, but he tells me to shut up. He comes around the table, and stands over me, his dressing gown gaping, his pallid skin too close to me. I can smell acrid sweat, nicotine, and sour beer. He says: Come on then, Ruby. How about it? There's no one else here. No one would ever know.

I stand up, nearly knocking him over, and I shout at him to leave me alone, but he grabs my arm. His grip is very strong, and I feel a jolt of fear. It's true. There is no one else about. The house is empty and isolated from the world, and I'm alone with a man who hates me. I look into his face and see the transformation in his eyes, like a shark. He will force me. I make a fist with my free hand, and swing it as hard and fast as I can, hitting him on the side of the head. His grip loosens and he shouts at me: You bitch!

I wrench free and run out of the house. I am running down the lane, I keep running, even though I can see he is not chasing me. My lungs begin to burn, and my legs feel like lead weights. I collapse inside the gateway to a field, and sobs force their way up my throat, my eyes stinging.

How long have I been here? I am freezing cold, no coat with me. This drab field stretches away into the distance, no trees or shelter. The icy wind makes me ache. My legs and arms are spattered with mud, seeping cold into my clothes. Who can I go to? Not Ben. How could I explain? Not Gretta, at work. There is only George who I can turn to.

The lodge is empty when I arrive, but as I turn from the door and stand in the porch I see George's figure, far away on the edge of the meadow. He looks as though he is mending a fence. The gusting wind brings me snatches of the sound of hammering. I shout, but the wind takes my voice and throws it in the opposite direction. So I tramp through the dripping grass, shivering with cold. George does not hear me approaching. He is crouched down in the grass, picking something up. It is a dead mole. I say: Oh, dear, poor little thing.

George jumps up in surprise. As he moves away from the fence I can see two more moles. They are nailed to the rail of the fence, their little pink hands spread out in crucifixion. I cry: Oh, my God! Who did that?

George turns his back on me, and nails the third mole next to the other two. He mutters: You have to control moles. Didn't you notice all the molehills in the meadow? They're wrecking it. If I make an example of one or two, the others might keep away.

I can't believe he means this. Is he serious? He turns to say something to me, but then his face changes: Shit, Ruby. What's happened?

He sees I am covered in mud, that I am a bedraggled mess. I collapse on him in a tearful heap, and he picks me up and carries me across the field back to the lodge. I am holding onto him and crying, feeling the safety inside his arms.

Inside, in the kitchen, he sits me down at the table and puts the kettle on. He makes me hot tea, and I tell him what has happened, about Charlie pursuing me, hounding me. George says I should tell Ben, but how could I now? If I do that, Ben will find out about us, and there will be so much pain. Perhaps I should try talking to Charlie again, try to explain to him, when he's not drunk, when he might listen to reason. George holds my face with both his hands and makes me look into his eyes: Don't you talk to him. *I'll* talk to him. He might understand me better.

I feel the weight of responsibility lifting slightly. He is kissing me gently, a protective, loving kiss. Heat rises up in me, his soft mouth coaxing me, drawing me in. I stand up and take his hand to lead him towards the stairs. But he stops me, he is tugging me back: Ruby. I'd love to do this. I dream about it all the time. But look at the muddle. We should wait.

Frustration is welling up inside me, a black mist. He keeps doing this to me. I try to push all these feelings down and then he kisses me like this, and expects me to feel

198

nothing. I feel so much, I think I'm going to explode some-times. I say: Can't we please allow ourselves this one luxury, some time together alone, just this once?

He hugs me, but says no.

I am leaving. He offers to come with me, but the thought of him colliding with Charlie is too much. I feel as though I have been stretched on a rack, barely able to hold myself up. I creep into my bedroom, lock myself in, and lie on my bed, exhausted.

There is a banging on the door, shouting. Ben. Ben is home. I crawl out of bed and find my way to the door in the dark. He looks horrified. I am still in my muddy clothes, my hair is sticking out in all directions. He says I look like a scarecrow. I think up a story about tripping over, and hurting my leg. He suggests taking me to hospi-tal, but I say no, I am better now he is here. I ask tentatively whether Charlie is around. Ben says he's gone up to London for a few days. Relief washes over me. Ben runs a bath, and I peel off my filthy clothes. I have a breathing space, time to think what to do. I wash the dirt of the day from my skin.

The wedding bed was beginning to take shape in Ben's loving hands. Hidden away in the workshop at Glandford he had carved four beautiful posts from oak. Each one represented one of the seasons. Holly, ivy and bunches of mistletoe crept up the first. The second was adorned with snowdrops, daffodils and fluttering birds, making their nests in a sinewy tree. Summer was sheaves of nodding barley and wheat, entwined with honeysuckle and dog roses, and autumn was a cornucopia of fruit, surmounted by showering leaves. He had never before produced anything so beautiful. He felt as though his love for Ruby was running through his fingers into the wood, making it as supple and workable as clay. Carving went smoothly, there were no mistakes, tools didn't go missing, and he hardly cut himself. When he entered the workshop, he took on a new character. The master craftsman stepped out and took over the workings of his hands.

As he chiselled away, day after day, he thought about how Ruby would react when she saw it for the first time, adorned with silks and downy pillows on the night of their wedding. The surprise and delight, followed by passion. He found it very hard to keep such a secret from her and, in order to do so, he had to be totally silent about what he was doing at the workshop. He knew she was puzzled, but that only added to his anticipation of the night, when suddenly everything would become clear, and she would think he was so talented and adorable. All these feelings of desire and love crafted every leafy sinew and every flower of his masterpiece, giving it life and movement. The tiny details of flower structure and corn ear and the practical nature of making one piece of carved timber fit into another filled his mind night and day. But now and then he would worry about the temple, and the lack of progress there. He mentioned it to Ruby one morning as they were clearing away the breakfast things.

'I wish I had time to go back up to Henford to look again at that letter from Rome. I'm positive it would throw more light on things. It would be so satisfying to pre-empt the professor.'

He was surprised by Ruby's response. 'Why don't I go up there and have a look for you?'

'Sorry?'

'Why don't I go and look at the letter for you? I was quite good at helping you with the pigment thing, wasn't I? I could take Gretta with me and we could make a little holiday of it. In fact, I seem to remember she did Italian at school. She might be able to translate some of it. What do you think?'

Ben was touched that she was interested enough to make the effort. 'That would be sweet of you.' He paused, not knowing whether to share his next thought with her. 'While you were away I could have a go at opening up that secret room upstairs.'

Ruby's reaction was immediate. She caught hold of his arm and looked at him with anxious eyes. 'I really wish you wouldn't.'

'Why ever not? What are you so worried about?' His voice was exasperated.

She took his arms, wrapped them around her and held him tightly. 'I don't know. I get this bad feeling every time you mention it.' She looked up at him. 'I know it's stupid, but it feels safer keeping it closed up.'

Ben's face softened. 'But what do you think's going to be in there? A dead body or something?'

She shuddered. 'You do hear about people being shut up in walls.'

'You don't really think that?' He held her at arm's length and looked into her eyes.

Ruby frowned. 'I don't have a rational thought about it. Just a feeling. Promise me you won't do it while I'm away. Maybe in a few months' time, when I'm feeling less stressed.'

His brow creased into a question. 'And why are you so stressed?'

Panic rose up inside her. Why hadn't she told Ben about Charlie when she had the chance, when things were more straightforward? What could she say now? 'Oh, nothing in particular. The wedding, I suppose.'

Ruby rang up Gretta. 'I need you to come to Derbyshire with me.'

'Where?'

'Henford. You know, where Ben's been going to find out about the temple.'

'And why would we be going?'

'I've got to get out of here for a few days. I'm going mad.'

'What's happened?' Gretta's voice was concerned.

'Charlie caught me and George together in the garden.'

'Oh, Ruby!'

201

'We were just sitting together, but Charlie obviously jumped to the wrong conclusion straight away.'

'What did he say?'

'He was disgusting, and then today . . . ' Her voice broke off as sudden tears welled up.

Gretta made soothing noises, and then said, 'I'll take the next couple of days off. Don't worry about it. Shall I come over this evening?'

Ruby managed a tearful 'Yes, please' and put down the phone. She lay on the sofa and imagined standing at the top of one of the peaks, looking out across the unfamiliar, expansive view of hills and dales, the wind blowing her head clean of all this fog. She started to feel a bit better.

Ben experienced a small judder of anxiety when he answered the phone and recognised the slightly wheedling voice of Professor Lal.

'Mr Fitzmaurice. How nice to hear you. I hope you are well?'

'I'm well. This is a surprise.'

The professor chuckled. 'Yes, it has been a long time since we spoke. I hope I did not offend, leaving so soon after your lovely New Year party, but, ah, business, you know.'

'Not at all.'

'It is like this, Mr Fitzmaurice. I hear that you have commissioned some conservators to carry out sampling of the paint layers in the temple.'

Ben thought to himself, the cheek of the man! Who has he heard that from? But he said, 'That's right. You have no objections, I hope?'

'No, no. As long as you are employing someone suitable, I think that on balance it is a good thing.'

'We are, of course, using a firm recommended by English Heritage.' Ben's voice was very clipped.

'That is good. And when is work due to begin?'

Ben's irritation began to boil over. 'I take it you've

decided it's permissible to discuss the wall paintings in the temple now? It's no longer a great mystery?'

Professor Lal had the grace to stammer slightly. 'I agree that the time has come to speak a little more freely.'

'And why should I tell you when the sampling is to begin?'

The professor's sigh rustled down the line. 'Dear Mr Fitzmaurice. I did not withhold information through spite, but for a substantive reason. Why would you feel the need to keep such information from me?'

'I may have my own research that I want to protect.'

Even to himself, this sounded petulant and childish. There was a tutting sound from Lal, and neither spoke for a moment. Then Ben said, 'They're starting next week.'

'I see, I see. Well, it is good of you to tell me. I wonder if you would be so kind as to keep me informed of progress? I am hoping to include the paintings in my new publication, if they are of any significance, which I think they will be.'

'Can you tell me why?'

The professor cleared his throat. 'Please don't get cross, Mr Fitzmaurice, but at the moment, no, I would rather wait and see. After all, I may be completely wrong.'

Ben just resisted slamming the phone down. 'This seems to be a rather one-way street, Professor!'

'Yes, I know. I ask for your patience. I think if any of the paintings have survived, you will be very amazed by them. I would so like to be there when they are uncovered. But that will be a long time, I think. These things cannot be rushed into, I understand.'

'We'll see.'

'Well, I am sorry to have troubled you about the paintings. Now, another thing, Mr Fitzmaurice. Could I ask you, have you noticed how George is at the moment?'

'Sorry?'

'George. I wondered if you had noticed how he is?'

Ben thought about George. He had hardly seen him since

New Year's Day, when he and Charlie had sat in grim silence munching away at the beautiful meal Ben had cooked, while Ruby was out wandering the park.

He replied, 'I haven't really seen much of him. Why do you ask?'

'Oh, well. We write, you know. Nothing to worry about. And now I must let you get on. I do hope you feel able to let me know how things go. Goodbye.'

Ben put down the receiver, seething over Professor Lal's nerve, ringing up out of the blue asking for information, but never giving any up. It occurred to him that the greatest triumph over the professor would be to have the paintings uncovered as quickly as possible, and be the one who informed the professor of their subject and significance. This idea appealed to him greatly.

The wall-painting conservators arrived to start sampling work in the temple. Over a period of two days they removed the upper layers of emulsion and whitewash in three small areas on each wall, using scalpels and taking innumerable photographs. The areas uncovered were only a centimetre square but they were enough to reveal that there was colour. Little patches of blue and green, just visible in the gloomy interior of the temple. Ben was keen to move things on.

'So, now we know the paintings really exist, what do we do next? Can we go ahead and take off all the white? What do you think we'll find?'

The young man from Chambers and Elliot Conservators shook his head. 'Unfortunately, it's a bit more complicated than that. For one thing, we don't know from these small areas that there is figurative painting underneath. It could just be different colour washes. The blues and greens may just be a result of chemical changes on a single original colour. We have no evidence so far of figurative work. But also, we really ought to do some analysis of the paint layers to see what they're made of, so that we can try to decide how to treat the paintings if we uncover a larger area. You see, the coloured surface has probably received a certain amount of protection from the layers covering it. If we suddenly remove them, we could create new problems.'

Ben's heart sank. 'What kind of timescale are we talking about, for the results from the sampling?'

'Well, I think we allowed a month in our quote, for me to analyse the results and then write them up for you.'

Ben peered again into one of the little patches on the wall. 'This one doesn't appear to have any colour in it. It looks black.'

'Yes. All three tests on that wall show various shades of grey.'

'What do you think that means?'

'Hard to say. That wall may have suffered from water ingress more than the others which might have affected the paint pigments. Or maybe it's just painted grey. I don't really know at this stage.'

'Couldn't you uncover a little bit more? Why not try an area more central?

The conservator looked doubtful. 'It's not really good practice to uncover lots of areas, in case the rest of the painting is never uncovered. You could get the painting decaying at different rates. Sometimes it's better for the painting's survival if it stays covered.'

This was not what Ben wanted to hear. He slipped into his father's authoritative voice, the landowner's sharp tone.

'What in heaven's name would be the point of leaving the paintings covered when we know there is something under there? That would be quite ridiculous. I am perfectly willing to pay to have them protected properly.'

'Well, it may seem odd, but the theory is, if we are not sure whether a painting will survive our present methods of uncovering, it's best to wait until a less damaging technique has been developed.'

Ben was exasperated. 'All I want you to do is uncover a

little more, so that we can see the nature of the paintings underneath.'

The young man from Chambers and Elliot thought hard for a few moments, weighing up the likelihood of losing the job against the possibility of damaging the paintings.

'OK. We'll uncover a small additional area, just to establish for certain whether there are figurative drawings here. It'll be charged at the same rate.'

Ben smiled enthusiastically. 'Wonderful! I take full responsibility, if questions are asked.'

The young man took out his scalpel and started the painstaking work of removing more flaky white pigment from the wall. The paint came off quite easily, and it did not take long before another two square centimetres were exposed, towards the right-hand side, fairly low down, where he hoped it would not be too noticeable. To his surprise, he uncovered a toe. There was no mistake. Rendered in shades of grey, with a strong black outline, there emerged a beautifully formed big toe. The young man considered it for some time before calling Ben in to have a look. Ben urged him to uncover more, but now the young man was adamant. Testing was absolutely necessary to find out more about the paint medium, in order to work out a conservation strategy. Did Mr Fitzmaurice want to be responsible for the loss of an historically significant work of art? Mr Fitzmaurice did not. The conservators went off to prepare their report.

Excerpt from draft first chapter of *Charlotte Wainwright – hostage to fortune* by Dr Jayne Greene

Charlotte Wainwright was the daughter of a Derbyshire mill owner. Her grandfather had bought in developing technology early, which allowed mass-production of cloth in enormous mechanised mills. By the 1790s the Wainwrights were one of the most cash-rich families in the land. Charlotte was therefore a sought-after prize amongst the young aristocracy, many of whom were rich in land and status but had little cash in hand.

In the second half of the eighteenth century the aristocracy was still a small club. Underneath the thin veneer of high art, ceremony and courtly manners, the pervasive culture within this elite encouraged debauched behaviour, with excesses of sex, drinking and gambling. Many sons of the best-known families lost enormous fortunes through drink-fuelled gaming and betting, purchasing of ridiculous fashions, the building of unnecessarily ostentatious country houses in the latest style, and the provision of households, clothes and carriages for their paramours. No wonder then that they turned, with voracious appetite, to the rich young northern heiresses who began to appear on the social circuit.

Of course, these heiresses whose wealth came from industry had their own agendas. Wealth could buy you material things, but could not give you pedigree. By marrying into the establishment, these merchant families attained status and respect only available to the aristocracy. It was, therefore, a mutually satisfactory arrangement.

This was the theory. In practice, of course, the forced intermarriage of the daughters of commerce and the landed gentry was seldom happy. The daughters had been bred within a culture of Protestantism, hard work and narrow respectability, which accepted the external rules of high society at face value. They found themselves married to men who scorned such values. The substantial marriage dowries the women brought with them only served to revitalise the coffers, and finance further frivolous pleasures.

Charlotte Wainwright was a typical daughter from a newly rich northern family. She had received some education through a governess, but was poorly versed in worldly knowledge. Her society was made up of other local tycoon families who met in the polite assembly rooms of Buxton and discussed the weather, and the latest fashions. The son of the greatest and most ancient family in those parts, Henry Faulkes, must have seemed like a peacock strutting amongst the sparrows. He was known to be wild and passionate, and rumour had it that he had almost killed a man in a duel of honour. To a young provincial girl of seventeen like Charlotte he presented an image of high romance, particularly when contrasted with her prosaic brothers, the only other men she had spent time with.

Charlotte would have had access to several contemporary novels where the fictitious heroine manages to bring the troubled hero back to the path of righteousness through her own purity and godliness, and she may have believed she could achieve the same feat. Unfortunately for her, Faulkes was not a character in a novel, but was very real. He seems to have made no allowances for her sheltered upbringing, and after their wedding in 1792 he immediately plunged her into his mad, bad world. Her initial idol-worship of him as a beautiful stormy hero quickly disintegrated. With no one to turn to for advice or guidance she seems to have been gradually infected with Faulkes' amorality, and found solace for herself in a series of forbidden relationships. The evidence for these is to be found in a private diary she wrote throughout her life.

Her first extramarital relationship was with Joshua Rackham, vicar of the parish at Oakstead, Norfolk, where she and Faulkes lived after their honeymoon. Initially she sees Rackham as a platonic friend with whom she can converse about ordinary things. It seems to have been a great comfort to her to find someone polite, and unchallenging, to drink her tea with. This was how she had imagined life as a gentle-woman. She also believed that the vicar might have a good influence on her husband, who was prone to indulging in wild parties with his debauched London friends. Then her first child falls sick. Faulkes seems to be inhumanly unaffected, repelled by her tears and emotions, preoccupied with his other projects. Only Joshua Rackham offers her sympathy, performing, one imagines, his curatorial duties diligently for the wife of his patron. However, during this troubled time for Charlotte her feelings seem to have grown, and her gratitude towards the vicar turns into love.

Whether this love is returned is not clear from her diary entries. She speaks of Rackham's 'gentle touch' as he sits with her next to her son's sickbed, and how he makes 'fervent speeches upon his wishes for her future well-being and comfort'. But the entries concerning Rackham are never as explicit as later entries on other lovers. Throughout the diary it is possible to trace her gradual descent into amorality as she becomes less and less protective of her own repu-tation, and increasingly explicit about what she gets up to.

Rackham certainly seems to have developed a strong aversion to Faulkes, perhaps as a reaction to the inhu-mane way the lord treated his wife, and he preaches an unguarded sermon from the pulpit directed against false leaders. No doubt, in normal circumstances, the lord of the manor would have been put out by such a speech, and perhaps the vicar would have lost his living. The content of the sermon does not satisfacto-rily account for the ferocity of the attack that followed. It is more likely that Faulkes had discovered the affair between his wife and the vicar, and used the sermon as an excuse to publicly humiliate Rackham.

Charlotte writes that Rackham's 'poor sweet face [was] disfigured and broken!'. A portrait of the vicar, taken when he was made bishop of Petersham in 1836 (and kept at the Bishop's palace there), bears out this description. His left eye is drawn down and hooded, and a thin scar line runs from its corner down to his mouth. The left corner of his mouth is turned down, in a kind of permanent palsy. His nose is lumpy, like a rugby player's, and is pushed to the right. Allowing for the portraitist's probable toning down of the disfigurement, it appears that Rackham was given a cruel beating by the lord of the manor.

The scene at the church must have been a terrifying one. Faulkes was well known for his vicious temper. The scar to Rackham's face is indicative of a blow from a lash, and it seems likely that Faulkes assaulted him with his horsewhip. Rackham, by all accounts, was a gentle, slight man. He would have had no defence against the attack. The first lash across his face would have caused him to fall to the ground. The broken and misshapen nose was probably the result of a kick to the head. It is likely that the vicar received other permanent injuries to the rest of his body, as Faulkes kicked and lashed him where he lay on the ground. Presumably, Charlotte was screaming and begging him to stop. The congregation would have gathered round, but were probably silent, in fear of their master. Perhaps at last, when it seemed that the raging lord would not cease until the man was dead, one or two of the more respected men of the village came forward and held their lord back with murmurs of 'That'll do now, sir. You would not wish to kill a man of God?'

A specialist physician was brought in by Henry's father, and the whole event was hushed up. Rackham was offered a new living in Burntbridge, Derbyshire, but was not able to take up the post for a full year, implying that his injuries were serious, possibly life-threatening.

It is interesting to note the last line of a letter to Rackham from Henry's father. It is clear that a deal was entered into by both families to keep a mutual silence about the beating, but the viscount writes: 'I could not guarantee your own immunity from censure, were news of these event to become more widely known.' The insinuation is that Rackham was indeed guilty of misdemeanour, which would not be defensible if made public. No wonder he accepted his new post and scuttled off, leaving poor Charlotte in the hands of her brutal husband.

March

It is a season in which much is to be done and he who would acquit himself to his own credit and his master's satisfaction must be every day busy.

Mrs Martha Bradley

Ruby had the reference for the box containing the Italian letter, so it didn't take her long to find it. Gretta sat shivering in her large furry overcoat and tutted about the dust. In March the dungeon-like room which housed the Henford archive was even more forbidding than Ben had found it. Mrs Sayer took pity on them and led them back to her flat to look at the letter. It was written on thick yellowish paper, all folded together. Ruby opened it and read the first lines, as Ben had done.

23rd October 1793
Roma

My dear Henry,
Your letter was very welcome, coming as it did during a week of extreme tedium brought on by the most diabolical rainstorms and freezing winds. I trust you remain well. Please pass on my good wishes to your wife.

At this point the style of the handwriting deteriorated suddenly, into a sloping scrawl which at first seemed indecipherable. Ruby wanted to make sure to do her best for Ben so she knuckled down and worked on each word, letter by letter, while Gretta sat curled up on the sofa reading a magazine. The letter went on:

I have been confined to barracks as it were, and have been unable to venture forth to further my acquaintance with all the attractions you mentioned in your last letter. But fear not! I have been to the one you were most anxious to hear news of and I must say it surpassed all expectations. Your taste is impeccable, of course. Where else, but in Rome, could one find such beauty and style available to the tourist at the turn of every corner? As you may imagine, I fell in love on the spot just as you did, and you may rest assured that I will strive in every way to protect that temple which is the source of such beauty and delight.

Here the letter became entirely unintelligible. After struggling with it for a few moments, it dawned on Ruby that this was where the writer had switched to Italian. She dragged Gretta away from her magazine and made her sit down and look at the text. Gretta groaned when she saw the state of the handwriting.

'I can't read this! I wouldn't even be able to understand it if it was in English. I was never very good at written Italian, anyway, let alone eighteenth-century Italian. It's impossible.'

Ruby would not be dissuaded. The mention of a temple in the last line made her certain that the letter was going to be useful. She got out the Italian dictionary that she had insisted Gretta bring with her.

'I'll write down the words as I read them, and you try and work out what they mean. OK?'

Gretta grumbled, but agreed to do it. The next two hours

were spent painstakingly deciphering each word and trying to string them together into meaningful sentences. It sounded rather wooden:

> Of all the Hyacinthus I saw, those petals have the most lovely shine. It is not surprising you miss them. Tell me more in your next letter about J. I think I remember something from the days before, and it could make me happy to renew that friend if I remember. I see ahead a long wait before we meet you again, when you have so much to make you remain. But please do not forget your poor friends, exiled in this city without a choice. Did you receive the last package I sent you? I hope you were happy with its contents. The sketches of Herculaneum are especially good and I am sure will be useful for you.

At this point the letter suddenly reverted back to scrawled English, much to Gretta's relief:

> I have only now received the package containing Mr Flaxman's illustrations of the *Iliad*. I am overcome by these line engravings and I am most grateful to you for sending me the copy so promptly. The rendering of Achilles lamenting the death of Patroclus moved me deeply. The unaffected simplicity with which these noble emotions are portrayed fills my soul with awe. There cannot be another subject which expresses so well the natural dignity of these ancient heroes and their deeds. I will treasure this gift all my life. Sir, my hand trembles with emotion as I write. I am, as ever, your most grateful friend.
> JS

Ruby and Gretta read through the letter once, twice, trying to make sense of it. Ruby said:
'He starts off talking about sightseeing in Rome and then

suddenly starts talking about flowers. Do you think there's any significance in the changes from English to Italian?'

Gretta frowned. 'There might be, or he may just have been bilingual and slipped from one language to the other. What do you think J is? Another flower?'

'Maybe. Though he goes on about "renewing that friend". It might be a woman.'

'Or servant or someone illicit. Perhaps that's why he slips into Italian. The trouble is, my Italian is so rusty, I could have read completely the wrong thing into it. It's years since I did any translation. Anyway, have we finished now? I'm hungry.'

Ruby smiled at her patient and loyal friend. 'OK. I'll let you off. Let's go into town and have some lunch, and look at some shops.'

Gretta leaped from her chair. 'Bliss! Let's go, quickly, before they stop serving!'

Back at Oakstead, Ruby showed Ben her copy of the strangely disconnected letter.

'What do you think it means?' he asked.

She shrugged. 'I don't know. It might be that the writer was just some flighty artist who wrote odd, disjointed letters. The bit about the temple, and looking after it, seems quite straightforward. Maybe Faulkes was trying to do some kind of conservation work. And the drawings of Herculaneum – would they have been of buildings?

'I think so. He might have based his temple design on them.'

'Mm. But the almost illegible scrawl and the slipping into Italian after such a polite and formal beginning still makes me suspicious. I think it's some kind of code. He's hiding something.'

'What, though?'

'I don't know.'

Ben read it through again. 'Why does he talk about hyacinths?'

215

He suddenly pushed his chair back from the desk, and got up to look at his bookshelves. 'Hyacinths. That begins to ring a bell with me. Hold on a mo.'

He took down a thick book entitled *Concise Dictionary of the Classics* and leafed through its pages.

'Here we are. 'Hyacinthus: a boy beloved of Apollo. He was killed when the god accidentally struck him with a discus'. I knew there was something. We read classics at school, and, if I remember rightly, there were lots of schoolboy jokes about Apollo and Hyacinthus. It's just the sort of thing that goes down well at boarding school. Lots of giggling about what Apollo actually did teach Hyacinthus.'

'Hyacinthus sounds like a girl's name.'

'Precisely. Just the kind of name you might use to describe somebody of, shall we say, an effeminate nature.'

Ruby raised her eyebrows. 'You think they might have been talking about gay men?'

'I don't know. What do you think? Is it likely that Faulkes was gay? He doesn't give that impression. All those children and everything.'

'Well, he seems to have been quite wild. Perhaps this was part of it. Perhaps our Henry Faulkes liked to keep his options open. How could we find out?'

They sat thinking about it for a few minutes and then Ben let out a long sigh.

'I can't think how. All the coding in the letter shows that they were being cagey about it, if it is true. It's not very likely that we'll find anything explicit. I could go up to Henford again and look for more letters, I suppose.'

Ruby felt panic rise in her. She didn't want to be left on her own with Charlie. She tried not to let the quiver enter her voice. 'You didn't find anything before, and it's a long way to go on a wild goose chase.'

'Mmm.' Ben was thinking about how much more work he had to do on the wedding bed, and only a few weeks left. 'You're right. Perhaps sometime after the wedding, I'll pop up there again.'

He considered phoning Jayne to discuss this new idea, but decided against it. So close to the wedding, he didn't want to be sidetracked by her husky voice.

Gretta was lolling on a large, exhausted-looking armchair in the corner of Ben's workshop at Glandford. She had come to take final measurements of the bed so that she could buy material to dress it up for the wedding night. Ben sat tense and excited on the workbench. He had just told her his new idea, which was to put the bed into the temple for the wedding night. She thought it was a fantastically romantic idea and had become very animated.

'How glorious it will be! We could fill the lake with floating candles and decorate the boat with lanterns. It'll be magnificent! You can ceremoniously row her across there, and we'll fill the temple with flowers and scented candles. God, it'll be amazing. I'm quite jealous.' She patted him affectionately on the knee, and then continued on her fantasy. 'We can swathe the bed in ravishing silks, and sumptuous cushions. We could have pure white silk, the really fine sort that looks like fairies' wings. It's magical. All the candles will make it glisten. Swathes of it drawn up at the top like a magnificent crown, flowing down like water onto the floor. Perhaps some delicate silver embroidery on the drapes around the bed, like cobwebs.'

'The state the temple's in at the moment, we'll have to be careful there are no real spider's webs.'

'Oh, don't worry about that. I'll sort it all out. I love makeovers. I'll get it cleaned out.'

'The only thing is, I'm hoping the conservators will have finished uncovering the paintings by then – otherwise it'll be a mess in there, with scaffolding and all sorts.'

'Can't it wait until after the wedding?'

Ben looked doubtful. 'I think I've set something in motion which it would be difficult to stop. And frankly, I can hardly wait to see what's under there.'

'But what if it turns out to be something really ghastly,

like devils or something? It wouldn't be very romantic. Couldn't we keep our nice white paint until after the ceremony? Please?'

'We'll have to see. We could always put the bed somewhere else. We could have it in the middle of the wood. No one would be able to see us.'

'Hmm. It might work. But you might find you have a drunken audience.' The thought of Charlie prowling around uncontrollably on the wedding night had occurred to her. She hesitated for a moment before speaking further, but then decided to plunge on. 'Do you have any idea whether Charlie is going to be around for the wedding?'

'I imagine so. He is one of my oldest friends. Why do you ask?'

At the sight of Ben's honest and open face looking so puzzled by the question, Gretta lost her nerve and tried to change the direction of the conversation. 'Oh, well, it occurred to me he might be upset that he's not best man.'

Ben laughed. 'You don't need to worry about that. Charlie would hate it. He hates churches and weddings. He'll sit at the back, get drunk at the reception, and try to seduce all the female guests. And will probably be successful. In fact, perhaps I should put warnings on the invites.'

Gretta laughed weakly, and went back to discussing silks.

I am sick with tension, my head constantly aches. Sometimes I wish Charlie would just tell Ben, get it over with, and I will be released from this permanent state of suspense. Every time he comes into the room I think: This is going to be it, he is going to say something. But he doesn't. He smirks at me, and makes lewd signs behind Ben's back. He reads out stuff from the papers about adultery, or talks about the plots of plays he has seen which involve unfaithfulness. And he looks at me with that cold, amphibian glare. Sometimes I think I am going to faint, the pressure in my temples is so intense.

The worst is if he finds me alone. I am getting better at avoiding this, keeping to my room, using the kitchen after he has gone. I never go to the sitting room on my own. But if he meets me on the stairs, or coming out of the bathroom, he harangues me, telling me it's only a matter of time, and that he'll tell Ben about George if I don't have sex with him. I say there's nothing to tell. In my heart I know that's not true but, if he does tell Ben at some point, I will be ready to deny it.

Sleeping and eating have become a trial, my stomach constantly churning. Ben thinks I'm suffering from nerves about the wedding, that I want to be thin to fit into my dress. It's fortunate that he's preoccupied with his own business, otherwise he would surely notice the strained atmosphere in the house? Charlie notices, of course. He loves to see me in pain. He says I was too fat for his taste before, that he finds the heroin addict look much more of a turn-on. He shoves his horrible naked body at me, he grabs at me when I pass. The thought that I might not be able to fight him off next time haunts me. He will hurt me, one way or another.

Charlie was biding his time. His thoughts were permanently occupied with plans to make Ruby suffer. His favourite fantasy was of the wedding ceremony. He imagined the vicar saying, 'If anyone knows a reason why these two should not be joined together in matrimony, speak now, or forever hold your peace,' and then Charlie would stand up at the back of the church and say, 'I know a reason. The bride-to-be is a whore.' He could see it like a corny old film running in his head, the outcry amongst the guests, Ruby's look of horror, Ben's face wiped clean of its smugness. The wedding service would definitely be the best time to do it, he thought. And he had not given up the possibility that she might have sex with him before the wedding if he frightened her enough. This was the other fantasy that preoccupied his waking

219

and sleeping hours. How he would give her a good seeing-to, if he got the chance.

One evening, after spending all night in the local pub, he was shuffling back along the pitch-dark lane when he heard footsteps behind him. Though his ears registered the sound, his brain did not attempt to analyse what this might mean. It only occurred to him to wonder who it was when he found himself flat on his face on the muddy bank, wet grass shoved into his nose. There was a knee wedged in his back and a hand on his neck, holding his head down so that he could hardly breathe. Soil was in his mouth.

Then a voice he vaguely recognised through the drunken fog said, 'This is a warning, Charlie. You keep out of Ruby's way. If I hear you've done anything that might upset things, you'll be sorry you were ever born. Do you understand?'

Charlie experienced a moment of confusion. Was he dreaming? He seemed to have wandered into a tacky 'B' movie, and bumped into the anti-hero. He thought, Oh God, why do I live out here in the sticks, and put myself at the mercy of every country bumpkin who can't hold his drink? The rough hand on his neck pushed his face into the grass again, then jerked him back by his hair.

'I said, do you understand?'

Charlie grunted something that meant yes, he did understand. The hand let go of his hair, and his head flopped back into the mud again. He heard the footsteps running away. He lay still on the bank for several minutes, listening to the silence. His neck hurt, twisted and sore. It had been a very strong hand that gripped him, a hand that could do a lot of damage. It was frightening. He sat up abruptly, suddenly conscious of his isolation out in the dark, before bolting for home, his head pounding, his stomach queasy.

Ruby had been invited up to the London gallery to discuss plans for further promoting her paintings. Thankfully, the gallery was now dealing with her directly, and she did not have to suffer Charlie's company. Instead, she had to put up with the oily advances of the gallery manager, Mr Bernard. It occurred to her that this was probably Charlie's doing, and that Mr Bernard was under the misapprehension that Ruby would not be slow in granting sexual favours.

Ruby felt a weight lift from her as she got on the train, which whisked her out of Norfolk. Oakstead had become claustrophobic. Even though Charlie seemed to have backed off slightly, to escape for a day was a real relief. Sitting in a café having lunch before her meeting with Mr Bernard, she had actually felt quite light-hearted. All the different people milling in the streets, the music, and the city sunshine made her excited and expansive. She realised how small and concentrated her world had become over the last few months, circumscribed almost entirely by the boundaries of the park.

Mr Bernard's attitude towards her, when she arrived at the gallery, soon brought back the sense that there was no escape. She found herself seated in a small office at the back of the building, her feet being shamelessly mauled under the desk by the feet of Mr Bernard. Above the desk he continued discussing plans as if nothing untoward was happening.

'I think a touring exhibition in the summer would be sensible, don't you? Let's try to reach out to some of the provinces. I think your work would transfer, you know, as it's highly accessible. Hmm? We could even explore the possibility of producing one or two of them in poster form. I think they could work very well, don't you? What do you think? How far do you think we should go, Ruby, my love?'

He leered at her, showing rather yellow teeth, as he leaned forward across the desk and tried to grasp her hand. Ruby retracted her feet under her chair and shrank back as far as she could from the desk. She was beginning to feel very depressed about men.

'I think, Mr Bernard, that I would like to continue this

conversation in the gallery. It's rather hot in here.'

She got up quickly and left the room before he could prevent her. He followed her a few minutes later, looking rather stony-faced. He grabbed her elbow, and steered her to a seating area in the gallery. As he did, he spoke softly into her ear:

'You know, you need to be careful with that attitude of yours, my dear. Attitude can make or break the reputation of an artist, as you must know. It won't do you any good if you put people's backs up. An artist is reliant on the good opinion of the patron. You should consider your future a little more, before you bite the hand that feeds you.'

He sat down and patted the seat next to him, inviting her to sit down too. But Ruby was hot with indignation and started to tell Mr Bernard what her opinion of him was. She was annoyed to hear her voice trembling, and her throat seemed to have dried up, making her squeak.

'How dare you speak to me like—'

She broke off as Mr Bernard caught hold of her arms and pulled her forcibly down on the seat. Through a fixed smile he muttered, 'Quiet! Customer.'

Then Ruby heard the tinkle of the doorbell. She turned, and was amazed to see that it was Professor Lal who had walked in. He looked similarly amazed.

'Ruby! What a lovely surprise! What smiling fates have brought us together, I wonder?' He came forward and took both her hands, and kissed them. Then he turned to the gallery owner. 'Mr Bernard. You see, we all know each other. How nice. You must be so pleased to have discovered a talent like Ruby.'

Ruby looked hard at the professor. Had he intended a double meaning? She wondered what he had seen through the gallery window, and how he had interpreted it. Mr Bernard, wondering the same thing, was lost for words for some moments.

The professor broke the embarrassed silence. 'Ruby is a good friend of mine. And it is so lucky that I also admire greatly her talent as a painter, as you know. I am staying nearby for a few days and I thought I would just pop in today, to look at Ruby's fruit. I thought it would brighten up my day. But look! A double treat! The artist herself! The gods are smiling upon me indeed!'

Ruby tried to sound suitably flattered, and Mr Bernard made spluttering noises.

Professor Lal looked from one to the other and said, 'But, please. I can see I have interrupted your meeting. Continue, continue! I will go and quietly look at the paintings while you talk. Please do not mind me.'

He strode off to the far end of the gallery and began considering a piece of sculpture. Ruby found herself feeling grateful for his presence. Since Mr Bernard could not continue harassing her, the meeting became more civilised, and the plans for future exhibitions were finalised quickly. When it was obvious that the meeting was over, the professor came up to Ruby and offered to take her for a drink somewhere.

Ruby, pleased with him for saving her from Bernard, said yes. They walked down the street a little way and found a decent café, with a table next to the window, overlooking the children's park.

The professor smiled in an avuncular way. 'And so, how are things with Ruby?'

She rolled her eyes. 'Better for escaping that man. Honestly! He's disgusting. Thank goodness you came in when you did!'

'You are pursued from all sides. It cannot be easy.'

Ruby looked at him with surprise. 'How do you mean?'

The professor looked down into his lap, arranging his napkin, as he said, 'I do not wish to intrude into your private life, but George has mentioned one or two things to me, and I can imagine that your situation is not an easy one at present.' He looked up and smiled at her, a sympathetic smile. 'Oakstead is a place of magic, but perhaps its spirit can be overstimulating at times.'

223

For once, Ruby felt he was being genuine. It made her cry. The professor passed her a napkin. She waited until control of her voice had returned before replying.

'It's nice of you to be concerned, but I'm all right really. Let's talk about something else.' She sniffed, and then continued. 'Have you heard about the wall paintings?'

The professor's sympathetic look transformed into an expression of keen interest. 'I haven't. What have you to tell me?'

Ruby told him about the toe. He looked pleased. 'Well, well. So something has survived. That is good news. I wonder to whom the toe belongs? Have you any ideas?'

Ruby shook her head. The professor put his hand up to his chin, and mused silently. Then he looked up, light shining from his face.

'Imagine! Gradually creeping out from underneath all the years of paint will come images that have not been seen for more than two hundred years! Hidden voices struggling out from oblivion! New things for us to understand and inter-pret! It is very exciting, don't you think?'

Ruby laughed. 'I envy your capacity for enthusiasm, I really do.'

The professor laughed too. 'It is a gift and an affliction, I assure you. My obsessions are not always appreciated by those around me. But to get to the bottom of things, some-times obsession is necessary.'

'Is it? I think obsessing about something can kill its spirit. In my painting, I feel if I get too involved with the minutiae of a subject it loses its life, and I might as well take a photograph.'

He nodded. 'Yes, I can see that might be a problem. But you are still obsessed with the process of painting, resist-ing the easy route of copying something rather than looking for its essence. Do you not agree?'

Ruby nodded slowly, thinking about it. The professor continued:

'For example, if you were to paint an apple, how would

you approach it? Would you think about how other people have painted apples, or would you try to see it fresh, with your own eyes, as only you see it?'

Ruby mused on the question. 'You can't help knowing how other people have painted an apple. It's almost impossible to be totally original, isn't it? Especially with something that has been painted so often. Everything you see feeds into the process but, yes, I would try to paint what is important to me about the apple, so that it's my perspective, and reflects my view.'

Professor Lal sat back in his chair and clapped his hands, laughing.

'Absolutely, absolutely! You see, this is also how I approach my work. Detail is often desirable but not accessible. There is so much so-called established fact, which later turns out to be propaganda from one side or another. That is why I relish the prospect of uncovering new evidence, new ways of seeing things. How dull life would be if we thought that there was only one way of painting an apple!'

'That's true.' Ruby was beginning to enjoy herself. 'And a painting doesn't just tell you what something looks like, does it? I mean, if I were to draw an apple, I would be thinking about its other meanings as well. You know, as the fruit of knowledge, and its connection with the fall from grace, and all that. So I might try to imbue it with a sense of voluptuousness, or sinful temptation.'

'That's right. And if you are lucky, when someone comes to look at the final painting they will bring similar knowledge to their way of viewing it so that they will interpret the apple in the way you intended. But, of course, if the viewer is a Hindu, or an animist, they will interpret the painting in a different way. That is why it is impossible to say that there is only one right way of interpreting something. Not just the interpretation of facts, but the facts themselves. For example, there is no way of proving that what I know as an apple looks the same to you as it does to me. Our optical instruments may register different colours, sizes, textures. We may smell it differently too. We may register different feelings when we take it in our hands. And it will provoke different tastes as well, so that some of us will like it, and some of us won't.'

Ruby laughed. 'I'll never look at an apple in the same way again.'

'Well, I hope not. That is my intention. Of course, the same theory can be applied to human beings also. We will all have different opinions of the same person and different interpretations of their behaviour.' The professor leaned forward across the table and tapped it with his finger, emphasising his words. 'I would like people to understand the impossibility of knowing. So many of the people I work with seem to think it is possible to tie a moment down, to understand it completely and sign it off as established fact. I do not like that idea. It will inevitably be a reflection of that person's view.' He paused, sipped his tea, and then looked up at Ruby. 'That is why I am so unpopular amongst some of my peers. They don't like me poking at their nicely contained theories. I irritate them.'

'Which is why you don't give much away.'

'In a nutshell, yes. Certain people are always keen to poke me back, if they have the opportunity. I have been particularly keen to keep the Oakstead temple to myself, because it offers entirely fresh, unseen evidence. I will have the opportunity to be the first to write its story using my ideas and ways of seeing. And the wall paintings will offer such great potential for interpretation. I am looking forward so much to seeing them reborn!'

'Well, I'll try to make sure Ben keeps you up to date with what's happening,' Ruby said, although she was privately unsure whether Ben would be prepared to share much with the professor.

The professor glanced at his watch.

'Oh! I must go. I have to pick up my daughter in half an hour.'

'I didn't know you had a daughter!' Ruby's image of the professor took on a whole new colour.

'Yes! Lila, she is called. Seventeen now.'

'You've never mentioned her.'

'I suppose we have not talked much about such things. It is always the temple and the paintings! And she lives with her aunt in Mumbai most of the time.' He gazed out of the window at the cars going by. 'My wife died when Lila was only a toddler, and so she became all the world to me.' Then he chuckled, and looked back at Ruby. 'She is thrilled to be in London, spending my money like water! You must meet her sometime.'

'I'd like that.'

Ruby was taken aback. Her opinion of the professor as a rather obstructive man, too interested in sex, and too excitable, had been overturned by her pleasant conversation with him in the café, his rescue of her from Mr Bernard, and his admission that he was a dedicated father. The professor paid for the tea and shook her hand warmly before setting off in the opposite direction down the road. She gazed at him as he made his way down the street, past shops and parked cars, and she suddenly thought: I've never seen him in the real world before. Only at Oakstead.

After putting Ruby on the train to London, Ben returned home and went straight up to the second floor, where the secret room was. He couldn't wait any longer to find out what was inside, and this time he had managed to keep his plan to himself, instead of discussing it with Ruby. He felt he would much rather know what was there than be prey to dark imaginings, as Ruby was. If he found something unpleasant – a dead cat perhaps – he could clear it away and patch the room up without her knowing. If it was all OK, he could take down the whole false wall, and make the existing room a more useful size. He armed himself with a jemmy and a torch.

It was messy work. The timber frame of the wall was

filled in with strong wooden laths, covered with thick layers of lime plaster on both sides. The plaster came off in big lumps, showering powder and grit. Ben had to bash the wooden laths several times with the jemmy before they gave way. Half an hour passed before he managed to make a hole big enough to climb through, by which time the air was swimming with dust.

It was very dingy in the room, the only light, apart from his torch, coming through the north-facing window on the other side of the partition. The smell was strong, of damp and rot, and it was cold. Ben felt as though he were stepping into different air, the memory of a two hundred-year-old day stagnating inside. He swept the torchlight over the room, and began to feel a slight prickle of apprehension. In the centre of the small space stood a solid structure, which appeared to be a tomb. It looked as though it was made from carved stone slabs – a long rectangular grey box, with a plain slab lid. Lying on top of it there was a figure. Ben stood stock still, and took in a deep breath to calm himself. Then he took a step nearer and shone his torch at the head. With great relief he saw that what had looked like a body, was in fact just an outfit of clothes. A blue jacket with wide lapels and tails at the back, some kind of shirt tucked inside a dirty looking waistcoat with a scarf arranged at the neck, pale breeches, stockings, and flat leather shoes. Venturing nearer, he saw something lumpy set at the top of the breeches. It looked like a large stone at first, but when he picked it up he saw that it was a crudely carved stone phallus. His fingers went limp and he almost dropped it. His sudden movement, and the exclamation he made, seemed very big and loud in the dead atmosphere of the room. When the silence seemed to have settled again, he placed the sculpture back where he had found it.

A crackling noise alerted him to something else hidden inside the breeches, which the stone had been weighing down: a piece of thick, yellowed paper peppered with black specks of mould. Gingerly, he extricated it from inside the cloth, and laid it on the slab. In the torchlight he read:

Sir
You find yourself in the midst of an experiment. You will be of a curious nature, and so I offer you an explanation – I hope to return to this world, and you see around you my preparation. Indeed, you may be I, reborn. Does this missive kindle the memory of a time gone before?
You will of course honour my wishes and leave this room as you have found it – or you may be sure I will return to haunt you.
HF

Ben shivered. He felt the spirit of Faulkes hovering over his head – ready to enter his body perhaps, so that he could be reborn – or to haunt him if his wishes were not complied with. He glanced up, his shoulders hunched, to see if there was anything there, some kind of glow or ectoplasm to indicate a presence. There was nothing. Even so, he was severely shaken, and he began to back out of the room, not wishing to take his eyes off the set of clothes, in case they rose up to throttle him. As he put his hand out behind him, to feel the edge of the opening, he cried out as his wrist was clasped in another's hand.

'Jesus Christ!'

'Sorry. Didn't mean to freak you out.' It was George.

'Bloody hell. You really put the wind up me.' Ben staggered out of the hole into the servant's room.

George was smirking. 'You were just about to put your hand on a nail, that's all.'

'What are you doing up here anyway?' To cover his embarrassment, Ben became gruff.

George stiffened almost imperceptibly. 'I wasn't being nosy, if that's what you're getting at. I was downstairs dropping off the veg and I heard a lot of noise up here, and

then nothing. I was worried that someone had hurt themselves. It sounded like a ceiling collapsing. I've been
wandering around up here for ten minutes trying to find the
right room. It's like a rabbit warren!'

Ben felt contrite. 'Well, that's good of you. Sorry. But
I've just had the fright of my life. Look in here.' He handed
George the torch, and pointed into the hole.

George stepped in, and Ben followed. 'Read that letter.'

George picked it up and held it close to his face. Ben
watched his expression of interest turn into a frown, and
then blank shock. The paper slipped from his fingers, and
he stood very still.

'Are you all right?'

George blinked, and straightened. 'Yes.' He was whispering. 'But it's a bit weird.'

He shone the torch around the room, and they both
noticed for the first time that there was a tall free-standing
cupboard covering most of the wall at one end. Tentatively,
Ben opened its doors. Inside was a collection of mouldering wooden boxes, corked bottles and jars, which looked
like they had contained food of some sort. Ben did not
venture to open them. One shelf was packed with bottles of
wine. On the top shelf was a large leather-bound book. Ben
lifted it down and laid it on the tomb. Bits of it had been
eaten away by some kind of insect or mouse, and the
borders of the paper were spattered with the same black
mould as Faulkes' letter. The typeface looked very old. It
was uneven, and the 's's were shaped like 'f's. The title
page read: *A Pagan Almanac: being a discourse on the rites
and customs of the ancient tribe of the Druids: with instructions on divers solemn ceremonies.* Ben turned some of the
pages. The language was archaic and convoluted and he
could barely understand it, but it looked like a book of
spells. There were strange diagrams and calculations. Some
seemed to show the path of the moon or the sun. On one
page there were illustrations of stone phalluses similar to
the one Ben had just found. On another, there was a series

of pictures of Venus figurines, bulbous figures with large breasts.

George was exploring the rest of the room. There was a box full of old banknotes and a chest full of clothes, including a razorblade and a brush. He whistled in disbelief. 'He was definitely planning to come back. Look at all this stuff! It must be worth a fortune.'

Ben looked up, and the flash of George's torch lit up something on the opposite end wall. Where the blocked window was hidden behind plaster, there was a painting: three large conjoined spirals in black paint. They were just like the ones on the portrait at Henford.

The two men spent another hour looking through the clothes, and trying to make sense of the book. They spoke little, both contemplating the meaning of this strange treasure trove, but keeping it to themselves. Ben felt that the air in the room had coalesced, as if contact with the outside atmosphere had made it react, and turn into a cube of thin jelly. His limbs weighed heavily as though he were moving against something, and his vision kept blurring. The little drop of fear, which had formed at the back of his neck when he first saw the shadow of the tomb, had gradually spread down his spine and into his legs. He kept repeating in his head, 'Ghosts don't exist, it's just old clothes,' but he didn't convince himself. He felt more and more strongly that the longer they trespassed, the more likely it would be that Faulkes would materialise inside the outfit and would leap up with murderous intent. The moment arrived abruptly when he could no longer bear to be in the room. He stepped out over the pile of plaster, and called back to George, 'You might think me mad, but we're going to have to block this all up again.'

George put his head through the hole and nodded. 'No, I think you're right. I wouldn't want to get on the wrong side of him.'

They stood for a moment contemplating the mess. Then

Ben said, 'If you could have a go at neatening up the hole, I'll drive into town and buy some plasterboard.'

Ben left, glad to breathe in fresh air. George went down to the kitchen for bin bags and a broom. While he was there, he looked in the cupboards and found some tins of food: tomatoes, sardines, beans. He put these in a plastic bag, together with an unopened packet of rice and some cans of beer, went back upstairs to the hidden room and placed the food in the cupboard. He contemplated the clothes lying on the tomb for several minutes, but then in swift movements pulled off his T-shirt, jeans, and shoes. He carefully slid on the old shirt and the breeches. They fitted perfectly. He shrugged on the waistcoat and overcoat, pulled off his socks, and gently rolled the stockings on. The leather shoes were not comfortable, having become misshapen in the damp and cold, but they fitted. He crept down the hall to a bathroom where there was a mirror, and stood looking at himself, in full Faulkes regalia, a slight smile on his face. When he returned to the secret room he lay down on the tomb and closed his eyes for a few moments. The room was completely silent and still, like the inside of a pyramid.

The sound of an aeroplane overhead finally broke the spell. He sat up, and blinked. Slowly, he took off his clothes, laid them carefully back in their place on the tomb, and put on the modern clothes. He went over to the cupboard, reached up and took a bottle of wine, padded downstairs, and hid it in his van. Then he went back upstairs and set to work clearing up the pile of plaster.

While out in the town buying the plasterboard, Ben calmed down, and started to feel a ashamed of his response to the room. It was only the silly whim of an eccentric after all! And the things in it – the books, clothes, and wine – would be worth a lot of money, as well as being of great academic interest. He decided he couldn't seal it up permanently. Once he felt ready, he could open it up again and perhaps ask Jayne Greene to come and have a look.

On his return to the house, he and George only blocked up the hole temporarily by nailing plasterboard sheets across it. By the time Ruby returned from London late that night, all the mess was cleared up. Ben and George had discussed what they would say, and Ben had rehearsed his lines with a nonchalant face.

'No, there was nothing much in there. We think it was something to do with keeping the damp out, so we left it.'

Ruby narrowed her eyes at him. 'I don't believe you. You're no good at lying. What did you really find?'

Ben tried to look offended. 'Nothing. Truly.'

'I'll go and ask George, if you don't tell me.'

He crumbled. 'Oh, OK. But you won't like it.'

'No, I don't expect I will. Which is why I didn't want you to do it.' Her voice started off angry and then dwindled into a sob. She took in a deep breath, sat down at the kitchen table and closed her eyes. 'Tell me.'

He sat next to her and held her hands. 'There were no dead bodies. Just some clothes, and a strange book, and some mouldy old food.' He paused.

Ruby opened her eyes. 'And?'

'There was a note from Henry Faulkes.' He stopped again as Ruby took in a sudden startled breath. 'It's all right. It's not sinister really. It seems he made himself a room, a bit like a mausoleum, with all the things he would need while he was waiting to be reborn. It's quite funny really.'

Ruby wasn't convinced. 'Oh, God. So he's been here all the time, in that room.' She closed her eyes again and her face was ashen.

'Don't be ridiculous! It's just some old clothes. He is dead and buried in Derbyshire.' He stood up abruptly. 'You're being too silly about this.' Ruby hid her face in her hands, and then Ben felt contrite. 'Look. I'm sorry I did something you didn't want me to, but I needed to know what was in there. I couldn't pretend it didn't exist. It was bugging me.' He sat down again, and tried to look into her

233

face. 'Ruby. Come on. It's all sealed up again now, no harm done.'

A sob escaped from behind her hands. She couldn't speak, but the thought going round in her head was: *The genie is out of the bottle.*

March 21st

Tomorrow the day will be longer than the night: the spring equinox, marking the festival of new growth. Eostre, the goddess, brings eggs to symbolise fertility, the smooth oval shell like cool skin, the nucleus buried inside ready to spring into life. The book says it is a time for clearing out the old, bringing in the new. I feel that I have received new life, the sun's energy running though my blood, burning away the dust and debris of the past.

There's an endless drive in all living things to reproduce, to continue the cycle: birth, death, rebirth. I'm filled with this potency. I feel the power within me to make new life, to emulate the Sun God, to bring the seed to the Earth Goddess. This is an energy that should not be wasted. Each moment of conception, the coming together of the male and the female, is a recreation of the first union of the sun and earth on the first day of the world. For that one moment we are merged into the great life force, we become part of the wheel. I will give myself up to the cycle of the seasons, I will be led by Nature's rhythms, and I will take her into the dance of life.

The report on the initial findings in the temple arrived from Chambers and Elliot. It contained photographs of the paint samples magnified under a microscope. They looked like juicy sandwiches of psychedelic, melted cheese, a thick white crust over thinner layers of blue and yellow and green. The report confirmed that the coloured paints were composed of minerals and binders compatible with use in the eighteenth century. On top of these were several layers of white limewash, followed by a layer of modern emul-

234

sion. The report said that the paints showed signs of some water and salts damage but that there was a good chance that significant areas of the original paintings had survived intact. The report went on to say that this, together with the documentary evidence supplied by Ben, and the discovery of the finely formed big toe uncovered in the first investigation, all supported a second, more extensive, phase of uncovering.

Ben was on the phone to English Heritage straight away. They recommended further monitoring and stated that, as the wall paintings were not at serious risk of decay, no grant would be available for any further work. Ben, beside himself with frustration, slammed down the phone. Then he stomped downstairs, and went across to the temple to have another look at the conservator's work. Why weren't these bureaucrats interested in his paintings? They seemed to have no sense of urgency. Of course, he thought angrily, they had been put off from the start by Professor Lal's involvement, his annoying secretiveness. They didn't seem to take the thing seriously.

He looked up at the pristine new ceiling. Now the temple was weathertight, what would be the point of yet more environmental monitoring? He went outside and sat on the tree stump overlooking the lake. His mind drifted on to the wedding, which was becoming imminent. In his despondent mood, this felt like yet another worry. The surprise of the wedding bed just wouldn't be the same if it wasn't in the temple with the paintings. He threw a couple of stones into the lake, feeling sulky. Then he thought: What could they do to me if I went ahead anyway? If a proper conservator did it, no harm would be done, and they couldn't criticise me for uncovering them at my own expense. He stood up abruptly and threw one more stone far out into the water before going back to the house to ring up Chambers and Elliot.

'Would you be able to come and uncover the paintings in the next month? It would be perfect if they were ready before my wedding.'

The secretary on the other end of the line sucked her teeth. 'The firm is pretty well booked up for the next six months, I'm afraid. Oh, hold on a moment.' Ben could hear muffled voices, as the secretary held her hand over the phone. Then she came back to him. 'Sorry to keep you waiting. You're in luck, though. My colleague tells me we do have two weeks free, because the grant for a booked job has fallen through. You are paying for the work yourself, I understand?'

Ben smiled to himself. 'Oh yes. Don't worry about your fee. There's no problem there. And I'll put them up at the Hall, if that will make it easier.'

Four conservators arrived a couple of weeks later. They began the painstaking work of removing several square metres of thick paint and limewash from the walls using only tiny scalpels and small stipple brushes. Having already found the toe, they decided to work their way up, so gradually revealing the foot, taut calf muscles, the bend of a knee, and then a powerful thigh, all rendered in sombre tones, with a strong outline. The painting had only suffered minor damage. They told Ben that this had probably occurred when the surface was prepared for limewashing with a stiff brush. Other small areas showed the tell-tale white frosting of salts caused by the damp, but it was thought this would recede now the internal environment of the temple was stable. The young conservators were impressed by the quality of the paintings and worked very long days, trying to uncover as much as they could as quickly as they could. They were spurred on by Ben, who fed them well, and visited the temple often to admire the delicacy of their work, and to watch the gradually emerging form of a reclining colossus, rippling with muscles. No leering satyrs, or orgiastic writhings. The man from Chambers and Elliot said the image seemed to be from classical mythology.

236

'Note on the possible interpretation of the spirals in the marriage portrait of Henry Faulkes' by Ben Fitzmaurice for *Derbyshire Archaeological Journal*.

The spirals on the piece of paper in the famous marriage portrait of Henry Faulkes have puzzled generations of art historians, but no new theory on their meaning has emerged in the past twenty years. I offer here a summary of some modern interpretations of the spiral motif as it appears in world art, in the hope that this may stimulate renewed debate over the hidden meaning of the portrait. The following four interpretations of the motif are by no means the only ones available but I have chosen them for their possible relevance to Faulkes. For example, the idea of the spiral as a symbol of movement forward may have been particularly apposite at the beginning of his new married life. The pagan fertility rites connected to some labyrinths may also have chimed with his interest in agriculture and the fertility of the soil. Of course, it is not clear whether he could have known the full spectrum of this potential symbolism of the spiral, although he did possess an extensive library. This would be a useful area to research.

Labyrinths: Classic seven-ring labyrinth designs, which are stylised spirals, are found all over the world, for example, in Sardinia (c. 2500–2000 BC), South India (c. 1000 BC), northern Italy (c. 750–550 BC), and Egypt (30 BC). The oldest in Britain is the Hollywood Stone, c. AD 550. The best-known labyrinth story is of the Minotaur at Crete, a creature with a human body but a bull's head, which lived in an underground labyrinth, and was fed human sacrifices. The Athenian prince, Theseus, survived the labyrinth because he was given a golden thread by Ariadne, which he used to find his way out after slaying the Minotaur. The story may be a myth but

Cretan coins between 430–67 BC carried images of both the classic seven–ring labyrinth, as well as a square version.

Possible symbolism: In the Cretan myth the gold thread may symbolise the umbilical cord; the dark passages the vagina; the monster a symbol of male fear of female sexuality/castration. Historic labyrinths are also portrayed as forts, castles, defensive systems – again this can be seen as symbolic of male attitudes to female sexuality – something rigorously defended, something to be attacked and broken down. The maze also features in pagan ritual and carries sexual imagery – the person entering is the seed penetrating to the hidden centre, which emerges new born, purified or reincarnated. Mazes are associated in northern Europe with May-time ritual processions and races connected with fertility – for example, a girl is placed at the centre and two men race to reach her first.

The maze was adopted and sanitised by the Christian church to symbolise the Path of Life, and the difficult spiritual journey to salvation. Examples can be found in many European churches and cathedrals (eg Chartres, Lucca, Amiens).

Altered states: spirals are seen by people in trance-like states, generated by the confused human neural system. The subjects of near-death experiences or drug-induced altered states commonly describe travelling down a long passage, sometimes described as a spiral vortex.

Possible symbolism: Spirals appear in the passage-ways of burial chambers, such as the famous one at Newgrange in Ireland. The artists may have been trying to recreate the sense of the trance-like state in order to symbolise the temporary nature of death – the long sleep, from which you wake when you are reborn. Or the spirals may have been part of cere-monies designed to make contact with the ancestors through entering into death-like trances. Drug-induced trance-like states form an important part of religious experience in many cultures. For example, it has been suggested that the bright red clothes of Santa Claus are a sanitised symbol of the bright red fungi fly agaric, which was used by pre-Christians to induce ritualised out-of-body states, such as flying.

Astronomy: Spirals exist on rocks in the Phoenix Mountains, USA, at a site which is thought to have been a prehistoric solar observatory. Similarly, the spirals at Newgrange, Ireland, have been interpreted as part of a complex calendar, in which a spiral running clockwise represents the winter sun, anti-clockwise the summer sun, and a double spiral the equinox. At another prehistoric site in Sweden groups of small round shapes and a closely drawn spiral have been shown to match ancient patterns of the constellations during times of total eclipse – the spiral being a symbol of the eclipsed sun. Following this theme, it has recently been discovered that Silbury Hill, near Avebury, was constructed originally in spiral form, as part of the enormous religious site there which maps the journey of the sun through the year.

Possible symbolism: straightforward pictorial symbol of the sun. Given the significance of the sun in the lives of prehistoric man, it is not surprising that the spiral is found on Bronze-Age objects in a land corridor running from Greece through to Hungary, Germany, Denmark and beyond.

Rebirth: The three conjoined spirals, such as the one found in Ireland, are drawn using one single line, without beginning or end. Spirals were also engraved on the bows of Viking ships. Similar spiral images are connected with the Celts, and more recently have been used as the logo of the Celtic-based separatist movement in Brittany, France.

Possible symbolism: This form of spiral has been

described as the 'spiral of life', representing the never-ending cycle of life, death, rebirth. In the Viking version, it implies movement away, followed by eventual return, so that the journey in the ship became symbolic of life's journey. This idea of movement and migration is the root of its appeal to the Celts who were forced out of England to the border countries of Wales, Scotland, Cornwall, Ireland and Brittany.

Editor's note: Reader's thoughts on how these theories could be related to the Henry Faulkes portrait would be received with interest.

April

Put your last hand to the fruit trees to prepare them for the summer's service.

Mrs Martha Bradley

Ben and Ruby drove along the coast to visit Sheringham Park, a landscape also designed by Repton. Ben wanted to look at the temple there, which was based on Repton's original design, to make comparisons. From the car park they walked down a narrow lane hedged with towering rhododendron bushes coming into bud. At the end of the lane the landscape suddenly opened up into rolling green parkland, the sea on the horizon, with the modest grey brick house nestling in the lee of the hill. To the right a temple was perched on a man-made hillock. It was very simple. An open circle with slender columns and a domed roof. It had nothing of the glowering power which emanated from the Oakstead temple.

Ruby sat on the steps around the base of the temple, enjoying the view, while Ben spent several minutes investigating the structure of the temple, and the materials. Then he stood looking at Ruby's silhouette in between two columns and thought how much that familiar shape had come to mean to him. He sat down and hugged her.

'Do you think I'm a boring old twit, dragging you round

to look at obscure temples and rambling on all the time about dead vicars?'

Ruby smiled, and gave his hand a squeeze. 'No. Not boring. Verging on the obsessive, maybe.' She laughed at the face he made. 'But it must be catching, because I was just imagining sitting here with an eighteenth-century dress on, wondering what would have been happening in the fields and the house.'

'I would like to see you in one of those low-cut muslin dresses, I must say.'

'But I would've been some lowly peasant girl in a raggedy dress, and scarred with smallpox. You never would've noticed me.'

'What makes you think you would've been a peasant?'

'I think my family have always been sturdy peasants. Red hair. Big bones. I expect in the eighteenth century we were probably living in hovels and working on the land. I bet we wouldn't even have made it to maidservant status. So I don't suppose the Fitzmaurices would have given me the time of day.'

'Well, thank God we live in the twenty-first century, that's all I can say. What would've happened to me?'

'You would've been married off to a rich heiress who you didn't like, and then you would have created havoc amongst the servants.'

'Do you think so? Like Henry Faulkes? Don't you think I might have been a kindly landlord who looked after his people, and went to church every Sunday?'

Ruby smiled and said, 'I suppose you might have been. I suppose some people had happy marriages and lived exemplary lives.'

'They must have done. Have humans changed so much?'

'I don't know. Maybe because everything else was so different, I expect people to have been different too. I mean, the fact that two hundred years ago we couldn't have contemplated being together seems mad to us now. But then it would have been perfectly logical, and unquestioned.

242

How can we really understand the mindset of those people?'

They sat watching sprays of white cloud spreading over the bowl of the blue sky, and the sea turning indigo blue. Ruby turned to Ben.

'When I was at college, I had this fanciful idea, which I've never told anyone else.'

'Go on.'

'I was struck by the way things seemed to have appeared to people in the past. So often, you can tell what period a painting is from by the look of the people in it. Not just the clothes. The shape of the eyes, the expression. There's a medieval type, an eighteenth-century type. They look different to us, even when the artist was aiming for realism.' She paused. 'This sounds silly, now I'm saying it out loud.'

Ben made encouraging noises, so Ruby continued. 'Well, I started to think about the air they were breathing. How much purer, how much less breathed, less polluted, almost like liquid it might've been. It would probably be too rich for us. And I thought, maybe the quality of that air really made everything look more vivid, some kind of light-refraction process, which changed colours and perceptions. Sometimes I think the air is still like that at Oakstead, captured in the hollow of the hill.' She looked at Ben warily for his reaction.

He said, 'Well, it's an interesting idea. An artist's view of the world. There might be some truth in it, I suppose. But surely if people were different, it was because they knew much less about the outside world. They weren't jaded with the knowledge of every car crash, or murder, or melting glacier. It must have affected their outlook on life. I feel that it was a much more hopeful time. People still believed in progress. We couldn't recreate that innocence. We see everything with knowing eyes, through so many layers of knowledge and information. It's rather difficult to escape.'

243

They both contemplated the peaceful artifice spread out below them, wondering how they would have perceived it two hundred years ago.

Then Ruby said, 'Maybe that's why those men and women who got married out of duty, like Henry's wife, were able to put up with it – because they knew less about what was out there in the world. Now we're overwhelmed with possibilities. You know, this boyfriend or that boyfriend, this car, that car. It's so difficult to escape being dissatisfied, wondering if you've made the right choice. In the past, it must've been easier to come to terms with your lot, if there was absolutely no alternative.'

'Especially if you believed in God and heaven and a sweet afterlife.'

'They wouldn't understand us at all. We seem to be so unhappy, when we have so much more than they had.' Ruby sighed a deep sigh.

Ben put his arm round her. 'What's the matter?'

'Nothing really. I feel guilty that I have so much. That I have you, and an amazing house to live in, and the park. I can't get used to it.'

'Don't feel guilty. Try to think of the house as an albatross which will eat all our money, and perhaps you'll feel better. And don't feel guilty about having me. You're doing society a favour, taking me on.'

She smiled at him, and said, 'How come you and Charlie are so different? Why did you manage to come through public school so unscathed?'

Ben thought about this for a moment or two. 'Well, Charlie had rather a rough time. His parents were ghastly to him, and he was sent away to school when he was six. I only started boarding when I was a teenager, and I always came home at weekends. I didn't ever feel that my parents were trying to get rid of me. Charlie did, and with good reason, I think. You have to feel sorry for him.'

Ruby looked doubtful, but Ben continued.

'I know he's been behaving particularly badly the last few weeks, but I'm trying to give him a chance.'

'Why?'

'I never thought I would say this, but I'm beginning to think he's jealous.'

Ruby attempted to look unruffled by this statement. 'Jealous? What about?'

'Although he wouldn't admit it, I think he would like to be in a relationship like ours. I suspect his gigolo lifestyle is beginning to wear rather thin and, secretly, he would like to settle down. I can see him in a few years from now with a very suitable wife and two children, living in a farmhouse somewhere.'

Ruby made a sceptical noise. Ben turned to her. 'I've noticed some animosity between you two lately. What's it about?'

She panicked. 'Oh, you know. The usual stuff. His way with women. We had a bit of a set-to about it. Don't worry. I'm sure it'll blow over.'

Ben looked concerned and said, 'Do you want me to speak to him? I don't want him making you unhappy.'

'No.' Ruby tried to sound as emphatic as possible. 'It would only make things worse. Don't worry about it.'

She got up from the step and stretched, trying to screen her nervousness. Then she turned round to give Ben her hands, to help him up. They walked down the slope together and along Repton's approach, which still brought them to the best view despite the passing of two hundred years.

It's getting dark. I am shut up in our bedroom. When Ben is out, I feel safer here. I have just read the last page of Virginia Woolf's diaries. There is no mention of any visit to Oakstead, but still I can't help imagining her standing by the window gazing out at the moon-soaked garden. I feel more and more that the house is full of these old energies, caught inside its own atmosphere; thick layers of emotions sinking through liquid time, tugged down by gravity. Brief moments, like short, flickering, silent films, playing over and over. Woolf walking up to the window and experiencing intense loneliness; the soprano singer running across the garden, a joyous little girl; the novelist reading about the First World War, sitting in the dining room, enveloped in sadness. And Faulkes. He is leaning against a tree in the garden surveying his land, and wishing for immortality. His longing drenches everything he sees, it seeps into the earth. I shouldn't think about these things, fear circles me like a vulture. I will look for the beauty.

It is a very bright evening. The full moon is high up in the sky, and a gusting spring wind blows frail clouds across its face. I can see right across the park, dancing trees silhouetted against the gleam of the lake. A movement sensed in the corner of my eye makes me look down, there is a figure hurrying alongside one of the walled gardens. It's George. I recognise the way he moves, his long fluid legs, his head up straight. He has a sack on his back, weighing down one shoulder. On impulse, I put on my coat and go out to find him.

When I enter the walled garden, I can't see George at first. He is crouched down in the soil at the far end. I feel a moment of doubt. What could he be doing out here in the gathering dark? Something I should not see? The image of the crucified moles returns to me. Perhaps he is setting a trap, or burying a slaughtered animal. What was in the sack? I hesitate, and think of turning back, but he stands up and sees me, his shoulders flinching: Shit, Ruby. I thought you were a ghost!

He strides over and hugs me tightly, asks me what I'm doing out there. I ask him the same thing. He laughs and says he is planting seeds. According to his 'planting by the moon' calendar, this moment will be the best in the season for planting flowers. The full moon is in Libra, and moonrise was at seven o'clock. I don't understand him. He says planting is always best when the moon is waxing. As it

246

increases, so does the fertility of the soil. Sowing at moon-rise increases yield. And Libra is an air sign, so when the moon is there, you plant airy crops such as flowers, cauli-flowers, broccoli, artichokes. I ask him if he thinks it really works. He looks at me, a hint of exasperation in his eyes: Didn't you read the prof's book? It's all in there.

He steps away from me: Anyway. I need to get on. Do you want to help?

I nod, and follow him up to the other end of the garden. Here the soil has been dug and raked, and raked again, and now it looks like muscovado sugar, dark and slowly soft. He has marked out a straight line with twigs and twine, and he draws another stick along in the soil, parallel to the string, to make a shallow channel. Then he rustles around in a basket full of brown paper bags. He says: Look. These are the seeds I collected last year. You remember? Love-in-the-mist.

He holds my hand open, as he did last summer, and trickles the seed onto my palm. They look the same as they did before, but then they were dormant. If we had scattered them onto the soil, they would have failed. Somehow, inside this tiny little black speck something knows that now is the right time to grow. A transformation will take place.

George mixes the seeds in with a handful of sand taken from the sack. He says: This will help you to spread the seeds evenly, especially in the dark.

He shows me how to sprinkle the sand and seed along the row, holding my wrist, measuring my steps, so that I walk slowly and evenly. It feels nice, working side by side, staking out the lines for the rows together, trying to read the names of the seeds on the packets in the moonlight, mixing batches of seed up in the sand for each other. After working for an hour we sit down for a rest on a bench by the wall, under espalier trees. We don't speak, but listen to the wind rustling through the branches, whisking the clouds along, the whole sky moving. George holds my hand for a few moments, and then I hear the sound of tyres on the gravel. Ben is home. I squeeze George's hand goodbye, and then run round to the front of the house, and greet Ben as he gets out of the van. He looks tired. I tell him I've been helping George with seed planting, and I ask him if he wants to join in. He smiles at me: You carry on if you like. I need a hot bath. It's absolutely freezing in my workshop.

I turn to go back to George, and then change my mind: No. I'll come with you.

When the conservator's report on the wall paintings arrived, Ben and Ruby took it over to the temple to read it there. It was a cool bright spring day, breezes ruffling up the lake as they rowed over to the island. Inside, the temple seemed dark at first, and the paintings were barely discernible, but gradually their eyes became accustomed. Square windows high up in the walls directed beams of light onto the interior, almost like spotlights, shafting through the floating dust, lighting up painted areas. Ruby gazed up at them. 'Tell me what it says.'

Ben read out the first paragraph. '"The previously undocumented paintings uncovered in the temple at Oakstead Hall's park are a remarkable survival of a complete neoclassical cycle of Greek myths. It is believed that they were either executed by, or at least closely super-vised by, Henry Faulkes, the fifth Viscount Faulkes, and they represent the emergence of an important new talent of the period."' His eye ran down the rest of the page. 'Blah, blah, late eighteenth century, etc. This is all the stuff I told them.'

'What does it say about the actual paintings? This one for instance.'

Ben leafed through the report. 'Let's see. This is the south wall. Here we are: Apollo and Hyacinthus. "A large and muscular naked man stands behind a naked youth. The younger man holds a discus while the large man leans over from behind and holds his arm, as if he is instructing him how to throw it. These figures may represent Apollo teaching Hyacinthus to throw the discus. The landscape shows a green valley and gentle hills, with a temple in the middle-ground, identical to the Oakstead temple. In a frieze around the picture are sprigs of white blossom and green leaves."'

Ruby studied the painting. There was the face of Apollo, in profile, with his long straight nose, even white teeth, his red lips curled back in a smile. His head was close to Hyacinthus', as if he was whispering in his ear, his arm curved round, holding the wrist of the younger man, directing him to hold the discus properly. The men stood at the foreground of a landscape that drifted off in a haze of green hills, delicate trees, and singing birds. Small, but perfectly rendered, a copy of the temple at Oakstead stood in a splash of silvery lake in the distant perspective.

'What was the story of Apollo and Hyacinthus again?' Ruby asked.

'Apollo killed him by mistake, throwing a discus too hard.'

'Oh yes. And what about these other ones?'

Ben shifted round to face the next one. 'This is the east wall so it must be Dionysus and Ampelos. It says, "Dionysus, represented as a bearded man, naked, with extremely muscular thighs, and torso, is shown wrestling with a naked youth, Ampelos, who is smaller and more slender. The larger man has one arm on the youth's shoulder, the other round his waist. His leg is hooked over the younger man's legs, as if to trip him over and force him to the ground. Bunches of purple and green grapes hang in heavy abundance, framing the picture. In the background, the hills, outcrops of rock and small copses of trees are populated with numerous animals: birds, lions, elephants, deer, and a large bull. In a frieze around the picture are images of harvest: apples, berries, stooks of corn."'

'And what's the story behind it?'

Ben quickly read the rest of the page to himself. 'It says here that Ampelos was killed, too.'

'By Dionysus?'

'No. Ampelos befriended all the animals. Dionysus warned him not to trust the Bull. But Ampelos couldn't resist riding it, and was thrown off. Afterwards, he turned into the first vine, and his blood was transformed into red wine. Which explains the grapes.'

The light from the window shone on the ruby-red grapes, which framed the view. The two wrestling men were surrounded by daintily stepping deer, diminutive grey rabbits, a fox shadowy in a copse of trees, hawks spreading their wings across the creamy blue sky and, in the further distance, an enormous, full-chested, solid brown bull, grazing harmlessly. The men's legs were intertwined, and their faces were close together, determined looks in their eyes, as they tried to make the other fall. The muscles of Dionysus rippled down his arm, highlighted with thin lines of reflected sun, shiny and sweaty.

'I like this one,' Ruby murmured. 'I like the way the animals are drawn, dotted around in the meadow like flowers. And the bull looks like it was Henry's prize bull from the farm.'

'This one is so different,' said Ben, standing in front of the third scheme. 'Patroclus and Achilles. I know about this one. We did it at school. They fought together in the Trojan wars, and Achilles almost went mad with grief when Patroclus was killed. It's in the *Iliad*. Nearly drove me mad, reading it in Greek at school. It was rather gory though, which appealed at the time.'

'It's very monochrome. Like all the colour has drained out. What does the report say?'

'"A large and muscular man lies almost naked on his side on a raised platform bed. This is Patroclus, killed in the battle of Troy. Behind him Achilles, dressed in armour, leans over him, one hand to his head as if he is weeping. On the floor in the foreground lie a helmet, a shield and a broken spear. The background is plain and austere, with blank stone walls partly draped with sheets. Instead of a frieze, the picture is framed by a black line. The scheme adheres to the strict neoclassical form, using sombre tones, very limited use of colour, and primitive architectural settings."'

'It's beautifully done,' said Ruby. 'Whoever did these certainly knew how to paint the male body.'

Ben turned to the last page of the report, and read it silently. Then he exclaimed, 'Listen to this! "These paintings represent a find of national importance. The quality of execution is high. In particular, the east wall painting is a fine example of neoclassical work. The survival of the entire cycle of paintings in relatively good condition is remarkable. In addition, the likelihood that both the temple and the paintings were designed and possibly executed by Henry Faulkes makes this one of the most important examples of neoclassical art to have been discovered in the last decade."' He looked up at Ruby. 'And if English Heritage had had their way, they'd still be hidden!'

They hugged each other, then Ben read the report again. After a few minutes he put the report down and took Ruby's hand. 'What I don't understand is, if Henry Faulkes was the painter, why don't we know of any other paintings by him?'

Ruby stood gazing at the face of Patroclus. 'Perhaps it's just because, up until now, no one thought he could paint like this. Now you've found this new information, it might be possible to start attributing other paintings to him. It could throw a whole new light on the stuff at Henford.'

'That's true! That would make a superb article. I'm close to getting enough information about all this to publish something in a proper journal.'

Ruby suggested to Ben that they should send a copy of the conservator's report to Professor Lal. Ben didn't agree.

'I don't want all and sundry to know I've uncovered them.' He let go of her hand.

'But he wouldn't tell anyone. He wants to keep it a secret too.'

251

'Yes, until he publishes them, and takes all the credit,' Ben retorted.

'Ben!' Ruby stood with her hands on her hips. 'You're being very childish about this. If you were being fair, you'd remember that it was the professor that set you on the right track in the first place, and he *has* apologised about not being straight with us. I think, if you shared things with him, he might tell us all sorts of stuff we haven't found out yet.'

'That's the point though! I want to find it out for myself.'

They brooded in silence for a few minutes, Ruby looking up at one of the windows, letting the sun soothe her face. Eventually Ben muttered,

'I'll send it to him in a week or two. When I've had a chance to really think about what the paintings mean. All right?'

Ruby's face broke into a smile. 'OK.'

That evening, Ben posted a copy of the report to Jayne Greene, with a note:

You are very welcome to come down and see the paintings any time. I'd appreciate your thoughts. Regards.

Draft of *The Lost Eden: sexualised landscapes of the eighteenth century*
by Professor A. Lal. (Excerpt 1)

One remarkable aspect of the neoclassical movement was its internationalism. All across western Europe from the mid-eighteenth century onwards there was a general revulsion against the baroque in the arts, together with a desire to return to pure forms and noble themes; what contemporaries called the 'true style'. This was a youthful, fiery and rebellious movement, with young artists railing against the blowsy and corrupt interpretations their predecessors

252

had produced of the eternal classical themes. It became an international movement, firstly because influential works such as Winckelmann's *Thoughts on the Imitation of Greek Works in Painting and Sculpture* (1755) were translated very rapidly and therefore became available to a very wide audience. Secondly, there was an unprecedented marketplace for both the philosophies and the products of this new movement, in the city which had become the honey pot for the swarming aristocracy: Rome. Nearly every artist of any importance spent some years in Rome in this period, studying the antiquities, and producing work influenced by their sojourn there. At the same time, the aristocracy of every European nation went to Rome to complete their education and were therefore exposed to the new 'true style' which they seemed to dutifully adopt and take home.

The role of Nature was central to the neoclassical movement. It was used to define, explain and excuse all aspects of life. In general Nature was seen as the ideal, as something which could be understood universally. But there were many tangential theories connected to this central one. In the same way that neoclassical art was regarded by its exponents as the 'true style' which sprung from Nature, and therefore cut across passing trends, some neoclassical philosophers argued that all sexual appetite was also a function of Nature, and superior to transient notions of morality. It should not surprise us then to find a movement in the eighteenth century which attempted to recreate the idyllic, classical portrayals of Nature evoked by Homer and Virgil, which had formed the backdrop to, and context for, the sexual freedom experienced by the ancient Greeks.

Sexual relationships, untrammelled by any moral structure, are the norm in ancient Greek mythology. The gods have sex with men, women, children; with their sisters, mothers and daughters; with mortals and gods; disguised as bulls, swans and snakes. However, the quality of these sexual relationships is governed by the gender of the sexual partner. Few of the women, particularly amongst mortals, have what we might call meaningful relationships with the fathers of their children. Most male/female sex is characterised by rape. Women are swept down from upon high and impregnated, or they are attacked by gods disguised as animals, or they are intoxicated by streams of wine. Sexual relationships between men, and between men and gods, in contrast, are characterised by friendship, admiration and a noble camaraderie. The theme seems to be that women are a necessary interruption for the sake of reproduction, but that the significant arena for qualitative relationships is between males. We have Apollo and Hyacinthus, Dionysus and Ampelos, Pylades and Orestes, Heracles and Iolaus, Theseus and Peirithous, Achilles and Patroclus. It is between such men that we witness loyalty, sacrifice, and a true meeting of minds. It is this legacy which was so appealing to English men of taste in the latter half of the eighteenth century.

It is generally accepted that the landscaped parks of this period were an attempt to bring alive the literary landscape embodied in classical texts. A well-known example can be found at the caves at West Wycombe in England, home of the so-called 'Hellfire Club'. Here, Sir Francis Dashwood created a symbolic landscape of Heaven and Hades during the second half of the eighteenth century. A steep hill, topped with a church, and a vast classical mausoleum, was excavated below to create a maze of caves. At the lowest level the last cave is divided from the others by a river. This is the River Styx, named after the river in Greek mythology, which divided this world from the Underworld. It is in this cave that the meetings of the infamous Hellfire Club may have taken place, including devil worship, and ritual sex.

It is my belief that these types of landscape were explicitly designed as part of an aristocratic cult of the erotic, which was widespread during the latter part of the eighteenth century, rooted in a profound belief in the supremacy of the classical period.

There was a strong belief that the ancient Greeks had produced the perfect society, with the most beautiful people. After its collapse, society had degenerated, resulting in uglier people with uglier lives. One aspect of this ancient society which, I believe, made it so attractive to the eighteenth-century art lover was its acceptance of homosexuality. In fact, ritualised same-sex relationships were at the very centre of classical social life. Rather than dividing the population into male and female, society was divided into passive and active sexual roles. There were three passive roles: woman, slave, adolescent male.

It is well known that Winckelmann, founder of modern artistic criticism, was a practising homosexual. This deeply influenced his approach to art and led him to believe that homosexual desire was at the root of artistic achievement in antiquity. Indeed he describes, with a great sense of nostalgia, how the ancient Greek gymnasiums where 'youths exercised themselves naked', were also the schools of art:

Here beautiful nakedness appeared with such a liveliness of expression, such truth and variety of situations, such a noble air of the body, as it would be ridiculous to look for in any hired model of our academies.

Male visitors to the gymnasiums were, of course, also viewing sexual exhibits. It was part of an adolescent boy's rite of passage to be taken as a lover by a male

255

adult. The beauty of a youthful boy was an accepted given, and as Diderot said in 1765, desire in ancient Greece was not divided into hetero or homo but was, rather, a homage to beauty in whatever form.

Winckelmann's homosexuality led him to spend a large proportion of his time in Italy, which was considered the home of sodomy. Other well-known homosexuals such as William Beckford, who fled England in the 1780s after a well-documented affair with an adolescent boy; and Payne Knight, who published his book on the phallic symbolism of ancient cults, *The Worship of Priapus*, in 1785, found welcome sanctuary in the more tolerant climes of southern Europe. Indeed, it would not be going too far to describe the Grand Tours undertaken by the English aristocracy as an early form of organised sexual tourism for which there was a large and enthusiastic market.

At the very end of this period, in 1809, we witness Lord Byron preparing to travel abroad specifically to visit the sites of classical history and to obtain access to the sexual freedom still available there. From Falmouth, where he is waiting for his ship, he writes, using a code based on classical myth:

We are surrounded by Hyacinths and other flowers of the most fragrant nature & I have some intention of culling a handsome Bouquet to compare with the exotics we expect to meet in Asia.

This use of the name of Apollo's lover, Hyacinthus, as a code to describe young gay men, has a precedent, in other letters exchanged between young aristocrats of the 1790s, and can therefore be taken as an indication of a sub-culture operating for some years at the turn of the eighteenth and nineteenth centuries.

Byron's well-documented sexuality gives a useful

insight to the predominant sexual practices within the small aristocratic clique of this period. He passed through a panoply of sexual liaisons – a sustained sexual relationship with his sister; a notorious passionate and destructive affair with Caroline Lamb; a marriage; a *ménage à trois* with Clare Claremont and Shelley; and numerous encounters with young men and female prostitutes. In the last weeks of his life he was still falling for Greek youths. He epitomises the idealised Greek citizen, of a type worshipped by aristocratic members of the cult that also created the landscaped parks of the eighteenth century.

May

This is the season when the housekeeper begins to
prepare for distilling. Plants are in their fullest perfection when they have grown up in their height and are
budding for flower. Some of them will be just in that
condition at this season. . .

*The British Housewife; or the Cook, Housekeeper's
and Gardiner's Companion* 1756
Mrs Martha Bradley

The ringing telephone woke Ben up. He recognised Jayne's
throaty voice immediately.

'Ben? Look. I've suddenly got a free couple of days and
I wondered if I could come and see the paintings. It's the
first chance I've had. What do you think?'

Ben could think of no reason why not, although he felt
uncomfortable about Ruby and Jayne being in the same
room. Ruby might be able to tell. But he said, 'Yes, of
course. You must come and stay.'

'Oh, good. Well, I'm at Derby station now, so I'll be
with you this afternoon.'

It was only afterwards, when he woke up properly, that
he remembered the wedding bed had been installed in the
temple the night before. To prevent any chance of Ruby
going over to the temple and seeing his creation, he had
hidden the rowing boat in the wood. He spent the whole of

the morning wondering feverishly how he was going to get Jayne over to the temple and prevent Ruby coming.

Jayne arrived in a taxi just after lunch. Ruby and Ben were still sitting in the kitchen drinking coffee. He felt hot and self-conscious as he introduced the two women to each other. They shook hands and Ruby started to make more coffee, but Jayne said she had already had too much caffeine on the train. Ben showed her to her room, and she came down ten minutes later looking fresher, with one of her short skirts on, and the stripy tights.

'Shall we go and see the paintings?' she asked.

Ruby, who was sitting at the kitchen table, looked up from the magazine she was flicking through, appraised Jayne and glanced at Ben. Then she looked down at her magazine again, saying, 'You two go. I've got things to sort out, phone calls to make.'

Ben tried to look disappointed, but inwardly thanked God. 'Oh, OK. That's a shame.' He clapped his hands, just like his father used to, when it was time to get moving. 'Right then, Jayne. Let's go.'

They started to walk through the meadow down to the lake.

'Nice place you've got here. My house would fit into your kitchen.'

'Yes, I'm very lucky.' Ben was stiff with self-consciousness.

She gave him a sidelong glance. 'Ruby seems nice.'

'Yes, she is.'

'Come on, Ben.' She poked him with her elbow. 'It's fine.' She was smiling her sparkling smile at him. 'Let's talk about the paintings.'

He managed to return a weak smile. 'Yes, let's. The thing is we'll have to get the rowing boat out first. I've hidden it up in the wood.'

On the previous evening George had helped Ben pull the wooden rowing boat up the track from the lake into the wood, after dark, when there was no danger of Ruby seeing. They had hidden it inside a thicket of dark fir trees, and covered it with brushwood. Now he and Jayne had to pull all the branches off again, and drag the boat back down the lane. It was heavy, and kept jamming on bits of flint sticking out of the track. They got hot and sweaty; Ben was constantly alarmed that Ruby would come and find them, and wonder what on earth they were doing. By the time they reached the bank of the lake, he was trembling with nervous tension. He rowed in silence. Jayne sat on the bench at the back of the boat, eyeing him quizzically. After a minute she said, 'You certainly know how to show a girl a good time.'

Ben grimaced. 'I know. Sorry.'

When they reached the island Ben leaped out, moored the boat, then offered his hand to her. She took it, but as he pulled her up she lost her balance, he staggered, and then stepped on her foot. He spluttered, 'Oh God. Sorry.' They stood looking at each other, slightly breathless. Then she brushed herself down, and said, 'Come on then. These paintings better be good.'

They entered the temple. Sun shafted in through the high windows onto the paintings, lighting up the gods and the idealised landscapes. But Jayne didn't notice these at first.

'Bloody hell! That's a bed and a half.' She sat on the pristine white covers, which Ben had put on the night before. He remained just inside the door, his hands sitting awkwardly on his hips, avoiding her gaze. The bed seemed to loom very large in the confined space of the temple. He hadn't noticed before. She patted the bedspread beside her, inviting him to sit down, but he said, 'No, thanks, I'm fine standing.'

She laughed at him. 'For Christ's sake, Ben. Stop being so stiff upper lip. What do you think I'm going to do?'

'Well, I don't . . . I mean, I wasn't . . . ' He was mortified. Of course! Why would she be interested in him, what had he been thinking? Making her out to be some sort of predator, after his flesh. The truth was it was his own

260

desire he saw reflected in her face, his own arousal that made him feel this sexual charge between them. She was a professional academic, schooled in discussing all manner of licentious texts in an esoteric, abstracted way. That is all that had happened in the pub. But he had shown himself to be a hopeless amateur, unable to keep his mind on an intellectual plane. Instinctively, his hands went up to cover his face, but then he translated the movement into a less emotional response, and wiped the sweat from his forehead.

'Sorry. I'm rather all over the place at the moment. Too much to do.'

He sat down next to her on the bed, and she turned to him and kissed him full on the lips.

I am going through the list of things to do for the wedding, which Gretta has sent me. I have to ring her friend the dressmaker, to arrange the final fitting. I have to arrange for the florists to visit the cutting garden here, to choose the flowers. I have to remember to have my hair dressed. The caterers want a decision on which puddings we require, which wine, how much champagne, and the final number of guests. The list is endless and pointless. All I want is for Ben and me to be safely on the other side of the wedding, to be married, to have said our vows, and to be beyond malice. I feel like a shroud of mist is around my head, a thin grey veil of anxiety, always there in the corner of my eye. What if Charlie is still planning some dreadful denouement? He is quite capable of something vicious. He is not in his right mind, so ridden with drugs and drink he is completely unpredictable. When Ben is not here I seek out George in the garden and sit where I can see him as he weeds, pricks out seedlings, and rigs up great frames for beans and peas. Sometimes I help him. Working together in the shelter of the walled garden brings me moments of respite, when I can feel that things will be all right. That George and I will be able to live side by side, knowing about how we feel. That Charlie will fade away.

Sometimes, when we are quite sure we are alone, George will hold my hand, or put his arm round my shoulder as we inspect our work. These moments are painfully sweet to me, like the last few days of summer.

I want to turn to Ben for comfort but he is never here. He is either up at his workshop, or writing down his thoughts on Faulkes and the paintings, doing more research, organising the wedding, or rushing around delivering vegetables. I wonder if he has really thought about what is going to happen in a few days' time? We will be the centre of attention, all those eyes on us, looking for palpable love, united souls. It is many weeks since I have felt that connection properly. We have lost the innocent pleasure of eating lunch together, talking idly about nothing. After the wedding, perhaps.

I drop the list of chores onto the table and gaze out of the window. There are Ben and Jayne Greene disappearing into the woods, distant figures, silent and shadowed. Should I be suspicious? She is obviously attractive, and has something about her, a pent-up energy, like a cork in a bottle. Ambition, I suppose. But I cannot muster any jealousy. Ben is probably just showing her around the estate in his polite way, telling her the whole story. Despite his preoccupations, I know he loves me.

After Ben and Jayne had dragged the boat back into the wood, and hidden it again, they were covered in dust and bits of twig. They hurried back to the house, and Jayne went off to have a bath. Then Ben realised he was supposed to be meeting up with George to discuss the vegetable orders for the coming week. After he had changed his shirt, he jogged over to the lodge. As he walked up the path to the door he heard shouting: George and another voice. Ben realised with a sinking feeling that the other voice was that of Professor Lal. He had hoped that man had gone away for good. The last thing he wanted now was for the professor to be snooping around the estate, finding out about the paintings. Especially with Jayne up at the house.

He couldn't catch what was being said as the two angry voices intermingled but he stood paralysed by the front door, wondering what to do. After a couple of minutes of incomprehensible yelling, the men seemed to have exhausted themselves and there was a moment's silence. Then the door into the hall opened and Ben heard Professor Lal say:

'Look, George. I am only trying to help you. You go too far. What you are doing is not right or fair. I cannot be associated with it. I am going out now.'

Ben heard steps coming down the hallway towards the door and, in a panic, rang the bell as if he had just arrived. The professor opened the door, looking shaken. There was sweat on his forehead, and his face was flushed.

'Mr Fitzmaurice! How nice to see you again. Do you wish to speak to George? Please come in. I was just on my way out.'

He brushed passed Ben and hurried away down the path. Then George appeared.

'Ben! Come in! I was expecting you.'

'What's the professor doing here? Have you told him about the paintings?'

George had his back to Ben, walking back down the hall to the kitchen. 'No, of course not. You told me not to. He's got a bee in his bonnet about something else. Don't worry about it.'

'But I *am* worried. Being on the estate, he's bound to get a look at the paintings.'

George turned round and looked Ben in the eye. 'Not without a boat. Anyway, does it really matter? You've found them, and they're stunning. Why shouldn't other people be allowed to see them now? The prof may be annoying sometimes but, it has to be said, he is honest. He won't pretend to have found stuff if you found it first. He knew the paintings were there, anyway. He's always very

263

nice about you. Why can't you give him a bit of slack?'

Ben stood amazed at this short outburst, but then found his voice.

'Now hang on a minute. "Nice"? He's been secretive all the way along, as well as leching over Ruby and writing mad notes.'

'What do you mean?'

'Oh, I found one of those New Year wishes things and it said something weird about Ruby on it.'

'What makes you think it was the prof who wrote it?' George smiled quizzically at Ben. 'It could've been anyone at that party. It was more likely Charlie.'

'Charlie! Why would he write anything like that? He and Ruby don't even get on.'

'Well, you're probably right. Forget I said it.'

'Let's change the subject.'

Ben was really shaken by this conversation. He had become used to George's mildly grumpy attitude towards him over the months, but this direct attack shocked him. With a sinking feeling, he recognised that his obsession with the paintings had not brought out his best side. He knew Ruby thought he was being unreasonable. Now the professor was here, wouldn't it be better to show the paintings to him in a grand gesture, rather than trying to keep them hidden? These thoughts ran through his mind, as he discussed with George the vegetable orders for a hotel in Holt. In mid-sentence, he said, 'Where was the professor going?'

'I don't know. He's left all his stuff here, so he'll have to come back. He's probably just gone for a walk to cool down.'

In normal circumstances, Ben might have tried to wheedle out of George what the argument had been about, but now he was too preoccupied with the whereabouts of the professor. He wanted to prevent Lal and Jayne encountering into each other, so he wound up the meeting and hurried back to the house.

He found Professor Lal in the kitchen with Ruby. She explained how they had bumped into each other as she returned from the village shop, and that she had invited him back for tea.

'Good! I was looking for you!'

'You were?' Professor Lal looked rather anxious.

'Yes. Look. I want to be straight with you. You may know this already, but I want to tell you. I've uncovered the paintings in the temple.'

Ruby and the professor exchanged glances before Ruby spoke up.

'I should've told you. I sent the professor a copy of the report a couple of weeks ago. He promised he wouldn't tell anyone else about it, and I believed him. I hope you don't mind.'

She winced, expecting Ben to be furious. But instead he stood looking blank for a moment, then rubbed his hands up his face and pushed his hair back, in a gesture of resignation.

'It was probably the right thing to do.' He turned to Professor Lal. 'Is that why you're here?'

The professor put his head to one side. 'One of the reasons, I must admit. I hope you will be generous enough to let me see the paintings. Are they good?'

Ben's face lost its slight frown, and his eyes lit up. 'They're amazing. In fact, now that you're here and it's all out in the open, you must have a look at them.'

Ruby interrupted. 'What have you done with Jayne? Is she still on the island?'

'No, she's upstairs, having a bath.' Ben felt himself blush.

The professor asked hesitantly, 'Is it perhaps possible for us to go to the island now?'

Ben felt exhausted at the very thought of dragging the rowing boat anywhere else that day. He quickly thought of an excuse.

'Well, actually, the rowing boat's out of action since this

afternoon.' He turned back to Ruby. 'It sprung a leak on the way back. We got soaked. That's why Jayne's upstairs.'

Lal took this disappointment surprisingly well. 'So no one can get to the temple today?'

'No, sorry.' Ben embroiled himself further in his lie. 'Perhaps tomorrow we could borrow something to get us across. I know someone in the village who has a canoe.'

The professor looked happy. 'I will look forward to it. But tell me, who did you use to uncover the paintings?'

Just then Jayne came in to the kitchen. She stopped abruptly when she saw the Professor. 'Oh, sorry. I didn't mean to barge in.'

Ben did not like the combination of Ruby, Jayne and Lal all in the same room together. He had the feeling of the floor falling away from under him as he tried to remember which story he had told who about the rowing boat, the paintings, and his research. Ruby filled the awkward silence by introducing Lal to Jayne. She said, 'I understand Jayne has been doing her own research on the park.'

Lal stiffened, and his smile was weak. 'Is that so?'

Jayne nodded, her face equally defensive, and serious. 'Yes, though I believe in quite a different area to your interests.'

'So Ben has told you something of my work?' Lal turned his gaze on Ben.

Ben laughed nervously. 'Your reputation goes before you, Professor. Jayne knows your work very well.'

'I see. And I can tell from your expression, Miss Greene, that you are not very impressed.'

Jayne bristled. 'It's *Dr* Greene, actually. And it's not a personal thing, it's a difference of ideology.'

'You do not approve of my methods.'

She gave a short shake of her head. 'It's not a matter of approving. I disagree from a purely theoretical standpoint.'

'Which is?'

Ruby interrupted them. 'Would you all like a drink? I'll open some wine. Why don't you sit down?'

266

Obediently, Lal and Jayne sat down at the kitchen table. Ben found the glasses, and Ruby uncorked the bottle. They stood by the sink together for a moment and she raised her eyebrows at him. He shrugged silently in response and made a face, which said: There's nothing I can do to stop them.

As they sat down, Lal turned to Jayne. 'Now, you were going to tell me, I think, what your theoretical standpoint is.' He said 'theoretical' as if it was a rude word.

'OK.' Jayne gulped some wine. 'Your book on garden myths is based on the premise that stories can be treated as legitimate sources of historical inquiry. To me, that makes a mockery of historical research.' Her voice became less husky as she got into her stride. 'For an ordinary reader, it creates this dangerous situation where stories and histories are completely interchangeable.'

Lal gave a slight nod. 'And why do you think this is dangerous, may I ask?'

'Well, for example, the intermingling of fact and fiction makes it difficult to argue against revisionist historians who claim that the Holocaust is a myth invented by Zionist propaganda!'

Lal put his hands to his head in mock pain. 'You see, you miss the point entirely! It is like this. Much of the so-called objective history which emerges from educational establishments is nothing more than myth. Do you know where the word *myth* comes from?' Ben muttered something about it being Greek, but Jayne was non-committal. Ruby was gazing out of the window, not listening. Lal continued. 'It is from the Greek, *mythos,* and it describes an authoritative pronouncement. Its authority requires people to accept its truth without question. A myth, you see, is any set of unexamined assumptions. Just this kind of uncritical acceptance of alleged historical truths has led to the rise of modern myths such as the denial of early civilisations in Africa, white supremacy, and the notion of progress. Disastrous!'

267

Jayne interjected. 'Yes, but that was propaganda. It wasn't based on fact. It denied the facts.'

'Surely you have read Foucault on the "regimes of truth"?' Lal sounded exasperated. He turned to Ben. 'It is clear. The history you study is entirely dependent on who is in charge of information. This prescribes the limits of what is knowable or sayable. It robs the minority cultures of their voice. This is the most dangerous thing for society, don't you agree?'

Ben was confused. He grasped at something he knew a bit about. 'But it's true, what Jayne said. Your attitude allows those right-wing historians to argue that the Holocaust was a myth. How can you argue against them if you say everything is a myth?'

Jayne continued the point. 'Yeah. You're saying that the terrible pain and suffering of every man, woman and child gassed, shot or tortured under Hitler has no more legitimacy as a true event than the scribblings of an unknown storywriter.'

Lal sat back in his chair, and let out a long sigh. 'Can you not see what I am saying to you?' They looked at him blankly. Ruby stood up and went over to the sink, and began chopping vegetables. Lal leaned forward with his arms on the table. He spoke rapidly, as if it were urgent that they get the message. 'Listen. It is like this. The Aryan doctrine at the centre of Hitler's ideology was a prime example of a myth becoming absorbed as fact into a society's psyche. It was done through the manipulation of systems of authority, and through the failure to scrutinise unexamined assumptions. The revisionist stance on the Holocaust is a similar attempt to create a new myth. My aim is to alert society to the dangers of prejudice presented as history. The Holocaust happened within the living memory of many people, and is recorded on film, and through the testimonies of millions of ordinary people. That makes it difficult for myth-makers to gain credence at the moment. But how do you think people will view this part of the world's past in a hundred years' time?' He did not wait for a reply, but tapped the table with a pointed finger as he answered his own question. 'It will depend entirely on who is in control of the truth.'

They all sipped their wine and thought about this for a moment, but Jayne was not beaten yet. 'What I don't like about your stance is your assertion that it's not possible to be objective. I agree it's necessary to be conscious of context, but all serious historians are aware of that. Everyone knows that the texts they're studying will have been influenced by the personal politics of the writer. That's why it's worth re-examining events in history over and over, checking previous assumptions. Isn't it?'

Lal put his hands up to his mouth, in his praying motion. 'All right. Consider this. Yesterday morning I saw an advertisement on a billboard for a new car. The style of the text, the colours, the shape of the car, its background of urban streets and skyscrapers, all of this signified to me that it was utterly contemporary and of the moment.' He smiled encouragingly at them. 'To understand this I needed to have lived a whole life assessing the different shapes of cars, absorbing the subtlety of changing fashions in colours, lifestyles, modern living requirements and so on. So much so that if in two years' time I came across that advert again I would perceive it as out of date. Indeed, I will never be able to look at that advertisement again with the same sensation of its modernity as I did yesterday morning. So how can I possibly believe I can understand the nuances of meaning, the subtleties of symbolism in a historical document or artefact made several hundred years ago? How can I stand in the maker's shoes?'

Ruby's interest was caught. She stopped chopping and turned towards the table. 'That's true. The way we see things can never be isolated from our life experiences. We probably absorb a million things subconsciously every day and it's all stored in there somewhere, colouring what we feel, or how we react to things. I don't know so much about history, but without those subtexts, art would be just a dull reproduction of life. We wouldn't have impressionism, or cubism, or poetry, or ballet.'

Lal was nodding vigorously, but before he could say anything, Jayne spoke.

'But I don't see history as comparable with art. History is more akin to science – there are facts, there are events and consequences of events.' Her voice had entirely lost its huskiness. 'It's OK for artists to be intuitive. Historians have to rise above the personal and look at the facts.'

Lal snorted. 'But again, you do not give sufficient weight to the problems of language, and that is why you believe in the possibility of objectivity. Do you really still suppose that it is possible for language to refer to some kind of independent world of facts, untainted by the mind of the reader? Are you so naïve?' Lal was becoming agitated, his hands waving around. Jayne tried to reply, but he spoke over her. 'No! *No one* has the key to meaning. There is no natural relationship between thought and word. Between the one and the other there is a chasm full of different possible interpretations.'

Feeling mildly snubbed by Jayne, Ruby was only half listening again. She had finished chopping the vegetables ready for supper and she stood drying her hands on a towel, looking out of the window. It was a beautiful evening, very still. She took her glass of wine, and stepped through the French doors to the steps outside, where she sat and looking down at the glimmering lake. Out there she could not hear the arguing voices. The serene beauty of this park on such a gentle May night made her cry. In a few days' time, she would be married, and everything would be different. Nostalgia and sentimentality churned inside her. She walked down the steps onto the lawn. Out of the corner of her eye she noticed a wash of pink: the apple blossom in the orchard, just catching the evening sun, transformed into pearly stained glass.

May 1st

Beltane. A year's full cycle. The long wait is over, our time has come. The moment of consummation when all of life, smouldering under the earth, is ignited once again. The Sun God delves down into the quiet chambers of the earth and lets loose the spark of life. The warmth of that pure flame licks around the slumbering world and melts away the death of winter. The friction of their union kindles a consuming fire. This is the evening when all men and women should go into the woods and make love. The seeds sown will encourage the goddess, and she will show life how to burgeon and multiply. As she ripens, so will the flowers bloom, and the trees will hang heavy with fruit.

New life is about to begin. There is a sacred bed for our union, a pure white altar for our devotional sacrament. My body is consumed with the creative fire. I will go now to find her and give her the gift of life.

I am standing in the orchard, in amongst the pink-blushed blossom, watching the light percolate through the branches as the sun goes down. An intoxicating smell of tropical islands wafts down from the heath, the buttery coconut smell of yellow gorse flowers. I close my eyes and inhale. An owl screeches, a pheasant squawks. The silence around these outbursts is intense. The night is filtering down through the trees and creeping down the hill, but the lake at the bottom of the meadow is still a bright mirror. The white temple gleams on the island. I can see no evidence of modern life. No telegraph wires, or pylons, no roads. I can't hear any traffic. I could be standing in the landscape of Henry Faulkes. He might be inside the house eating his dinner at the great table, his wife perched at the other end, attended by servants. Or perhaps he is writing to his friend in Italy, telling him about the triumph of his new temple. He may even be in the temple admiring his work. Perhaps he is not alone there. On a night like this, the temple would be the perfect place for a lovers' tryst. His wife? Or a lover from the village?

He would saunter out through the French doors after dinner, leaving his wife to embroider, or sew or read by the fire. He would breathe in the fresh night air and imagine himself in the magical land of Arcadia. He would hear the distant clanging of cowbells on the herd grazing in the meadow, and imagine the goatherds in ancient Greece, clattering down the mountainsides, their bells ringing out through the gloaming. He would sense the barley and wheat in his fields, burgeoning in the rich loamy soil, quenched with soft spring rain, warmed by the primrose spring sun. He would walk down to the lake through the water meadows, past the dark shapes of the cows and their bull. Then he would step into the punt at the side of the lake and quietly push himself across to the island. Inside, someone waits for him, nervous, excited, expectant. The door creaks open, letting in a small ray of dusty, dwindling light. The silhouette of a tall, muscular man, and then the door shuts and it is dark...

And then there are arms tight around me, I hear the scream of adrenalin pump through my arms and legs, the impulse to run. A voice in my ear: Ruby. It's OK. It's me.

I turn in the circle of arms, and see George. I say: For God's sake! I thought you were—

I nearly say Faulkes, but feel silly, and stop myself.

George doesn't reply. He puts his hand behind my head and pulls my face to his and kisses me. And keeps kissing me. The kiss goes right down into the centre of me and starts up a thirst. I cling to him, and drink his kisses, as if he is a dark well of water and I have been lost in the desert. He is ice-cold water on a hot, blistering day. Lime and sharp lemon zest amongst dusty sand and parched treeless plains. The ice cubes slide on my tongue, they are crushed against my teeth, they cool my aching throat. The thought that Ben may look down from his study and see our shadows in the moonlight flickers through my head, but I can't stop. My body has become enmeshed in his and my thirst is unquenchable. I want to lie down, to feel pressed into the earth, to get him as close to me as possible. My legs are weak. I tug him, but he resists. He says: Come with me.

I follow him out of the orchard. We are walking round the side of the house, across the meadow, down to the lake. I can see the rowing boat, nuzzled into the bank, not leaking, not sinking, magically complete. He leads me to it and we climb in. He rows across the water, we slide through the liquid silver. And now we are walking to the door of the temple. The door is ajar; there is a glimmer of light. I step inside and pass into another world.

All around the floor are a myriad of candles forming a path that leads to a bed. But bed is too prosaic a word. It is a ship in full spate, with sails of white silk billowing around its masts. It is carrying a cargo of abundance, fruit, flowers, wheat, barley. Inside the gossamer curtains there is a pristine white sheet of silk, and plump white cushions all scattered with apple blossom. I can see branches of white lilac standing in a huge vase at the head of the bed and they scent the air: sweet, musky, piercing. On the floor by the bed there is a bowl of liquid spangled with delicate white flowers. George fills a wine glass from the bowl and tells me to drink it. It is syrupy, a melting potion of wine and flowers, seeping into my senses. He stands behind me, his head buried in my neck, his hands on my breasts. He says: Let's not wait any longer.

His breath travels through my ear and into my body with the intensity of a drug injected into my bloodstream. I don't know why he has decided we can do this, but I don't care. I am so glad to be able to let go. His hands are persuasive, luxuriant. He picks me up and lays me on the cool, silken sheet. He unties my hair and spreads it across the pillows, taking up tresses and kissing them. He carefully removes all my clothes and stands looking at me. I am strangely unabashed, excited by the glimmer in his eye. He stands

273

watching me as he slowly takes off his clothes. He looks like the image of Apollo flickering on the wall behind him. Now he kneels on the bed and sprinkles me with blossom. The petals land lightly on my stomach, slightly moist against my hot skin, like cool fingertips. He kisses me and we are at the start of a long, sweet journey. My body is a vessel of ambrosia, which runs in floods from my head to my toes. I feel the relief of letting this love flow out. My body relinquishes all fear and suspicion and opens to him in full trust. I hunger, I thirst, I invite him to replenish me, salve the longing, soothe my need. The scent of him drenches my senses, I am feasted with honey and cream. Shimmering nectar on my skin wherever he touches me. Heat and moving shadows engulf me. He plays with me, persuading me with his warm fingers, moulding me, teasing me. He fills me with suffused heat, I am drawn up and recede like quicksilver mercury. He whispers, warm breath against my ear: The moment is coming. Give yourself up.

And now we approach the lip of the hill. I am caught in the vortex, it sucks me up with the clouds, the sky, the ground, condensing it into a single point, a concentration of all matter into one atom. A moment, a split second of terrified anticipation. Now. White light. Everything shatters. Molten honey. Sugar rain. Warm red rivulets of wine.

Ben, Jayne and Professor Lal adjourned to the study to re-examine the report on the paintings. The atmosphere was frosty. Jayne and Lal had not been able to agree on anything. Ben desperately tried to diffuse the situation, making polite conversation, but his words fell into empty pools of silence. Jayne sat in an armchair, flicking through the report. Lal stood by the desk while Ben searched through a pile of paper.

'I've got some photos of the paintings here you might like to look at.'

Lal shook his head and put up his hand. 'No, thank you. I would prefer to feel the full impact of the paintings in real life, undiluted by previous knowledge of the images.'

There was a slight 'humph' noise from Jayne, but she did not raise her head. Lal continued to direct himself to Ben.

'You see, the choice of subject for the paintings supports everything I have come to feel about Henry Faulkes. But, no doubt, seeing the paintings themselves will also be influential.'

'In what way?'

'The tone of them, the emotional depth, colour, and so on. Whether the paintings are an intellectual exercise on a classical theme, or whether they are infused with an emotional intent.'

Jayne looked up, unable to resist. 'I thought you said it was impossible to stand in someone's shoes, and relive what they were thinking?'

Lal smiled at her, a hint of condescension in his eyes. 'It is, of course, impossible. And so we must make the story that we think is most likely, and be honest about it.'

Ben wanted to avoid the argument starting up again, and so he interjected. 'Why don't you tell us what you think the story is.'

The professor glanced at Jayne, who had returned to report-reading, and then looked intently at Ben. 'It is difficult for me to talk about my research, as you know.'

'Jayne knows about the letters, and the sermon. Unless you have something else up your sleeve, I think we are on a level playing field.' He rustled around in the papers again to deflect attention away from his blush. He was still keeping Faulkes' reincarnation room a secret. If he told them about it they would want to see it, but the thought of opening it up again filled him with blank fear.

Jayne looked up, smiled briefly at Ben, and said. 'Why don't you tell us what you think? You have the least to lose.'

Lal nodded. 'Yes, indeed. What is your interpretation of the documents?'

Ben sat up straight, as if an interrogator's light had

275

been shone on him. 'Well, I don't know.' Lal and Jayne continued to look at him expectantly. 'Let me see. There are a certain number of facts. Henry Faulkes designed the temple, and the paintings inside, and the paintings are based on classical stories, maybe on things he'd seen in Rome.'

Ben paused. The professor nodded, and said, 'Go on.'

'OK.' He looked at Jayne, who held his gaze intently. He spoke hesitantly, as he tried to remember what he was supposed to know, and the things that were secret. 'So . . . I think Faulkes . . . showed the temple to the vicar, who was . . . outraged and preached a sermon against him about idolatry. And then . . . Henry's father stepped in. He set Rackham on the path to promotion and sent Henry off on a tour researching farming practices . . . Which was when he really started to develop his interest in intensive farming and so forth.'

'Anything else?'

Ben turned his gaze from Jayne, and looked at Lal. 'No, I don't think so.'

Jayne stood up, stretched and yawned. 'Look. This is all very interesting but I'm knackered. When were you thinking of eating?'

Ben looked at his watch. 'I think Ruby was planning for half past eight.'

'Well, if it's all right with you, I'll go and take a nap. I started very early this morning. Could you wake me up when dinner's ready?'

Ben followed her out of the room, on the pretext of checking she had clean towels. In the hallway he whispered, 'Don't worry. I won't tell him about Charlotte. Were you worried I was going to spill the beans?'

She ran her finger down his cheek. 'Nope. I know whose side you're on.'

He grabbed her wrist and pulled her hand away from his face. In a low whisper he exclaimed, 'Jayne! Stop it. You'll get me into trouble.'

She chuckled, then went off to her bedroom. Ben stepped back into the study. Lal was sitting on the sofa, sipping his wine. 'She is an interesting girl,' he remarked. 'Earnest. Ambitious. She will go far, no doubt.'

Ben sat in the armchair. 'So now she's gone, are you going to tell me what you really think?'

The professor laughed. 'I do feel a certain obligation to tell you. You have been unstinting in your hospitality, and you are the owner of the paintings. But you can imagine, I am uneasy about the presence of Ms Greene. Can I rely on your absolute discretion?'

Ben swallowed, and then nodded. 'Of course. I won't tell her anything you don't want me to.'

'All right then.' The professor put his hands in his lap and leaned forward. 'You see, you have all your so-called facts but now we have to read into them, behind them, between them. We must make connections, and interpretations, and weave these things into a coherent story. We must ask "why", and "what for"? Always we must see these separate small events as bricks in a huge three-dimensional model, you understand. If we look through each window we have a very different view of the same building. Let us look at the subject of the wall paintings again.'

'OK.'

'What is there in the paintings that would have outraged the vicar so much? These are fairly run-of-the-mill classical scenes, the kind of thing you might have found in any other country-house setting. Do you agree?'

'Well, yes, I suppose so.'

'So if it was not the paintings what could it have been, which made our poor Mr Rackham so horror-struck?'

Ben blinked. 'I don't know. But you have an idea. Tell me.'

The professor leaned back in his chair and sighed. 'It is like this. The more we know about the context the more we will understand the possible stories about a thing. Are you with me?'

Ben nodded impatiently.

'Well then. Let us look inside the temple. For many years, decades, it was considered that all there was to know about the interior was that it was painted white. Nothing unusual about that. But in fact the walls, far from being blank and innocent, were actually concealing something, deceiving us. If we analyse the covering paint we may be able to tell when it was put on. Was it soon after the paintings were finished, or long after? This in turn could tell us whether the paintings were covered up because they were considered unseemly, or merely painted over because they had decayed and were no longer fashionable. Did the conservator do any such analysis?'

Ben shook his head. 'I don't know. Should they have done?'

The professor made a face. 'It would have been helpful. Never mind. Let us consider now the paintings uncovered. Some men wrestling, some discus practice, a death. Sport and war. This could be all that the pictures signify. Some interesting pictures of male past times. Do you think that is all they are?'

'Well, no. The report says they're Greek myths.'

'And I agree. But had I not studied Greek mythology I might have understood them differently. I might have thought they illustrated some historical event, or some kind of religious ritual. Who knows?'

'The design of the temple is a big clue, isn't it?'

'It is. Which is why understanding context is crucial. If the subject matter was merely described to you as men wrestling and dying in battle, there would be no clue to their origin. They could be Norse, Anglo-Saxon, Persian, Egyptian. The style of the temple, and the drapes, the features, the scenery in the paintings all indicate Greek influence. And because we are in England it is unlikely that it dates from the first classical age. What do you think?'

Ben laughed. 'I think it's unlikely.'

278

'Good. So we have Apollo and Hyacinthus, Dionysus and Ampelos, Achilles and Patroclus. Do you know anything about these characters?'

'A little. I've been reading up on them.'

'So why do you think Henry Faulkes chose these subjects? Do you think they reflect things he was interested in? Sport and fighting?'

Ben's face brightened. 'It could be, couldn't it? He certainly did a lot of fighting.'

'That is true. My feeling is that the choice of subject can tell us much about the chooser. It might be something as straightforward as an illustration of his favourite past times. But I think there is a deeper symbolism here.'

Ben opened his mouth to say something, but paused, twisting his mouth in concentration. Then he started again. 'There was one thing. I mentioned it to Ruby. But it's probably silly.'

The professor smiled encouragingly. 'Tell me. Many things seem silly at first.'

'Well, when we were at school, we thought Hyacinthus was a hilarious name for a boy, and we used to think that something funny went on between him and Apollo.'

The professor's smile broadened. 'Now I think we are getting somewhere. If we look at the facts about the paintings here, in the light of what we know about the sexuality of the late-eighteenth-century aristocracy and their attitude to the landscape, certain aspects immediately become illuminated.'

'Do they? I'm afraid I don't know very much about the sexuality of the eighteenth-century aristocracy.'

'Well, let me tell you then. You know, of course about the grand tours— '

The professor was interrupted abruptly by the entrance of Charlie, who crashed the door open, strode over to Ben and stood in front of him where he sat in his armchair.

'Come with me! I want to show you something.'

'Charlie! I'm in the middle of talking to the professor!

And you're drunk.'

'I'm not drunk. I don't get drunk. Come on. We may miss the show, if you don't come quickly. Pardon the expression.' He giggled to himself.

'What are you talking about?'

'Your lovely wife-to-be and your gardener. I just saw them in the orchard, being very friendly, I can tell you. She must prefer brawn to brain. That's probably where I went wrong.'

Ben's mind went blank for a second, blotted out by panic. What was Charlie saying? Grasping at the nearest idea, he latched onto Charlie's last words. 'What do you mean, "where you went wrong"? What's it got to do with you?'

Charlie was slightly wrong-footed by this, and struggled for his next words. 'Look. All you need to know is that your so-called angelic fiancée is off having it away with your gardener in the wet grass somewhere. Do you understand?'

Ben's stomach churned. What if Charlie was telling the truth? Where was Ruby? Could she do something like this to him? Suddenly, his old nihilism about relationships returned with a fat thud. What would be so surprising about such an infidelity? Only that afternoon he had been seriously tempted himself. Images of Jayne slipped across his mind, the softness of her kiss, the smallness of her as he had hugged her, before saying no. The kisses that had followed, despite his weak protest.

Charlie started to tug at his sleeve. 'Come on. I want you to see what a slut she is. Just like all the others.'

Ben stood up suddenly and pushed Charlie away, so that he staggered backwards.

'Don't use that language about Ruby. Or anyone, for that matter. Your drink-sodden mind has made you see things that aren't true. Just go away.'

'I saw them, snogging like there was no tomorrow. In the orchard. No mistake. I've seen them before, anyway. This

280

isn't the first time. She's been cuckolding you for weeks, you sad bastard. And I could've had her too, if I'd really wanted.'

Ben lunged out at Charlie but he managed to get behind the sofa out of Ben's reach. At this point, the professor stepped in.

'Gentlemen. Please. This is not worthy of you. Please calm down.'

Charlie stayed cowering behind the sofa but Ben drew himself up with a sigh and then sat down heavily in the armchair, his face in his hands.

'Look,' the professor said, 'it is probably not my business, but I do have some experience, some knowledge about these things. My advice to you, Ben, is do not go and look. It would serve no good purpose. What value is a relationship if there is no trust? You must trust that whatever Ruby is doing, she is doing what she has to, and that she has always your best interests at heart. I am sure that Charlie is wrong and Ruby is probably just walking in the park somewhere. If you go and look for her with this feeling of distrust, you will undermine the foundation of your love. If she is really somewhere with George it will not make you happy to find them. Believe me, I have been on both sides of the story.'

The professor came over to where Ben was slumped. He squatted on the floor, and took Ben's hands away from his face so that he could make Ben look at him.

'There is a time to speak and a time to remain silent. My advice is, overlook this. Forget it. It is nothing. It is a spring fairy story, a figment of the evening's imagination. If you do not know that something has happened, then it has not happened. Trust her.'

The professor gave Ben's hands a squeeze and then stood up. He addressed Charlie, saying, 'I think that you would benefit from a cold shower, and a good night's sleep. Then in the morning you should think hard about your life. You are slowly killing yourself.'

Charlie turned on the professor shouting, 'What the fuck do you know?' He lashed out at him. 'Your fucking stupid mumbo-jumbo!'

At which point Ben stood up, grabbed Charlie by his shirt, and threw him down on the ground. The two men rolled about on the floor in an undignified heap, Charlie shouting at Ben to get the fuck off him, and Ben shouting back that he deserved everything he was getting. Ben felt a surge of violence pump into his fist. A new strength came to him and he managed to pin Charlie down. Then he thumped him hard in the stomach. Charlie made a satisfying 'ooph' noise as the wind was forced out of him. Ben lifted his fist again, his body taken over by a sudden rush of savagery. Just at that moment the professor grabbed a vase of flowers and threw the contents over the two men. The shock made them stop for a moment, so he tried to separate them. Ben put up his hands, as if he was surrendering, and slowly got off Charlie, who was prostrate on his back. Ben slumped back down in the armchair and began to cry. Charlie picked himself up and shuffled out of the room, holding a hand to his stomach. The professor said, 'I'll go and get us a drink.'

She drinks down the potion willingly, and I lay her on the sacramental bed, she is mine for the taking. Like soft, ripe fruit. My body pulses, she lies expectant, her legs apart, wanton. I lower myself onto her, my cock delicious on her sweet flesh, my hands on her breasts. I want to sink into her, eat her, press myself through her skin. Her body rises up to meet my touch as if my fingers are magnets. Her breath comes in short gasps, she is trembling. I flick her breasts with my tongue, and she moans. I taste her skin, tracing a line down her belly, down between her legs, where it is hot and soft. A long kiss, my tongue inside her, feeling the tender walls, the place where life enters. Sharp, ravenous lust shoots through me as I slide into that softness, deep into her centre. Her body arches, her head thrown back. I bite her neck, her nipples. I push myself further, I can feel the entrance to that mysterious place, where the seed will grow. I turn her, so that I can see her long strong spine, see her muscles moving under the skin, like an animal. My fingers explore her, the soft lips, the little hood, and she begins to moan rhythmically, her breathing heavy. And then I fill her again, my cock is molten, urgent, as I ride her, she cries out, my hands enclose her breasts, her buttocks crashing against my thighs, my body is the life force, I am finding the core of her, feeling her womb open to me. Her back is curved, I hold her pelvis, feel the bones of her, pull her deeper onto me, waves of sheer pleasure, she spreads wider, opening herself, her body begging me to find the centre. I feel the seed rushing up through me, a flame, the life giver, inside her, in the depths, I feel her shudder, and the seeds explode, they burst into her, her bones, the skin, the heat inside, wet ... new ... life.

An hour or so later Ruby crept into the house, with a sense that her guilt was stamped all over her skin. She listened at the study door, and could hear the murmuring voices of the two men. It seemed they must still be immersed in the story of the wall paintings. It occurred to her that they might not have missed her at all, and this calmed her nerves slightly. She slipped into the bathroom and washed herself, while she rehearsed over and over again what she would say if Ben asked her where she had been. Then she walked down the hall to the study.

Ben was still sitting in the armchair, his eyes red-rimmed, his nose pink. Professor Lal was perched on the edge of the sofa holding a box of tissues, one hand resting on Ben's knee. Ruby was astonished.

'What's going on? What's happened? Are you all right?'

The two men looked up at her as she stood in the doorway. Then they glanced at each other briefly, before Ben said, 'It's OK. I had a bit of a bust-up with Charlie.'

Ruby's skin began vibrating again. Her voice came out as a faint little croak: 'Why?'

There was a lifetime's pause. Ruby was isolated from the world by the arctic wind which encircled her. Ben looked at her, and she tried to look back at him with open, guiltless eyes.

He said, finally, 'Oh, he was being disgusting about women again, and I just lost it. The professor had to pull us apart. I feel so stupid now, for letting that drunken oaf get to me.'

Ruby's legs almost gave way as relief swirled through her body. She stumbled over to Ben and put her head in his lap. She mumbled incoherently into his trouser leg, 'Did he hurt you? Did you hurt him? Where is he? Has he gone?'

Ben looked down at her tousled, guilty head, and stroked her hair. 'He's gone,' he said.

There was a light tap on the door and Jayne stepped in. 'Sorry. But can you smell burning?'

The roast chicken was burned to a frazzle. Ruby made cheese sandwiches for Jayne, Ben and the professor but said she was not hungry, and slipped off to bed. Ben followed shortly after. They lay next to each other for some time, trying to sleep, but not managing it. The silence of the night was pounding in their ears. Ben's arm was aching, hurt in the fight. He was shocked with himself. He had never before experienced the brutal instinct which had welled up in him that evening. For one short moment he had understood how Henry Faulkes must have lost his temper, drawn his sword, and forgotten the consequences. No doubt, Henry would have had a go at killing Charlie and George. The frenzy had felt very powerful at the time, an immense relief to let go of habitual restraint. But now Ben felt ashamed of himself. He lay next to Ruby, tortured by Charlie's words, by the recurring sound in his head of Charlie's winded stomach, by the look in Ruby's eyes when she had come in. He found himself unable to speak, tongue-tied by a miasma of thoughts, images and the painful throb in his hand.

Ruby felt that the bed must be vibrating with the unsteady beat of her heart, the anxiety seeping out of her.

Eventually she whispered, 'Are you awake?'

She felt Ben's head turn on his pillow. 'Yes. Sorry. Am I keeping you awake?'

'No. Why aren't you asleep?'

'Why aren't you?'

Ruby rolled her eyes to herself, but quelled her irritation. 'I'm worried about you and Charlie fighting. It's not like you.'

She heard Ben let out a long breath. There was a gap of silence, and then he spoke quietly. 'He said some horrible things, and I'd had enough of it.'

Ruby's mind raced. How could she find out what Charlie had said without incriminating herself? She spoke hesitantly. 'Can you tell me what kind of things they were?'

The duvet slipped off her as Ben turned over roughly, away from her. 'I don't really want to talk about it.'

Ruby lay still, looking up into the black for a few seconds, before she decided to risk going further. 'Were they horrible things about me, by any chance?'

Ben's voice was very thin, almost broken. 'Yes, they were.'

A wave of heat ran down Ruby's body. She let it pass, then turned over onto her side, put her arm round him and pulled him into the crook of her body. Conscious that whatever she said now could affect the rest of her life, she spoke very carefully, choosing her words.

'Ben. You must've noticed how Charlie's been towards me lately. You mentioned it yourself. He hates me. Whatever he told you, it was probably made up, to make you hate me, too.'

'But why? What have you done?'

A quiver of irritation entered into her voice, despite herself. '*I* haven't done anything! At Christmas he told me he loved me! He's mad!'

Ben hurriedly rolled onto his back, his head turned towards her. 'He did what?'

285

Ruby told him about the terrible scene on the day of the yule log search. 'Ever since then he's been horrible to me. I suppose because I didn't react in the way he wanted me to.'

To Ruby's relief, Ben finally turned towards her and put his arm over her shoulder. His voice sounded warm and sympathetic. 'Why on earth didn't you tell me about this?'

The feeling that danger had passed was so palpable, Ruby could sense it whisking out of the window, a dark shadowy bird. Tension left her body and her voice became suspended with tears.

Ben held her tight, thanking God she had told him something he could believe. 'Shush, shush,' he said, trying to comfort her. 'It's over now. I'll tell Charlie, he must leave. He's been poisoning the atmosphere for too long. I should have done it before.'

Ruby sniffed, and managed to say, 'I'm sorry. I didn't know what to do.'

'Let's not talk about him any more. Let's pretend it didn't happen, and start again.'

'OK.'

The darkness protected them, allowing Ben to conceal the lingering doubt which stretched his mouth down, and creased his forehead, despite himself. They fell asleep, Ben's arm still over Ruby's shoulder, half protective, half possessive.

The next morning Gretta arrived early. She had come to stay for the two days left before the wedding in order to help get everything ready. She found Ruby, Jayne and Professor Lal taking refuge in the kitchen, as a huge row could be heard coming from upstairs.

'What's happening?' she whispered.

Ruby held up her hand briefly, and said, 'Shh!'

They listened to Ben and Charlie shouting.

'I don't want to hear any more about it, Charlie! I've had enough. Get out of here.'

286

'You fucking sucker! She's really taken you in, hasn't she! How long have we known each other? But you believe *her*! Well, believe what you like! I'll be glad to get out of here. While you're at it, you better chuck George out as well, or she'll be at it again before you can say jack shit!' Scuffling could be heard as the two progressed along the landing, and down the stairs.

'Just shut your mouth. If you say another thing, I'll bloody well shut it for you. I mean it.'

Gretta could not resist peeping through the crack of the door. She saw Ben standing defiantly at the bottom of the stairs as Charlie searched for his jacket.

'And you can give me your keys. I'll pack up your stuff and send it on.'

Charlie turned and swore at Ben. 'No bloody way. I'm not having you go through all my stuff. And I need my laptop for work.'

Ben faltered. 'Oh, I see. Well, go and hire a van and get it sorted out today. I want you out of here.'

'I'll be fucking glad to go. Can't think why I've stayed so long!' Charlie strode to the open front door and slammed it behind him without another word. Gretta watched Ben slump down onto the bottom step of the stairs and put his head in his hands. She quietly shut the door before turning back to the others.

'What's going on?'

Ruby's head was in a fog of involuntary memories of the evening before. She closed her eyes in a gesture of weariness. 'Ben and Charlie had a huge row. Ben's very upset.'

Gretta held Ruby by the arms, as if to steady her. 'And you? What's happened to you? Did Charlie do anything to you?'

'No, it's not that. Look, let's go for a walk. Do you mind?' She addressed herself to Jayne and Lal. Jayne shook her head. 'My taxi's due any second.'

Lal jumped up from his chair and said, 'Not at all. It will do you good. And I must sort out my things at George's and then perhaps Ben will be ready to show me the paintings. Thank you so much for your hospitality. Off you go.' And he gently pushed Gretta and Ruby towards the doors.

The two women walked in silence for a few seconds, then Gretta said, 'And?'

Ruby looked at her friend with anxious eyes but said nothing. Gretta persisted.

'Has Charlie said something?'

Ruby inhaled a huge gulp of air, then exhaled it slowly, trying to calm herself before replying. 'I don't know. Ben won't tell me the details of what happened, but he hasn't accused me of anything. He just said Charlie was being horrible about me.'

Gretta frowned. 'I can't imagine Charlie not telling him about you and George, if they were arguing.' She looked at Ruby. 'Where were you, anyway, when all this was going on?'

Ruby looked away across the field, in an attempt to hide her guilty face, but she failed to fool Gretta.

'You were with George.'

Ruby hid her face with her hands. 'Yes. Oh God, Gretta, I didn't mean to. It just all happened in a whirlwind. I wasn't prepared.'

'What happened?'

'He came along yesterday evening, and swept me off my feet. I'd given up on him, honestly. We've been very sensible the past few weeks. I'd thought, OK, this is how it's going to be. I'll marry Ben and no harm will have been done. I'd got used to the idea. But then last night we went off into a fantasy world, and ended up in the temple.'

'The temple!'

'It was incredible. I don't know how he'd arranged it, but there was a massive bed in there. A four-poster! All draped with silk and muslin, and loads of candles. It was amazing. What's the matter?'

Gretta had stopped stock still and was looking horrified. 'You had sex with George on the four-poster?'

288

'Well, yes. Why? What do you know about it?'

Gretta took both of Ruby's hands and shook her. Then she said slowly, enunciating every word separately, 'That is the bed that Ben has made for you, for your wedding night. That's what he's been doing up at the workshop all this time. He wanted to make your wedding night special. And now you've had sex on it with another man, you idiot! Didn't you think?'

Ruby froze as another wave of horrible remorse washed over her. 'Oh, God. What have I done? That beautiful bed. Oh, God.'

Gretta put her arm round her. 'Think. How did you leave the bed? Was it all in a mess? Will it be obvious it's been slept in?'

'I don't know. Yes, probably.'

It suddenly dawned on Ruby that Ben and the professor were planning to visit the temple later that morning. 'What am I going to do?' she wailed. 'They'll be able to see what happened!'

Gretta grasped both of Ruby's arms, to try and calm her. 'It's all right. We'll sort it out. I don't want Ben to find out about this. You'll have to pretend to be utterly amazed and overcome by the bed when he takes you there after the wedding. What a dreadful mess.'

Ruby sat down on the ground and cried. All the shame, which had been temporarily kept at bay by mesmeric recollections of the previous night, suddenly arrived in a sliding heap. She imagined Ben working on the bed, so guileless and full of hope, planning a night of shared love, and she felt a terrible pain in her stomach. How can you undo what has been done? Her mind flitted through the past year, from one event to another, trying to see where she went wrong, how she could have done things differently.

Gretta sat down and put a comforting arm round Ruby's shoulder. 'What are you going to do about George?'

Ruby shrugged helplessly, but then a sudden thought made her sit up straight. 'Do you think George knew the bed was Ben's?'

'Yes. He helped Ben put it up the other day.'

Ruby wailed, 'Why did he do this to me? After all these protestations about being Ben's friend. Why?'

Gretta made a tutting sound. 'We don't have time for this. We need to go and sort the bed out. Come on!'

Ben found Jayne sitting in the kitchen on her own. 'Where is everyone?'

'They've all scarpered. You can be scary when you're angry.'

He sat down at the table and put his head in his hands. 'Sorry. You must think this is a madhouse.'

She chuckled. 'It's been interesting.' She placed a hand on his arm, but he pulled away.

'Seriously, Jayne. I don't want any more complications. I'm getting married in a couple of days, for heaven's sake!'

She picked up her empty mug and walked over to the sink. 'You're right. You just make me misbehave, you're so bloody proper.' She peered out of the window. 'My taxi should be here in a minute.'

'You're going already?'

She gave him one of her brilliant smiles. 'I've got places to go, people to meet.'

They both heard the sound of tyres on the gravel drive. Ben picked up her suitcase and carried it out to the front steps. She looked up at him. 'So will you tell me sometime what that was all about?'

He shrugged. 'I'm not sure myself. But I will ring you. In a couple of weeks. I may have something I want to talk to you about.'

She raised her eyebrows. 'OK. Sounds mysterious.'

The taxi pulled up, and he helped her slide the suitcase in onto the back seat. 'Safe journey.'

She smiled and waved. He thought to himself: she *is* lovely. The least I could do is tell her about the secret room sometime.

*

Ruby and Gretta hurried towards the lake, to where George had moored the boat on the previous evening. But it wasn't there. When they looked more closely they could see marks in the muddy grass at the water's edge which suggested the boat had been dragged away along the track. Gretta smacked her hand to her forehead.

'Of course. They've been hiding the boat so that you wouldn't be able to see the bed.'

'Then George must have been up here this morning to move it. We left it here last night.'

They walked along the track a few steps towards the edge of the wood, looking for clues. Ruby suddenly exclaimed, 'Oh!', which made Gretta jump, and clutch her arm.

'What is it?'

Ruby laughed. 'Oh, nothing really. I've just realised why I saw Jayne and Ben up here yesterday. I did wonder what they were doing, going off into the woods.'

Gretta released Ruby's arm and gave her a scornful look. 'That's the pot calling the kettle black, isn't it? Or, what's the other one? What's sauce for the goose is sauce for the gander?'

Ruby made a face. 'Yes, OK. I get the message.'

They carried on walking in silence, inspecting the ground for signs of the boat, but looked up at the sound of running steps. George was coming down the track but stopped abruptly when he saw them. The three stood awkwardly together, not quite meeting each other's eye. Ruby looked across the lake as she said, 'We need the boat. Can you show us where it is?'

George looked at Gretta. 'Er, yeah. It's not far. But Ben . . . ?'

Gretta barely concealed a sneer as she said, 'What do you think's more important? Ben finding out that Ruby has seen the bed, or Ben finding out you've slept with her on it?'

George rubbed his chin with his hand, and looked

towards Ruby's unsmiling profile. 'If you're worried about the bed, I've sorted that out. But I think Ben knows already.'

Both women gave him their full attention. 'What?'

He looked at his feet, but glanced up once or twice at Ruby. 'The prof rang me this morning and said there'd been some kind of fight last night, between Ben and Charlie, about us. Charlie saw us going off.'

Ruby closed her eyes, as a shot of anxiety ran through her body. George took a step towards her, then hesitated. He spoke to Gretta. 'I really need to talk to Ruby.'

Gretta began to protest but Ruby nodded. 'It's OK. You go back to the house and check Ben is all right. I'll come back soon.'

Gretta stomped off down the track, and George took Ruby's arm. 'Don't look so worried. It's good that Ben knows. We would've had to tell him some time.'

'Would we?' She pushed his hand away. 'Don't. Someone might see.'

He looked puzzled. 'Come on, Ruby. This is it, now. Ben knows, Charlie knows, Everyone knows.'

Ruby turned away and started walking towards the wood, seeking privacy. 'Ben hasn't said anything to me.'

George grabbed at her arm to stop her. 'What do you mean? What about last night? We connected into something. You can't just ignore it.' He had raised his voice and his grip was hard. 'I've been waiting for this for a whole bloody year!'

'You're hurting me.' Her eyes were brimming with tears. As he let go she ran into the wood where they couldn't be seen from the house, and slumped down on the trunk of a felled tree, her head in her hands. He followed, and sat down beside her.

'You'll have to tell him when the baby starts showing.'

Ruby tensed and raised her tear-streaked face to him. 'What baby?'

George put both his arms round her and pulled her

towards him. 'The one we made last night.'

Ruby pushed him away again, her eyes anxious. 'We didn't make a baby last night.'

George laughed. 'Course we did. How could we fail? I've been reading the signs since last May, for Christ's sake! It was Beltane, we drank the magic May bowl together, we made love in a sacramental bed in a temple. I felt it happen. It's been going on since time began, Ruby. You must have felt it?'

She looked into his eyes, and her own eyes widened. She stood up abruptly. 'George. I don't think you're feeling very well this morning. I think maybe you've been working too hard. Why don't we go back to the lodge, and you can have a rest.'

George laughed again. 'I don't need rest! Who needs sleep at this time of the year? Can't you feel the energy coming off the grass, out of the trees?' He grabbed both her hands and pulled him towards her where he was seated. 'You and me are part of this. Can't you see how beautiful and shiny everything is? We showed the earth what to do, we were part of the ceremony. We were meant to be together.'

He tried to manoeuvre her onto his lap, but she resisted, stepping back from him. She stammered, 'I ... I don't understand ... I don't know what you're talking about.'

He gazed at her and spoke slowly. 'No. You're right. I haven't explained.' He held out his hand, his face more gentle, more like his usual self. 'Come and sit next to me. I'll tell you.'

She perched on the end of the log, just out of his reach. 'What's happened to you, George?'

A broad, elated smile spread across his face, and his eyes closed, as if he were meditating. 'I have felt the energy of the earth flow through me, the connection of everything ... like a bright light shining out of my skin.' His eyes opened suddenly, looking at her. 'You must be able to see it?'

She shook her head slowly. Then she stretched out her

293

hand and felt his forehead. It was burning hot. She felt somewhat relieved. 'You have a temperature, George. You're feverish. We should go back to the lodge, and put you to bed.'

He stood up, irritated. 'No, no, no. I'm not ill! I've never felt better.' He began to pace up and down in front of her, gabbling. 'This is the best day of my life. All the waiting, the months of work, it is all coming together today. I have woken the Earth Mother, and brought her essence here. Look at the trees, you can see the leaves growing, the buds shooting.' He stopped and stared at her. 'Have you been into the vegetable garden this morning?' She shook her head. He started moving again. 'I was there at sunrise, and I could literally see the stems growing, the fruits filling out, like speeded up film. We couldn't have done it better!' He suddenly dropped to his knees at her feet. 'You were the goddess last night. You *must* have felt it, you *must* understand.'

Ruby scanned his face, trying to find his familiar warm look. 'It was lovely last night, George. But we just made love. We haven't changed anything. I didn't know you were into all this stuff. You should have told me.'

He barked out a laugh. 'You *did* know. Deep down. Your body knew, even if you won't recognise it.' His hand went to her stomach. 'Your body knows it right now. It's answering the call, and growing new life.'

Ruby leaped up off the tree trunk, and pushed his hand away. 'I think . . . this is not . . . let's not talk about this at the moment. Let's go back to the lodge.'

He struggled up from the floor, put his arm over her shoulder and spoke down her ear. 'You're worried about Ben. But I don't think he'll want you once he knows you're carrying my baby.'

'For God's sake, George! There is no baby!' She pushed his arm off her and stood facing him with her arms folded. 'You seem to have forgotten a small detail when you were planning all this. I'm on the Pill.'

294

We are staggering back to the lodge, George leaning against me, his arm round my shoulder, but unthreatening, slumped. He is crying, a flood of tears. Professor Lal waits at the door, anxious, attentive. George allows us to take off his coat and shoes, like a child in a trance, and we put him to bed. He pulls the cover over his head, and we leave him, hoping sleep will come.

The professor shows me a copy of *Reaching Paradise*, which he found by George's bed, full of manic underlining, circling and exclamation marks; and scrawled notes in the margins, stuff about fertility and rituals. George's mad plan. I feel so stupid, so duped, but the professor tries to soothe me. He says: Madness is a consummate actor.

I walk away from the lodge, this horrible feeling of love washing away, the foundations collapsing. All the pain George has caused me over all these months, these things that moved me so deeply, they are all thrown back in my face, made meaningless. The George I thought I knew was an illusion; he has dissolved into thin air, leaving me with all these feelings, unconnected, doomed to collapse in a heap on the floor. That look in his eye, the light that seemed to shine out at me, was potent, but it came from a strange place, like a man possessed.

I should have seen he was working too hard, that he was up at all times of the night, sewing and planting, digging and harvesting. When did he sleep? I was blind. He drew me in, with this beguiling energy, the intensity it brings, the heat. I have been in a daze, breathing in this air infected with desire. Looking back over the year I see myself, sleepwalking, thoughts never reaching the surface, clogged in cotton wool. As if I have been asleep in the wood all this time and the dreams have taken over. It is time now to wake up, shake off the leaves and twigs, and open my eyes.

I walk into the kitchen. Gretta and Ben sit chatting at the

table, planning the wedding, making lists. They look up and smile at me. They are real, I am awake.

George lay under the covers listening to the murmuring of Lal and Ruby down below. He heard the front door close, and Ruby's goodbye. Some time later he heard the professor open the bedroom door, pause, and then close it again, followed shortly by the click of the front gate as he set out towards the Hall.

George spent the next couple of hours in careful preparation. He threw all his clothes into a suitcase, placed his precious books in one box, his few other possessions in another, and loaded them in the van. Then he drove up to the walled gardens, and harvested all the ripe produce he could find: lettuces, rhubarb, seakale, leeks, radishes, spinach, broccoli, cauliflowers and cabbages, all crammed into bags. When he could find nothing else ripe, he quietly took out an old scythe from the long sheds and systematically cut down all the vegetables and fruit bushes, all the flowers, everything that he had grown. They formed soft piles of feathery leaf under the steady, clean strokes of the curved blade.

Afterwards he drove his van up to the lane above the memorial to Ben's parents, where Ruby had left her bike a year ago. He took out his jemmy, a torch, and a thick pen which he used for labelling plants, and put them in a large empty holdall from the back of the van. He walked through the wood, past where Ruby had lain sleeping when he first saw her. Creeping along the ride, which was flowering again with campion and stitchwort, he caught a glimpse of Ben and the professor striding off towards the temple. Down at the rear of the house, the door was unlocked. He could hear the murmur of voices, Ruby and Gretta, who were still sitting in the kitchen. After listening for a few moments he slipped up the back stairs. In the old servant's quarters, he carefully prised out the nails which held the plasterboard across the entrance to the secret room. There

296

were a few creaking noises, as the nails gave way, but no one downstairs noticed. Using his torch to see, he gathered together Faulkes' clothes, the book of magic, the phallic stone, and as many bottles of wine as he could fit into the holdall, padded in amongst the clothes. Then he took out the black marker pen and scrawled on the wall in large spidery letters: *I am reborn*. He smiled to himself, placed the torch by the door, and made his way back to the van.

Ruby and Gretta were about to start lunch when Ben came crashing into the kitchen, red-faced and breathless. 'Come and look at this,' he gasped.

They followed him, half walking, half jogging back to the entrance of the walled vegetable garden. 'Look.'

They stood in a line gazing at the sad, crumpled heaps of wilting foliage. Gretta spoke first. 'Oh, my God! Who could've done this?'

Ben stood slightly bowed, one hand on his waist, trying to catch his breath, the other hand at his forehead. Through his teeth he muttered, 'I don't know. The professor and I just popped over here, after looking at the paintings, and this is what we found.' He stood up and stared out over the garden. 'Could it have been Charlie?'

Gretta looked at Ruby swiftly, a question in her eyes. 'It could've been.'

Ruby shook her head silently.

Professor Lal arrived, also breathless. His face was creased with anxiety. 'George has gone.'

Ben glanced up and saw the exchange of looks between the other three. 'What? How do you mean?'

Nobody said anything. Ben suddenly lost his temper. He shouted, 'Somebody bloody well tell me what is going on!'

Professor Lal held up his hands, as if to ward off Ben's anger. 'Mr Fitzmaurice, please, it is upsetting, I know.' He twitched his head. 'I can hardly believe my eyes.' He took Ben's hand and held it between his own. 'I am afraid that it is George who has wreaked such terrible havoc.'

Ben wrenched his hand away. 'What are you talking about? Why would he do such a thing? He's dedicated to the gardens, they're his life!' He stood staring at the professor, but then his face suddenly tightened. He took a step towards Ruby and grasped her arm, squeezing out words through his teeth. 'He hasn't ... done something to you, has he? Charlie said ... something, perhaps he was mistaken. George didn't ... hurt you?'

Ruby put her arms round him, and held him tight. 'No. It's nothing like that.'

The professor laid his hand on Ben's back. 'From what I have seen of George since yesterday, I would say he is having some sort of nervous breakdown. Too much work, not enough sleep. It seems he has turned his anger towards the thing he loved most. A common reaction, is it not?'

They remained standing at the entrance to the garden for some time, as if transfixed. But then Ben shook himself, and let go of Ruby. 'I've got a hundred phone calls to make. I'll have to ring the shop, the restaurant. I'll need to get someone in to replant, see what we can do. I might even ring the police. He's cost me a bloody fortune!'

Gretta joined in. 'And the flowers for the wedding, and the caterers! What are we going to do for salad? This is a disaster!' She and Ben hurried off towards the house. Ruby remained standing next to the professor. He glanced at her now and again, as she gazed miserably at the mess. After a few minutes, he spoke.

'Perhaps you, too, should go back, Ruby. Ben will need your help.'

She sighed deeply. 'It's all my fault.'

He wagged his finger at her. 'No. That is not the case at all. George did not have to do this. It is unworthy of him. He must be very sick. Do not for a moment take the blame.'

'How can I explain it to Ben?'

The professor lifted his shoulders, made a rueful face. 'Ah. A difficult case. But I will say one thing to you. It is my belief that truth is a much overrated commodity.' He turned towards the hall, looking at her out of the corner of his eye, his head slightly cocked. 'And everyone knows that there are no facts. Only interpretations.'

Ruby met his eyes for a moment and then looked at her feet. 'Let's go back.'

As they entered the house they heard banging noises from above; Gretta came scuttling down the back stairs. She spoke quickly. 'The back door was open – Ben went up to check. Get upstairs, quick, Ruby. He's going bananas!'

Ruby followed the noises to the old servants' quarters. She found Ben wielding a hammer against the dangling plasterboard panel, his face distorted with rage. 'That bloody bastard! That shit!'

'Ben! Stop it. Please!'

He looked up before throwing the hammer down hard on the floor. 'Look what he's done in here.' He shone the torch into the darkness, the beam flashing onto the scrawled writing: *I am reborn.*

A ringing sound filled Ruby's head, a shriek of blood rushing in her ears. She cowered involuntarily, feeling something creeping up behind her. 'It's like the abandoned sepulchre. As if someone's rolled away the stone,' she mumbled.

Ben let out an irritated snort. 'Oh, for heaven's sake! He's *stolen* valuable property. It's not some bloody ghost walking. It's George, flesh and blood, stealing my bloody property! Playing tricks on us!' He kicked the table, then he turned angrily on Ruby. 'Why has he done this? You must have some idea. You were with him last night.'

Ruby closed her eyes, unable to look him in the face. 'I don't know. He might be angry with me.'

'Why?' Ben stood looking belligerent, his hands on his hips.

Ruby's voice was a whisper, her throat closing up with anxiety. 'He ... I ... didn't give him ... what he wanted.'

'Which was?'

Ruby looked up at him, her hand to her throat, her breath short. 'I can't stay in here. I'm going to faint.'

She staggered out of the hole, and went out onto the landing. Ben found her sitting at the top of the stairs, leaning against the wall, tears streaming. After a moment or two he sat next to her, and put his arm round her. 'What a bloody mess.'

He could feel her body vibrate as she sobbed silently. He stroked her hair. 'Ruby?'

She looked up at him, all blotchy, and streaks of mascara. Wiping away her tears with his fingers he said, 'Do you still want to marry me?'

She hid her face in his shoulder and said in a choked voice, 'I need a tissue.'

He searched in his pockets and found a moderately clean one. 'Here.'

After blowing her nose she took a deep breath and then looked at him intently. 'Yes, very much. If you'll still have me.'

He nodded, and put his arm round her again. They sat at the top of the stairs for a long time, the silence broken only by the rhythmic sound of a cuckoo, wafting up thinly through the open door.

Draft of *The Lost Eden: sexualised landscapes of the eighteenth century*
by Professor A. Lal. (Excerpt 2)

At Oakstead, a moderately sized house in the county of Norfolk, England, there is a remarkable survival of a park created by the foremost figure of the aristocratic sex cult, which attempted to recreate the landscape of the ancient Greek world. The park is a perfect example of the symbolic use of landscape to provide the setting in which to recreate that classical idyll, when every form of sexual practice was devoid of shame. The park is a well-preserved example of the

300

work of Humphry Repton, the best known landscape gardener of this period in England. At Oakstead, his patron was Henry Faulkes.

Faulkes was a complex and interesting man. He is best known for his pioneering work in agriculture, where he was instrumental in pushing forward innovative farming practices for increasing fertility of the land. Many of these theories were based on detailed research he had conducted into fertility rites, including those of ancient Greece. He was, in fact, deeply interested in pre-Christian culture and seemed to practise a form of hybridised paganism, which incorporated ancient British fertility rites into a framework built on the worship of classical gods. It is clear from accounts of life at Henford Hall that he marked the important pagan moon festivals (Samhain, Beltane, Imbolc and Lammas) and the sun festivals of equinox and solstice, with appropriate ceremonies. In one document there is a detailed description of his celebration of Saturnalia, a Roman festival, in the days running up to Christmas.

Sex played a vital role in ancient fertility rites. For example, in spring, to encourage the earth to reproduce, it was customary, up until relatively recent times, for couples to go out into the fields to have sex en masse, this act of procreation being intended to encourage the earth to follow suit. This aspect of paganism must have appealed greatly to a man whose reputation for sexual promiscuity was well known in contemporary circles.

Faulkes studied classics at university and then went on an extended Grand Tour of Europe, staying for over a year in Rome. This self-imposed exile was partly prescribed by the result of a duel in England in which he almost murdered his opponent. A further reason for this extended holiday was the freedom it offered for sexual relationships with other men. On his return to England, his father seems to have taken him in hand by organising a suitable marriage and rusticating him in a minor country seat in the backwaters of Norfolk: Oakstead. Faulkes, unrepentant, immediately set about transforming this forgotten place into Arcadia. Repton, whose career was burgeoning at this time, was brought in to oversee the work. He produced an idyllic landscape, a perfect balance between trees, water, sky and grass as well as the practical needs of a large estate, catered for by enormous walled gardens and greenhouses. Though Repton supervised the work, the deep involvement of Faulkes in the park concept is clear. In a portrait of him and his wife, painted in 1791, he is shown pointing to his plans for the estate, which provides, in an exaggerated form, the background of the painting. There is also a clue to his enthusiasm for pagan worship in the three spirals, which can be seen on the plans. These shapes are commonly held to represent the Earth Mother, the interlocking circles being symbols of the cyclical nature of death and rebirth.

In the Red Book produced for the park by Repton, we can see in the reported conversations of the text the strong opinions of the patron: he wants certain views, he wants enormous kitchen gardens. The most significant point about this Red Book, however, is the omission. Nowhere in the design or in the text is there any mention of a temple. However, it is the temple at Oakstead which makes the park so important.

The temple sits on an island in the lake, in splendid isolation. It is austere in design, following the precepts of stark neoclassicism, with heavy emphasis on the contrasting masses of the square and rounded elements. The columns supporting the portico are in the plain Doric style. The Doric order was perceived by this period as the architectural symbol of an uncorrupted people living close to nature. It was the style which most resembled the cut trees from which it was believed Greek architecture derived its basic form. The windows are expressed as deep, square recesses, emphasising the thick massing of the walls. The entablature is reduced to a plain band, with no ornamentation. The design is uncompromising, primitive, masculine. The temple at Oakstead is one of the most extreme examples of neoclassical architecture to have been built in this country, and is certainly far too radical to have come from Repton's moderate and conservative pattern book.

In fact, the temple is entirely the design of Henry Faulkes. Apart from the obvious influence his extended stay in Rome must have had on his design, contemporary correspondence with friends still in Rome proves that he was being supplied with drawings and engravings of Roman ruins and landscapes, which he used as an inspiration for both the park and the temple. It is also clear from this correspondence, though allusions are coded, that his links with the homosexual circle in Rome were still very strong. One correspondent describes to Faulkes in coded terms how he has taken over the care of one of his former lovers, described as a 'temple' which is 'a source of beauty and delight'. From the accounts for the work it can be shown that the real temple at Oakstead was built after Repton's park was completed, and was Faulkes' pièce de résistance. In it, he expresses his deep commitment to the aristocratic cult of antiquity with its reverence of the male form.

It is Faulkes' treatment of the interior of the temple at Oakstead, which finally makes explicit his celebration of the erotic culture of the classical world. Recently uncovered wall paintings have revealed the homoerotic nature of Faulkes' sexuality. The main painting depicts Achilles mourning Patroclus. This was a subject close to the heart of every committed neoclassicist, and was explored by several eminent

303

artists of the movement at the end of the eighteenth century, including both Flaxman and Fuseli. In their renderings of the heroic myth we are presented with the image of a naked, powerful man racked with grief for the loss of his beloved friend. Of course, it was common knowledge that the Greeks believed the relationship between the two warriors to have been homosexual. This is the key to the *Iliad*, the masterpiece by Homer, the poet who was regarded in the last years of the eighteenth century as the supreme primitive. Thus the bond between the two warriors was the most favoured symbol for homosexual love in its purest and noblest form.

In the seclusion of a private temple, Faulkes was able to explore the homoerotic nature of his subject explicitly. Patroclus lies on his side, almost entirely naked and exposed. He has a magnificent muscular body. Though the phallus is covered by a thin cloth, its shape is perfectly discernible. Achilles lies behind him, his head resting on the warrior's shoulder, and his arms draped along his thigh, resting suggestively close to the penis. The implicit sexual nature of the position is unmistakable. The picture could quite easily be of two lovers, the closed eyes of Patroclus portraying sexual ecstasy rather than death. It is only the iconography of the discarded helmet and shield which acts as a clue to the identity of the two men.

Other paintings around the temple deal with pagan themes, some classical, some from Celtic folklore. There is Apollo, leaning amorously over Hyacinthus, teaching him to throw the discus, there are Dionysus and Ampelos wrestling in a bower of grapes. There is also a series of friezes illustrating the four Celtic moon festivals: Imbolc, Beltane, Lammas and Samhain. In the winter section for example, we see Brigit, a Celtic goddess who revived the earth after winter on 1 February, the Celtic festival of Imbolc ('in milk', referring to the suckling of newborn lambs).

It seems clear that, having created the appropriate context for his beliefs and desires, Faulkes then approached the object of his passion: Joshua Rackham. Joshua Rackham was the young local vicar. My research has shown that Rackham was at Harrow at the same time as Faulkes, although in a lower year, and he quite possibly caught the eye of the heir to the Oakstead estate while still at school. This may explain why Rackham was offered the Oakstead living. Rackham appears to have been a rather highly strung and sensitive young man, who had a breakdown of some sort at the death of his mother and so never completed his education. He was obviously beholden to the lord of the manor. However, once he had been shown the temple by Faulkes, there followed a serious and violent breakdown in relations. From contemporary correspondence between Rackham and his family, it is clear that the vicar became highly agitated and overwrought.

But why should a vicar be so outraged? It was not so out of the ordinary at this period for the landed gentry to experiment with temple designs, and decorate them with pseudo Greek and Roman paintings. It was perceived as a fashion by those unaware of the aristocratic sex cult. As far as I am aware, no other vicar was moved to attack their patron for the use of pre-Christian, classical subjects. The conclusion must be that, during the visit to the temple, Faulkes made sexual advances towards the vicar. One can only speculate on why Faulkes thought the vicar would find such advances welcome. Perhaps he mistook Rackham's obsequious gratitude for love. It seems he made a grave error of judgement. Soon after the visit, Rackham denounced Faulkes from the pulpit.

The content of the sermon is centred on the pagan and idolatrous nature of the temple, rather than on the sin of sodomy. However, an allusion in the sermon to the citizens of Sodom and Gomorrah, though brief, would have been clearly understood by the congregation. Despite the evidence for an influential homosexual presence in the higher echelons of eighteenth-century society, sodomy was still regarded as heinous by the law and, if proven, could carry the death penalty. The voice of homosexuality was forced to remain stifled, and is only beginning to be heard now, as western society becomes more liberal and therefore more willing to listen. However, without understanding its influence, the artistic movements of the eighteenth century cannot be properly understood.

Allegations of homosexuality against the lord of the manor could have had very grave consequences indeed for everyone concerned. After the preaching of the sermon, it appears that Rackham was violently assaulted by Faulkes. After such a public attack on his character it was no doubt expected of him. The whole episode was then smoothed over by Faulkes' formidable father. Henry was sent off on an extended tour, and Rackham was given a new living in the north.

Of Faulkes' passion there is only one clue extant. Browsing through books in the extensive library at Henford Hall, while researching this book, I came across his Greek edition of the *Iliad*, to him the equivalent of the sacred Bible. Leafing through this aged book I noticed some lines heavily underscored, presumably by Faulkes himself. The lines, which surely refer to his doomed relationship with Rackham, translate thus:

the memory burning on. . .
the all-subduing sleep could not take him,

not now, he turned and twisted, side to side
he longed for Patroclus' manhood, his gallant heart
. . .

I am sitting in the rowing boat again, surrounded by a thousand floating candles, the lake glittering. I can hear violins
across the water. On the shore, all my friends and family
stand waving, and shrieking, and laughing. The blushing
bride being cheered off on her wedding night. How terrible
it must have been, to be sent off with a virtual stranger, to
be deflowered, while everyone waited with bated breath. I
am wearing the shimmering white silk dress that Gretta's
friend made for me. The symbolic virgin parcel in her pristine wrapping, one in a long line, passed from man to man,
in a grotesque fertility ritual. But I am spoiled goods. I was
here only a couple of nights ago, in the same rowing boat,
being taken to the temple by another man, for another kind
of fertility rite. How strange, that despite our supposed
sophistication we are still immersed in these age-old preoccupations, the taking of the bull to the cow.

I have been acting all day, we all have. Everybody
pretends not to notice the devastated gardens, the bitterness
glowering inside the walls, the rotting plants in heaps. I
know that there is a malign spirit out in the world, a
mischief maker, who would like to trip us up, make us fail,
watching us with a gleeful grin. We will have to pick our
way through the obstacles thrown at us.

My greatest challenge will come when the boat nudges the
bank of the island, and we will go into Faulkes' temple, and I
must be astonished by what I find there. I look at Ben, who is
seated facing me, rowing. He smiles but I know that Charlie
and George have sown the seed of disappointment. He
doesn't want to believe bad stories about me, and so we
haven't talked about it again. I won't be able to lie if he asks
me straight. But if he has decided to avoid it, I will too.

Ben manoeuvres the boat next to the bank, and jumps
out. He offers me his hand, and helps me step out of the

boat, my dress gathered over my arm. We walk in silence to the door of the temple, which is open, light spilling out. Inside, there is the same bed swathed in silk, the floor lit with candles, the smell of lilac blossom. And yet, it is different. I am here with Ben. He loves me. I love him. I turn to him and say: This is perfect.

A slightly damaged perfect thing.

Author's note

Just prior to publication it has been revealed that Faulkes' greatest legacy is now under threat. Unfortunately, his remarkable wall paintings are decaying, possibly as a result of too much exposure, too quickly. The colours, so well preserved when first uncovered, have begun to deteriorate, and the plaster surface has started to flake and powder the floor of the temple. Despite every effort, it appears that this deterioration cannot be halted. Tragically, these unique works of art will soon be no more than a memory.